ANGIE'S DES

Cattleman's Club 7

Jenny Penn

MENAGE EVERLASTING

Siren Publishing, Inc.
www.SirenPublishing.com

A SIREN PUBLISHING BOOK
IMPRINT: Ménage Everlasting

ANGIE'S DESTINY
Copyright © 2015 by Jenny Penn

ISBN: 978-1-63259-539-3

First Printing: July 2015

Cover design by Les Byerley
All art and logo copyright © 2015 by Siren Publishing, Inc.

Printed in the U.S.A.

PUBLISHER
Siren Publishing, Inc.
www.SirenPublishing.com

ANGIE'S DESTINY

Cattleman's Club 7

JENNY PENN
Copyright © 2015

Prologue

Sunday, June 1st

Angelina Montes took a deep breath and pressed the doorbell before her. It chimed with a serious tune she recognized instantly as the famous "Carol of the Bells." While Angie had nothing against Christmas carols, they seemed out of place given it was summer, but that was Patton. She was a lover of all things tacky and melodramatic, which included an obsession with Christmas. Not that Angie could cast a stone, though.

She wasn't known for being either calm or cautious, just the opposite. Angie knew people thought she was weird with all her premonitions, but the truth was she couldn't help what she felt. Besides, she was very rarely wrong. A fact that only unnerved the people around her all the more. That included her family, which may explain why she wasn't in love with the holidays.

They reminded Angie of just how alone she was and just how much her parents had given up on her. She unnerved them with all her dreams and with her rather sharp insights. That was actually her intuition at work. It helped her see through the lies. Her parents tended to lie a lot.

Now that they'd both remarried and grown busy with their new families, they used that as an excuse to avoid Angie. Some might think it was strange that a woman who had more than seven siblings could be without family on the holidays, but Angie was generally the one left out.

She was also the passed-around one. In grim reminder of just how her teen years had been spent, her parents had actually fought over who had to put her up this past Christmas. Her mother didn't have room at her house for Angie to stay with her. Her father had gone to his in-laws.

Angie had gone to Hawaii and spent a ton on herself, having long ago found that retail therapy did actually help. At least a little. That, though, had been last Christmas. The next one held the promise of so much more because Brett and Mike Mathews were finally coming home.

Home. Home to her.

That thought put a smile on Angie's face even as it fueled an ache deeper below. Who wouldn't ache for Mike and Brett? They were tall, broad, and filled out with rock-hard muscles. That's what they'd looked like at eighteen. From the pictures Hailey had shared with her, Angie knew they'd only grown thicker and more lick worthy over the years.

Sometimes just the thought of them made Angie want to purr. Identical twins, they both had been blessed with thick, lush brown hair that was tinged with a hint of auburn highlights that matched the sharp cut of their features. It softened them, making them all but smolder as those dark eyes glinted with a promise of pure ecstatic delight.

That's what Angie's future held, which explained the smile curling at her lips as the door flew open. Louder, and definitely more piercing than the doorbell, Patton's squeal of delight had Angie wincing, even as she found herself swept up in a damn near crushing hug.

"Jesus, girl, have you been working out or something?" Angie stepped back the second Patton released her to finally get a good look at her childhood friend. "Holy crap! When did you start wearing stripper outfits? You know you're about to fall out of that shirt, don't you?"

Far from being insulted by Angie's blunt questions, Patton just laughed and responded in kind. "You're just jealous because you forgot to grow boobs."

"Please," Angie huffed as she grabbed her breasts and bounced them at Patton. "I bet these puppies outweigh yours."

"That's right. You got puppies, and I got melons."

"Everybody likes puppies better than melons."

"Yeah, but guys don't nibble on puppies," Patton shot back triumphantly, and Angie had to give it to her. She had a point.

Not that Patton was waiting for her agreement to take a victory lap. "Score one for the redhead while the brunette..." Patton drew out that last word as she paused to consider the matter with a smile that held more than a touch of mischief. "Gets an invitation inside. Come on. There is somebody I want you to meet."

"Oh God," Angie groaned, refusing to take that first step as she narrowed her gaze on Patton. "Please, tell me it's not a man."

"Nope." Patton held up her hands in surrender. "I know better than anybody not to bother fighting that war."

That she did.

Patton and Angie shared more than history and a sense of humor. They also shared a dedication to the men they loved. Patton was one of the few people who hadn't made Angie feel like a freak for her devotion to a dream almost as old as her. Angie had been thirteen when she'd had her dream about Mike and Brett. Everybody had laughed at her, including Mike and Brett. But not Patton.

She'd understood.

Of course, Patton wasn't exactly sane or normal. She'd made her own choice a long time ago that intimacy could best be explored with the men who owned her heart. The only difference between them was that Patton had finally managed to seduce her men, whereas Angie's battle was just about to begin.

After having been stationed overseas with the marines for the past decade, Brett and Mike had finally retired. Retired and returned home briefly before skipping back out of town to go fishing for damn near a month. Actually, Angie wasn't upset about getting a little extra time to come up with a plan that ended in their seduction.

That plan would have been easier to come up with if Angie knew the two men better, but it had been years since she'd seen them. While she'd written to them almost every single month they'd been gone, Angie's dedication had not been returned. She'd received only the occasional letter back from Brett and barely a single word from Mike, never a nice word

It would have been easy to be disheartened, but Angie was far from that. She was determined. That was another trait she shared with Patton.

Throwing her arm over Angie's shoulders, Patton all but dragged her into the house. It smelled of wood and leather but was bright and welcoming, just like always. It felt like a home, like the dream Angie had of building a happy family with Brett and Mike.

"You have got to meet Casey," Patton insisted, leading her toward the kitchen. "She's my business partner, and you're just going to love her…though, she's having some men problems, so she is kind of acting a little mopey."

Patton imparted that bit of information out of the side of her mouth and in a low enough tone that the redhead slouched over the kitchen table didn't hear her. Angie heard her, but she wasn't paying any attention to her longtime friend. Her attention, instead, was riveted on the other woman and the realization that she recognized her.

Worse, Casey recognized her.

She could tell the other woman was about ready to say something but, thankfully, held back as Angie gave a quick shake of her head. Luckily, Patton didn't notice, but then she was too busy shaking the empty wine bottle and complaining that it had been full only minutes ago. Angie didn't doubt her because Casey looked as though she was full of something more than just surprise.

Of course, Patton being Patton, she was more than eager to raid Chase's office for the good stuff he, apparently, hid from her in there. No sooner had she disappeared than Angie plopped her ass down in the seat beside Casey and gave her a pointed look.

"I didn't know you knew Patton."

"*I* didn't know *you* knew Patton," Casey shot back with a definite slur to her words.

"What were you doing at the club?" they asked simultaneously.

The club being the Cattleman's Club, an adult entertainment resort that helped keep Angie in business and Patton's men rich.

"What were you doing at the club?" Casey retorted at the very same time as her, though, Casey answered without hesitation while Angie ignored her question. "Checking the place out for Patton."

That made sense. Patton's men owned and ran the club but refused to let her in. Nobody refused Patton anything without risking her taking up the challenge. While generally, Angie admired Patton's gumption, this time it could spell real trouble. Not just for Chase, Slade, and Devin.

Angie's entire business was built on the club. She was technically a travel agent, but she specialized. That translated into her traveling the world and visiting other resorts where she identified rich, single females who might be interested in a more entertaining vacation. Patton could ruin it all.

"And have you told her anything?"

"Not yet." Casey frowned and slumped even closer as she gave Angie what she suspected was supposed to be a sly look but really just highlighted the woman's tipsy state. "Why? What don't you want her to know?"

"That I go there at all." That wasn't the whole truth, but it was as much as Angie needed to admit to.

"But—"

"I'm a travel agent," Angie cut her off to explain as she offered Casey a pleading look. "Do you know how hard a profession that is with the Internet taking over? So to make a living, I specialize."

That was a polite way of saying she helped women indulge their deepest, darkest, most erotic fantasies. Of course, it didn't hurt that the Cattlemen tended to be not only hot but also very good at making a woman beg for more, even as they took total command of their bodies.

They just didn't know how to touch a woman's heart. At least not Angie's.

"And you think Patton wouldn't understand that?" Casey asked, drawing Angie's attention back to her scowl, but she didn't get a chance to answer before Patton reappeared.

"Look at this." Patton waved a bottle under Angie's nose.

Angie looked, but the only word she recognized on the label was cabernet. "I'm sorry, honey, but I don't know enough about wine to know what I'm looking at."

"Three hundred dollars," Patton informed her, making Angie's eyes widen as she glanced back down at the bottle.

"For wine?"

"Yep." Patton nodded, plunking the bottle down on the table and heading around the kitchen's island to retrieve the corkscrew left out on the counter. "Chase has got a little collection going. He keeps saying he's going to lay down a…pipe? A pike? I don't know."

Patton shrugged as she moved back toward the table. "It's something like that, which is basically to say he's going to buy a bunch of wine when we have our first kid…or is it port? Is there a difference between the two? Isn't port a wine?"

"Again, you're asking the wrong person. I like liquor with a little fruit, not fruit with a little liquor."

That was the truth. Angie could outdrink almost anybody, but she rarely touched wine. That didn't mean she didn't know a few things about the types of people who drank wine. More importantly, she knew Chase Davis. He didn't like people to touch his stuff.

"But I'm pretty sure you aren't supposed to open a three-hundred dollar bottle for no reason. Isn't Chase going to be a little ticked that you're drinking his wine?"

That question had Patton stilling for a moment before she popped the cork and chunked it, along with the corkscrew, onto the kitchen table. The message was clear, at least to anybody who knew Patton.

"Oh, I see." Angie smirked. "That's the point."

"Do you know that butthead still won't take me out to his club?" Patton shot back before nodding to Casey, who held up her glass for a refill. "I had to send her in undercover just to find out what the place looks like. That isn't right."

And, in Patton's book, two wrongs made everything right.

"Of course, they found my mole," Patton huffed as she snatched Casey's tilting glass out of her hand and poured it nearly to the rim before handing it back.

The half-drunk redhead promptly spilled a good chunk onto the wooden tabletop. Without blinking or missing a single beat in her tirade, Patton wiped up the spill and continued to pour two more glasses.

"Then tortured her into confessing, and now he's giving me that silent, brooding look, like I've betrayed him." Patton snorted and rolled her eyes. "Of course, I'm not the one spending all day surrounded by naked women, which really wouldn't bother me if he'd stop acting like he was up to something.

"Not that I think he's cheating on me, but then how many women out there say the same thing and then come home one day to find their men sticking it to the help, which is just why I got rid of that slut

Charlotte and got us a real housekeeper, but that still doesn't explain what the hell Chase is up to."

"But you're going to find out," Angie concluded, following her friend's twisted tale to its clear conclusion. "And, in the meantime, annoy him by drinking all his wine, right?"

Patton smiled and raised her glass as she settled down into her own seat. "Here is to irritating the crap out of the men we love."

"I'll drink to that." Angie tapped her glass against Patton's as they both ignored Casey, who appeared to be brooding in the corner. "Though I would point out that, at least, you're getting compensated while I'm still making do with a plastic vibrator."

That had Patton giggling as she offered Angie up the same assurance every other woman ever had. "Trust me, real dick is so much better."

"Only if it's the right dick," Angie corrected.

"I'll drink to that."

Angie kind of thought Patton would drink to just about anything if it meant emptying Chase's bottle. That wasn't why she was there, though. As much as she might love Patton, Angie hadn't come over just to catch up. She had an ulterior motive.

"So…Brett and Michael are coming home finally, huh?" Angie pointedly steered the conversation in the direction she wanted it to go.

"Yep." Patton nodded. "You now stand the chance of becoming a real woman, virgin. That is if you can convince the two biggest sluts I've ever met to give up their roaming ways and settle down."

"Please." Angie snorted up a laugh. "Brett and Mike are not the two biggest sluts you ever met. That would be your own men, Patton."

Actually, Brett's and Mike's reputations were far overblown from what Angie could tell. She didn't doubt that they had some wild times in the military, but most of their days and nights had been spent as soldiers, not as lovers.

"Nah, that would be Hailey's men." Patton smirked, clearly on the verge of giggles. "You should been there when they met Brett and Mike. That was one hell of an introduction."

"I've heard the rumors. Something to do with them crashing through a window at an inappropriate time."

"Hailey was tied naked to the bed," Patton whispered, the laughter breaking into her words as she tried to continue on. "And Brett and Mike thought that Cole and Kyle were *forcing* the issue. They...they..."

Patton couldn't get the rest out, but Angie already knew. "They beat the tar out of them and had Hailey's boyfriends arrested."

"That's why Hailey's looking for revenge." Patton waggled her brows at Angie as her laughter subsided.

"Yeah." Angie knew all about Hailey's quest. That was partly why she was there. "When is Hailey supposed to get here by the way?"

"I don't know." Patton glanced over at the clock. "Soon. Just do me a favor. Don't get her arrested again."

"She got herself arrested," Angie shot back. "I can't help it if she can't outrun the police."

"Well, that's because she's short. She's got them little legs."

"Oh my God, it's Lana!" Casey erupted, her bellow, causing both Patton and Angie to start.

Angie glanced instantly around, feeling her heart jolt at the very thought that Lana had dared to show up in Patton's territory. She hadn't, but that almost didn't matter as Patton also glanced around in confusion.

"Who is Lana?"

That question had Casey blinking and seemingly appearing to realize that she'd spoken out loud.

"Nobody." Casey couldn't have looked guiltier or sounded drunker.

"Casey," Patton pressed.

"She runs things down at the club." Casey cringed, refusing to meet Angie's gaze as she spilled those beans in a rush that stood in stark contrast to the way Patton slowly repeated them.

"She runs things down at the club..." Patton went still, her eyes rounding in an almost comical look. "You don't mean Lana Vey? About five-eight with a killer body and an enviable head of black silk that never has a single strand out of place? *That* Lana?"

"Uh..." Casey blinked rounded eyes as she stared back at Patton.

Patton didn't need an answer. She already knew it. That didn't stop her from grilling Casey, as if she were in any condition to answer. With every question Patton shot her way, she stared back like a deer caught in a set of headlights until the doorbell rang and put her out of her misery.

Patton disappeared long enough for Casey to glance over at Angie, belch once, and ask, "I did wrong, didn't I?"

"Yeah."

Angie nodded, not surprised at all when Patton reappeared with Hailey and a thousand dollar bottle of wine. Chase's collection would be decimated by the end of the night, but that wasn't Angie's problem. She knew Chase well enough to know he could handle Patton, just as she knew Patton could handle him.

It was Lana that she worried over.

Angie counted Lana as a friend, even if she didn't dare to reveal that fact to Patton. Not that she was keeping the secret to protect her own interest, but she didn't want to end up in a war between the two of them. After all, Patton had a right to hate Lana just as Lana had the right to hate Patton. They were both in love with the same man, and that was never good news.

There was nothing to be done about it. Chase was in love with Patton. Whatever he felt for Lana paled in comparison. In the end, that meant she was the one who was going to get hurt. So, she was the one who had Angie's sympathy.

Hailey, on the other hand, would have Angie's undying gratitude if she helped Angie finally get her chance with Brett and Mike. That possibility had Angie offering Hailey an oversized smile and hopping out of her seat to engulf the other women in a big hug. Angie greeted Hailey with an enthusiasm that was not wholly returned.

"Hey, Hailey! It's been years."

"Hey, Angie," Hailey returned with a caution that spoke volumes about their past relationship. So did the way she eyed Angie as she released her. "You look good."

"Good enough to seduce your brothers?" Angie asked as she did a turn and showed off what she knew was a killer body.

Hailey, though, didn't look too terribly impressed. "It's not your body that you have to work on. It's the crazy."

"Hey! I resent that." Angie didn't really, and the laughter in her tone assured Hailey knew it. "I come by my crazy naturally. No work needed."

"Is that right?" Hailey lifted a brow as Patton filled a new glass with Chase's precious wine. "Well, let's hope my brothers have developed a taste for crazy because, if you can convince them to settle down and stay home, I'll love you for the rest of my life…What is this? I don't like wine."

Hailey's nose wrinkled as she leaned away from Patton, who was trying to hand her a glass.

"This is Chase's punishment. So drink," Patton commanded.

"Do you know you're bossy?" Hailey shot back.

"And sit!"

Hailey rolled her eyes at that and yanked out a seat. She plopped down into it and shot a glare back up at Patton. "Happy?"

"Very." Patton smiled as she settled down into her own chair and glanced around the table. "And why wouldn't I be? I'm with three of my best friends and on my way to getting drunk."

"I think Casey has beat you there," Hailey muttered as she eyed the other girl.

"What?" Casey blinked at the sound of her name. "Did I do something?"

"No, honey, you didn't do anything," Angie quickly assured her, honestly afraid of what might come out of her mouth next. "Why don't you rest your head on the table and take a little nap?"

"Or I could have another glass of wine," she suggested, appearing to perk up all of a sudden.

Patton was way too eager to pour Casey one as far as Angie was concerned, but she kept her opinions to herself. After all, she wasn't anybody's mother. God only knew how her children would turn out. They'd probably inherit her gift for foresight. Just the idea left her unnerved because she knew how much trouble that kind of intuition could be.

Then Angie remembered that all of her kids would have Brett and Michael as fathers. They were reasonable enough men. Soundly logical. Sort of. After all, it wasn't completely rational to swear that they'd marry her if they de-hymenated her. They'd meant that as an insult, an expression of their total lack of interest in her, but Angie had taken it as a challenge. It had been one the whole town had taken an interest in.

Was she right? Was her gift real? Her dreams prophetic? Or did Mike and Brett mean what they said? Did they really have no interest in her?

Those questions had burned through the gossip mill all those years ago and most people had come to the conclusion that she was nuts. That Mike and Brett had run all the way to the marines to escape her. That had led to painful jokes about how they'd rather be dead than be with her, but Angie hadn't let those snickers bother her.

She knew the truth.

They'd come back for her.

They had. Only the question was, who were they now? Angie didn't suspect they were the same men who had left. Brett had always been the wild one, but she'd seen him grow in the letters he sent back to her. His notes had been randomly infrequent but long and honest when she'd received them.

More than once, she'd felt like his confessional as he expressed opinions about his job, coworkers, and lifestyle that often held a note of discontentment. They'd also held a hint of the man he'd grown into. He was curious and cared about people. Most of his frustration came from an inability to help or even know what to do to help.

Mike, on the other hand, had left Pittsview a thoughtful over-achiever who was known for his understanding and kindness. Angie suspected those qualities might have rusted over the years, given his notes had been all too brief and abrupt. She had read between the lines, though, and knew things were difficult for him.

Angie suspected that Brett wasn't the only one questioning his role in the world. Or, maybe, that was just her being hopeful and refusing to believe the obvious. Mike wasn't interested.

If that were true, he'd have to be clearer than that. Soon, he'd have the opportunity to be.

Chapter 1

Wednesday, June 25th

Brett woke up to the sound of running water and smiled as he blinked the sleep from his eyes. His grin dipped as he glanced down at the clock on the nightstand and realized how late it was. It was almost eight in the morning, and he was still in bed.

He should be ashamed of himself.

Out of the marines almost three months now and he'd already fallen out of the habits they'd drilled into him. There were only two excuses for sleeping late, but there wasn't a woman in his bed and he hadn't spent the night working. What he had been doing was existing off fast food and alcohol for the past several weeks, but then that had been life on a fishing boat.

Fishing meant fish. Fish were good for a body.

Not good enough, though. Swearing there and then to get in at least a five-mile run that morning, Brett rolled to the side of his bed and sat up, almost banging his head against the ceiling. He'd long outgrown the top bunk of the bed he had shared with his twin brother as kids. The problem was the room hadn't grown with him, and it was still too small to fit two twin beds.

Hailey's room, though, was big enough for a princess. That was just what he thought of his sister. She was a future queen in jeans and way too good for the two turds she was dating, or had been dating.

Last night Brett had gotten the call he'd been waiting for. Finally, Hailey had come to her senses and kicked both of her boyfriends to the curb. That meant they were fair game, and hunting season had just started. That thought put the smile back on Brett's face.

As a matter of habit, Brett tended not to like any man who showed any kind of interest in his sister, but with Cole and Kyle, it was even more personal. He hadn't forgiven either one for what he'd caught them doing to his sister. The thought that they were doing it every damn night...Brett took a deep breath and let it out before he popped a vein.

It was fine.

It was over.

Hailey was back home where she belonged. Of course, her return meant only their mother's room was available, but it had been turned into a shrine. They'd lost their mother years ago. That had been a rough time, though, one Brett suspected had been harder on Mike. His brother was a deep fucker and tended to internalize things, he and Hailey both, which was why Brett wouldn't even consider disturbing their mother's bedroom for a second.

Instead, he kept his chin buried in his chest and jumped down to the floor. Brett paused long enough to tug on a pair of jeans before heading down the hall to bang on the bathroom door and remind Hailey that other people had to brush their teeth.

He didn't get a response, not that he expected one. Hailey had always been stubborn and a little vindictive. He knew she was still carrying a grudge about what had happened when they'd returned home a month back. She might have a little bit of a right to be annoyed. They had crashed through her windows, but they'd bent on rescuing her.

How were they supposed to know that Hailey had been corrupted by two perverts? As far as Brett was concerned, Hailey should get the hell over her hissy fit. After all, he was the one who had that horrible image burned into his mind. Brett was going to need therapy to get rid of it.

Of course, his definition of therapy, though, didn't include some tweed-wearing twit sitting on his leather padded seat. No. It came from revenge. That was just what he'd come home for. Cole and Kyle, the two idiots Hailey had made the mistake of falling for, were going to pay for ever touching his sister.

Now that she'd dumped them, Brett could get around to making their lives miserable without having to worry about Hailey making his that way. That thought put the smile back on his face as he shuffled into the kitchen to find his twin relaxing at the round table tucked into the corner.

"Mornin', sleepyhead," Mike called out without even looking up. "You missed the morning run."

Wearing a pair of gray sweats and nothing else, Mike had his bare feet propped up on the table with his nose buried in the morning paper. The heady aroma of coffee filled the air, drawing Brett toward the counter where Mike had left out a mug for him.

"I don't see you wearing any sneakers," Brett muttered, well accustomed to the gloat in his brother's tone.

"I left them out on the porch." Mike peered over the paper to waggle his brows at Brett. "You might even find old lady Hinkle out there, too. I think I'm going to have to start running with a shirt on. Otherwise, there might be a rash of heart attacks breaking out all over the neighborhood."

Brett rolled his eyes at that. Being identical in almost every single way but for personality did not stop Mike from assuming he was the good-looking one. It didn't help that women bought into that lie. Hell, if Brett wanted to, he could douse himself in cologne and press his clothes, too, but he wasn't into pimping himself, especially not when it would have been a lie.

He looked tough, and he liked it rough.

He also liked to brush his teeth before he drank his coffee.

"How long has Hailey been in that shower?" Brett asked, ignoring Mike's smirk.

"Long enough to assure we don't have any hot water left," Mike retorted as he lifted the paper back up, no longer interested in the conversation.

"And you haven't harassed her?"

"I'm reading the paper."

Brett rolled his eyes at that. The Pittsview paper had to be the biggest journalistic joke out there. After all, what did they have to report on? Mailbox smashings? Cows being tipped over? Or perhaps Mrs. Hinkle dying of a heart attack in her front yard as Mike jogged on past?

"Well, then I guess you won't mind waiting until I'm done," Brett shot back as he plunked his mug back down on the counter and headed back toward the bathroom.

Hailey might think she was being clever, trying to run them out of hot water, but he was still the older brother. Besides, he was used to cold showers. After all, the marines didn't provide spa-like retreats for soldiers in the field. Hell, they were lucky to get to bathe daily.

There were all sorts of things the marines hadn't allowed them to do, but then there were all sorts of tricks that they drilled into Brett, tricks Hailey was about to get a taste of if she didn't get her ass out of the shower right then.

* * * *

Mike watched Brett storm out of the kitchen and rolled his eyes. He didn't see why his brother felt the need to go piss off Hailey. They should just be thankful that she'd come to her senses before either Cole or Kyle managed to knock her up. Just the thought of those pricks touching his sister had him tensing.

He really didn't like them, and now he didn't even have to pretend to. Not that Mike had ever bothered to put much effort into pretending, but he hadn't pounded the bastards into the ground, and that seemed like a very gracious consideration on his part. Hailey probably wouldn't agree, but women tended to be funny about those kinds of things.

Thankfully, Hailey wasn't too funny.

He and Brett had seen to that. They'd had no choice. Without a father around to help make sure she didn't end up harmed or too prissy, he and his brother had taken up the task. They'd turned her into a proper tomboy, one most of the other guys had been afraid of, but they'd been gone a long time.

It was clear their absence had been felt. Hailey had turned into a girl over the past ten years. Worse, she'd turned into a woman. A woman with bad taste in men. Thankfully, she'd realized that truth. Mike was grateful it hadn't taken too long and was more than willing to sacrifice a few hot showers for the cause.

Brett, on the other hand, clearly wasn't.

Mike rolled his eyes as he heard his twin pound on the bathroom door and holler out that he wasn't above turning the water off if Hailey didn't hurry her ass up. Threatening was a waste of breath as far as Mike was concerned. Everybody knew actions spoke louder than words.

Hailey's rang out in silence. She didn't respond to Brett, and neither did the water cut off. It was going to, though, one way or another. Mike glanced up as Brett stormed back through the kitchen, wearing a scowl and muttering to himself about bullheaded redheads.

He slammed out the back door, no doubt headed for the main pipe's cut-off valve. It was an asshole thing to do, but then Brett was known to be an ass. Hailey was known to be meaner, which was just why Mike turned his attention back to the paper in his hands.

He was content to let his siblings settle their dispute between each other. Besides, there was actual news in the newspaper for a change. Lana Vey had confessed to arson last night. Lana Vey. Now there was a looker. She'd been real friendly during high school. Hell, more than friendly.

She'd been creative.

She'd also been Brett and Mike's first shared girl. That wasn't shocking. Lana had been a lot of men's first something. She got around and her reputation had preceded her. Apparently, though, the scarlet letter A they were pinning on her wasn't for adultery, but arson.

As if that wasn't weird enough, she hadn't just confessed to any fire. Lana had confessed to setting the barn fire that Patton Jones had nearly died in. Mike didn't need the paper to tell him that Lana and Patton were long-time archenemies. He knew their story already and could well imagine how Chase was feeling that morning because he was the thing that the two women fought over.

Unfortunately for Lana, she'd never stood a chance of winning that war. Mike, Brett, and Chase had been friends from the cradle. Mike knew that the only woman Chase had ever or would ever love was Patton, which was a little weird actually.

They'd known the Davis brothers since they'd been in diapers. Their bond went deeper than mere friendship. They'd formed a family of sorts, all five men having the same problem in common—no-good dads and ailing mothers. That meant it had been up to all five of them to watch out for Patton and Hailey.

It might have been years since Mike had seen Patton, but he still thought of her as another little sister. It didn't matter that she wasn't anybody's sister, at least not by blood. That was the way he felt. That made it weird for him to think of her with the men considered to be almost like brothers.

Weird, though, seemed to be the mood of the day. As if Lana's confession weren't enough to keep the gossips' tongues wagging for the next several weeks, there had also been a murder in town. There hadn't been a murder since Chase's daddy had stuck a knife into Patton's daddy's heart all those years back.

Nobody knew what that had been about, but there were a lot of rumors. Mike figured there would be even more now, given there was no suspect or person of interest as of yet. There was no doubt it was a murder, too. Gwen Harold had been found with her head bashed in, which was just a damn shame, given the picture the paper ran.

She was quite a looker, and Mike was looking. After three weeks spent on a boat with nothing other men and fish, he wouldn't have turned down a little female companionship right about then. An easy woman, one who knew how to make a man sweat, that was what he needed. That was what he liked. Mike knew of a club full of just the right type of women.

The sound of running water in the background falling silent had him glancing up as, a second later, Brett slammed back into the kitchen. His twin paused to catch Mike's gaze and issue a maniacal-sounding laugh. Brett was enjoying himself, which wasn't shocking. Harassing their sister had always been one of Brett's favorite pastimes, one he indulged in with glee.

Brett took off for the bathroom, hollering out to Hailey as he taunted her with a bold gloat that would, no doubt, have their sister squawking all over the place as she pitched a fit like she was still eight…or, maybe, she wouldn't.

Mike glanced up in confusion as Hailey stepped in through the back door. She shot him a smile and opened her mouth to offer him a greeting that got cut off by the sound of Brett demanding she get her ass out of the bathroom now. As the words echoed through the house, Hailey's smile took on a wicked curl, and Mike knew instantly that Brett was walking into a trap.

"Brett! No!"

Not even certain what the danger was, Mike still nearly fell out of his seat as he scrambled to catch his brother before it was too late. All he managed, though, was to get ensnared in Hailey's trap himself.

Mike burst into the hall at the very same moment the bathroom door flew open. There stood Angelina Montes, wearing nothing but the towel wrapped around her head and the sunlight beaming through the bathroom window. She was all golden tanned and curved to perfection with long, silky black strands of hair dripping water down her body.

Despite the warning screaming through his head to shut his eyes and block out the image, Mike's gaze locked on a single glistening bead of water and tracked it as it slid down between the gloriously big mounds of her breasts. They lifted with each breath she took, setting more droplets into motion and drawing attention to the luscious-looking pink nipples all puckered and begging to be played with.

God help him, Mike was all but drooling with the sudden intense need to take a taste of those puppies. They looked soft and tanned, just the way he liked his tits. Actually that was the way he liked his women, and Angie fit that bill. She was long and toned and so damn perfectly built that it made him ache to simply touch her, but he didn't dare.

Angie came with a price.

She wanted a wedding and had made that clear well years ago. Mike could still remember that day. She'd been sixteen and bossy as hell. She sure as shit hadn't looked like this. Mike's fingers curled into fists as his eyes slid down over the gentle flare of her tummy and hips to the smooth, naked mound of her cunt. Not a single hair marred the sight of the plump, swollen lips of her pussy and the cream dripping from them.

She was hot and ready to be fucked.

He was hard and aching to give it to her.

"Hey, boys. Bathroom's free."

With that, she turned to saunter down the hall, the full globes of her ass bouncing with each step as her hair swooshed, a hypnotic lure. Like a dog on a leash, Brett jerked forward, no doubt ready to either pick a fight or fuck it out. That was just his nature. There was only one way to stop him.

Mike latched onto his brother's shoulder, jerking him back hard enough to send Brett, flailing, down to the floor. His brother crashed into the wood planks, sending a shudder racing down the walls of the hall. At the end, Angie paused to glance back, and Mike caught the smug smirk that tugged at her lips before she disappeared into Hailey's room.

Hailey!

This was her doing. Turning with a swiftness that had saved his life more than once, Mike pinned his sister with a glare that would have had most people cowering in fear. Not Hailey. She stood there in the doorway to the kitchen, grinning as if she'd just won the lottery.

"What did you do?" Mike stalked forward, forcing Hailey back into the kitchen in a blatant attempt to intimidate her, a blatant and pointless attempt.

"What?" Hailey blinked innocently, even as she gave way, retreating toward the coffeemaker and snatching up Brett's mug in the process.

"Don't what me, young lady," Mike snapped, not in the mood for Hailey's games. "Why is Angie walking around my house naked?"

"Your house?" That gave Hailey pause as she turned to snort at him. "Ha! Check the deed, my dear brother, because your name is not on it."

"What the hell is going on here?" Brett roared as he came charging into the kitchen and into the middle of their conversation. "Why is that woman in my bathroom?"

"It's not yours," Mike informed him, drawing Brett's outraged glare in his direction. "Your name's not on the deed."

"*What?*"

"I'm just saying." Mike held his hands up in surrender. "Our dear sister is the *sole* owner of this here house."

Brett held Mike's gaze for a long second before he turned back toward Hailey. "You got thirty seconds before I take things into my own hands."

"And what are you going to take into your hands?"

That bold question came from Angie herself. She strutted into the kitchen, barely dressed in a mini-skirt and a tank top that left a whole lot of smooth, golden skin uncovered. She looked good. Good enough to lick. Good enough to eat. God help him he was hungry.

The little witch knew it, too.

Both he and Brett quickly got out of her way as she strutted on past with a shake of her ass and a smile that held all sorts of promises.

"Mornin', boys. Hailey."

"Angie," Hailey returned with an amused welcome as she handed her Brett's mug. "Coffee?"

"Thank you."

Mike watched the two women fawn over each other as they both prepped their cups, unable to take his eyes off of Angie. She'd changed from the tall, lanky girl she'd been when he'd last seen her. He knew that, though. He knew it because she'd written to him every day that he'd been gone.

Mike had written back only occasionally, and only out pure boredom and loneliness. Every time he had written to her, he'd pretty much told her to get lost. To get a life and forget him because he wasn't interested in her.

That had been a lie.

It didn't matter. It didn't matter if he'd saved every one of her letters. It didn't matter that he reread them over and over again. It didn't even matter that, at some level, he'd always been anxious to see if another one came. What mattered was what was right. Angie was too young, too naïve, too sweet and trusting. She relied way too much on her infamous intuition.

That scared the crap out of Mike. It made her vulnerable to getting hurt, and he didn't want to be the one to hurt her. He could. He would if he didn't control himself. She deserved better than him. That truth had been self-evident in her letters.

Every few weeks Mike had received another one, and as the weeks passed into years, he'd watched her evolve from a wide-eyed teenage optimist to a funny, faithful woman. A part of him had fallen in love with the woman in those letters, but Mike knew better to believe in that fairy tale.

Love was an illusion. So were prophetic dreams. Relationships came at a price. It didn't matter if he was willing to pay. Mike wasn't willing to let Angie pay because he knew, in the end, he would hurt her.

That was just the brutal truth.

"Hailey's grown some teeth," Brett snarled softly into Mike's ear as he pressed in close to Mike's side. "I say we punish them both. They wanted war. War they'll get."

"The best thing would be to ignore them." Mike kept his tone low and turned to pin Brett with a pointed gaze. "Ignore them and prove that we're not interested in playing along with whatever game Hailey's dreamt up. Engaging them, on the other hand, is a surefire way to drag things out."

Brett appeared to consider that for all of a second before he shrugged. "Let the games begin."

Before Mike could argue with him, Brett brushed past his brother to bark at his sister like the commander he was.

"Hailey!" Brett narrowed his gaze on their sister with a hard look and issued a simple threat. "You've got *one* minute to tell me what the hell is going on here."

"Don't take that tone with your sister," Angie snapped back instantly, drawing herself upright in a mocking imitation of Brett's stance that drew Mike's gaze straight toward her breasts.

He couldn't help but wonder if she had some work done because the last time he'd seen Angie she'd been a little more normally proportioned. She'd also been a giggling teen who ogled them with blatant lust. Now she was shaped like a *Penthouse* centerfold with attitude to spare.

Where was his sweet Angie? She'd been there in the letters. That woman certainly hadn't sounded like the vixen strutting past now.

"And *you*," Brett snarled as he tried so hard to glare Angie down he looked ready to shit bricks. "What the hell do you think you're doing walking around naked?"

"Air drying?" Angie shot back with enough of a lift to her tone to leave her words sounding more like a question instead of an answer, but there was no denying the smug satisfaction tugging at her lips. "Why? Didn't you like what you saw?"

A man would either have to be dead or gay not to like what Angie had to show them. That thought led Mike to wonder if she really had lived up to her vow and saved her virginity for them. If she had, then they were screwed. If she hadn't, then he'd fallen in love with a lie and he'd screw her.

"So, it's like that, is it? Okay." Brett answered his own question as he held his hands up in surrender and began to back up toward the door.

He was chuckling, a sound Mike knew too well. His brother was up to something.

"Fine. You can have the last word for now, but this isn't *over*."

All three of them watched as Brett slammed out the back door.

"Where is he going?" Hailey lifted a brow as she glanced between Angie and Mike.

"Probably to turn the water back on." Angie shrugged.

"What? Why?"

"It's a long story." Angie smiled as she cast a glance over at Mike, who still stood there eyeing her with what he feared was blatant lust. "So, Mike, it's been a while."

"Are you still a virgin?"

Mike knew that was a blunt question to ask, but he couldn't respond to her until he had an answer. He received one almost instantly, though Angie didn't say a word. She didn't have to. Her smile and the glimmer that sparkled in her eyes said it all. That was all he needed to hear to sigh heavily and silently curse fate. Things would have been so much easier if Angie was that easy.

Brett banged in through the back door, drawing everybody's gaze in his direction. He knew it, which was why he stuck his chin in the air and marched straight through the kitchen without a word to anybody. A second later, the bathroom door slammed and was quickly followed by the sound of water running through the pipes.

"So…" Mike breathed out that word, trying to release the tension and the frustration along with it, but Angie wouldn't give him the second to gather his thoughts.

"When did your brother go crazy?" She directed that question at Hailey, who just shrugged and pointedly looked toward Mike.

"Oh, no." He shook his head at them both. "I'm not playing this game. I got nothing to say to you, virgin."

That gave Angie a moment's pause, and Mike could sense her amusement as he turned pointedly to address only Hailey.

"I'm assuming you *didn't* have a fight with those two blockheads you're dating, right?"

"What can I say?" Hailey shrugged. "I tried to resist Cole and Kyle, but they can be *very* persuasive."

"And so you…"

"Rented my room to Angie," Hailey filled in cheerfully.

"Hi, roomie!" Angie waved at him, but still he refused to look in her direction.

Mike didn't dare. It was clear she wasn't wearing a bra, and it was a little cold in the kitchen. Unfortunately, there was nothing little about his body's response to the sight of those luscious tits straining beneath the cotton of Angie's tank top. She didn't have to know that, though.

"Since when did the two of you become besties?" Mike prodded. "I thought you were all pissed that she got you arrested."

"That?" Hailey looked taken aback, as if she hadn't held a grudge for years. "That was forever and a day ago. Really, Mike, you've got to learn to let things go."

That was rich coming from her, but before Mike could comment on that fact, the water running through the pipes cut off, and a second later, the bathroom door slammed open. Brett strutted out, dripping wet and naked as a jaybird with his dick pumped up nice and hard so it could lead the way.

"Oh for God's sake," Mike groaned as Hailey shrieked and clenched her eyes closed.

Angie, on the other hand, just stared and grinned as Brett walked right into the middle of the kitchen. Without a word of explanation, but with a bold laugh, he started shaking, spraying water in all directions. That included Mike's.

"Hey, man, this is the kitchen!" Mike complained, not that his twin seemed to care.

Brett stilled, fisting his hands on his hips and grinning triumphantly back at Angie, who hadn't flinched. Her gaze had remained locked on Brett's dick with a hungry look that was so damn sexy it was hard to remember that turning her down was for the best. It didn't matter how hot Angie was or how much he wanted her. It would end only in disaster.

How could it not?

After all, it had started as a crazy dream years ago. It had seemed like such a simple thing at the time. Angie had been harassing them as usual about her dream and how one day they'd all live happily ever after together. Brett and Mike had found the whole thing funny, at first.

Angie hadn't let it go. She'd pestered them every day for several years before they'd finally broken down. It had been on the last night before they headed out for boot camp. Both Brett and Mike had been looking forward to having a wild send off, when Angie had crashed the party and chased away their dates.

It had been a joke, but they hadn't been amused. So, full of annoyance and outrage, they'd sworn they'd never touch her, and if they did, they'd marry her.

Who knew the woman would actually hold them to it?

Angie had done more than that. She'd responded with her own overly dramatic vow, promising to save herself for them. And according to Chase Davis's frequent calls, she had. Angie had waited for them. Never in his life had anybody waited on him. That made Mike feel things that honestly scared the crap out of him. He didn't like being scared.

"Okay," Hailey said, interrupting Mike's thoughts. "As the landlord around here, I'm instituting a house rule. No naked people in the kitchen. Now out!"

Hailey issued that order without ever opening her eyes. She even jammed a finger blindly in the direction of the door, but Brett didn't move.

"As the bigger, stronger, older brother, I'm instituting a new rule. All women must be naked in the house at all times...except for you, Hailey," Brett qualified after a second's hesitation in which he seemed to recognize just what he was demanding.

"Okay!" Angie agreed as she reached for the hem of her shirt.

"Don't—" Hailey didn't even get a chance to get a second word out before Angie's tank top hit her in the face when the other woman whipped off her shirt.

"Okay!" Hailey retreated blindly toward the back door. "I'm just going to leave you all to sort this one out yourselves, but when you're done, Angie, you can find me at the police station."

Chapter 2

"I'm innocent." Angie held her hands up as she felt both Mathews brothers' glares turn in her direction.

She knew exactly what they were thinking, but she hadn't gotten Hailey into any trouble. Hell, one could have argued that it was Hailey who had just landed Angie in hot water. No doubt, it was payback for the past. If it were, then Angie would count herself lucky because she wouldn't mind being punished by these two.

Just the thought had her nipples puckering and their gazes zeroing in on her chest. That was just what she wanted. Actually, what Angie wanted was to feel the thick length of dick Brett was waving around doing something a little more useful, like pounding into her.

It had been hard, real hard, not to give in to temptations all these years. There had been more than one occasion when she'd almost broken, but the wait was worth it. The painful agony of waiting just made it cruel for Brett to stand there naked, taunting her with an erection she really wanted to play with.

Maybe it was time to teach him not to wave his boner all around. Not unless, of course, he wanted somebody to come along and take a taste. Angie licked her lips and reached for the waistband of her skirt.

"But I could be guilty of anything else you wanted," she offered, forgetting about Hailey as she shoved her skirt down and stepped around the counter. She began to advance slowly on Brett, who held his ground, though he looked shaky doing it.

"After all, you have to admit this body is built for sin."

Angie ran a hand down her side, drawing their gazes to the smooth curve of her naked mound. She ran a finger down her slit, gathering the heated proof of her desire onto her fingertip and raising it daringly up toward Brett's lips as she leaned in close enough to brush her breasts against his chest and her cunt against the wet tip of his dick.

"Tell me, Brett, would you like to taste my cherry?"

His lips parted, and his tongue slipped out, but at the last second, he wrenched himself backward with a denial that sounded painful.

"No! No. I will *not* give in." But he would retreat, not that he went quietly. Pausing in the door, he turned to pin her with a heated look that promised retribution. "This isn't over."

Angie blinked and couldn't help grin. She wondered if Brett realized he was repeating himself. Turning, she cast her smile at Mike and found his gaze riveted on her finger. He looked hungry, and she couldn't resist tormenting him by lifting her finger to her own lips and sucking it dry.

That had the big man swallowing hard and stumbling backward. Mike looked so cute and serious, with his hair cut short and his dark eyes narrowed on her. Actually, he looked a little strained, which just made it all the more amusing when he banged into one of the kitchen table chairs and then fell into it. Angie smirked. Thanks to her time spent out at the Cattleman's Club, where women were required to be naked, she was very comfortable standing there wearing nothing but her smile and the morning sunlight while he sweated in his seat.

"Your brother does know that he sounds like some movie star villain, right?" Angie asked, deciding to toy with Mike by simply pretending she wasn't crowding him back into his chair, or slipping onto his lap.

"I mean really, it's not like I'm trying to rule the world," Angie purred as she spread her thighs across his and ground her cunt into the fabulously thick bulge of his erection.

Twining her fingers into the soft strands of his hair, she leaned up and pressed her breasts against Mike's chest as she forced his head down until their lips almost touched. He didn't fight her, but his chin didn't dip willingly either. He sat there stiff as a board, his muscles drawn tense and his breath caught. It was almost as though he was afraid.

"Or maybe I am." Angie pulled back, uncertain of his response but not about to show it. Sliding back off his lap, she paused to stare straight down into his eyes. "You never know."

With that, she turned and sauntered back toward the coffeepot, leaving him sweating in his seat. He didn't stay there long but scrambled back to his feet and fled out the door without a single word to her.

Angie sighed, the doubts and fears she'd carried with her nibbling on her conscience once again. The truth was that she didn't know Brett and Mike that well. She hadn't seen them once in ten years. Other than a few letters from Brett and even fewer from Mike, she didn't know what their lives were really like.

But her dreams were never wrong.

Angie believed in them, but that didn't mean she sometimes didn't wonder if everybody else was right. Maybe she was crazy. Maybe she was chasing an illusion. Or maybe she was just horny and obsessed with an overgrown crush.

Angie knew she'd find out the truth in the coming days. Of course, she was hoping to find all sorts of stuff, like what it felt like to finally take a man into her body. Not just one. That thought had her smile curling with wanton anticipation as she gave her pussy another quick stroke before pulling back on her skirt. Her shirt followed, and by the time she was settling down at the table with her morning cup of coffee, she was fully dressed and still not ready for the surprise of the day.

* * * *

"Well? Did you find anything out?" Brett demanded to know as Mike slammed into their shared bedroom looking worse for the wear.

That was just how Brett felt. He'd thought he'd one-up Angie by
strutting around naked, but the truth was, if he didn't keep his pants
on, he might end up sticking his dick someplace nice and tight, like
Angie's pink, creamy cunt.

God but did he want a taste of that pussy.

Who could blame him? Angie was so damn hot not even a saint
would be able to resist her forever. Brett was far from that pious. In
fact, he was pretty far from that high standard. Normally he'd already
have the woman bent over the table, but this was Angie. Angie was
different.

She was funny, smart, spunky, and sweet, and a little nutty with
all her premonitions. Normally, he'd snicker at such talk, but Angie
had been right about one thing. She'd said all those years ago that
they couldn't beat fate and wouldn't be able to resist her. It was that
last one that Brett had a sick feeling she was right about.

It was the rest he wasn't sure about, which was just why Brett had
never encouraged her. That had been easier when he'd been busy and
far away. He wasn't either of those things anymore. So, maybe, it was
time to re-evaluate the situation. Re-evaluate and then tie Angie down
with her legs spread and paddle that pussy until she was wet and hot,
begging him for more.

Then he was going to eat her out and make her come so hard, so
many times, that by the time he fucked his hard length into her tight
cunt there would be no pain for Angie, not even when he rode her
roughly through a dozen more climaxes.

When he was done with her, she'd be so far under his thumb that
she'd do whatever he asked. That thought put a smile on Brett's face.
He liked the idea of having Angie at his beck and call. Maybe he'd
keep her home, naked and leashed to the bed.

"Hey!"

Mike snapped a finger in front of Brett's face, breaking him out of
his hypnotic fantasy. He turned a glare on his brother as he tried to

pretend as if he wasn't weakening. "Well? Did you find anything out?"

"I just told you—no!" Mike huffed and rolled his eyes. "I know all you know, which is Hailey has rented her room to Angie."

"Did I know that?" Brett didn't remember anybody telling him that, but they must have because the question clearly irritated his brother.

"You were standing right there," Mike snapped back in exasperation.

"Like I was listening to anything Angie had to say," Brett scoffed as he broke into a grin. "All I was thinking that entire time was she grew some pretty big tits while we were out of town."

Mike heaved a sigh at that confession and shook his head. "You are so going to end up married to that woman."

"Oh, and you're made of such stronger stuff." Brett snorted at the very idea.

Mike just stared at him and blinked, not answering, but that in itself was an answer. When he finally did speak, his tone was distant and cold sounding.

"I think the smart thing to do would be to move out and not engage the enemy."

"Are you kidding?" Brett blinked at that, shocked his brother would even suggest something like that to him.

"Brett—"

"Don't start with that reasonable tone." Brett cut Mike off, not interested in the lecture he sensed coming. "After all, this is an irrational situation, so logic really shouldn't apply."

"That's the stupidest thing you ever said," Mike snapped, straightening off the door as he stiffened back up with his agitation.

"No, it's not." Brett scoffed as he bent back over his boots. He jerked on his laces, setting the double knot into place before straightening up himself. "The stupidest thing I ever said was I would marry her ass after I fucked it, but it wasn't as if I was expecting her to actually consider that an invitation instead of a dismissal."

"Which is just why we should—"

"What? *Flee?*" Just the idea was outlandish. "I am not a yellow-bellied coward and will not run from any woman."

Mike's mouth fell open. "You are not seriously considering marrying that woman."

"I don't know." Brett shrugged. The truth was the idea didn't really panic him, but still, he wasn't in a rush to marry anybody. "I am going to fuck her, though. So if you don't like the conditions she's set, maybe you ought to figure out a loophole or re-negotiate our terms."

"*Me?*" Mike gaped at him. "Why me?"

"Before it's too late." Brett nodded, perfectly content to let Mike sort out this problem. After all, he was the smart brother.

"Oh, for God's sake."

"Maybe we could goad her into making a new bet," Brett suggested, liking the sound of that. "Like convincing us to marry her by fucking our brains out?"

"You're crazy." Mike shook his head at his brother in disgust. "And this is going to end badly."

"Maybe." Brett couldn't deny that the possibility was great that things would snowball into an utter disaster. Maybe that's what Angie meant by fate. All Brett knew as that it didn't change anything. "That doesn't mean it won't be fun. Besides, what is the worst that could happen? We end up married to her? I mean, seriously, we could make her life a living hell. Convince her to divorce us."

"You're nuts." Mike snorted and rolled his eyes in disgust before pointing out the obvious. "You can't make her life hell without making yours that way. Talk about cutting off your nose to spite your face. Really, man, do you think before you speak?"

"I think you think too much," Brett shot back. "This isn't complicated, and she can't make us marry her, no matter what we do."

"Don't doubt it. You're going to end up married."

"Maybe." Brett shrugged, knowing that his cavalier attitude was just fueling Mike's irritation. "But that doesn't mean it won't be fun."

"I can't talk to you when you're like this." Mike waved him away as he turned around and wrenched open the bedroom door. "I'm going to get a shower."

With that, he stormed off, leaving Brett chuckling in his wake. Mike was such a drama queen. It was almost amazing he was straight. Even more shocking, the women actually tended to prefer Mike. They seemed to think he was a mature, responsible adult, or, at least, they didn't think Brett was any one of those three things. He was just fine with that, especially given their low opinions of him didn't stop very many women from having sex with him. It just normally meant they expected more of Mike before they did him. So, in the end, who really had it worse? The answer was clear.

Maybe that was the loophole he was looking for. Despite what she might think, Angie didn't really want to be married to him. No woman did.

Chuckling to himself at that thought, Brett followed Mike out the door and headed back to the kitchen, but all his hastily plotted-out plans were forgotten the second he stepped into the room to find Angie bent over the dryer in the back of the room. She'd put her mini-skirt back on and still wasn't wearing any panties, giving him a clear view of the pink folds of her pussy as she dug out a lace thong from the dryer.

Even once she stepped into them, they barely hid anything from his heated gaze as she fished around for the matching bra. That gave him a perfect opportunity to come up behind her and pin Angie in place with a hand flattened down over her spine.

"Hey!" She jerked against his hold, trying to squirm free but couldn't match even half his strength. That didn't stop her from mouthing off. "What the hell do you think you're doing?"

"Punishing a naughty, naughty girl," Brett retorted, making no attempt to disguise the laughter in his tone as he leaned down to whisper right in her ear. "You wanna be Mrs. Mathews? Well, here is a taste of what that means."

"Wait!"

But Brett was done waiting. Shoving her skirt right up to her hips, he exposed the beautifully curved cheeks of her ass. They were golden tan, just like the rest of her, but in a moment, they'd be glowing red.

"Can't we talk about this?" Angie pleaded.

"Nope."

Brett was having way too much fun to stop now. So was she because there was no denying the heady scent of a wet pussy filling the air. It intoxicated him, drugging Brett into thinking this wasn't just a good idea but the best damn one he'd had in a long time. Of course, he might not be thinking with his brain right then.

That worry didn't stop him from bringing his hand down hard, cracking his palm over the rounded curve of her ass and spanking a gasp right out of her. Just as he had imagined, her golden flesh flushed a beautiful, rosy hue that spread out as he brought his hand back down. This time Angie panted out a sexy moan and arched into the blow, making Brett's dick pulse hungrily as the swollen and wet folds of her pussy peeked out at him from behind the thin, lacy crotch of her panties.

The glistening beads of her desire only thickened along those pink lips as he paddled her hard and fast. Brett allowed his fingers to curl around and brush up against her cunt in an occasional teasing caress. Angie hips lifted even higher in a silent demand as her legs opened wider in a blatant invitation Brett didn't have the willpower to resist.

He had to touch.

Sliding a finger beneath the edge of her panties, he lost himself in the heated softness of her cunt. Stroking over her delicate folds, he couldn't help but test the tight depths of her velvety sheath. He stretched her wide with first one finger and then another and another until she moaned and shifted, fucking herself against him as she began to beg for something more.

"Oh, that feels so good," Angie murmured. "So good, but it could feel better."

Glancing over her shoulder, she caught his gaze and held it as she pumped her hips against his hand. It was the sexiest damn thing, and the moment only got better as she smiled and suggested that he take a taste, or give her one. Who knew which one he would have taken? Brett didn't get a chance to make that decision before Mike was there, whipping him away from temptation.

"Damn it!" Mike spat, keeping one hand fisted in the towel wrapped around his hips as he sent Brett crashing backward into the floor with the other. "I can't leave you two alone for a minute, can I?"

Brett was getting kind of tired of being pushed around, but before he could offer his own objection, Angie was snapping hers out as she turned around to confront his brother.

"You're a kill-joy, you know that?" Angie shot back as she yanked her skirt back down.

"And you're a cheater," Mike retorted, causing Angie to reel as far back as she could with the dryer behind her.

"I am not!"

"And walking around naked is *normal* for you?"

"Well…" Angie smiled as she caught Brett's gaze. "Cattleman Club rules, no clothing allowed on the women."

"You're a member of the club?" Brett lifted a brow at that, jumping to the very logical conclusion. "Then you've had sex, and our deal—"

"—is still on," Angie cut in. "Because while those men may have gotten a good look at all I have to offer, and a few lucky ones have even had the joy of getting me off on occasion, none of them have fucked me."

"You're bullshitting us." Brett didn't buy that lie for a minute. "There is no way they'd let you in the club and not have more fun than that with you. We know about the club, Angie. We're good friends with the Davis brothers, remember? So why don't you try a new lie?"

"Why don't you try giving your buddies a call?" Angie suggested with a smug smile. "And they can tell you all about how I supply them with women. Speaking of, I have to get down to the police station, and I should probably put on a more appropriate outfit. But since these are all wet, I might as well just throw them into the wash."

Angie lifted up her skirt and pulled down her panties, causing Mike to turn like a damn prude toward the wall while Brett acted like a man and stared. Hell, if Angie wanted to put on a show, he'd be more than willing to watch. Besides, it wasn't like ogling the woman could do any harm. Or maybe it could, because he really was hurting.

If he wasn't going to get to fuck her, he was going to need somebody else to take care of the need boiling in his balls, but strangely, that thought just didn't interest him.

* * * *

Mike watched Brett all but pant after Angie as she sauntered past him like a cat who knew the dog eyeing her was leashed, though he doubted she'd mind getting eaten. In fact, she'd been seconds from a devouring when he'd shown up, which left him with only one question echoing through his mind.

"What the hell do think you were doing?" Mike demanded to know the second he was certain Angie was out of earshot.

"I was just trying to teach the woman a lesson." Brett huffed indignantly as he turned back toward Mike.

"And what lesson was that?"

"I don't know." His brother shrugged, a small smile tugging at his lips. "Can't remember."

"Oh for God's sake! We just had this conversation."

"Well, I'm sorry, but I'm horny," Brett shot back. "You had me out on that damn boat fishing for the past three weeks. I'm a young man. I've got needs."

"Fine!" Mike snapped. "We'll go out and find you a woman. Just keep your hands off Angie!"

"Fine." Brett sulked as he threw himself into the kitchen seat, and Mike could tell that it really wasn't fine.

Hopefully, though, his brother could manage for a minute or two on his own because Mike needed to get dressed. He made it quick, not even bothering with shoes, keeping an ear out for Angie. It wasn't a shock that she was moving slower or that he made it back to the kitchen before her.

Brett knew Mike had rushed. His brother shot him a look and shook his head sadly as Mike stepped through the door. He ignored Brett. After all, his brother didn't have any right to cast a stone. Brett was the one who had been treating Angie to a quick finger fuck.

Mike knew his brother. If he hadn't interfered, he had no doubt that Brett would have ended up taking Angie right there against the dryer. Really, that was no way to treat a virgin. That was just why Angie deserved better than them.

Both brothers stilled as the sound of her bedroom door opening echoed down the hall. It was followed by the click-clack of heels on hardwood, and then Angie was strutting into the kitchen looking like a million bucks in a custom-tailored suit with a skirt, though she'd clearly forgotten one important item.

"Aren't you supposed to wear a shirt with that?" Mike grouched as his gaze narrowed on the sexy swells of her breasts revealed by the deep *V* of her jacket.

God but she looked good, and just seconds from being naked, but really he should have kept his mouth shut because no sooner had he spoken than Angie was rubbing up against him, her leg sliding up his thigh as she ground her hips into his.

"That's not all I left off," Angie purred with a smile that promised all sorts of erotic delights. "Wanna see?"

"Oh, yeah," Brett breathed out, all but leaping out of his seat. He came rushing forward, and Mike knew exactly what he intended to do, but they didn't need to indulge Angie with any kind of sandwich, even a meatless one.

"No." Stepping quickly back from the sudden rush of panic that flooded through him, Mike masked the frantic sensation with a scowl that he aimed at the woman causing him to sweat in a way he never had before. "If you're going to live here, we need some rules."

Mike straightened up, trying to reclaim his dignity, despite the disgusted look his brother shot him. He didn't know if he was fooling Angie, but Mike wasn't fooling Brett. Not that it much mattered. Angie clearly wasn't interested in hanging around to discuss the matter.

"Oh, please spare me the lecture." Angie waved him away and turned to march off toward the door. She paused with her hand on the knob and cast a pointed look back over at him. "I'm not your sister, and you sure as hell aren't my big brother. There is no fighting destiny. Go ahead and try, it won't change anything."

With that grand pronouncement, she swept the back door open and promptly walked into the large man filling in the doorway. They didn't come much bigger than GD, which explained why Angie literally bounced off of him and stumbled backward. Big he might be, but slow he was not. GD managed to catch Angie by the elbow before she ended up on her ass.

"Watch out, now," GD warned her, though it was clearly too late. "Oh, it looks like I'm interrupting something."

"A grand exit," Angie informed him as she shook off GD's hold. "So if you don't mind stepping out of the way…"

"By all means." GD stepped back on to the small landing that led down to the patio out back. "I assume you are headed down to the police station given your outfit?"

"Of course." Angie paused on the porch to glance up at him. "Have you already been there?"

"Yeah." GD frowned as if that answer weighted heavily on him.

He cast a quick glance back at Mike, who didn't even bother to pretend he wasn't listening in. The big man shot him a dirty look before turning a shoulder on him. That might have muffled their conversation, but it didn't stop Mike from catching GD's plea to Angie.

"I was hoping you might have a word or two with Patton on Lana's behalf."

"A word or two about what? About how Lana tried to kill her?"

"It wasn't like that, and you know it."

"I don't know anything." Angie shook her head. "I haven't been to the station yet."

"Yeah? Well, you know how these things work," GD shot back. "The DA is going to do whatever the Davis brothers insist he do. They're going to do whatever their woman tells them to, which means that *crazy* is steering this ship, Angie, and it isn't just Lana's fate hanging in the balance. It's the whole damn club's. Think about it."

Angie shot him a dirty look but didn't take up the argument as she turned and continued on with her grand exit. Mike watched her go until she was out of sight. Then he turned his attention on the big man crowding into the kitchen.

"What the hell was that about?"

Chapter 3

"Nothing for you to worry over," GD shot back as he closed the door and moved to help himself to some coffee. "I heard you two were back in town, and I came—"

"Anything that has to do with Angie is now officially our business." Brett cut him off, causing GD to pause as he glanced up at the other man.

Normally he was the biggest guy in the room, assuring that GD didn't take much shit from anybody, but that didn't hold true when Brett and Mike joined the party. They weren't little by any measure. Neither were they above using their size to their benefit.

Today they looked ready to brawl. That was fine by GD. It might be early, but his day was already chock-full of shit. That didn't mean it couldn't get worse. With his cousin's sudden appearance that morning, it probably would.

"So, it's like that, huh?" GD snorted and shook his head. "You two idiots realize you are taking all the fun of the chase away from the woman, right? I mean, everybody expected you to put up a little fight, at least."

"Everybody?" Mike's scowl darkened at that revelation. "Who is everybody? Why do they know our business?"

"Everybody is everybody," GD repeated, not intimidated in the slightest by either brother's frown. "And nobody has forgotten Angie's crazy dream or your over-melodramatic response. So, welcome home, where your business is everybody's business, and their business is yours."

"Well, you can just go tell *everybody* that this fight has just begun." Brett smirked, his glower giving away to a grin GD recognized well, even after ten years.

Of the two brothers, Brett had always been the charmer. Relaxed, easygoing, athletic, and always there to help, Brett never had a bad word to say about anybody it seemed. Mike, on the other hand, was a little weird. The man ironed his T-shirts, and he'd been athletic but never really put much effort into it. GD remembered Mike had always had his nose buried in some book.

That had paid off. Mike had managed to graduate fifth in his class and had been accepted to West Point. He hadn't gone. Instead, he'd enlisted with his brother. That was just weird. Then again, twins tended to be a little weird, especially about each other. GD figured Brett and Mike were a little odder than most, given they almost never agreed about anything.

Even what to do about Angie, apparently.

"There is no fight," Mike said, contradicting his brother. "We're not engaged in any battle. Whatever Angie is up to, whatever she does, it's not our problem."

"Yes, it is," Brett snapped.

"Brett—"

"Mike!" Brett shot back with the same plaintive exasperation his brother had used.

It was an obnoxious gesture, one that had Mike's lips thinning as he clenched his jaw and glared at his brother. Brett glared back. They stood there like that, the seconds ticking past with heavy silence until GD had had enough. He didn't have time for this bullshit.

"Well, this is just fascinating and as glad as I am to see you two back in town again, we've got some business to discuss," he declared, interrupting their staring contest and drawing both annoyed gazes in his direction.

"Yes, let's," Brett agreed with a nod. "We'll start by you explaining what you and Angie were whispering about."

"I take it you haven't read the paper." GD sighed. It was a long story, and he really didn't feel like going through all the details. So he shortened the tale to just the important facts. "Lana confessed to setting the Davis brothers' old barn on fire. I'm sure they told you all about that."

"Uh-huh." Mike nodded as GD fished a mug out of the cupboard and turned toward the coffeepot. "Patton got caught inside and damn near went up with the building."

"It wasn't that close," GD muttered. "She wasn't even burnt."

"I'm sure that makes Chase feel so much better." Mike snorted, and GD had to admit he had a point.

Chase was fit to be tied, not that GD could blame him. He knew how he'd feel if one of his exes almost hurt his girl. The guilt that thought alone stirred in him had GD cringing. Brett wasn't shying away, though.

He was stepping up.

"I still don't understand what that has to do with Angie." Brett crossed his arms over his chest, blocking GD's path back around the island counter. "While you are explaining things, I'd like to know just what the Angie meant when she said she was supplying you guys with women."

"Trust me, you don't really want to know."

Of that, GD was certain, but he knew nobody was listening to him. The brothers were back to picking on each other.

"Who the hell cares about all that shit?" Mike scoffed. "What I want to know is how a club full of so-called *studs* can't manage to de-hymenate one damn woman? You couldn't help us out there, huh?"

"You fuckers have been doing with my Angie, it stops now!" Brett snapped, shooting GD a dangerous look.

"Your Angie?" Mike gaped at his brother. "You've been around the woman for all of two hours! Now she's yours?"

"She wrote to me almost every week I was gone," Brett said, defending himself. "I know Angie better than I know most people."

"Oh please." Mike rolled his eyes. "Next you're going to be saying you fell in love with her mind."

GD waited, but Brett just stood there smiling. He didn't know what to make of that, and Mike had clearly worn out of the argument. He flopped back into a seat with a sigh as Brett turned a pointed look back in GD's direction.

"I believe I asked you a few questions, and I'm still waiting for my answers."

The command in Brett's tone irked GD a little, and he considered taking exception, but things were bad enough. He'd eaten enough attitude already that day. So he shrugged and offered the other man a response that was sure to irritate.

"I don't know what else I can tell you. You seem to have all the details. Angie supplies us with women."

"And?" Brett pressed.

"And?" GD repeated back.

"Why is she going to the police station?"

"Yeah," Mike spoke up, finally seeming to agree with his brother on one thing. He did want some answers. "Why's Hailey down there?"

"Probably because Patton's down there." At least, that was what GD figured. He also figured neither brother was going to let him get to the real point of his visit if he didn't satisfy their curiosity about everything else.

"Okay, look." GD set his mug down and tried to lay it all out for them. "Angie supplies us women. Lana manages them. Patton is engaged to the owners. Patton and Lana hate each other. Angie is good friends with both of them. Until today, Patton didn't know Lana was working down there. Chase didn't know that Lana had burnt his barn down. If this all comes out…"

Hell, GD didn't even want to think about the ramifications. Not that it really much mattered to him anymore. He was done with the club, which was exactly why he'd come to have a chat with the Mathews brothers.

"You guys are screwed." Brett snickered as he finished GD's thought for him.

"And here I was thinking you two would want to become one of us guys," GD retorted.

"You offering us a membership?" That had Mike perking up. "Because Brett here was just complaining about a lack of pussy."

"Yeah, I'm sure that is a problem for you with Angie around."

Everybody knew about the challenge the two idiots had dared to issue to one the most stubborn woman around. It had been years and Angie still hadn't let go of the issue. She was damn near on a holy mission, saving her virginity for Bret and Mike. All it was going to cost them was a wedding ring. As if that was just the dumbest thing in the world, the legend around their epic battle had only grown larger when people learned that it had all started with a dream Angie had had where she'd been married to both brothers.

Of course, everybody knew that Angie put a lot of stock in dreams, which just went to prove that she was nuttier than Patton. Patton was the only other woman known to be crazy enough to save her virginity into her twenties for a set of brothers that kept turning her down. Of course, the good money had always been on Patton. From what GD could see, the woman was still the one to bet on this time.

"Not a membership, a job." GD glanced pointedly from brother to brother. "I hear you two are without one of those."

"Actually, hadn't been looking." Brett shrugged and nodded toward his brother. "And big brains there plans on applying down at the community college in Dothan, though he hasn't got a clue as to what he's going to go for."

"I know I'm only going part time," Mike quickly corrected. "After all, a man's got to eat."

GD had a feeling he knew just what Mike was dreaming of snacking on.

* * * *

Angie parked her car across the street from the police station and sat there behind the wheel, trying to figure out what the hell she was really going to do once she walked into the station house. The easiest thing would be to side with Patton. After all, she was the one who had almost been killed.

Still, Angie knew Lana well enough to know that the other woman would never intentionally harm anybody, no matter what. Didn't she deserve to at least explain what happened before Angie judged her? Even if she didn't, what about the club?

GD, that jackass, was right to be concerned. This was a tangled mess. Worse, it was a public one. Clubs like the Cattleman's could survive only in secret. The club shouldn't come before justice, though.

Should it?

Angie could go around and around all day and grow a headache the size of the Grand Canyon, or she could get out of the car, cross the street, and see what she did once she got to the other side. That was how she normally handled stressful situations. She let her gut guide her because it knew best. So, with a deep breath, Angie shoved open her door and hurried on into the lobby before she lost her nerve.

Not large by any measure, the station was mostly one big room separated by a large counter. On one side, deputies milled about while civilians remained on the other side. Normally there would be only one or two deputies around and absolutely no civilians, but that morning the lobby was full and bustling.

There were the Davis brothers, all three pacing round and round in endless circles. Then there was Patton, firmly planted on the long wooden bench seat that ran the length of one wall. To her right was

Hailey, who had a hold of her hand and was practicing her "there, there" pat. Then there was Rachel, the local reporter, dating the very deputy she was talking to as she leaned against the counter, looking anything but professional right then.

There were others loitering about the lobby. Angie recognized a few as councilmen, another as a lawyer, and even a few of the busiest gossips had come to linger about and try to overhear the latest news. That was the curse of a small town. Nobody's business was ever private, which just went to prove that GD was right to worry over the club.

Angie, though, wasn't. She'd find a different job if the club shut down, but Lana was still screwed, no matter what. Really, as far as Angie was concerned, this was all Chase Davis's fault. He was the one who had led Lana on, who had toyed with her emotions for years, who had denied the obvious and allowed her to believe in a fantasy he had known wouldn't come true.

In short, he was an asshole.

She made sure he got that message, too, when he glanced in her direction. Shooting him a dirty look, Angie turned toward Patton as she rushed up to offer her a quick hug.

"Angie!" Patton stepped back and gave her a smile that contradicted her words. "You didn't have to come down here."

"Yeah," Angie drew that word out with a heavy sigh, realizing what she had to do. "I'm sorry, Patton, but I didn't come for you."

"What?" Patton blinked. "Then what are you doing here?"

"I've got a confession to make."

"Oh God, no!" Patton rolled her eyes and reeled backward, shooting her own dirty look at Chase before turning her attention back to Angie. "Not you, too. I'm kind of full up on confessions today, if you don't mind."

"I'm sure you are, and I know this isn't going to be easy to hear, but…at least, I can answer some of your questions." Angie tried to put a positive spin on the moment, but all she did was add to Patton's confusion, which darkened her scowl.

"What do you mean?"

"I mean"—Angie paused to take a deep breath and then just rushed right through the words—"I've been working for the club for years. I supply them with women, and I...am a good friend of Lana's."

"I see."

"Patton—"

"Nope." Patton held her hands up, cutting Angie off. "I don't want to hear it."

Angie could respect that, but she couldn't leave it there. "When you're ready—"

"You're going to tell me everything I want to know," Patton said, cutting her off and speaking loud enough to assure the three brothers covertly watching them as they paced. "No more secrets."

That had Chase stopping, offering her a plaintive, "Patton—"

Patton cut him off, too, not bothering to glance in Chase's direction even as she pointed toward him with a finger. "I'm not talking to you."

Chase growled, his jaw locking for a second before he resumed his pacing. He was like a dog on a leash, not that Angie had any sympathy for him. He deserved what he got. She was sure Patton would make him pay. It was just her nature. Forgiving was not.

"So? Do you have a plan?" Angie prodded carefully, not certain of the response she would get. What she got was classic Patton. That came with an eye roll and a disgusted sigh.

"Of course I have a plan." She glanced over at the brothers before leaning in to whisper softly. "I got plans for everybody. They start with seeing how far I can push those three before they snap."

"And..." Angie pressed when Patton left it at that.

Apparently, she didn't think there was much more to add. She did so in a tone full of exasperation. "*And,* hopefully, they'll get really creative when they punish me. It's going to be tons of fun."

Patton visibly fought back a smirk before turning to glare at the three brothers who had stopped, all pointedly trying to overhear their conversation. A fact that did not escape either Patton's notice or comment.

"What are you three looking at?" she barked at them, drawing another round of grumbles, this time from all three brothers.

Patton was definitely pushing and clearly enjoying herself, but that didn't concern Angie.

"Focus, Patton," Angie snapped, desperately trying to keep her own impatience out of her tone. "I'm talking about Lana."

"I know," Patton shot back, this time letting her smirk run free as she glanced back at Angie. "And that's my plan for you."

With that obnoxious retort, she turned to rejoin Hailey on the bench seat, waiting for God knew what. One thing was for sure. Patton wouldn't be telling Angie anything, not that she could blame her for that either. At least she was still speaking to her, and obviously she wasn't really out for blood.

That didn't mean they weren't all going to suffer. Lana, no doubt, more than the rest. The only question was who was really in charge of her future. Chase or Patton? Angie got her answer the moment she turned to head for the counter.

Chase cut her off, issuing his demands without preamble or even an attempt at a hello.

"I need you to take over Lana's duties at the club." Blocking her way, he issued that order as if Angie was actually under his command.

"Really?" She cocked a brow, making her opinion of him known with just a look. "And why should I do *anything* for you?"

"Because you are the only one qualified," Chase shot back. "So, yes or no?"

"That depends." Angie wasn't about to let him go so easily. "Are you going to press charges against Lana?"

Chase hesitated, and she could see that he wanted to say no. For a second, he looked guilty as he glanced over her shoulder. "That's up to Patton."

She couldn't argue with that. It would have been pointless to try, so Angie went for something more attainable. "Okay, then can you tell me why GD came by to see Brett and Mike this morning?"

Chase hesitated, but she could see he knew exactly what was going on. He didn't even try to deny it. "GD's offering them his job."

"His job? You mean out at the club?"

"Yeah."

That was not happening. Not on her watch. Those boys belonged to her, and they weren't escaping this time. "You give it to them and I quit."

"Angie—"

"No women. No membership privileges. Those are my terms." She was sticking to them, but she could tell Chase wasn't convinced.

"Seriously, if they wanted to be with you, they would be," Chase pointed out with the blunt harshness that had always left her wondering what either Lana or Patton saw in him.

"And if they didn't really want me, they'd fuck me and not marry me. Right?" Angie shot back. "After all, there is nobody making them live up to their word but them. Think about it."

With that, she shouldered her way right past him and up to where Rachel was fawning over her boyfriend. She and Angie had never socialized much, Rachel being a member of the good-girl club and Angie being a member of the wild-girl one. Rumors, though, were that Rachel had turned over a new leaf.

It probably had something to do with the big brute smiling down at her. If any man had ever looked in love it was certainly Deputy Kregor. The tenderness in his gaze hardened into a serious look at

Angie approached. The tall man straightened up to stare down at her with a look that more befitted his uniform.

"Can I help you, ma'am?"

"I'm here to see Miss Vey."

Angie stuck her chin into the air, realizing in that moment her outfit wasn't going to get her past this guy. So much for using her assets to flirt her way in to see Lana. Now she'd have to use her brains.

"She's not available for visitors," the deputy informed her.

"Do I know you from somewhere?" Angie asked, narrowing her gaze on him, knowing that she did. Deputy Kregor was a Cattleman. A fact she wasn't sure Rachel would approve of, or maybe she would.

"From the club." He nodded, clearly not embarrassed to discuss the matter not only publicly but also in front of his girlfriend.

"Then you know the kind of power I have," Angie snarled, threatening him directly and still getting nowhere.

"I don't need you to hook me up, lady," the deputy assured her, proving that he not only recognized her but also knew just what she did for the club. "I got all I need right here."

"Aren't you sweet." Rachel giggled, blushing under the look he shot her way and proving that while the rumors might be true some things never changed.

One thing that never changed was Chase Davis's ability to command authority, no matter what the situation. That included this one. Stepping up behind Angie, he pinned the deputy with a pointed look and demanded the man let Angie see Lana. That was all it took. Not a minute later she was being shown into a small room with nothing more than a table and a couple of chairs filling it out.

There sat Lana, looking more dejected than Angie had ever seen. She glanced up as the door opened, and there was a hopeful flash of optimism that lit up her gaze for a moment. It lingered, sounding in her voice as she pressed Angie for information almost the second the deputy stepped out of the room.

"Have you seen Chase? Is he very mad?"

Angie's heart about broke at that, and she couldn't help but sigh as she shook her head at Lana. "Honey…"

"I know," Lana whispered as her shoulders slumped forward and her chin dipped down. She didn't make Angie say it. Instead, she said it herself. "I'm pathetic."

"No!" Hurrying across the room to drop her purse on the table, Angie whipped around it to offer Lana a big hug. "Never say that. You're just a woman in love with an asshole. We've all been there."

"Yeah, but we didn't all burn down the asshole's barn with his current girlfriend in it," Lana muttered, not appearing the least bit consoled by Angie's heartfelt affection.

"Well…that's true." She couldn't help but admit to that. Stepping back to pull out a chair next to Lana, Angie settled down, keeping a hold of the other woman's hand and giving it a squeeze. "You want to tell me what happened?"

"It was an accident."

"The fire?"

"No." Lana heaved a heavy sigh, glancing up to meet Angie's gaze as she admitted, "I set that on purpose. I just didn't know Patton was in there. I never meant to hurt her or anybody."

"I believe you." Angie did. She had known Lana long enough to know she wasn't that kind of spiteful.

"Yeah?" Lana smirked, all but reading Angie's mind. "Is that your famous intuition at work?"

"Hey, don't knock it," Angie warned her.

"I wouldn't dream of it," Lana assured her. "After all, you may be the only one who believes in me."

"I don't think so." Angie glanced back toward the door, assuring it was closed before she leaned in to whisper. "Nobody wants this to go to anywhere really."

Lana contradicted her instantly. "Nobody but Patton, no doubt."

"I don't know about that." Angie couldn't help but smile slightly as she pointed out what she considered to be obvious. "I'm not going to deny that Patton wants blood, but she can't enjoy watching you bleed if you're in jail. Beyond that, she has to know that Chase would care and that would make you, actually, somewhat sympathetic, and that's the last thing she wants."

"Are you kidding me?" Lana blinked at her as though Angie had lost her mind, but she really hadn't.

"No. I'm not," Angie insisted. "I did see Chase, and you know what I saw?"

"One really pissed-off man?"

"A guilty looking one," Angie corrected, determined to force Lana to put the blame where it was due. "Chase may be an ass, but he's not stupid. He knows he made this situation what it is."

"Your loyalty is touching." Lana offered her a small smile as she shook her head. "But I did this. Not him."

"He drove you to it."

And that, as far as she was concerned, was that.

"You really are a sweetheart." Lana squeezed her hand before proving why she'd always thought Chase would eventually see things her way. They thought alike. "But I have a different favor to ask you. I need you to take over for me at the club."

Chapter 4

"This place is amazing," Brett whispered reverently, afraid to raise his voice and make the dream shatter. "If I'm asleep, please don't wake me up because this was just what I always thought heaven would be like—naked women everywhere."

That comment earned a laugh from GD, who shook his head at Brett as he led and him and Mike through the sea of not just naked but also beautiful women. There were short ones, tall ones, dark ones, pales, and everything in between. The Cattlemen obviously liked their variety, and not just in women. They clearly liked to have their women in almost any way and position physically possible.

It was a smorgasbord of forbidden delights.

Brett couldn't wait to indulge his own imagination. The real question was what to try first. He could pick a beauty or two and put them on display in the cubes or have them entertain him in the main hall, possibly treat him like a king in the sultan's cabana, or he could even hunt them down like naked prey in the lush garden mazes.

It was all too much. Brett didn't know where to start.

That wasn't true. The problem wasn't where. It was who, and who would be hurt. Angie? Mike? Him? All three of them? Those were weighty thoughts, and he purposely brushed them aside as GD led them to the very gates of the most wonderful place on earth.

They called it the Harem.

It was the women-only spa, where the ladies were primped and pampered. It was a privileged area where only male servants were allowed to wander. Male servants, and now Brett and Mike. It was prime pickings, and he could see the luscious fruit on the vine.

Brett's gaze lingered on a blonde, curvy and glistening with suntan oil. He studied her for a moment, waiting for the rush of hormones to flood his blood and harden his cock, but all that whipped through him was a whisper.

She doesn't have anything on Angie.

That was just a rude, annoying little voice, and Brett refused to listen to it. He'd never been that picky before and didn't believe for a second that his dick was about to start turning blondes down now. It just needed a little encouragement.

"Why don't the two of you go on, and I'll just catch up later," Brett suggested as he flashed Mike and GD a quick smile before nodding toward the woman sunning herself down by the Harem lagoon-styled pool. "I think it's time for a swim."

"No picking up the ladies in the Harem," GD instructed him.

Slapping a hand down over Brett's shoulder, he forced him to turn toward the small, thatched-roofed bungalow tucked in between the oversized palms. He shoved Brett toward the red-painted door as he continued his explanation.

"The master of ceremonies is only allowed to come here to discuss business with the director of female services. Technically, that's Lana Vey."

"Didn't she just get arrested?" Mike scowled, barely sparing any woman a glance. He'd been focusing on GD's explanation as if the scenery wasn't any more interesting than an old folks' home.

"Yeah..." GD drew that word out with the heaviness of a man who had given up all hope. "It's a mess."

"So, there is a job opening?" Brett asked, coming to the obvious conclusion. "Because, you know, there are two of us. Mike could be the master, and I could be the director."

"How come you get to boss around the naked women?" Mike took immediate exception to that suggestion. "Maybe I want to be the director."

"Neither of you want the job," GD cut in. "All these women do is bitch, and, really, the point of the club is to get away from that."

"There is a point to all this?" Brett shot back with a smirk. "That sort of takes the fun out of it, doesn't it?"

"Trust me, there isn't much fun about being the master either," GD warned him. "Because the men bitch, too."

"About what?" Brett couldn't even conceive of what they had to complain about, but the answer was kind of obvious.

"Each other," GD retorted succinctly. "This a den full of alphas, and that can blow up. Part of my job is to keep the flames from becoming infernos."

"Then get me a hat and a bright red truck. I'm ready to volunteer," Brett assured him, earning a laugh from the big man and an eye roll from Mike.

"You're more likely to start the fires than put them out." Mike spoke as though he wasn't a kid with a pack of matches himself, but Brett wasn't fooled.

Everybody else might think his brother was the calm, sensible one, but Mike was the one who got them into the most trouble. That was what came from too many brains. Fortunately for Brett, he hadn't gotten his fair share of those, a fact that he relished.

After all, he wasn't interested in being considered smart so much as good, and that he was. Brett was good at a lot of things. Fixing engines, hitting a mark, escaping the enemy, playing just about any damn game of chance there was, not to mention sports, he was good at all the things that counted.

Who the hell wouldn't want to be him?

Mike.

"I think we best get moving before Brett sets a spark off," Mike suggested as he eyed his brother. "I know that look. He's getting ready to do something stupid."

Brett rolled his eyes as GD continued on with the tour. It ended up in the men's den, where formally attired butlers and attendants waited to see to any order and a fully stocked bar was packed with the finest of liquors, all for free.

"This place just keeps getting better and better," Brett whispered, eyeing the selection of liquors in amazement.

"Just don't forget this isn't just about having fun," GD warned him. "It's a business."

"Now you're just letting the air out of my tire," Brett grouched, turning away from the bar with a sigh.

"I hate to tell you this, buddy, but there isn't any air in your tire," GD pointed out. "Which brings me to another point. There are no drugs allowed. No pumps, no blue pills, no anything. Understand?"

"Like I need an aid." Brett snorted at that but couldn't deny GD's original point. Glancing down, he shook his pelvis as if he could wake up his penis, but it didn't respond. "Maybe he's broken."

"Or maybe he's just not seeing what he really wants," GD shot back, causing Mike to scowl.

"Maybe we ought to stick to the business at hand," Mike insisted, shooting Brett a dirty look as GD nodded and turned to gesture to the wall of mirrors. Each one glowed with internal screens.

"This is called the big board," GD explained before moving over to a table and picking up what looked like a remote. "The big board is the club's main communication hub. As you can see, you can watch what's going on in any of the areas where the cameras have been turned on, and there almost isn't an inch of the club that isn't covered by a camera."

"We can see that." Brett nodded, his grin growing even larger as he tilted his head to study some of the funky positions being tried out. "You guys offer a yoga class or something?"

"No, we don't even have a gym. Most the guys have them at home, though. The members tend to be pretty much all in shape. Wait until you're challenged to a hand-stand sixty-nine competition." GD snorted. "Takes a lot of strength and focus and the guys love to practice that one."

"You're kidding, right?" Mike echoed Brett's thought, though his brother's tone was tinged with disbelief while Brett waited in anticipation of GD's answer.

"Nope." GD shook his head. "And, trust me, the women got the easy part. They always do because there is only one thing that these men love almost as much if not more than fucking, and that's competing. You can see here. We've got a betting book."

Using the remote to flip through the menu options, he began going over the club's computerized systems. Through any of the tablets provided, a man could access a catalogue that listed not only available women but also provided pictures of them along with their preferences. After picking out a woman or two or three, a man had to decide where to host his private orgy, and there was a catalog for that, showing vacancies and areas available.

Available didn't mean free.

The club had its own currency, known as buckles. Men earned buckles through competitions and activities that were routinely held. They could also win them through betting, and that was where things got interesting. Brett found himself fascinated by the club's betting book. Only the most perverted kind of wagers were placed, and one of the biggest ones had Angie's name attached to it.

Brett went cold as he stared at the sheer quantity of men who had anted up to be the first man to pop that cherry. The only comfort he could take was the fact that the bets were old, and clearly all were losers. That was Angie, more stubborn than a pack full of alphas. Alphas who had absolutely no respect for Brett or his brother.

The heated flush that had scorched across his cheeks flared hotter as Brett caught sight of his own name and the bets being placed against him and Mike. He wasn't the only one who took note of the cattleman's lack of confidence in either of them.

"What the hell is this?" Mike demanded to know as he pointed at his name. "Who the fuck is Dean Carver? And why does he think he's going to be the one who gets to train Angie after we disappoint her. *Disappoint?*"

"I have never disappointed a woman in my life," Brett declared indignantly as he straightened up, but GD looked far from impressed.

"You can't blame them for thinking…"

"Thinking what?" Mike pressed as GD's explanation faded into silence. "They don't even fucking know us, so how can they be thinking anything about us?"

"Angie's popular." GD shrugged. "So, it stands to reason that these guys would all kind of think you're idiots for turning her down."

"Do they *know* that we'd have to marry her if we didn't turn her down?" Mike shot back, clearly outraged at the savaging of his reputation.

"She can't make you marry her," GD pointed out as if Mike didn't already know that, but it was Brett who answered for him.

"We gave our word."

That was all that needed to be said, or maybe not.

"You were eighteen." GD chuckled. "She was…what? Sixteen?"

"You're forgetting her dream," Mike grumped. "The crazy woman actually thinks we're her destiny."

"My point is that only a crazy person would consider your vow binding," GD insisted.

"Who said we were sane?" Brett asked, wondering what planet that person lived on.

"Hey!" Mike shot him a dirty look. "Are you saying I'm crazy?"

"Yeah. Hell, you're the one who has been keeping me on a leash, so that must make you the crazier one." That sounded reasonable to Brett, but he didn't think Mike agreed, given the look his brother shot him.

"Anyway…" Mike pointedly turned the conversation and his glare back on GD. "If we're going to work here, Angie's got to go."

"Uh…yeah, that's not happening." GD hesitated to take a deep breath that warned Brett things were worse than they appeared, which was saying something. "She's our recruiter. And, like I said, she's popular."

Brett could see. He could also see notations he didn't understand. "What does this mean? Jarrod ten in the back? Five hundred buckles? Is that a lot?"

"You don't really want to know the answer to that, do you?"

"Oh, I think we do." Actually, he already feared he knew. "What does ten in back mean?"

"Just what you think." GD confirmed Brett's darkest suspicions. "Jarrod had ten minutes to make Angie come while riding her ass."

That was blunt and crude and filled Brett with a sense of outrage he probably didn't have any right to feel.

"Hey, what about this?" Mike pointed out a bet that wasn't even a year old.

It read clear as day and needed no interruption. GD had competed in a sixty-nine competition with Angie as his partner. They'd won, or, more specifically, he had. Brett stilled at that revelation, his gaze cutting from Mike to the big man as he felt the burn of a nastily heated emotion flare through him. It was unrecognizable, but he didn't like it. It made him want to hit something, like GD's smug face.

"What the hell does that mean?" Brett demanded to know, even though he already knew. Part of him just couldn't accept it.

"Just what it says." GD didn't back down for a second. Instead, the gloat in his tone only thickened. "Angie rewards men who are good with their mouths. After all, she only promised you *one* kind of virginity."

"You son of a bitch," Mike whispered, echoing Brett's thoughts exactly. "You've fucked her."

"Been a while but"—GD shrugged—"I've won more than just five hundred."

"*What the hell does that mean?*" Brett was on his feet now, his fingers clenched into fists and ready to swing as he glared down at the big man.

"It mean's giddy up. The girl likes it from behind."

That was it.

Without thought, without hesitation, without consideration for just how big the damn man was, Brett launched himself at GD.

* * * *

Chase heaved a deep sigh and wondered what deity he'd pissed off because his day was just growing uglier and uglier. Now not only did he have a pissed-off Patton, a locked-up Lana, and a dead Gwen, he had three beaten and bloodied men littering his office. He figured he might consider himself lucky that there weren't any more bodies, given the size of the three men who had busted up the men's den.

GD wasn't little, and neither were the Mathews twins. The twins, though, were known to be brawlers. Hell, he'd gone several rounds with them himself. GD, on the other hand, normally had a little more sense than to pick a fight, but apparently, his new girlfriend was having a negative effect on him.

Chase hadn't met the infamous Kitty Anne, but he'd heard about her. He'd also been warned to keep Patton away. GD feared Patton would be a bad influence on his Kitty Anne. Apparently, she lacked impulse control.

And, as if having a second Patton running amuck around town, Wanda was back. Wanda Davis. The name sent a chill down Chase's spine, an old reflex from childhood. He had right to his fear. Wanda had beaten the crap out of him.

While most men might think it was embarrassing to admit to having his ass handed to him by a girl, those men had not met Wanda. She was big, strong, and just a little shy of sane, but that didn't make her impulsive. Wanda was that cunning kind of crazy that made her a whole lot more dangerous.

Angie, on the other hand, wasn't dangerous. She was just weird. She liked to make decision based on her gut feeling. Chase couldn't deny that Angie's intuition had served them all well when it came to her recruiting abilities, but that didn't make her qualified to run the club.

Nobody really was but Lana. Chase admitted he probably should have had her training somebody to take over, but he hadn't. Now he was stuck with Angie.

The Mathews brothers, on the other hand, he could get rid of. They did have a well-known feud going on with Angie. Now they were supposed to work with the woman? The place would be in shambles before the end of the week.

GD couldn't leave.

"I need to speak to you." Chase nodded toward the big man before casting a dirty look at the two brothers drinking his best liquor. "Privately."

"That would be our cue to get lost." Mike nodded toward his twin as he shoved out of his seat. "Maybe we ought to go find ourselves some ladies to kiss our boo-boos."

Brett snorted and rolled his eyes as he shoved out of his seat. If Chase hadn't had enough on his plate, he might have wondered about his lack of enthusiastic response. As it was, he noted and then dismissed it as he focused in on Mike's comments.

"I don't think so." Chase felt like an ass for doing what he was about to, but Angie hadn't given him much choice. He hoped the brothers understood. Actually, he tried to make sure they did. "Angie's taking over for Lana, and she had one stipulation. I bet you can guess what it is."

They could. Chase could tell from the way both brothers turned outraged gazes on him as they sputtered.

"But...but...that's not fair!" Mike spat, sounding desperate.

Brett didn't. He sounded more confused than anything. "But we're working here."

"No pussy for you." Chase couldn't make it clearer than that.

"You would chose a woman over your best friends?" Mike demanded to know.

"I chose the running of this club over your carnal urges. Besides, I'm sure you can pick a woman up in town." Hell, Chase knew it. The two brothers were trouble, the kind that attracted women.

"Yeah, but they're not already naked," Mike grumbled.

"We're not arguing about this." Chase couldn't afford to. "Angie made her demand, and it's not like it's not fair. She's not getting any dick."

"Not in her pussy, at least." GD smirked from his seat as he taunted the brothers anew. "Her ass, though, that's up for grabs, and let me tell you the woman knows—"

"Enough!" Chase cut him off, reading the violence flaring in both brothers' eyes and recognizing it for what it was.

So maybe Angie had a point. Maybe that infamous intuition of hers was right again. Maybe Brett and Mike hadn't touched her for the same reasons Chase had held out on Patton, because it was the right thing to do. Not that he'd been able to deny her forever. He didn't think Brett and Mike would be able to resist Angie either.

Maybe there was hope that things would work out after all. It certainly would make his life easier if Brett, Mike, and Angie settled down together and agreed to manage the club. It could be the perfect, long-term solution to Chase's problems.

One thing was for sure. Lana couldn't come back.

"Just get gone," Chase snapped, shoving both brothers toward the door. "And if you want pussy, then I suggest you buy a ring or convince Angie to lift her demand."

"Fine," Mike huffed. "But you wouldn't know where Miss Bossy is?"

"In her office." Chase jerked opened his door and stood back. "Go argue with her."

They went grumping off, and he was glad to see them go, slamming the door behind them and turning on the big man still snickering in his seat. GD shook his head and sighed.

"This is not going to end well."

"What?" Chase lifted a brow. "Brett and Mike attempting to persuade Angie to let them have sex with other women or the conversation you and I are about to have?"

"I would have said the former, but given that tone, I'm guessing it's the latter," GD grumbled as his smile faded. "You're pissed."

"You got that right." Actually, pissed didn't even begin to touch on what he was feeling. "You lied to me."

"About?"

"Lana."

Sucking in a deep breath and trying to control his temper, Chase moved around his desk, putting the large, heavy piece of furniture between them before he did something rash. Starting a fight with GD wouldn't improve his day, even if the thought was tempting.

"I didn't know she started the fire," GD denied, sounding as sincere as he ever did. "I swear it."

"And you couldn't figure it out either?" He didn't buy GD's excuse for a second.

The big man was the best damn investigator in the county. If he hadn't managed to deduce Lana had set Chase's barn ablaze, then that was because he didn't want to know. Not that Chase could really blame him. He didn't want to know it either.

Until that morning, when Alex had called Chase to tell him that Lana had confessed, his emotions had been simple. He was going to kill the bastard who had dared to threaten his Patton. That bastard turned out to be the man in the mirror because Chase knew he was the one who had driven Lana to lash out.

"Honest, man, I thought it was somebody else." GD put his hands up and dug his heels in. Chase just wasn't up for the battle.

"Yeah. Right." Slumping back down in his seat, he stared down at the desk and heaved a deep sigh. Lana really wasn't the problem. The problem would be arriving in the morning. "Patton cut Lana a deal. She's buying Lana out."

"What?" GD gaped at Chase in horror. "Patton? She's going to own a fourth of the club?"

Chase nodded slowly. "And she's got plans."

"God save us all," GD whispered. "Angie and Patton are going to be working together."

"Along with Brett and Mike."

"And Wanda," GD breathed out with a heaviness that left, no doubt, about how he felt about their cousin.

Chase couldn't claim to feel any different. Wanda was a nightmare. A strange kind of nightmare, because she wasn't mean or vindictive. Instead, she had an iron-clad conviction of what was right and the strength to enforce her beliefs. That made her prone to trouble. Real trouble.

"Yeah, about her, what is she doing here?"

"Hiding."

GD caught Chase's gaze, and they shared a look.

"It's that bad, huh?"

"Does pissing off a serial rapist sound like a good thing?"

No, it certainly didn't. Chase hesitated, but couldn't help but ask, "And just how did she accomplish that?"

"She shot him in the balls."

"Oh, God." Chase cringed, but wasn't shocked. That sounded like Wanda.

"He broke free and is on the loose. We don't know if he's coming after her or not." GD shrugged, but it was there in his eyes. The big man did know. "Her daddy's concerned, so he's the one who sent her this way to get lost until him and Jonathan catch the bastard."

If Wanda's dad was unnerved, then there was reason to be worried. Danny Davis, better known as the Bull Moose, made his nephew, GD, look small by comparison. Hell, Wanda was damn near as tall as her cousin, and she was the short one in her family. She was also the only crazy one, which probably had something to do with being the only girl in a brood of seven siblings.

"He told me to sit on her," GD grumbled before snorting and rolling his eyes. "I was thinking of trying to distract her with a little side action."

Chase perked up at that, a terrible thought darting through his head. "Oh, don't say it."

"But I'm not sure if I know any men brave enough to take her on."

"You're not bringing her to the club." Chase didn't have time to deal with that.

"But if I don't find that rare breed of man, then I know what Wanda will find." Again GD met Chase's gaze, and they shared a moment.

"Trouble."

"Gwen," GD clarified, reminding Chase of the one last problem he had to deal with.

Gwen.

Dead Gwen. Murdered Gwen. Murdered, blackmailing Gwen. Murdered, blackmailing, Cattleman club member Gwen. Murdered, blackmailing, Cattleman club member, ex-lover of the current sheriff, who also happened to be a Cattleman, Gwen.

Sadly enough, it got worse from there.

Chase shot GD a pleading look and came as close to begging as he ever would. "You can't leave me."

Chapter 5

Angie sat behind Lana's desk feeling completely disoriented. This was the wrong side. She never sat in the big chair. It felt weird. Even stranger was the sense that this was her command post and she had a legion of servants at her beck and call.

Servants!

The notion was just too weird to a woman who didn't even have employees. Even if she had, Angie would have let them call her by her first name, but here she was Miss Montes. As if that wasn't weird enough, they catered to her. Nobody ever catered to her.

Just the opposite. Angie was a travel agent, a glorified sales person. She was normally the one making the pitch and seeking to convince others, but all of a sudden, she had a whole harem full of women seeking her approval. They needed it to get past the gates that led to the Cattlemen.

The Cattlemen had needs as well.

She was the grease in the well-oiled machinery that made the club run smoothly, and Angie didn't have a clue as to what the hell she was doing. Lana and Chase might think she should have one, but they were crediting her with paying more attention to what the hell Lana did for a living than she ever actually had to.

It couldn't be that hard, though, to figure it out. All she had to do was return calls, authorize bills to be paid, pat hands, input data, and sit back and enjoy making Brett's and Mike's lives a living hell. That last one was the real reason she'd accept this temporary position. The payback was worth any difficulty she might encounter over the next few days.

Just in case Angie forgot that fact, fate brought them right to her door, and they came storming in, only to stumble to a halt. Almost instantly, Brett's eyes narrowed on her breasts as Mike wheeled around like some virginal prude who had never seen a naked lady. It was almost laughable, and Angie couldn't help but smile as she leaned back, making sure Brett got a full look as she stretched and sighed.

"I was wondering when the two of you would arrive." Angie gestured to the chairs across from her as she rose up and moved toward the small wet bar in the corner. "Please, have a seat. Is there anything I can get you?"

"A taste of that pussy?" Brett asked hopefully as Mike snapped at her.

"Will you please put on some damn clothes?"

"Nope." Angie shook her head at both of them. "No free tastes for you, and going naked is the only option at the club. At least not for the women, which I'm sure you've noticed."

"You're different," Mike insisted.

"Not really," Angie denied with a smile as she eyed the thick bulge growing bigger by the second beneath Brett's zipper.

His eyes had dropped with his request and now remained fixated on the lips of her pussy, making her cunt go all soft and wet. Mike, on the other hand, was growing tenser.

"Angie—"

"And you're proving it right now. Obviously I'm harder to resist, or are you ready to have that seat?"

That challenge had him turning around and marching stiffly over toward one of the chairs set on the opposite side of the desk. He plopped down, his back straight as a lance, his gaze locked on the wall, his attitude clearly in place. Brett was just as obviously ready to take up the challenge.

He smirked as he settled down into the chair that was about two sizes too small for his oversized frame. Not a little man by far, Brett looked rock hard and solidly male next to the floral fabric. Mike, with his features gathered into a scowl, looked darkly dangerous and sexy as hell. If only he walked around naked, then they could have some real fun.

That thought put smile on Angie's face as she repeated her earlier offer. "Something to drink?"

"Oh, screw the damn drink!" Mike pointed to the chair on the opposite side of the desk as he tried to boss her around. "Sit the fuck down. We've got some stuff to discuss."

"Well, when you put it like that, how can a lady resist?"

Angie smirked, intentionally taunting him by sauntering up to plop her ass down into his lap. There was no hiding the welcome waiting for her there. He was hard and large. That just fed her lust all the more, making her brazen enough to grind her ass into the thick length of his erection as she wrapped her arms around his neck and pumped her breasts against his chest as she gazed up at him.

"So? What exactly is it that you wanted?" Angie purred as if she couldn't tell. Want it Mike might, but take it…the bastard just refused.

"Don't make me dump you on the floor," he ground out, barely managing to loosen his jaw enough to get the words said.

Angie blinked, remaining still and silent as she all but dared him to try. Of course, he had to. She knew he would, but she'd practiced long enough with a stripper pole to know how to hang on as he stood up. Mike's expression was almost laughable, and Angie couldn't help the giggles that escaped when he actually tried to shake her loose. Brett's deep chuckles rumbled beneath her lighter laughter, his tone filled with amusement.

"Hey, brother, I think you got a woman stuck to you," Brett informed him as if Mike didn't know, earning him a glare from his brother and another laugh from Angie.

"Let go!" Mike snapped but didn't force the issue.

He didn't have to. Angie could tell he was feeling stubborn and grumpy. With an indignant sigh, she released him and stepped back to shake her head up at him.

"Well, aren't you grouchy?" she muttered as she cast a frown in Mike's direction.

"Yes, I am," he shot back. "You're denying us women."

Angie snorted at that as she retreated around her desk. "I'm just evening the odds. No dick for me, no pussy for you."

That sounded reasonable to her, though the truth was much simpler. She was jealous. Angie hated the feeling. It made her sick and irrational and made her do stupid things. Looking stupid was her greatest fear.

Actually, it was her second. Being alone was her first, but she didn't have to worry about that. Fate had assured her long ago that these two brothers were the men meant for her. Of course, fate was a screwy thing, and Angie had to admit she wasn't sure if it had done her right or wrong.

"Don't you have any pride?" Mike demanded to know in a blatant attempt to shame her, but Angie had no shame. She just shrugged.

"What does pride have to do with this? We're talking about sex. It's not exactly a dignified sport, at least not if you're any good at it."

"And how the hell would you know, virgin?" Brett retorted, answering before she could. "Oh, that's right. You take dick in a whole lot of ways, just not the best one."

"That's a matter of opinion."

Angie had no complaints, but she could tell Brett did, thanks to the tense line that had formed over the bow of his very kissable lips. He was forcing his smile and gritting his teeth. There could only be one reason for his sudden sourness.

"After all, I like variety," Angie pressed, secretly thrilling at the glower growing in both brothers' gazes. "And around here, what Angie likes, Angie gets. Got me?"

"That's fine." Mike's soft tone didn't blunt the menace echoing in his words as he leaned forward over Lana's desk and pinned Angie with a feral look that sent both a thrill and warning racing through her.

He really was a handsome fellow. Mike's scowl only highlighted the rough, rugged cut of his features. It was as though he'd been carved from stone by a master sculptor, one who had captured the dark, tormented depths of his soul. The sight made Angie's heart ache.

She wished she could soothe away his worries and fears, assure him everything would be all right, but Angie knew Mike would never accept that kind of gesture. He'd see it as pity and was way too hard to tolerate that kind of weakness.

"Go get yourself whatever the hell it is you want and leave us alone."

"And would that really make you happy, Mike?" Angie lifted a brow, daring to taunt him with the most outlandish of threats. "I tell you what. You agree to sit and watch, and I'll let you pick out the man."

All he had to do was say yes and Angie would have known that he wasn't the one for her, but Mike didn't say it. He didn't even respond to her offer but sulked deeper into his seat with a belligerent frown drawing at his brow.

"This is about that stupid fucking dream, isn't it?" Mike grumbled of disgust. "That was years ago. I would think by now you'd grown up enough to realize the idiocy of basing your whole life on a dream!"

"You think I'm any more thrilled about this situation than you?" Angie snorted, deciding on trying a different angle. She was going to prick his pride because everybody knew he had a lot of it. "For God's sakes, Mike, look at yourself."

"What?" Like a dumbass, he looked down at himself and scowled. "There is nothing wrong with me."

"Please," Angie snorted and rolled her eyes. "Maybe if I was…well, I mean, do you really, honestly, think that a woman like me wouldn't want to aim a little higher?"

"*What the hell does that mean?*"

"It means the princess here thinks her delicate ass is too good for us," Brett answered, sounding far from insulted. Mike, on the other hand, was red enough to make a tomato envious.

"Is that right?"

"I'm sorry." Angie offered him that apology with a half-hearted, pitying smile. "But I make like four times what you do. Not to mention I'm better educated and, honestly, a lot more popular. I've got to figure I'm, at least, four steps above you. Crazy or not."

"Steps?" Mike gaped at her as if she'd lost her mind. "There are steps now?"

"Of course there are," Brett agreed, leaning back smugly in his seat and making it clear he knew just what Angie was up to. "And princess likes the idea of getting dirty with the big, bad boys, don't you?"

"You may be that big," Angie assured him. "But you're not that bad."

"You're all but begging us to corrupt you."

"I never beg." Angie never would.

"And what do you call grinding up against us naked at every opportunity?" Mike asked in exasperation.

"Marketing." Angie smiled.

"Ha!" Brett erupted with a spontaneous laugh that rumbled on as he shook his head at her. "You are too much, and I think Mike's right. It's time we set some rules."

"Rules?" Angie heaved a heavy sight. That sounded so confining. "Must we?"

"Absolutely." Mike nodded as he finally settled down in his seat. "Get a pen out. We're laying down the law."

"Really? And what's the penalty if I break it?" Angie lifted a brow, certain that the answer didn't matter. She would be breaking it. Mike knew it just as she knew he didn't have a clue as to what to do about it.

"Get a pen!"

* * * *

Mike glared across the desk at Angie, refusing to let his eyes stray as she made a show of getting up and bending over to retrieve a pad and pen from the lowest drawer in the desk. She might have the best ass he'd ever seen, but he cared more for her than that.

And he did care.

That was what was eating up. He knew what kind of guy he was, and it wasn't a good one. He'd done things, horrible things. Not just to the enemy. He'd broken more than one woman's heart. He'd broken too many to count. He was that kind of bastard, and Angie deserved better.

That was what Mike was trying to do there, save her. Save himself. He would do it to. It was that simple determination that had made him such a good solider. He latched onto that goal and refused to let go. He was a marine. He wasn't about to let some little girl take him down.

Of course, the Corps had never trained him to handle the kind of temptation Angie presented as she settled back down in her seat and scooted her chair forward in a motion that had those perfect tits bouncing. She knew exactly what she was about. Her smile assured Mike of that.

Angie held his gaze, the light twinkling in her eyes as all the secrets of the universe seemed to shine out of them. The promise of a life full of love and happiness, of tenderness and joy, of frustration and aggravation, and every other thing that scared the living crap out of him. Mike knew who he was, and he was not that man.

Neither was Brett, but then his twin wasn't particularly insightful either. Left to his own devices, he'd probably end up married to Angie—married and divorced, leaving behind kids and a broken-hearted woman. That was the fate Mike was trying to save Angie from, but it would have helped if she didn't seem so eager to throw herself into the fire.

"Okay." Angie licked her lips and wiggled in her seat as she clearly settled into the role of the leader. "Rule number one—"

"No running around the house naked," Mike cut in, asserting his dominance, not that she paid him any mind.

"No sex of any kind with anybody else."

"I don't think so."

Keeping Brett entertained with a little pussy on the side would definitely help keep him out of Angie's, and Mike wasn't going to let his brother take him down. That was what would happen if they limited themselves, but Angie wasn't listening.

"Rule number two, all hard-ons are to be attended to promptly."

"I don't get it," Brett cut in, sounding honestly confused and more than a little amused. "If we're not allowed pussy than how—oh, wait. I get it. I can agree to that rule, but I've got to point out something—"

"Brett—" Mike tried to cut him off, knowing exactly where his brother was heading, but there was no stopping him.

"I got about twelve inches that need attending to, darlin', so, according to your rules…"

Brett didn't finish that thought. He just smiled and leaned back in his seat, thrusting his hips slightly up and drawing everybody's attention to the prominent bulge growing behind his zipper.

"Oh, I think now it's thirteen," Brett warned Angie. "You better get up and over here, darlin', before it reaches fourteen and I decide to take that ass for a ride instead."

Angie tipped her head back and laughed, enjoying the moment. She took her time as she shoved her chair back, clearly planning on giving Brett exactly what he asked for. Mike knew what would come next. Fear and panic shot through him.

This was all happening too fast.

He didn't have a plan. He always had a plan. What was he going to do? Mike didn't know, but that didn't stop him from catching Angie's wrist as she came around the desk and tried to saunter past him. He meant to tell her to sit her ass right back down, but those weren't the words that came out of his mouth.

"Have a seat."

That sounded more like an invitation than a command thanks to the husky want thickening his tone. Angie heard the difference. Her smile grew wider as she glanced down at the bulge in Mike's jeans before looking back up and pinning him with a pointed look.

"On that thing? It might poke me."

Brett bust out laughing once again. Angie began to sink down to her knees in a sexy motion that had the blood roaring through Mike's veins as his dick swelled painfully harder.

"Maybe I ought to take care of that for you before you hurt somebody," Angie purred as she pressed herself between his knees.

Her tits, all flushed and full, brushed against his thighs and had his fingers digging into the arms of his chair as he fought the need to touch. That wasn't all he wanted. He wanted a taste, too. A taste of those tits, and to make a whole damn meal out of the wet pussy scenting the air with the sweet aroma of feminine arousal.

Mike's gaze dipped down past the graceful curve of Angie's waist to the naked folds of her cunt. They were swollen and glistening with cream, and he swore right then and there that before this war ended he would know just how good she tasted and how hard she could come. In that second, a primitive, feral urge rose up through him, defying the logic and reason that assured him he should run.

Run now before it was too late.

The panic damn near overwhelmed him, and instinct kicked in as his legs kicked back, sending him toppling over in his chair. Mike crashed into the floor and scrambled to his feet, taking off without a thought as to what he was fleeing or where he was running to.

* * * *

Brett sighed as he watched his brother flee like a little girl being chased by a bee. It was humiliating, but he understood. Angie clearly didn't. She stared after Mike with a confused scowl, replacing the sultry look that had set her features aglow seconds ago. She glanced over at him, and he could see the doubts clouding the brilliant glimmer in her eyes before she swallowed them back and forced a smile, no doubt for his benefit.

"Was it something I said?" Angie joked, but Brett knew Mike had hurt her.

"Mike gets panic attacks sometimes," Brett admitted with a sigh. Shoving out of his seat, he avoided her gaze as he turned toward the door. "I better go check on him."

"Brett?" The uncertainty in Angie's voice had him pausing by the door to glance back her, still kneeling there looking almost lost.

"It's not you...well, maybe it is, but it's not because of you." Brett knew that didn't make any sense, but he didn't know what else to say.

Even if he did, he didn't want to talk about it. What they'd seen, what they'd endured, those were their demons to carry and cope with. If they had to be shared, then they would be shared between them. Brett wasn't about to tarnish a creature as soft and sweet as Angie with all the horrors he'd seen during war.

Turning, he left her kneeling there and walked away. Brett didn't have to look for Mike. He knew where he'd run off to, and sure enough, a half hour later when he pulled his truck into the shade of a cluster of oaks, he could see his brother's legs hanging down from the old gnarled branch they used to climb up to and stare out over the massive, man-made lake.

Back then, they'd been young and had shared their dreams of the wild life they intended to live. Their stories and tales had been so full of excitement and victories. They'd been so naïve about the price of that kind of life. Now that they knew, the question really was what they were going to do next. There was no better place to find that answer than here.

It might have been a decade since he'd climbed their old oak, but the motions were still trained into his muscles. The only difference this time was that the limb he settled down on to next to his brother groaned beneath their combined weigh. For a moment, Brett worried that they might be taking the expressway down, but the branch held, even if it did dip a little.

"You need to lose some weight," Mike commented without bothering to look over at Brett, who scoffed instantly at that monotone reprimand.

"You weigh more than me."

"Six percent body fat," Mike shot back, touting his most favorite number because he knew Brett's was seven. No matter how hard he tried, his brother was always just a little harder than him.

"Well, at least I didn't run screaming from the room because a naked girl was about ready to give me a blow job." Brett knew that was low and insensitive, but that was him. He didn't do serious talks. They made him feel strange and uncomfortable.

"I wasn't screaming," Mike muttered as he rolled his eyes. "And I wasn't running. I was *escaping*."

"A naked woman?"

"A failed marriage," Mike corrected him, giving voice to the fear Brett knew had lived within his brother since their father had walked away.

The bastard had just upped and left years ago without a single word or ever once looking back. That didn't mean that Brett didn't know that he'd moved down to Dothan, married another woman, and started a whole new family. Apparently, he liked that one better.

Only Hailey had seen him since, and only once. Apparently, their dad had shown up at the lawyer's office to claim his half of their mom's life insurance after she'd died.

Brett hadn't been there, which was probably a good thing because God knew he'd like to beat the crap out of the man for what he'd done to his brother and sister. Both Hailey and Mike were sensitive souls. Both had been devastated. Not Brett, though. He was just angry. He'd put that anger to good use over the years, so maybe he should have been thankful.

"Maybe we should move out of the house," Mike suggested, bringing up that topic once again.

"So, that really is your solution." Brett cast a disappointed look in Mike's direction. "You just want to run away."

"Knowing when to retreat isn't running away," Mike shot back, returning Brett's look with his own dark one.

"Yeah, it is." Brett snorted up a laugh.

"Well then, what the hell do you suggest?" Mike demanded to know defensively.

"Why not give things a chance and see where they lead?"

"To love?" Mike spat that word out as if it left him feeling dirty. "Now who sounds like the girl?"

"Men can love," Brett insisted before shooting his brother a big smile. "I love you."

"Oh, shut up."

"What's wrong?"

"Brett—"

"Don't you love me, too?"

"Brett." Mike breathed out his name on an aggrieved sigh as his shoulders slumped under an imaginary weight, but Brett wasn't going to let his brother wiggle out of saying it.

"Don't you?" he pressed, earning a growl and a snarl as Mike finally gave in.

"You know I do. Otherwise, I'd have beaten you to death by now."

"Well, that's sweet." Brett snickered, not the least bit put off by his brother's scowl. "Just say the same thing to Angie and see how she feels about you then."

"Crazy as she is, she'd probably put on boxing gloves and take me on."

"Likely naked, too," Brett added on, finally causing his brother to snort up a half-smile.

"Yeah, likely, too."

That eased the tension, and they sat there for another half-hour in silence before Brett dared to say what he was really thinking.

"What are we going to do with her?" Brett glanced over at Mike, who turned his chin to meet Brett's gaze. For a moment they shared a special kind of acceptance. "I'm sorry, man, but I'm not going to last."

"You really think we're good enough for her?"

"No." Brett shook his head. "But that is not exactly our decision to make, is it?"

"Yeah, it is." The corners of Mike's lips lifted in a smile Brett knew meant trouble. "All we've got to do is prove the point to Angie."

"And how you going to do that?" Brett was almost afraid to ask.

Chapter 6

"Why are men so intent on being difficult?" Angie asked that question of nobody in particular. Flanked on either side by Patton and Hailey, she looked up and pinned the big, bald bartender with a pointed look as he slid a beer beneath each woman. "I mean, really, all I wanted was to give him a blow job, and he ran away like a little girl."

All three women waited and watched as the stiff-faced Riley blinked that question in. He didn't crack a smile or flush with any kind of blush as he responded with a flat, uninterested tone.

"That's six bucks, plus a two buck tip for asking a stupid question."

"What's so stupid about that question?" Angie bristled as Hailey reached for her wallet.

"You been hanging out with the wrong type of man if you don't get how scary you are," the man shot back as he snapped up the money Hailey offered him.

With that, he turned and sauntered off, leaving all three women staring after him before finally Hailey broke the silence.

"He might have a point there, actually." Hailey cast a critical eye over Angie. "I mean, you're putting a lot of pressure on them with all that destiny crap. You ever consider how overwhelming a man might find that kind of idea? After all, there is such a thing as trying *too* hard."

"No there isn't." Patton snorted and rolled her eyes. "Don't let Hailey make you doubt yourself. You know your destiny. You feel it in your heart. You got to follow it…and you haven't gone too far even if you have tied the man to your bed and mounted him."

"Now there is an idea."

One Angie would have loved to try, but she didn't think Mike would take kindly to being restrained like that. Brett, now, he might let her get away with it. She'd probably have to return the favor, though. Not that that was a problem.

"Don't even think about it," Hailey warned her. "And don't listen to Patton. Trust me, none of her men would dare to let her tie them up."

"Oh, I don't know." Patton straightened in her seat with a smug smile. "They're all at home squirming, and I bet they'd do just about anything to be forgiven, particularly Chase."

That comment had Angie's thoughts shifting away from the two brothers intent on driving her nuts to the two women, who, thankfully, had settled their differences. Well, maybe not settled, but they'd negotiated a true of sorts. She knew just whom she had to thank for that.

"That was real nice." Angie shot Patton a grateful smile as she qualified her compliment. "What you did for Lana. I mean it was a little weird—"

Patton cut her off with another snort. "There is nothing weird about it, and I wasn't being charitable. I was getting rid of the damn woman."

"You could have sent her to jail," Angie pointed out. "That would have gotten rid of her a lot longer than just a few weeks."

"Yeah, and then what about Chase?" Patton shot back. "The man reeks of guilt, and that isn't just because he lied to me. I can tell he feels like the monster that kicked the puppy, and I don't need him obsessing over her like that or putting himself down. Besides, I got what I wanted."

"Her share of the club."

Angie knew the contracts were being drawn up, just as she knew that Patton could afford to buy out Lana only because Lana had agreed to her price.

"That's right. The Cattlemen are under *new* management." Patton gloated outright as she lifted her drink up into the air in a salute. "And I can't wait to walk around naked!"

"Like Chase is going to let you get away with that." Angie paused to narrow her gaze on Patton. "Unless, of course, you want him to have a stroke."

"No. Not hardly," Patton assured her. "I just don't want him brooding over his mistakes. I have found nudity does tend to distract a man."

"Hear, hear." Hailey raised her glass to that.

They all drank, but it was Patton who smacked her glass back down and offered them up another evil smile.

"Besides, I need the leverage. I've got plans."

"Plans?" Angie lifted a brow, not liking the sound of that at all. "What kind of plans?"

No goods ones. That answer became obvious as Patton started rattling out all her ideas. Angie and Hailey listened to her go on for nearly another hour before Patton's phone rang and she finally took a break to answer it. It was then that Hailey finally gave voice to the worries Angie had sensed brewing in her since they'd met up.

"So, Mike really took off, huh?"

"I'm sure he was just messing with me." Angie forced a smile, not wanting Hailey to worry.

"I don't know." Staring down into her drink, Hailey seemed to weigh the options before finally giving voice to her worries. "Mike's always been the sensitive one, you know? I think things might have been a little harder on him in the military than Brett."

"Don't worry. I'm not planning on being hard on them," Angie assured her as Patton's indignant tone rang throughout the bar.

"Oh, don't take that tone with me, mister! I'm allowed to ride my motorcycle if I want to. After all, it's mine!"

"I'm just saying, he's always been weird about letting people in. Our dad walking out didn't exactly help."

"Then it's time he broke out of that shell, or he'll spend the rest of his life alone and locked in it." Angie would know. Hadn't she locked herself away in her destiny? Her fantasy of them, of Brett and Mike.

"Yes, but that doesn't mean you have to keep flashing him." Hailey puckered up somewhat indignantly. "Maybe you should take things a little slower. You know? Like keep your clothes on."

"Oh." Angie considered that for a moment and could admit, at least to herself, that Hailey might have a point. That didn't stop her from teasing the other woman. "But I look good naked."

"Oh, yeah? Then come and find me because I'm not coming home till I *feel* like it." Patton slammed her phone closed and glanced back over at them with a smile. "Now, where were we?"

Before either one of them could answer, the bar's phone let out a shrill ring. Riley answered it, barely speaking a word, but he didn't have to say anything. His gaze spoke for him as it landed on Patton.

"Yeah, man, she's here."

"Well, I guess I've got to go." Patton hopped off her seat, pausing only to give Angie and Hailey a quick goodbye. "See you two ladies later."

With that, she sauntered out of the bar, sticking her tongue out at Riley as she strutted on past him. A few seconds later, the roar of a motorcycle's engine boldly revved up in the parking lot. It growled loudly before speeding off with a whine, and Angie couldn't help but offer up a prayer that Patton didn't end up a splat on the road.

"I mean, really, do you want to end up like that?" Hailey asked as she turned back to pin Angie with a pointed look. "Always at war? Because my brothers deserve a little peace."

Angie couldn't deny that Hailey had a point. She deserved a little peace, too. She felt certain she could find it. After all, Hailey had.

"Oh, don't even pretend like you and Kyle started out all lovey-dovey. He was your archenemy in high school," Angie reminded Hailey, knowing the other woman hadn't forgotten. "And from the rumors I've heard, you and Cole started out with a pretty antagonistic relationship."

"I guess," Hailey admitted somewhat reluctantly. "But we confined our battles to the bedroom and adopted a porno night."

"Excuse me?" Angie blinked, not certain what that had to do with anything.

"We have porno night," Hailey repeated, and this time she expanded on her explanation. "You ever see that documentary about the monkeys who have sex as a way to settle every dispute?"

"No." And Angie really wasn't interested in seeing it either. "Please tell me that's not the porn you are watching."

"No! God." Hailey huffed as she rolled her eyes. "I didn't mean it like that. I meant that Kyle, Cole, and I are all real competitive, so to keep peace, we have game night…sometimes more than once a week, but the point is that it's hard to fight when you're fucking."

"I see." Actually, Angie really didn't, but she didn't figure she would no matter how Hailey explained it. "Well, maybe you ought to give that advice to your brothers because I am trying to convince them to have a porno night, and they keep telling me no."

"That's because you keep making marriage a string attached to the sex," Hailey retorted before also pointing out what Angie could begin to see was kind of a flaw in her plan.

"And men hate to feel pressured."

"Mike more than most." Hailey nodded. "That's probably why he ran. You scared him."

Angie didn't think it was her that had sent Mike fleeing so much as what she represented, the possibility of a relationship and a future. The reason didn't matter, though. Hailey was still right. Angie needed to find a way to take the tension out of the moment. Thanks to Hailey, she had a pretty good idea of how to do that.

"I've got to go." Angie picked up her purse and hopped off her stool. "This has been a good talk. Next time I'll get the drinks."

"Where are you going?" Hailey swung around in her seat, calling after Angie. "It's still early!"

"Sorry, I've got some business to take care of," Angie tossed back as she reached the door.

It flew open before she could push into it, and Chase came storming into the bar, damn near running Angie over in the process. He stumbled backward, his gaze cutting from the room at large to her, and she could read more than anger there. He was panicked.

"Sorry," Angie offered him a quick, sympathetic smile. "Patton already took off, and no, I don't know where."

"Damn it!" He spat that out as he turned to storm right back out of the bar, but Angie caught him by the elbow, bringing Chase to a quick stop.

"You know she's just messing with you, right?"

Angie didn't feel any qualms about ratting Patton out. Not when she knew Patton was looking forward to getting punished. Hopefully, this would help with that goal because Angie really didn't like Patton racing all over the place on that damn bike.

"It's payback for lying to her all this time, but still, she's not really hurt," Angie assured him, expecting instant irritation at that revelation. She got it. It just wasn't directed at the right person in her mind.

"Don't you think I know that?" Chase snapped.

"You do?" Angie released him to pull back and scowl. "Then why are you running around cussing at everybody?"

"Because I don't want all my underwear dyed pink again," Chase shot back as if that made any sense.

It didn't, but then again, it didn't need to, which was a good thing because Chase wasn't waiting around to explain himself either. He slammed out of the bar, leaving Angie to wonder if he knew that Patton had forced Lana to sell her half of the business to her.

Something told her he didn't, or he wouldn't be faking being panicked.

That was tomorrow's problem.

Tonight she had a bigger obstacle to surmount. Unfortunately, he wasn't home when she got there, but Brett was. He was vegging out on the couch, watching TV and drinking a juice box. He glanced up as she came strutting into the room.

"Hey." Brett lifted his juice in a greeting that Angie didn't bother to return. Instead, she started right into her proposition.

"I want to make a deal with you."

"Yeah?" Brett lifted a brow at that. "What kind of deal?"

"I'm talking about a porno date night." Angie sucked in a breath and laid out her idea without bothering to consider the details. "We'll each get one day a week to tempt the other. If, on my day, I manage to get you or your brother to fuck me, you marry me. If, on your day, you manage to make me beg you to fuck me, it's a free ride."

Brett blinked up at her and then burst out laughing. Angie didn't know what to make of that. All she knew was that he looked good, relaxing there on the couch. While the same artistic hand had cut Brett's features from the very same cloth as Mike's, the light of his personality animated his expression with such mischief that Angie had always been able to tell them apart. She always would.

"I'm sorry, Angie," Brett apologized as he got himself in hand. "I'm not laughing at you. I'm just laughing at the situation."

"Why?" Angie narrowed her gaze on him, certain that didn't sound good. "What's the situation?"

"I'm sure you'll figure it out soon enough." Brett straightened up in his seat as he reached for the remote and hit the mute button. "As for your proposal, I'm curious if you're offering this just to me or to both Mike and me?"

"It's open to both of you." But Angie didn't expect both brothers to take her up on it. At least not at first.

"Yeah, but you don't think Mike is going to say yes." It was like Brett was reading her mind. "But you do think I will. What's more, you think I won't have the control to stop."

"Does it really matter what I think?" Angie couldn't deny he was right on all three of those points.

"Oh, yes. I think it does," Brett insisted with a wicked little smile that hinted at a deeper meaning. "But, like I said, you'll figure that out soon enough. What I want to know is just what is allowed, that is if I agree to this arrangement."

"Anal, oral, and everything in between." Angie could tell that her bold bluntness amused him. More than that, it had him shifting as his jeans began to bulge with a great deal of interest. "Even vaginal if you can make me beg for it…even if you can't, you can always use a toy. Hell, it's not like others haven't."

That last comment had Brett's eyes flashing with a sudden heat that played directly into Angie's plans. She had Brett hooked and halfway reeled in. He was going to agree, or he would have if Mike hadn't chosen that moment to come slamming through the front door.

"I got the liquor," he declared, not bothering with a greeting. At least not bothering to offer his brother one. Instead, he cast her a big smile that warned Angie something was definitely up. "Hey, Angie, want to get drunk?"

"Why would I want to do that?" Angie lifted a brow as she fought back a smile, suspecting she knew exactly why he wanted her to do that.

Mike didn't answer, though. Instead, he moved deeper into the living room to drop the box of booze on the coffee table. It was an impressive pile, and she didn't think for a moment he planned on finishing that off alone. She was probably supposed to help. Then, once inebriated, who knew what would happen? What vows might get revoked? What conditions overturned?

Angie rolled her eyes at those thoughts, wondering if Mike really thought she was that easy. Or that it was that easy to get her drunk.

Many had tried to get Angie liquored up enough to make a mistake. None had succeeded because the one thing her parents had given her was a good alcohol gene.

That didn't mean she didn't enjoy playing along with the guys, though normally her fun began after they passed out. Just the idea of what Angie could do with Mike had her grinning as she moved to close the door. She had it halfway there when the door swung back inward and two men came huffing in as they lugged a keg with them.

"Hey, Mike, where you want this?" Duncan, a local deputy and well-known Cattleman, called out as his buddy shot Angie a devilish smile.

"Hey, Angie." There was no hiding the mischievous glimmer in Daryl Watts' eyes. He was a new member to the club and clearly fitting right in with the rest of the guys. "You ready to party?"

"Oh, yeah." Angie smiled and peered around the door. "So how many of you are there?"

So the game wasn't exactly laid out the way she'd imagined it. Maybe Mike thought she'd make a different kind of mistake. Angie wasn't certain. All she knew was that he was the one who had made the mistake.

Chapter 7

Thursday, June 6ᵗʰ

Mike smacked his lips, trying desperately to swallow the foul taste that permeated his mouth. There was no help for it. He needed to get up and brush his teeth. Only he couldn't seem to move. His limbs felt heavy, and his head as if it was full of cotton, except when he tried to move. Then his head felt like it was full of rocks, clacking against his skull and unleashing pounding waves of pain.

Staying still seemed like the best option. Besides, he was quite comfortable. The mattress beneath him was soft but not as soft as the woman curled up in his arms. She smelled good and had big boobs. That was all he really knew right then, and he only knew that much because his face was buried in the silken strands of her hair, his hand curved around a very plump breast.

Mike couldn't help but give it a little squeeze, smirking to himself when he felt the nipple buried in his palm harden. That wasn't the only thing growing harder. The woman in his arms murmured and shifted, grinding the plush globes of her ass back up against his morning wood.

He might be hung over and feeling like shit, but he still had it. Mike would even be willing to brave the pain of moving to prove that point and figured that as long as he kept his bedmate face down in the pillows she wouldn't be able to tell how bad off he actually was. Hell, he couldn't even crack his eyes open without grimacing and wincing away from the light.

That didn't stop him, though, from capturing her tit between the sides of his fingers and giving the puckered bud a roll or two. The woman moaned and matched the motion as she rotated her hips in a blatant invitation. Mike was never one to turn down a naked woman, especially not one who smelled as good as this one.

The sweet scent of her cunt filled the air, and he knew she was hot, wet, and ready for him. Mike couldn't resist testing those waters. So, he risked the pain and slid a hand down over a soft stomach, a smooth mound, and into the swollen folds of a pussy weeping for his touch. She was tight, wet, and had muscle control that made his dick thump against her ass in silent demand to be buried in her.

The cunt clenched around his fingers responded to his cock's motions, pulsing and rippling with a welcome that had Mike ready to roll the woman in his arms over and bury himself in her, but she moved first. Arching her hips and capturing his dick in the crease of her ass, she pumped herself against him as she moaned and begged for him to take her there.

Mike was halfway there, rolling her over and rising up onto his knees as he gripped her waist and lifted her up. Then he opened his eyes to find his way and blinked against the harsh glare of sunlight only to find himself staring down the graceful curve of Angie's back.

The tanned, plush globes of her ass were caught between his hands, even as the swollen, flushed length of his dick pumped up and down the sweet crease that divided her cheeks. She was bent over before him, moaning into the pillows as her hips followed the motion of his hand…the hand he had buried in her hot, wet cunt.

That was when it hit him. He was about to fuck her. About to fuck Angie. Mike couldn't stop. The want, the need, it was all too much, and his body was moving without command. Despite the voice screaming a warning through his head, Mike felt his hips rear back and watched the swollen head of his cock slide down to the shadowed entrance.

He was one breath from taking what he wanted when the panic finally rallied through him, and Mike found himself falling backward. Wrenching himself away from her, he tumbled off the bed and crashed into the floor. He didn't feel any pain, though. Nothing could penetrate his shock as he watched Angie heave a deep sigh and she scrambled to her knees and frowned down at him.

"I take it you're not going to take my ass for a ride, huh?"

* * * *

"She offered you *what*?" Slade gaped at Brett as if he'd lost every marble in his head.

"A porno date night," Brett repeated with a shrug before pointedly glancing around at the bodies piled up on the floor. "Then this happened."

This being the rager that had the cops showing up at their door at the three in the morning. It had been impossible at that time to really stop the party. The deputies had helped Brett chase off those who were still standing, but a good half of the partiers had already collapsed in either exhaustion or inebriation, his brother included.

Of course, that had been after Angie challenged him to a drinking competition. Mike had lost, and Angie had won in more ways than one. With his brother barely capable of forming words, she'd led him back to her bedroom. Brett wasn't sure what had happened from there, but he did know his brother had been way too drunk for anything good to happen. That was just why he hadn't followed them. After all, somebody had to remain sober and watch over the party.

Brett hadn't gone to sleep until he was sure that everybody was down and in no danger of drowning in their own vomit. He'd checked in on Angie and Mike then and saw them cuddled up and naked in her bed, but a hard look had assured him nothing had happened.

Neither was sweaty or mussed. More importantly, nothing was sticky. He didn't know if that was for the better or the worse. Brett had considered the matter as he crawled up into his own bed and had come to no answers before he passed out.

It seemed as though he'd just closed his eyes when a pounding at the back door had him tripping over the bodies still littering the floor to reach the damn thing and make the racket stop. Brett had found the middle Davis brother on the back porch, looking way too wide-eyed and awake for the hour.

He hadn't offered up an explanation for his visit and Brett was way too tired and hung over to ask. He was trying to catch up, but the coffeemaker worked only so fast. He stood there behind the counter, keeping an eye on the pot as Slade started to pester him with way too many questions.

"Yeah…" Slade drew out that word as he took in the mess all around him. "What exactly was this?"

"A kegger."

"A kegger?" Slade scowled as if the notion were idiotic. "What are you, eighteen?"

Brett shot him a dirty look for that shot but didn't bother to respond to it. He decided to pull the coffeepot out before the maker was done. There was enough for a cup. He didn't care about the sizzling splats that came dripping down onto the burner. He'd clean the damn thing later. Hell, he had a whole house to clean, so what did it really matter?

"What is really going on here?" Slade prodded, clearly unwilling to give up until his curiosity was satisfied.

"Mike thinks he can dissuade Angie by being an ass," Brett muttered, barely sparing Slade a look as he savored his first sip of bitter heaven.

After two more, he began to feel normal again. Normal, but still tired. Stepping over the two girls crashed out on the floor, Brett ambled around the kitchen counter to settle down into one of the kitchen chairs. Beside him, a man sat slumped over the table, snoring loud enough to irritate.

"So Mike threw a party to be an ass?" Slade pressed with a smirk. "That doesn't sound right."

"He's got a plan." Normally Mike's plans were pretty good, but not this time. "Mike's going to drink too much and whore around until Angie decides he's too disgusting to bother with."

"And how is that working for him?" Slade asked, and as if in answer, the sound of a door crashing open echoed down the hall.

It was followed by the thunder of footsteps and the groaned complaints of the people being tripped over. A second later, Mike darted past the doorway. He was naked and appeared to be running for his life, though nobody was chasing him. Mike disappeared, and Brett waited for the slam of their bedroom door before he shrugged.

"I'm not sure, but I'm going to say it's probably not going well."

"I think I can see that." Slade snorted and shook his head at Brett. "You know this isn't going to help your reputation, don't you?"

"I'm not worried about my reputation," Brett assured him.

"No? Then what are you worried about?"

"Mike." That was the God's honest truth. "I mean, this thing with Angie…it could be good. Really good. She's a great lady and hot. Man, does she look good…"

Brett sighed as he remembered how good. He couldn't help but smile as he considered how much better she'd feel, but he didn't dare linger on that though. Not unless he wanted to be more uncomfortable than he already was. Shaking his head to clear it of the memory of Angie walking out of the bathroom wearing nothing by a golden tan and a glistening sheen of water…

"Hey!" Slade snapped and kicked Brett's chair. "Whatever it is that's got you smiling like that, either do something about it or stop thinking about it."

"Yeah, see that's the problem." Brett smiled sadly as he focused once again on Slade. "I want her. I'm going to have her. The only question is what it's going to cost me."

"You afraid of losing your freedom?"

"No." Brett shook his head. "That's not it."

He didn't elaborate. He didn't have a chance. Mike came slamming out of the bedroom and storming into the kitchen, looking like a man who had just lost a serious battle. His hair was a mess. His clothing wrinkled. His eyes were bloodshot, and the stubble on his chin was thick and dark. He paused at the first sight of Slade and glared at the man.

"What the hell are you doing here?" Mike didn't even give Slade a chance to answer before he turned his scowl on Brett. "And what the hell happened last night?"

"Shhh!" Brett lifted a finger to lips as the mass of people strewn about the place grumbled and shifted, roused by Mike's thunderous tone.

It was too late, though, and people started to wake up enough to need assistance in finding the door. Mike sure as hell didn't offer it. He was too busy with the coffee and then trying to find something to eat. Brett heard Angie moving about, too, which explained the people who came stumbling out of the hall.

Angie wasn't actually one of them, and from the sound of water running through the pipes, Brett guessed she was getting a shower. She'd finished by the time he'd managed to clear everybody out of the house. He ambled back into the kitchen to find Slade at the stove, frying up a batch of bacon while Mike sat at the kitchen table with his head hung over.

"How you feeling this morning, man?" Brett stopped to ask his brother that question as he picked up the two mugs from the table.

It earned him a dark look as Mike's eyes shifted upward. His chin remained buried in his chest, and he looked like a wounded, feral animal. Brett didn't want to get bitten. So he held his hands up in surrender and backed away.

"Forget I asked."

"I'd like to forget the whole fucking night," Mike grumbled.

"You remember it?" Slade turned from the frying pan sizzling before him to cast a curious look over at Mike, whose scowl only deepened at that question.

"No, but I woke up naked in Angie's bed. I think that speaks for itself."

"Trust me, nothing happened." Brett lifted the coffeepot out of the maker, filling both mugs before returning Mike's to him. "Even if she'd mounted you, you weren't in any condition to take that ride...unless you took one this morning?"

Brett was guessing no but that it had been a near thing given the look Mike shot him. His brother didn't answer, though. He didn't have to. The heat racing across Mike's cheeks spoke for him. He was blushing. Mike didn't blush. That never happened.

"Man. Oh, man." Brett plopped down in the seat across from Mike and leaned forward eagerly. "Tell me everything."

"No!" Mike drew back as if Brett was the pervert, but it wasn't as if they hadn't had these conversations before. Then again Slade was there, and this was Angie.

"Later then."

"No!" Mike snapped. "Nothing happened."

"Uh-huh."

"I swear it."

"Sure." Brett didn't believe that for a moment, but he did believe his brother would never admit to what had happened.

"You know who you remind me of?" Slade asked as he came to dump a plate full of crispy bacon right beneath Mike's nose. "Chase."

"I'll take that as a compliment, even though I know you don't mean it as one." Mike also took the bacon, beginning to devour it like a man who hadn't eaten in months.

"I didn't mean it as an insult," Slade assured him as he stepped back to attend to the rest of the strips he still had frying in the pan. "But you're wearing the same constipated face that Chase kept making when Patton came home to claim him. Let me tell you, fighting it doesn't solve anything. Fucking..."

"Shut up, Slade," Mike grumbled. "This situation with Angie isn't anything like yours with Patton."

"Well, that might be true," Slade allowed. "After all, Patton is crazier and so is Chase. This whole Lana business has him twisted in knots, and Patton running wild isn't helping, which is just why they're sorting things back out at home right now."

"Yeah?" Brett quirked a brow at that. "He got her tied up?"

"Actually, he spent most the night dismantling her motorcycle." Slade's grin grew, making it clear he approved of his brother's destruction. His smile dipped, though, as he admitted, "Of course, she's probably online ordering up another one."

"She could just ask Hailey to put it back together," Mike suggested, his words sounding as worn out as he looked. "Hailey could rebuild the bike faster than Chase can tear it apart."

That was the truth. Hailey was a hell of a mechanic and an amazing blacksmith. She was also, apparently, tamed, which was just depressing. Brett sighed as Slade shook his head and shot down that idea.

"Chase has already talked to Cole and Kyle. They got Hailey under control. She won't be bringing her tools out to the ranch any time soon."

"I don't even want to know what you mean by that." But Brett would take care of the matter because nobody controlled his sister, or his brother. "Oh God. I know that look. You're planning on making trouble."

"Me?" Mike snorted at that before finding his first smile of the day. "I have no idea what you are talking about."

"Uh-huh," Brett agreed with clear disbelief, making a mockery of his words.

"See, just like Chase." Slade sighed and dropped another plate of bacon on the table before plopping into a seat. "I do not envy you having to put up with what's coming."

"And what's that?" Mike demanded, stiffening up in his seat.

"You breaking her heart."

"Please." Mike snorted and rolled his eyes. "That is exactly what I'm trying to avoid."

"I'll tell you what, man, prove me wrong."

"And how am I supposed to do that?" Mike scoffed. "Live happily ever after with the girl?"

"Why not?"

"Because nobody lives happily ever after."

That truth popped out, and Brett knew Mike hadn't meant to reveal that much. That depressing bit of pessimism was their father's damn fault. Brett really hated the man for what he'd done to his siblings. At least Hailey was willing to take a chance, even if she did have poor taste. Mike, Brett feared, would never be able to get over their dad's desertion.

Even if there had been any point to arguing with his brother, there wasn't time. All three men fell silent at the sound of a door being opened. It was followed by the shuffle of footsteps. Seconds later, Angie came shuffling into the kitchen.

Wearing a pair of faded gray sweats that hung low on her hips and a white tank top that molded to her breasts and flat stomach like second skin, she looked so damn good it made Brett ache in all the best ways.

"I see you decided to put on some clothes this morning." Despite his best attempt to sound as though he was joking, there was no disguising the strain in Mike's tone. It added a sharpness to his words that had him sounding like an ass yet again.

Angie paused to cast a dark look over at Mike. "Don't worry. I'll strip down when I get to work."

"Wait a minute." Brett spoke up from his corner, drawing Angie's gaze toward the table and the two men sitting there. "You're not prancing around all day naked at the club."

"Club rules." Angie shrugged. "Isn't that right, Slade?"

"That's right."

The man nodded in agreement, though his gaze and smirk remained firmly fixated on Brett. Brett paid him no mind. He was too busy trying to ignore the acidic bite of jealousy at the idea of all those men ogling Angie.

"Well now, there is a new rule," Mike declared, not shockingly siding with Brett. "Angie remains clothed, or we quit."

"It's a club rule," Angie shot back but Mike remained unmoved.

"Slade is making an exception."

"He can't do that…can you?" Angie frowned as both Mike and her turned to glare at Slade.

Slade frowned then sighed and finally shrugged. "Yeah. We'll make an exception."

"Fine," Angie snapped. She turned back around to storm out of the kitchen.

"And don't forget panties!" Brett hollered after her. Angie's response came seconds later as her bedroom door slammed closed.

"That was fun," Brett admitted as he broke into a round of chuckles.

"I don't think it was for Mike," Slade commented as both men turned to study him.

His fist was clenched around his mug, his knuckles white, his fingers tensed. A tick even began to twitch above his brow and only by a visible force of will did he manage to relax his muscles enough to force a smile.

"I have no idea what you are talking about."

"Mmm-hmm," Slade murmured with blatant amusement.

"You know what the sad part is?" Brett asked as he leaned across the table to whisper loud enough for Mike to hear him clear as day. "The bastard hasn't even kissed her yet."

"Really?" Slade lifted a brow.

"I think he's scared."

"Chase was the same way. Too afraid he wouldn't be able to stop once he got started."

"I am not afraid," Mike spat. "And I can start and stop whenever I want."

"Mmm-hmm."

"You want proof? I'll give you proof."

"Don't be doing anything on my account." Slade held his hands up in surrender, but the laughter was still there, lurking in his gaze. "I don't want to get blamed for you being an ass."

"I am not an ass!"

"Mmm-hmm."

"You're the ass," Mike muttered as he sulked back into his seat.

* * * *

Mike was not an ass, he assured himself. He was the victim. After all, he was the one so damn drunk last night he couldn't remember what the hell had happened. He suspected Brett was right and the answer was nothing, mostly because he'd been way too drunk. How he'd gotten that way, he wasn't sure but knew Angie was to blame.

She's turned the tables on him and used his own damn party to lead him astray when Mike had meant to spend the night flirting with every other woman and maybe doing a little more just to make sure Angie got the message. Well, now he was the one who had gotten it.

This war.

If he had any doubts about that, Angie cleared them up as she came storming back into the kitchen dressed like a hooker ready to go pick up johns on the street corner. Mike's eyes weren't the only ones damn near bugging out of his head as she strutted past wearing white thigh-highs along with six-inch, fuck-me-now stilettos. She had a skirt on that barely covered her ass and a shirt that molded itself like second skin to the breasts that were damn near falling out of the top.

Turning her ass on all three men at the table, she bent over and shook it at them. "See? Panties."

"Is that what you call that scrap of lace." Brett snorted. "Strippers wear more than that."

Angie shot him a middle finger salute and turned to pin Mike with a pointed look, clearly awaiting his response. She was at it again, taunting him, but this time he wasn't going to let her get to him. He had a point to prove, and he was still intent upon it.

Aware of all the eyes tracking his progress as he shoved out of his seat and came around the table, he stepped up to confront Angie directly. The tension in the room thickened with anticipation. Mike knew not a single one of them, not even his brother, could guess at what he planned to do next. He certainly caught Angie off guard as he swept her up into a passionate kiss.

Unfortunately, she was not the only one caught by surprise.

The heat and lust that had been simmering beneath the surface now for twenty-four hours exploded into a raging boil as the sweet taste of her flooded his senses. Angie needed no prodding and offered no resistance as his lips broke over her softer ones, forcing them open so that he could plunder the deep, heady depths of her kiss.

It was too much, a voice shrieked through his head. He was drowning, and if he didn't flee now, he'd be caught forever in her web. Still, Mike didn't have the strength to pull back as Angie fitted her curves perfectly against him and started to grind with the skill of temptress who knew she had her prey cornered.

With the expert precision of a snake, Angie struck, clamping her lips around his tongue and sucking him deep as she pumped her hips against the painfully hard and throbbing length of his erection. He was going down, fast and hard.

It was time to abort, and there was no way to do that smoothly or retain his dignity. Mike just had to shove her back before he took her to the floor right then and there in front of Slade and his brother. That is probably what he should have done. At least then they wouldn't have laughed at him.

That Mike could handle, but Angie's smile… Something had to be done about that. That and her smug attitude.

"You okay there, stud? You look a little shaky."

Mike growled, curling his fingers into fists in a pointed attempt to stop them from trembling. The gesture and the reason behind it weren't lost on Angie, who boldly strutted past him with a seductive suggestion.

"Don't worry, stud. We can work on that tonight."

"I have a date."

That had everybody in the room pausing, but if he had expected that to dent Angie's confidence, Mike was sadly mistaken. Her smile just grew, and the mischievous twinkle in her eyes assured him she'd seen through his lie. Now he was in real trouble, but at least, he wasn't an ass.

"I look forward to meeting her," Angie assured him as she opened the door, causing Slade to hop out of his seat.

"Hold up, Angie," Slade hailed her as he darted across the kitchen. "I'll give you a lift out to the club."

"And one home?"

"I got ya," Brett offered. "I'll be out there later to meet GD."

All eyes turned toward Mike, and he shrugged. "I've got other plans."

Angie snorted at that, and there was no disguising the laughter in the sound or just what she thought about his "other plans."

"Sure thing, stud. You've got a date to go find."

Mike snarled, about to become the ass that he was trying to avoid being, but Slade moved quickly to head off disaster. Hustling Angie out the door, he slammed it before Mike could do anything stupider than he'd already done. As if he didn't know that he'd totally screwed everything up, he had a brother to remind.

"Now what you going to do…stud?"

Chapter 8

Angie took a deep breath, forcing her nerves to settle as Slade jogged around the front of his pickup to climb into the driver's seat. It had taken an extreme force of self-control not to melt into a puddle at Mike's feet. The man really knew how to kiss.

He'd left her shaken and weak. Her only consolation was he hadn't been in any better shape. Thankfully, everybody had been focused on him. Nobody noticed that she'd had a hell of time recovering. It wasn't until Slade started to ease his truck away from the curb that she realized she'd forgotten to even greet him.

That was how off the mark she was, but it was way too late to back up and say hello. That would only draw attention to the fact that she was as off her game as Mike. So, instead, Angie let out her breath slowly and continued on as she had started, with attitude to spare.

"This is a nice ride and all, Slade, but we both know you didn't come all the way into town to play taxi out of the goodness of your heart. So what's up?" Angie asked, certain something was.

"Patton."

"I can't help you there," Angie cut in, taking a guess at which direction this conversation was headed. "Whatever happened with Lana, it's between you and her…and her."

"I'm not talking about that," Slade shot back, a hint of annoyance in his tone.

"No?" That surprised Angie, and she couldn't help but cast him a questioning look. "Then what?"

"Patton…wants your job." Slade sounded as though he'd tasted something foul, and he looked as if he'd smelled it. Angie, on the other hand, couldn't help but laugh.

"Yeah, I know. She told me last night, and I'll tell you what I told her. She can have it. I've got other things I can do, like get back to work."

"Like we're going to unleash Patton unsupervised on the club." Slade snorted. "And the club accounts for ninety percent of your sales, so this is your work."

Angie felt her amusement sour as she figured out just what was coming next. She should have known, not that knowing would have any effect on her answer.

"Oh no."

"Yes."

"No." Angie shook her head. "I am not being responsible for whatever she decides to do, and I'm not ratting her out to you whenever she decides to do something. No."

"Yes."

"You can say yes all you want. The answer is still no."

"Please?" Slade batted his lashes at her, and Angie had to admit that the man had some enviable lashes.

He had enviable everything. Tall and hard, with eyes that sparkled in the daylight, the man was a walking sex dream, just like his other two brothers. Yet, he did nothing for Angie. That wasn't to say she hadn't enjoyed his attention in the past, but he didn't make her heart race or her knees go weak, which was a good thing because Patton would have killed her if he did.

She didn't want to be at war with Patton over anything. Not even the club.

"No."

"Fine," Slade huffed, heaving an aggrieved sigh. "How much is it going to cost me?"

"You think my loyalty is for sale?" Angie asked, shocked and more than a little offended that he thought so little of her.

"I think you might need some help with those two idiots back there." Slade hit on the one thing she couldn't deny.

"Help?" Angie eyed him, tempted despite herself. "What kind of help?"

* * * *

Brett couldn't help laughing as he headed toward the Pittsview's town center. Mike could be a real idiot sometimes, but Angie turned him into a complete dumbass. Only love could do that to a man. Even Mike had to see the truth now. He was in love.

In love and pissed off about it. Worse, Mike seemed intent on following through on his stupid plans to try and harass Angie into abandoning him. Why? Brett still didn't get it.

That was because it didn't make any sense. Mike was afraid of getting his heart broken, so he was breaking it? He was afraid of hurting Angie, so he was hurting her? Brett had made those points to Mike right after Angie and Slade had left, but his brother hadn't been in the mood to listen.

So Brett had taken off to go pick on two men who had no choice but to listen to him. Cole and Kyle had broken his sister's spirit. Now, he was going to break them. That put a smile on Brett's face as he drove into town.

Hailey didn't answer to any man, especially not Kyle Harding. That ass had been a complete prick to her all through high school. Back then he hadn't dared to cross the line, and Brett had barely spared him a moment's notice. Now, though, the man had gone too far. Now he was sleeping with Brett's sister.

He wasn't the only one.

That was reason enough to hate Kyle Harding as far as Brett was concerned. There was no reason that he could see not to visit that hate upon the man. That was just what he planned on doing as he pulled into the parking lot of Cole and Kyle's garage.

It didn't matter to him that the two idiots had managed to build their own successful business, or that they clearly weren't frugal about spending their money on Hailey. That was clear from the rock they'd bought her and the home they were restoring for her. None of that changed Brett's opinion of either of them.

He hopped out of his truck and headed in through the open bay, intent on causing trouble. Brett could hear one of Cole's cousins complaining loudly as all the men clustered around an RV some sick mind had turned into what looked like a big pile of poo. It looked completely out of place next to the classic cars that the garage was known for restoring, but Brett didn't care.

He didn't even wonder what the hell was going on. All that mattered was that he could hear both Kyle and Cole teasing Cole's cousins. They were on the other side of the RV, and the phone was across from Brett, which gave him an idea. Snapping his cell out of the holder clasped to his waistband, he flipped open his phone and dialed up the shop and then waited against the side of the RV as he listened to Cole's laughter ring closer and closer.

Just as the asshole came past the bumper of the RV, Brett stuck his foot out and tripped the idiot, sending him stumbling forward before crashing down onto the cement floor.

"*Shit!*" Cole cursed, proving he had absolutely no manners and was way too low class for Brett's sister.

"You all right, man?" Kyle came jogging around the corner of the RV just in time for Brett to trip him, too, sending him crashing right down on top of Cole and earning Brett another obscenity.

"Son of a bitch! Get off me!" Cole shoved Kyle back, who quickly scrambled to his feet and turned to confront Brett.

"Oh, it's you."

"Yes, ma'am." Brett nodded. "And I'd curb the impulse to swing that fist, lady, because you know how Hailey feels about us fighting."

Of course, Hailey wasn't there. She was busy right then back at the house, where she kept her studio in the garage. He'd kissed her on the cheek before he'd left her to her work not but ten minutes ago.

"What do you want, asswipe?" Cole demanded to know as he pushed himself off the floor and rose up to take a stand with Kyle. "Other than stinking up my shop, I mean."

"Very good, little girl," Brett shot back. "I'm so insulted I might cry."

"And I'm so amused I might call the cops and have you arrested for assault," Cole retorted.

"Watch it now, sweetheart, or I might just have to go find *your* sister and see if she feels like playing a round or two of cow to my boy."

"My sister's married."

"You think that would stop me?"

It would, but Cole didn't know that, and he took the bait like the moron he was and surged forward. Brett would have enjoyed beating him back down, but Kyle got in the way, placing a hand on Cole's chest and shoving him back.

"Don't take the bait, man." Kyle smiled slightly. "There are other ways to deal with bullies like him."

"Really, Nancy?" Brett lifted a brow. "What you going to do?"

"Aaron? Jacob?" Kyle called out.

"Four against one?" Brett snorted, not intimidated by those odds at all. "Because I can take you of all just—"

His words got cut off by a foghorn that actually blew stink along with its steamy blast. Almost instantly, an odor so foul filled the garage that Brett was left gagging and stumbling for the open garage door as his eyes began to tear. Kyle and Cole followed him, laughing and smirking as they enjoyed their momentary victory.

"Jesus." Brett sucked in a deep breath of fresh air and tried to throw off the smell that felt as if it was permeating his very skin. "What the hell was that?"

He hadn't asked that question of anybody in particular, but Cole answered nonetheless.

"The world's biggest stink bomb." He smirked as if that was some kind of prize to brag about.

"And it doesn't get to you?"

"We've burnt out our ability to smell long ago." Kyle shrugged. "Now, *Nancy*, what the hell are you doing here?"

Brett drew himself up at that and narrowed his gaze on Kyle. He'd be getting his revenge, but pounding on him was just too damn easy. He'd have to think of something special. Until then, he had a few words to share with the obnoxious twits snickering at him.

"I heard a rumor that you weren't *allowing* my sister to do certain things, like fix her friend's motorcycle." Brett paused, giving them a chance to deny it, but neither man responded. "I don't like hearing that. My sister does what my sister wants, or I'll be doing what I want. Got me?"

"Your sister negotiated a truce," Cole informed him with a smile that left no doubt about how those negotiations had gone. "In the end, she got some things she wanted, and we got some things we wanted. The rest of the details ain't none of your business."

"Everything about Hailey is my business," Brett assured him. "And I take my business seriously."

"And we take keeping your sister happy seriously," Kyle shot back.

"Which is why we decided to issue you a challenge even Hailey can't object to."

"Yeah?" Brett cocked a brow in Cole's direction. "And what's that, Sally?"

Kyle's gaze narrowed, his grin tightening, but he didn't take the bait, proving that he was serious about keeping Hailey happy. Brett still didn't like him, though.

"It involves us humiliating you on an obstacle course," Kyle suggested, pausing until it became obvious he wasn't going any further without some kind of response from Brett.

"You've got my ear."

* * * *

Angie stared down into her glass and told herself she deserved this. Her day had been that difficult. *Patton* had been that difficult. She really was as crazy as everybody said. Angie didn't know how she'd missed it.

Patton wanted to open up the Harem as a day spa, wanted to expand the club to include couples, thought adding a golf course would only add to its appeal as a resort, and, of course, wanted to set up a small retail boutique for her lingerie line and possibly cosmetics and lotions and other sexual aids that the ladies could take with them when they left the club.

Some of her ideas had a little merit. Others were just outside any realm of logic or reason, but the worst part hadn't come until the end of the day. That was when Patton had let it slip that she'd copied every file from the club's membership onto a flash drive back a few weeks ago. She'd given it to somebody for safekeeping, and hopefully, she could get it back. Angie sure as hell didn't want to be around if Patton couldn't because God only knew what Chase's response would be.

Just the thought of it had sent Angie to the bar, where she had ordered up her favorite and most forbidden treat, a triple-decker milkshake made of coffee, vanilla, and chocolate, topped with whipped cream and toffee crunch. It had to be the most fattening creation the club had ever whipped up. Normally it was shared, but that afternoon, Angie was miserable enough to tackle the thing alone.

"Oh, man!" Brett slid into the seat beside her, eyeing her dessert instead of her breasts for the first time ever. The gleam of excitement glinting in his eyes, though, was strangely the same. "That looks good."

"I'm not sharing," Angie informed him, protectively pulling her glass closer as she shot him a dirty look that warned the big man not to even try to sneak a taste.

"Please." Brett snorted. "I want my own. Yo, barkeep!" he hollered out, drawing the man's attention toward them as he pointed at Angie's glass. "I want one."

The man scowled and nodded, clearly not pleased with Brett's less-than-sophisticated behavior. Not that Brett seemed to mind or care as he turned a big goofy smile on Angie.

"So? How was your day?"

"Miserable," Angie admitted as she began to dig into the delicious layers of frozen goodness. "I'd ask you the same, but I think it's fairly obvious how yours went."

"I'm working at a club full of naked women." Brett grinned like a boy up to no good. "There is live-action porn everywhere I look. My day was fan-fucking-tastic."

"Yeah? Well, give it a few years. The glow wears off," Angie warned him.

"Wow, aren't you Miss Grumpy?"

"I said I had a miserable day," Angie reminded him.

"Wanna talk about it?"

"No." Angie really didn't. "I want to sit here and eat ice cream."

"Fine. You just sit there and sulk, and I'll tell you about my day."

That was just what Brett proceeded to do. He talked non-stop, though Angie didn't think he was trying to annoy her. He was just that excited. Strangely enough, despite his original comments, the things that seemed to thrill him the most were operational. Brett seemed amazed at how well the club was organized and how smoothly it ran.

Those were not subjects that normally tickled Angie's fancy, but she couldn't help but get sucked into his enthusiasm. They spent over an hour, lingering there they discussed his ideas for the club. They weren't half as outlandish as Patton's, but that didn't mean Brett didn't approve of some of the new owner's ideas. He certainly had his own spin on them.

As they sat there laughing, Angie couldn't help but remember Slade's advice to her that morning. He was right. She had them primed and ready for a full-on assault. Now was the perfect time to switch gears and go for the under-the-radar friendship connection. It wasn't as though it was hard or that she had to pretend to find him funny and engaging.

Brett was both of those things without trying, just like he was sexy without any effort. Angie watched him dig into his own milkshake and smiled as she felt her heart melt. He really was just an overgrown kid, and she couldn't wait to experience that fun-filled enthusiasm between the sheets. She got wet just thinking about it and had to focus on something else before she did something really outlandish like tackle him right then and there.

"So, Cole challenged you to a duel? An actual duel? Like pistols at dawn?" These men, they never stopped competing.

"Please." Brett snorted. "He may be a Sally, but he isn't stupid. I am, after all, considered a hell of a good shot."

"I can imagine." Actually, Angie didn't want to. Guns were not her thing. "But if not guns, then what? Swords?"

"Like Hailey would let me run her girlfriend through." Brett shook his head. "Nope. We're going to run an obstacle course. Apparently, they got one out at someplace called Camp D. Ever heard of it?"

"Run by the notorious Nick Dickles." Angie nodded. "He's never made the rounds here at the club, but his reputation precedes him nonetheless."

That earned her a quick look from Brett, and she could all but read the thoughts swirling through his head. Angie could have put him at ease and assured him that Nick had not cut his reputation on her ass, but then she might have to admit that Cole had. She suspected he'd view that as a worse sin, so she just smiled politely and waited until he shrugged and continued on.

"Well, apparently, he's trying to rehab his reputation and help a bunch of kids at the same time."

Brett paused to glare down into his glass as if offended to find it empty. Angie could sense that he was debating having another, and she couldn't help but tease him.

"If you're going to be running an obstacle course, don't you think you better lay off the ice cream?" Angie suggested with a little smile as Brett cast her a dark look.

"I might have to paddle you for suggesting that I might lose," Brett grumbled with mock outrage. "I could wipe the floor with those two pussies Hailey's fallen for with only one leg and a beer belly hanging down to my knee. If I can't, then I don't deserve to be called a marine."

Angie smiled, oddly warmed by his outrageous confidence. Warmed and enticed, which was just why she slid to the edge of her seat and into the heady heat of his body before responding.

"It's not *those* pussies you have to watch out for, stud," Angie murmured as pressed in slightly, allowing the hard tips of her breasts to brush against her arm as her feet touched the floor. She shot him her best sultry look and matched it with a husky tone. "And if you can't keep up with me, then you don't deserve to be called a Cattleman."

With that, she turned and started across the room. On cue, Brett came following after her.

Chapter 9

Mike stepped back and checked himself out in the mirror. He was looking good, completely recovered from that morning. His slacks were clean, pressed, and matched the crisp cut of his shirt. He'd debated over a tie, not sure what the etiquette was anymore. It had been a long time since he'd gone on an actual date.

Over the past several years, most of the women he'd spent time with had been marines. They hadn't dated. They'd done things more entertaining than going to dinner. Things like what he'd almost done with Angie that morning. The minute that thought popped into his head, he crushed it.

He would not give in to those thoughts or the dangerous places they led him, kind of like the alcohol last night. Mike had heard enough tales that day from the men he knew to know that he and Angie had engaged in a drinking competition. He hadn't won. Mike didn't even know what to think about that, and he wasn't going to get hung up on his failures.

So, Angie had won the first round? So what? Tonight was his chance to get revenge and hopefully prove his point. She was better off without him. Actually that should have been obvious to the woman this morning, but instead of being outraged that he'd planned to use her to drain the wake-up wood, she'd been begging for it...begging for it in the ass.

Once again, Mike refused to let that thought lead him astray. Instead, he forced himself to focus on the moment at hand. He had dinner plans. He had an official date with a brunette sure to make Angie fall over with jealousy. More than just having a large set of breasts and an ass a man could bounce a quarter off of, she was also a pre-med student, meaning she was smart. Smart and hot…Mike scowled as he tried to remember her name.

It was something like Stacy, but that didn't feel right. It didn't matter, and that went to prove what kind of bastard he was. Soon Angie would know the truth because Mike planned to flaunt whatever her name was in Angie's face.

She deserved it.

Hell, she and Brett had been flirting up a storm ever since the two of them had returned from the club. They'd been laughing and teasing each other and making plans to veg out for the night. God help him, for the first time ever, Mike had been jealous of his own brother.

He wanted to be the one having fun.

He'd tried to have a little. He'd gloated over the fact that he had to get ready for his date, but Angie had simply smiled and strutted past him. She didn't believe him. Well, she'd learn the truth soon enough. Mike glanced at his watch and frowned. Stacy…

Tracy?

Definitely not Casey.

What the hell was her name again?

The chime of the doorbell assured him it was too late to figure it out. He'd call her honey or darlin' or something like that. Women ate that shit up. Shooting his reflection one last look, Mike headed out into the living room where Brett and Angie were hunkered down, watching some reality show that sounded like chickens squawking at each other.

Thankfully they muted it as he strutted past, both lifting their gazes toward the door as they waited for him to open it. Before he could, the doorbell rang again, and again, and again, and was mid-ring as he finally threw it open to find…*Stacy? No. Tracy.* Oh God, he really couldn't remember.

What Mike did remember was that she'd looked better that afternoon. She certainly had been dressed better. Mike couldn't help but scowl as he took in the circus costume the brunette was wearing. It looked like plastic beach balls encased her boobs, making her large rack look more vulgar than enticing.

Hell, he'd worry that if he grabbed one it might honk at him or shoot a spray of water in his face. That thought had him biting back a snicker as he took in the rest of her outfit. There wasn't a single color in the rainbow that she wasn't wearing or hadn't painted on her face. It looked as if a three-year-old had assaulted her with a box of crayons.

As humorous as Mike found that thought, his good mood faded with the realization that he was going to have to be seen with her. While he didn't care about most people's opinions, there were two sitting behind him that counted a whole lot. Both Angie and Brett were clearly fighting back the giggles as they rose up to greet his date.

"Hey, honey, you look...colorful." He couldn't bring himself to say good or smile with any sincerity, not that it much mattered.

The woman not only had the audacity to scowl up at him, she snapped at him in a waspish tone only a longtime girlfriend should ever use on a man. "That took long enough. You going to leave a woman standing out here all night? I could be assaulted, or bitten. Who knows what's lurking in the bushes! Well? Are you going to invite me in or spend the whole night staring at my breasts? Oh, never mind, I'll invite myself in, and you can stare at my ass instead." That was just what the woman did, shoving past Mike without missing a single beat.

"Hello, there. I'm Gracie." She paused to snort and wipe her nose along her arm before extending her hand toward Brett. "And you are clearly Mikey's twin. Rhett, right?"

"Brett." Brett eyed her hand and shook it quickly, wiping his own against his jeans discreetly as Gracie prattled on.

"Yes, of course, I'm sorry. It's just that I had this dog named Rhett when I was a kid. Oh, he was so sweet but incontinent. He left these stains all over the hardwood floors, and don't you know that my mother always blames me, telling people they're *my* stains, and I tell her, mother, if you say it like that, people will think I peed on the floor, and really, how gross do you think I am?"

Gracie paused as if she expected a response, but Angie and Brett clearly didn't know what the hell to say to that. They stood there silently glancing between each other as if they expected the other to save them. Of course, Gracie didn't stay silent for long.

"I'm Gracie," she repeated as she stuck her hand out toward Angie, who shook it reluctantly. "And you must be Hailey, the sister."

"I'm—"

"I heard all about you today." Gracie waved away Angie before she could correct her. "And let me tell you, for the record, I think your brother is right. Men shouldn't be tying women up. That is just backward, honey. We got the pussies, we got the power, and they should bow down to it, am I not right?"

"You are on the money," Angie agreed with a snicker, casting a smirk right over Gracie's shoulder at Mike.

His plan was blowing up all over him. He couldn't get Gracie out the door fast enough. Neither could he get her to shut the hell up. It wasn't until halfway through the dinner, as she actually lifted up her plate and licked it clean, that it dawned on him that he might have just been set up. There was only one way to find out.

"And so I said to her—"

"Enough."

Mike didn't raise his voice or snap that word at her, but it still carried the weight of his years as a commander and cut straight through her act, causing Gracie to still for a second before regaining her balance and her role.

"Excuse me? That is—"

"I'm the new Master of Ceremonies out at the club," Mike warned her, taking a big gamble that he knew just what was really going on here. Of course, if he was wrong, he'd sound crazy, but it wasn't like Gracie was all that sane.

"I don't—"

"And you won't," he assured her as he cut her off again, leaning forward and dropping his tone to a dangerous whisper. "I'll make sure that you *never* again participate in any club events. Understand, Gracie?"

The brunette hesitated and broke into a big smile. "I was wondering when you'd catch a clue."

"And I'm wondering who set me up." Mike leaned back, certain now that he had the upper hand. "And I'm assuming it was Angie."

Gracie didn't respond to that but just grinned. There was something about the glint in her eyes, though, that warned him things were not that simple. Others had been involved.

"Who?" He didn't clarify that at all, knowing she understood him perfectly.

Gracie didn't even try to pretend as though she didn't. Neither did she tell him. Instead, she simply shrugged and offered him a clue that left no doubt over where the Davis brothers' loyalty truly lay.

"Let's just say the orders come from higher up."

"You're lying." Mike stiffened up in his seat, honestly shocked by that admission. "They'd never betray me like that."

"Old lovers versus old friends, loyalties sometimes get messy, and let's face it, you haven't been around much."

No, he hadn't. Nor did he miss the implication of her words. "Old lovers? You're not talking about Angie…and the Davis brothers?"

Mike could barely get the words out. He was about to have full-on heart palpitations. They'd slept with his woman, and given they hadn't fucked her pussy, that could mean only one thing. They'd had that ass. They'd had his Angie!

"Are you going to have a stroke or something?" Gracie's grin faded into a look of concern as her gaze narrowed on the flush Mike could feel consuming his face.

* * * *

Angie smiled as she watched Brett study her toes intently. They'd vegged out in the living room, eating peanut butter and jelly sandwiches and drinking sweet tea as they argued over what to watch. He liked cheesy sci-fi shows. She liked competition reality shows. They'd both won a few rounds, but when the last one had gone to Brett, Angie had gotten up and fetched her pedicure kit.

Strangely enough, Brett had become obsessed with the feminine routine and taken over, first massaging her feet and now painting her nails. Angie had a sense he just might be a toe sucker, which she never would have expected but didn't object to. What was there to object to?

Men who dug feet liked to massage them, and Angie was always up for a good rubdown. In fact, she was debating how to get his hands from her toes to her shoulders when her phone rang. She glanced over at it sitting on the coffee table, swearing that if it was the club she was quitting. The name flashing on the little phone's screen, though, couldn't be ignored.

Frowning, she reached for it, having to twist at the hips as Brett refused to release her foot. He'd already finished with one and was almost done with the second. Clearly, he wasn't letting go until he was done. Angie didn't object, just stretched and pulled the phone close enough to pick up.

"Hey, Gracie," she greeted the other woman without any worry over Brett's reaction.

He'd deduced that Mike's date was a setup not two seconds after Mike had hustled the other woman out the door. It had been kind of obvious, which made it all the more amusing that Mike hadn't figured it out right then and there. She suspected that hadn't lasted based on Gracie's greeting

"I just got ditched."

"What?" Angie frowned as Brett bit down on his bottom lip in a gesture so sexy it made her want to rub her legs together like some damn cricket in heat.

"Your boy figured out the game," Gracie warned her, sounding more than a bit concerned, but Angie wasn't disturbed in the slightest.

"Hmm." She sighed. "It's about time. You make it all the way through dinner?"

"Yeah, but—"

"Oh." Angie's head popped up as she heard a truck pull into the driveway. "I think he's here. He must have really sped. When did he leave you?"

"Not even five minutes ago, and that's what I'm trying to tell you. You're in trouble."

"Trouble? You think I'm about to get spanked?"

Despite the grimness in Gracie's tone and words, Angie couldn't help but share a smile with Brett as the sound of the engine cut off and the slam of a truck door followed almost instantly. The heavy pound of footsteps assured her he was tearing down the front path.

"Angie—"

"You know, I never have had my pussy spanked." Angie directed that comment more at Brett than Gracie. He lifted a brow and shot her a look that assured her he was putting that on his list.

"I think you ought to take this a little more seriously, Angie," Gracie grumbled. "The man about blew steam right out of his ears."

She wasn't lying either. The front door slammed open, and Mike charged in like a bull that had just been hit with a branding iron. Angie couldn't help but admit she was a little taken aback as he leveled a finger right at her and roared, "*You!*"

"I see what you mean," Angie muttered to Gracie as Brett straightened up, his smile fading into a concerned frown.

"What's wrong, man?"

"She...*she*..."

Whatever it was, the man couldn't actually get it said. He was shaking that bad. Angie had a feeling this wasn't just about Gracie.

"I'm missing something, aren't I?" She directed that question at Gracie, who answered almost verbatim along with Mike.

"He knows."

"I know!"

That really didn't tell her anything. "About?"

"The Davis brothers," Gracie clued her in while Mike sputtered over the words.

"About? About! You...you and....ah! *How could you?*"

"I think that's my cue to let you go," Gracie murmured, clearly having heard Mike through the phone.

"Night, Gracie." Angie sighed and closed her phone as Brett's frowned continued to deepen.

"What the hell is going on here?" he demanded to know, and Angie could tell that Mike was in no condition to answer.

"Your brother just found out that I've been with the Davis brothers." Straightening up on the couch, she could sense the night had come to an end and began to collect the pieces of her nail kit while Brett continued to blink in confusion.

"What do you mean, *been with?*"

Angie paused to give him a pointed glance, not certain Mike's blood pressure could take hearing the words outright. Not that he had any right to his little tantrum. Neither did Brett have any right to glare at her like that. Perhaps, it would be best to make that point once she confessed to everything, and that way, hopefully, she wouldn't have to keep making it.

"I mean that I've *been with* a lot of men." Angie stressed those two words with enough force to assure both men tensed, their expressions going equally dark.

"Define a lot," Brett demanded with a snarl, but Angie wasn't falling for that.

"No. That's none of your business." Snapping her beauty bag closed, she rose off the couch and hit him with the lowest blow, knowing they'd have to get past it at some point. "But I have enjoyed the company of the Davis brothers in the past...as well as Cole and Kyle."

There. She'd said it. Sure enough, it had both brothers reeling backward as they gasped and stuttered.

"Not Nancy!"

"And Sally!"

"Oh God. I think I'm going to be sick." Mike bent over, grabbing his stomach as sank to the ground in an overly dramatic display as far as Angie was concerned.

"Just stop!" She snapped at them both. "It's sexist and archaic for the two of you, who have no doubt been sticking it to every slut you've come across, to carry on because I've enjoyed the company of a few men.

"*And*"—Angie raised her voice when it looked like Brett was about to object—"I have saved the best for you. Now, I'm sorry if the truth hurts you. That wasn't my intention. Hell, I wouldn't have even thought you would care, Mike, given the way you've treated me over the years. I got like a letter or two a year telling me to get lost. And you."

Angie turned on Brett. "You barely wrote more than that. Never once did you indicate that you returned my affection. Hell, you used to sign your letters *respectfully*! Like that sets a lady's heart fluttering. So you really have nobody to blame but yourselves."

That was the honest truth. If they'd wanted her, she was theirs, but instead, they'd run in the opposite direction. That hurt a hell of a lot more than the thought of them with other women. It hurt enough to have her turning and rushing out of the room before the old wound broke open and they saw the depths of the pain she kept hidden from everybody, including herself.

* * * *

Brett watched Angie turn and run away, but she wasn't fast enough for him not to catch the glint of tears in her eyes. The sight left him sighing, as it drained all his outraged indignation better than anything else could. She was right, of course.

She'd been theirs for the taking, and they'd left her for others to have. It had been the right thing to do back then. Angie had just been a girl, a girl obviously desperate for acceptance. That made sense. After all, she was the forgotten daughter, and that was something Brett and Mike and Hailey knew about.

At least they'd had each other. Angie had clung to them. She, Patton, and Hailey had hung out so much it had been as if he and Mike had three sisters instead of just one. That was just why they'd rejected her, but Angie wasn't their sister, and she wasn't a girl anymore.

Mike wasn't half as disinterested as he was trying to pretend to be. Brett eyed his brother as he knelt there on the floor, staring at the wood boards, looking utterly dejected.

"It hurts, doesn't it?" Brett asked quietly, daring to say out loud what he was actually thinking.

For a moment, he thought Mike would ignore him, but slowly his brother's chin lifted, and he met Brett's gaze before nodding. "Yeah."

"Me, too." Brett was hurt, but he wasn't angry, not the way that Mike sounded.

"I just want it to stop."

"I know." Brett did, just as he knew it wasn't going to. He didn't figure his brother needed to hear that, though. "What I don't know is what you are trying to accomplish here."

"I don't know." Mike shrugged before heaving a heavy sigh and shoving up to his feet.

"No, seriously, man." Brett wasn't about to let the point go. He kept his gazed fixed on Mike as he flopped down in the loveseat next to the couch. "One day you won't look at her because she's naked. Then the next day you're kissing her passionately in the kitchen and then going out and picking up other women. What does that really get you?"

"I don't know. Okay?" Mike admitted defensively. "I don't have a plan. I just know that this isn't right."

"What isn't right?" Brett pressed.

"Us with her." Mike waved a hand toward the hall. "Angie was right. She's too good for us, and how long will it really be before—"

"Before you walk away like dad?" Brett cut in, knowing exactly where this conversation was now headed.

"Before she gets hurt." Mike stubbornly finished his point but still didn't seem to see the flaw in his thinking.

"So you're trying to hurt her to spare her future pain?" Brett lifted a brow at that. "You do realize that makes no sense, right?"

"You know what? Never mind." Mike shoved to his feet.

"So we're done talking about this?" Brett asked as his brother turned toward the hall.

"Yep."

"You know I'm—"

"Yep."

Mike walked away, dismissing both Brett and his concern, but that didn't make it vanish. His brother was on edge, distracted and clearly not in full control of himself. That made Mike unpredictable because Brett had honestly never seen his brother out of control.

Of course, Brett was also known for his self-restraint, which was a good thing for Hailey's two boyfriends. Just the thought of those two had him scowling. He couldn't believe Angie had let them touch her.

She was going to get spanked for that.

The real questions were—when, how, and where. The endless possibilities put the smile back on Brett's face as he slumped back onto the couch and picked up the remote before glancing back at the doorway and wondering if Angie really had gone to sleep.

She really did have nice toes.

And Brett really didn't want to go to sleep in the top bunk again.

Chapter 10

Friday, June 29ᵗʰ

Angie didn't wake up alone the next morning. She found herself cuddled into the warm, hard shelter of Brett's body. He had his arms wrapped around her, and one thick thigh shoved between hers. The scrape of his jeans felt deliciously rough against the sensitive skin of her inner thigh, and she couldn't help but rub her leg up and down his.

The seductive little motion had Brett's arms tightening around her as he growled softly in her ear, heightening the tension slowly thickening in the air. It was aided by the feel of his hand sliding down her stomach toward the soft folds of her cunt. Already wet and swollen, the parted lips of her pussy blossomed beneath the callused invasion of his fingers, and Angie gasped as a bolt of pure, frenzied pleasure bloomed through her.

Her hips jerked back up against his, burrowing the rock-hard bulge restrained behind his zipper between the cheeks of her ass. Angie ground herself against Brett, taunting him even as he pinned her clit beneath his finger and began a slow massage that had Angie drooling into her pillow. This was how she wanted to wake up every morning.

Well, sort of.

In Angie's fantasy, it wouldn't be his fingers pressing deep into her cunt, nor would he have his jeans on. Not that she had the breath to complain or even the words. Brett stole them from her mind as he pumped his fingers in and out of her in a slow, hypnotizing rhythm that had her hips following until she was moaning with the need for more.

Moaning, but not begging.

That was just what he tried to coax her into doing as his breath washed over her neck in heated strokes that were followed by the velvety glide of his tongue and sharp nip of his teeth. Brett nibbled his way up the sensitive arch of her ear.

"Is there something more you want, baby?" The husky timbre of his voice didn't disguise the hopeful lift tinting his words.

Angie smiled and pulled free of his hand so she could turn in his arms. Brett fell backward at the gentle press of her palms against the hard wall of his chest. She could feel the heavy pound of his heart and read the anticipation glinting in his eyes as she slid upward, straddling his thighs as her hands dropped to the top button on his jeans.

Knowing he was watching her every move, Angie licked her lips and lowered her gaze to the sight of his thick dick. It sprang free as she lowered the zipper's small metal tab down. There was nothing small, though, about his cock. Swollen and flushed with a hunger that had the blind eye crowning his head weeping up at her, he was bigger, thicker, and longer than any man she'd ever had.

As they'd pointed out last night, Angie had had quite a few. She might be a virgin, but she was no blushing prude or innocent girl to be swept up in the passion of desire. No. She a woman who knew how to make a man beg. Brett was about to find that out.

Lifting her pelvis up, Angie reached down and spread the lips of her pussy wide and over the thick length of his cock. She settled down, capturing his dick in an intimate embrace that had her clit pinned once again. With a flex of her hips, that little bud lit up with the most amazing sensations as she slid down the hard, velvety length.

Angie panted out with delight, repeating the motion as she began to slowly ride Brett. He felt so good against her that she couldn't help but savor the moment, even as she knew she was tormenting him. Every flex of her hips set off another deliriously thrilling sparkle of pleasure, but only for her. All Brett got was being taunted with the wet slide of her pussy and promise of what he could be getting.

That thought brought a smile to Angie's lips as she caught his gaze and bent slowly down until the tips of her breasts teased the heated wall of his chest. Her mouth brushed against his. She didn't kiss him, though. Instead, she whispered softly, challenging him in a way she knew would drive Brett nuts.

"This how I ride my men. They've begged and pleaded to be allowed to take the reins, but they weren't man enough to tempt me into giving into their demands." Angie leaned back until she was once again upright and smiling down into the scowl that darkened his features. "I guess the question is, are you man enough? Or should I keep looking?"

That question got an instant response as Brett growled, his arms snaking around her to jerk her back down into a frenzied kiss that assured Angie he'd broken his chains and had lost all reason. He was wild and crazed, as she'd always wanted. Wild, crazed, and demanding. His lips forced hers apart, his tongue taking instant possession of her mouth as he ravaged her with a hunger that she couldn't help but respond to.

This was the moment Angie had waited all those years for. It was perfect…except that Mike wasn't there. She didn't know if that meant anything and didn't have the capacity to really consider the matter. Drunk on the lust pounding through her veins, Angie was only distantly aware of his absence.

Even that small concern vanished as Brett released her lips and settled his hands on her hips. With one hard jerk, he lifted her cunt up and over his mouth, capturing her pussy in an open-tongued kiss that had Angie squealing as she clawed at the headboard. He fucked her with quick, rapid strokes of his tongue, licking his way right up the spasming walls of her sheath, even as his fingers curled around the flushed globes of her ass.

He bounced her up and down his tongue, the callused tips of his fingers dipping down to tease the puckered ring of muscles guarding her back entrance. Gathering up the thick cream slickening the path from her cunt to her ass, he began to fuck his fingers deep into her tight rear channel, widening and stretching her in a clear promise of what was to come.

Angie moaned, all but ready to beg for it as she pumped her hips in rhythm to his fingers, enjoying the burn of his penetration and yearning for a true fucking.

* * * *

Brett knew it. He knew just what she wanted. He was more than ready to give it to her, but first he wanted to make her come. He needed to. Drunk on the taste of her, he couldn't deny that for the first time ever a woman's pleasure had become more important than his.

This wasn't just about making sure she remembered this moment or trying to erase any memory of her past. This was about Angie and knowing that she belonged to him. That she had given herself to him and that he was worthy.

So Brett drove her from one screaming fit to another as he relentlessly devoured her cunt. She was trembling so hard that he could feel the shudders echoing through her sheath and the thick avalanche of heated cream coated every inch of both her pussy and ass. Only then did he pull back, allowing Angie to collapse against the headboard in a trembling, sweaty heap.

Not that he was done with her.

Rising up behind Angie, Brett grasped her hips and angled her ass backward, far enough that the sticky head of his cock kissed the warm, trembling globes of her ass. He paused there, giving Angie a second to catch her breath and glance back at him. He knew instantly from the wicked curl of her lips that she was far from intimidated.

"What you waiting for, cowboy? Giddy up and let's see what you got."

What he had was twelve painfully swollen inches and a set of balls that were on fire. Those flames flared into a full-on inferno as Brett slammed Angie back into the headboard and fucked the full length of his dick into the heavenly, tight clutch of her ass. There was no stopping him after that.

He took her rough and hard, pounding into her with a speed he'd never unleashed on any other woman. None had been up to taking him like this, but Angie was. She laughed and flexed her hips backward, meeting him stroke for stroke as the headboard began to crack against the wall. The bed groaned beneath them, threatening to give out before Brett did, but he didn't care.

All that mattered was the rapture racing through him and making every single one of his nerve endings sparkle to life. Nothing had ever felt this good. Nothing ever would. Brett knew that instantly. He didn't fight it, but he reveled in the certainty that he had found what so many didn't even believe existed. He'd found perfection.

Then it consumed him in a searing tide of ecstasy that had him straining as he slammed into her once, twice, three more times. Angie screamed, convulsing with her own release and collapsing with him in a heap on the sheet below. They stayed like that, a tangle of sweaty limbs and heaving breaths that slowly evened out. Then Angie was wiggling for freedom.

Brett loosened his hold, grimacing as Angie slid her ass free of his still-hard dick. With a frown, he glanced down at the damn thing, wondering what the hell was wrong with it. He'd come harder than he'd ever had before. Normally, right about then, he would be as soft as pudding, yet he was ready to go for round two.

He should be so lucky.

"I hope you're clean." Angie rolled over and reared up onto her knees.

"Huh?" Brett smacked his lips and eyed her breasts. He couldn't believe he'd forgotten to pet those puppies.

"Clean," Angie repeated, stressing the word as she slapped his hand away. "As in STDs."

"I don't have anything," Brett sulked, pulling his hand back and shooting her an injured look.

"You better not." Angie shoved a finger into his chest and pinned him with a pointed look. "I don't normally let men go in bare."

"I thought I was special," Brett reminded her, not about to admit that, for the first time in his life, he'd been so overwhelmed he'd forgotten the most basic rule—always wear a condom.

He always had. He was glad that so had she. Brett wasn't so pleased that she hadn't answered him yet. Instead, Angie offered him a little smile before leaning down to press a hard kiss against his lips. It was quick and over before he could respond. Then she was scrambling off the bed.

"I'm going to go get a shower," Angie tossed over her shoulder before disappearing out of the bedroom door without bothering to even slip on a robe.

Brett rolled over onto his stomach to watch her go, enjoying the sight of her sauntering down the hall. She had such a nice ass. The best damn one he'd ever ridden. That was saying something. It also made him question what he was doing watching when he could join her in the shower and do a little scrubbing.

That thought had Brett scrambling off the bed and rushing after her, but the scent of bacon thickening in the air had him changing directions. Mike was cooking. He only cooked when he was pissed. Brett didn't doubt that he knew what had his brother upset right then.

Betrayal always burned.

That was just what Brett had done with Angie, betrayed his brother for the first time ever. Now it was time to try to set things back to right. If they could be set that way.

* * * *

Angie showered wearing a smile the size of the state of Texas. It only grew bigger as caught the heady aroma of bacon and coffee as she stepped out of the bathroom. Somebody had cooked breakfast, maybe Brett. How sweet would that be?

It would also have explained his absence in the shower. Angie had been half expecting him to show up at any second. She'd forgive now for not joining her, but she'd never forgive herself if she didn't get in there before all the bacon was gone. Angie knew Brett well enough to know he wouldn't be saving her any.

Not bothering with panties but slipping into a bra, Angie tugged on a sundress and headed for the kitchen, only to find both Brett and Mike brooding over the table. It was piled high with platters of bacon, eggs, biscuits, sausage, and gravy. While all that looked good, the kitchen looked like a bomb had gone off in it.

Angie didn't figure that was her problem. After all, she hadn't made the mess but did plan on eating the results. She was eager to find out if it tasted as good as it smelled and chose to ignore Mike's scowl and Brett's snicker as she settled down to begin filling the plate set for her with heaping piles of food.

"Hungry?" Mike lifted a brow, managing to infuse enough irritation into that one word to assure that he was pissed. She could guess why, and she wasn't apologizing for it.

"Yeah," Angie shot back, glancing up to catch his gaze. "Brett and I got a morning workout. Its shame you weren't there to join us."

"I don't think you're ready for that."

"Why don't you try me?"

That taunt had Mike's gaze narrowing dangerously on her. Angie could sense that he was about to try and teach her a lesson, but no sooner had his lips parted than the back door erupted with a mad pounding, followed by a panicked holler.

"Angie! I need you!"

It was Patton, and it couldn't have been good.

"Angie!"

"Don't think we aren't going to pick this conversation back up later," Mike warned her before lifting up and heading for the door.

That had her looking toward Brett for an explanation of what his brother meant. He wasn't in the mood to offer it. Instead, he was giving her a look that made Angie's nerves tingle with an almost ticklish sensation.

"What?" Angie lifted a brow at him, all but daring him to give voice to the glint shining in his eyes. Brett was never one to back down from a challenge.

"I had fun this morning."

"Why am I not shocked?"

"Because you are smart enough to know that I'm hooked now. A free taste, and the next one is going to cost me what?"

Angie had a response to that. She just didn't get a chance to get it out before Patton was rushing into the kitchen. Barely sparing Mike a glance or Brett a hello, she latched onto Angie's arm and yanked her right out of her seat.

"We need to talk. Now!"

"Please tell me there hasn't been another fire," Angie begged as she allowed herself to be shoved back through the doorway and into the hall.

"Trust me, this is worse than death."

"What the hell is worth than death?" Angie asked as Patton continued to hustle her back toward her borrowed bedroom. Patton threw the door open and all but shoved Angie into the bedroom.

"Life," Patton answered succinctly, slamming the door closed behind her as she turned to confront Angie. For the first time, she paused, her gaze cutting over Angie's shoulder and widening. "Jesus, what the hell happened in here?"

"What?" Angie turned to glance around.

"It looks like a clothing bomb exploded all over the place."

"I haven't had time to straighten up," Angie shot back defensively. It wasn't that bad.

"You better learn to straighten up a hell of a lot more often if you're going to be shacking up with two marines." Patton spoke as if she were some kind of authority in shacking up with marines.

"Ex-marines," Angie corrected her as she turned to narrow her eyes on Patton. "And you didn't rush me all the way back here to discuss my housekeeping habits because I was enjoying my breakfast, and I could—"

"The flash drive is gone." Patton cut her off with that cryptic confession, as if that made any sense.

"What flash drive?"

"Don't you remember?" Patton huffed. "I told you yesterday that a few weeks ago I copied the club's membership files onto a—"

"Flash drive." Angie did remember now that Patton had mentioned it. She could see now why the other woman was panicking, too. The tinge of hysteria began to tint her tone as well. "What do you mean it's gone?"

"Well, I gave it to Heather…Heather Lawson, you know, the very responsible, solid, reliable—"

"You can just call her uptight and be done with it, Patton," Angie snapped. "Not that it much matters. Are you telling me she lost the flash drive?"

"I don't know if I would use the word lost so much as misplaced."

"Patton!"

"She put it in her desk drawer at work, and it's not there now." Patton grimaced, slinking backward as Angie felt her face begin to heat and her temper, rarely stirred, begin to boil.

"So it just grew legs and walked off?"

Patton didn't have an answer for that, just a shrug.

"Patton, this isn't a joke," Angie stressed. "That flash drive could destroy the club if it became public."

Worse than that, it could destroy the Davis brothers. Their names wouldn't be worth spit in a bucket after the club's members got done with them. Their lives would be utterly ruined and, no doubt, their relationship with Patton, too. She knew it. That was obvious from the pain and fear in Patton's tone.

"Don't you think I know that?" Patton looked up helplessly at Angie. "Chase is going to kill me."

Angie knew she was expected to say that he wouldn't but couldn't bring herself to lie. He just might. Hell, he wouldn't even have to pull the trigger. All Chase had to do was throw Patton out and her world would come to an end.

Part of Angie rebelled at that thought, wanting to see her normally strong and confident friend take on this challenge with her usual exuberance, but another part of Angie understood Patton's terror. It had been a long, lonely rode to Brett and Mike's door. If they slammed it in her face, she didn't know if she could turn toward the darkness.

So, despite her better judgments, Angie found herself trying to offer Patton some assistance and heartfelt advice.

"He'll be more likely to forgive you if go confess to him right now." Less likely didn't mean quickly or that there wouldn't be hell to pay, and they both knew that. "Beg his forgiveness and give him a chance to get out in front of this thing."

That was the reasonable, rational, mature thing to do, but if Patton were any of those things, she wouldn't have copied the damn files onto the flash drive to begin with.

"Are you nuts?" Patton gaped up at her. "Did you just hear me? Chase is going to *kill* me!"

"Then what the hell are you going to do?"

That appeared to stump Patton for a moment, but all too quickly, the crazy gleam returned to her gaze. "I know. We'll conduct our own investigation."

"No."

"But—"

"No." Angie cut her off, not about to be sucked into Patton's lunacy. Angie wasn't a teenager anymore. If she got arrested, she'd be tried as an adult. "I don't know anything about conducting that kind of investigation and neither do you."

That bought her a moment of sanity, but it didn't last. "Then we'll hire a professional."

"Who?" Angie demanded to know. "You can't bring an outsider into this. Chase will really kill you then."

"GD."

"GD gave his job up at the club because he wanted to spend more time out at the camp with his new girl."

Not to mention that Slade already had him looking into Gwen's death. Apparently, the woman had been blackmailing a whole list of men. Angie didn't know all the details, and didn't want to. What she did know was that Patton didn't know the details either, and Slade wanted it kept that way. He and his brothers didn't want her to worry, which just went to prove that Patton wasn't the only one hiding things.

"Oh, I know!" Patton exploded off the bed in a rush of excitement, drawing Angie's attention back to her with a scowl. Whatever had Patton happy couldn't be good news.

Chapter 11

Patton barreled past her to throw the bedroom door open wide and take off down the hall, leaving Angie to chase after her. "Where are you going?"

To the kitchen, apparently. Patton came to an abrupt stop, causing Angie to plow into her and drawling both Mike's and Brett's attention in their direction. The brothers had finished breakfast and were cleaning up, though they had left her plate untouched. Angie counted her luck to have two such domestic and thoughtful men. Or she would have if she hadn't been in a panic over just what Patton intended to do.

"Mike." Patton turned on him where he stood by the sink. "Rumor has it that you had a nightmare of a date last night."

"Patton—" Angie tried to cut her off, but it was to no avail. There never was any stopping Patton when she started going.

"You know you were set up, right?" Patton ignored Angie to taunt Mike with that and bring up a point that was still clearly sore.

"Yep." Mike cast a dark look in Angie's direction, one Patton clearly misread.

"It isn't Angie's fault," Patton rushed to assure him, defending Angie, but not out of the goodness of her heart. "It was Slade."

"I know that." Mike's gaze assured Angie that Patton didn't know the rest.

Thankfully, Patton didn't give him a chance to enlighten her on those details because, while Patton had seemed to completely forget that Angie had lied to her for these past few years about the club, she didn't think her friend would be nearly as forgiving for what she'd done with the Davis brothers.

It probably hadn't been right of her, but in Angie's defense, they were that good. It wasn't as if they weren't doing it with everybody else, she assured herself, but that didn't make her feel any less guilty or cool the heat warming her cheeks.

"Oh, well…you want revenge?"

"Oh yeah."

Mike nodded, his gaze darkening with a look that had Angie's breath catching. There was an ominous note to his tone that assured her he was issuing a warning, one that had her tingling with anticipation. He knew it. The satisfied smile tugging at the edges of his lips curled higher into a full smirk as he shifted his attention back to Patton.

"What have you got in mind?"

"Well….really, you'll just be….kind of…..*helping* me out, and just not telling Slade…or Chase or Devin." Patton stumbled through that request, ending with a hopeful smile as both Brett and Mike narrowed their eyes on her.

"That doesn't exactly sound like revenge," Brett commented slowly, pausing to give Patton a chance to respond, but she didn't really help her cause when she smiled and shrugged.

"I can't really tell you the details until I'm certain of your loyalty."

"Oh for God's sake." Angie rolled her eyes. They were in serious trouble, and Patton was playing games. "What she means to say is that she—"

"Angie!"

Angie continued right on over Patton's objection and ignored the outraged look the other woman shot in her direction. "Copied the entire membership list along with all personal files onto a flash drive. She gave it to Heather Lawson, who, apparently, left it in her desk drawer, and now it's gone."

"Well, thank you very much, Miss Helpful," Patton spat. "Now I might have to kill them!"

"Hold up." Mike raised a hand into the air, asking for silence before shooting Patton an appalled look. "You did *what*?"

"I think the question you want to ask is why," Brett corrected him, appearing more amused by the moment as he shook his head at Patton. "Because you know Chase is going to kill you."

"I know," Patton huffed sulkily.

"I mean, he really is going to *kill* you," Brett repeated, clearly fighting back the chuckles.

"Are you going to help me or not?"

"I don't know if I'm ready to die yet." Brett appeared to consider that as his brother took the matter a little more seriously, or at least, he was a little more curious.

"Help you do what?" Mike asked cautiously, as if he almost half expected the answer to bite him.

"Find the flash drive, duh!"

"And why do you think we would know how to do that?" Mike pressed, appearing fascinated despite himself. He was even, perhaps, a little amused.

Patton wasn't. Her gaze narrowed on him as she all but snarled. "I just thought you might be able to figure it out. After all, you are marines. Aren't you supposed to solve problems?"

"You know that attitude isn't helping," Brett shot back as he glanced down pointedly at the floor. "But begging might."

"Oh, screw you, Brett!" Patton snapped as she stormed toward the back door. "I'll just go find the damn thing myself."

With that grand declaration, Patton slammed out of the kitchen, leaving Angie staring after her while Brett burst into laughter and Mike scowled.

"She's not kidding, is she?" He directed that question at her, and Angie couldn't help but shake her head.

"Nope."

"Great," he groaned.

"So?" Angie lifted a brow, completely ignoring Brett. "What are you going to do?"

"I'm not an investigator, Angie. I'm an ex-marine." That sounded reasonable, but that didn't change the situation. There really was nobody left to ask for help.

"I could make it worth your while," Angie offered.

"Is that a fact?" That question came from Brett, who sobered up quickly as he cast her a big grin. "And just how you planning on doing that?"

"I'll lift the no-pussy-at-the-club rule."

It took a momentous amount of faith and courage to make that offer, but really it didn't matter. They could always have broken the rules. The decision to be faithful, to choose her, had to be theirs. Destiny was theirs to choose.

"And what about you?" Mike seemed far from pleased with her graciousness. In fact, his expression only darkened as he pressed her. "Are you allowed to stray as well?"

She never would. He should know that. So, instead of offering him the reassurance he clearly wanted, she dared to search for some herself.

"Does it matter?"

* * * *

Did it?

Yes. It did, and he couldn't fight that truth anymore. Mike had considered Brett's comments for a better part of the night to finally admit that his brother might have a point. Attempting to hurt Angie wasn't exactly a rational thing to do if he wanted to prevent her from getting hurt.

That didn't mean he was completely ready to give in.

"Whatever." Mike shrugged as if it meant nothing to him.

"Let me interpret that for you, Angie." Brett stepped in, ignoring the dark look Mike shot him. "That's Mike's way of saying it matters."

"Shut the fuck up, man. I can speak for myself," Mike snapped, hating the betraying heat he could feel flooding his cheeks.

"Then why don't you?" Brett shot back.

"Because I don't have anything to say." That was a lie.

His brother knew it. God knew what Brett would have said next, but he didn't get a chance before Angie drew their attention back toward her as she stepped around the counter to reach a hand up and cup his jaw. She turned Mike's head until his gaze connected with hers and he could see the depths of her affection shining there in her eyes. It about damn near undid him.

"If I wanted dick, I would have gotten some a long time ago," Angie stated without a single hint of hesitation. "So it doesn't really matter. What matters is Patton and the mess she's about to make. I have a feeling she's headed for trouble."

"Fine." Mike sighed as he gave in with ill grace, eager to end this conversation and escape the soft, gooey emotions trying to weaken him. "I'll help her out, but somebody does really need to tell the Davis boys before they find out the hard way and we all suffer their displeasure."

That dour warning earned him a smile from Angie, as she seemed to relax, though he had no idea why. "Worried they might kill you?"

"I'd like to see them try. Of course, I have to go find her." Mike glanced over toward the door, wondering where he should start looking. "Either one of you got any idea where Patton took off to?"

"Probably to go talk to Heather or tear apart her kitchen," Angie suggested. "Which should be interesting, given Heather is dating the sheriff. I'll put fifty down on the two of you being arrested by the end of the day."

"You wanna bet?" Brett perked up at that. "Because, while I am not going to take your money, we could do something like what they have at the club. Bet ourselves some buckles."

"Yeah?" Angie's brow lifted as her smile grew outrageously suggestive. "What are you going to do with buckles?"

"Give me fifty, and I'll show you." Brett wagged his brows back at her.

"Since it's my ass on the line, I should be the one who gets to enjoy winning," Mike weighed in, reminding them both that this was his challenge. It wasn't the only one.

"Really? You think you're up to claiming a victory?" Angie asked too innocently.

"What the hell is that supposed to mean?" Mike demanded to know, recognizing the insult and guessing at its source as he all but dared her to say it aloud.

"That, when the time comes, I'm figuring I'm going to have to tie you down to the bed or else find myself alone in it at a pivotal point," Angie stated with no hint of concern for his growing scowl.

"And what the hell is *that* supposed to mean?"

"That you like to run away like a little girl," Brett called out cheerily.

"Brett!"

"Hey, I say it like it is." Brett held his hands up in surrender, even thought he was far from contrite. "And we all know the truth here."

"*And what the hell does that mean?*"

"You do know you are repeating yourself, right?" Brett frowned at him as he studied Mike with mock concern. "Isn't that like a sign of a stroke or something?"

Mike clenched his jaw closed and growled as he tried to stare down his brother's smirk. It didn't work, but then he didn't have long to really try before Angie stroked the backs of her fingers up his cheek. Her touch was electric, her skin as soft as the finest silks. His gaze met hers, and he felt the fire of recognition shoot through him.

There were no words to describe the sensation, and no denying its pull. As Angie lifted up onto her toes, his head dipped, his lips brushing over hers as all his former vows were forgotten. All that mattered was the sweet ambrosia drugging his system and addicting him to her taste. It was the flavor of lust, flooding his system with a pure, white-hot need. Her lips forced his open, her tongue darting out to duel with his as they fought for control of the kiss. He, harder, bigger, stronger, and more determined.

Angie never stood a chance.

Giving into the feral instincts that he'd honed as a marine, he gave them the freedom to claim control. Wrapping his arms tight around her and crushing her tightly against him, Mike ravaged her mouth, forcing her tongue backward just as he forced her ass up tight against the island counter. He pinned her there as she clung to him whimpering, sexy little sounds that shredded whatever decency he might have, even as his hands began to tear at her clothes.

Mike needed to feel her, to touch her, to finally appease the ache within him that had been driving him crazy these past two days. Just one touch, one taste, and, maybe it would be enough. That was a desperate hope, and he knew it. Angie tasted too good, her curves too plush and soft against him, and she smelled like a heaven he wanted to drown in.

That was when the panic hit.

* * * *

Angie felt Mike's hand on her thigh begin to tremble. Half shoved up her skirt and warming the skin beneath the curve of her ass, his fingers hesitated, bringing their forward march to a stop and leaving her dangling there with her breath caught and little more than a hope to cling to. She knew what came next, and sure enough, Mike thrust her away from him in the next breath.

Leaning back against the counter, she lifted her gaze to his and saw the fear lingering in his eyes. Then he was stumbling back and fleeing for the door. Angie might have taken it personally that he couldn't even seem to touch her without panicking, but instead, her heart broke for him.

She knew what he feared, but there was no way for her to assure him she'd never leave. Not like his father. It would just take time. The only problem with that was Angie wasn't known for her patience. On the other hand, she did have Brett to entertain herself with while Mike sorted out his issues.

Turning around to eye Brett, she caught his gaze, sharing a smile with him, even as he faked confusion.

"What?" Brett smirked and lifted his chin in a defiant angle. "You going to come over here and try to scare me off next."

"Actually, I was thinking of coming there and expressing my gratitude for this morning's pleasantries."

"Oh, well." Brett sank down onto one of the kitchen chairs and leaned back, spreading his legs wide in a gesture that drew attention to the large, hard bulge tenting his jeans. "Giddy on up and show me what you got."

There was no way Angie could resist that challenge. She put an extra swagger in her walk as she came around the counter. In a smooth move, she slid onto his lap and pressed herself against his long, hard frame. Brett fairly rippled with muscles that most men never bothered to develop. He was big and trained to kill, but she felt no sense of danger as his arms lifted and his blunt, callused fingers curled around her chin to tilt her head up so that their gazes met and locked.

For a moment they stayed just like that, as a recognition that went deeper than the flesh filled the air with a tension that only added to the sultry awareness growing between them. She knew he'd planned to say something clever, something teasing, but the words never made it off the edge of his lips. Instead, his mouth dipped down to meet hers as she stretched up, giving into the moment as she discovered his taste for the first time and found herself addicted within a second.

Just like his brother, he fought her for control, flooding her sense with both the heady thrill of battle and the certainty of defeat. She was going down, and Angie couldn't wait to get there. Even as she clamped her lips around his tongue and sucked hard, her hands were fumbling with his belt.

Brett growled, his whole body clenching with the sound as his hips flexed forward. He pressed the hard ridge of his erection up against her stomach as his buckle bit into her hands. The silent demand had her all but melting. He wanted her, needed her, was being eaten alive with the same hunger as her. Angie didn't need words to know those truths.

Neither did she need any further encouragement.

* * * *

Pulling back, Angie released Brett's tongue to capture his gaze and hold him locked within the dark, erotic promise glinting in hers. His breath caught, and his whole body tensed as she sank down between his knees, holding him spellbound with her eyes. The confidence and hunger reflected there was so damn sexy that Brett knew he wasn't going to last.

He was harder then he'd ever been and on the verge of coming before she even managed to get his belt undone. Angie knew it, knew how close he was. Her smile assured him of that, and so did the slow motions of her hands as she drew out the moment until his balls were ready to explode and his dick painfully swollen, but Angie had no mercy.

Instead, she taunted him, leaning forward to grasp the metal tab of his zipper between her teeth and lower it slowly down with an expert skill that assured him she'd practiced this move before, possibly even on his archenemies—Cole and Kyle. That thought only inflamed the need searing through his veins. She was never going to go down on those two idiots again.

He'd kill them first.

That thought put a smile on Brett's face and had him relaxing back against the counter as his dick finally sprang free into the warm, welcoming grip of her hands.

"Go on, baby," Brett murmured, still holding Angie's gaze. "Measure me if you want because we both know I'm the best thing you ever had."

Angie responded to that with a gentle squeeze of her fingers as she did as commanded. The pleasure she gave him with that simple touch had his voice dipping into a low, husky murmur as he encouraged her to do it again. The twinkle in her eyes grew as she obeyed him once more.

Squeezing, tugging, and pulling, Angie began to pump his length like a pro, making his head swell with a delight that had Brett's lids drooping even lower as he gave himself over to her expert touch. She stroked and petted him, taking her time as she drove him slowly crazy. Brett was clenching against the need to force her to move faster when finally her fingers dipped down to measure and weigh his balls while her tongue flicked out to lick over his head and leave Brett straining against the sudden rush of rapture that tore through him.

The intense bolt of molten bliss shot through him again and again as she began to lap at the sensitive head of his cock with long, slow, velvety strokes of her tongue. All the while her gaze remained locked on his, heightening the moment into something more intimate than it had ever been before. Then his eyes were closing, his head dipping back as Angie's lips broke open around the flared knob of his cockhead.

Then she took him to heaven, sliding straight down his length and sucking hard as she growled deep in her throat. The sexy little sound assured him she was enjoying the moment, though there was no way she could be having as much fun as him. Nothing had ever felt this good, except maybe when her head started to bob.

Pumping and licking and fucking him with slow, torturous motions, Angie drove Brett to the very edges of his self-control, something that normally didn't happen until he was buried balls deep inside a woman, normally her ass because most cunts weren't that tight. Angie's mouth was, and she took him all the way back and down her throat without ever choking once, but she did swallow, making him growl a little himself.

The deep, feral sounds rumbling out of his chest lacked the plaintive hunger that hers had contained. Instead, the rough purrs held a warning that his patience was thinning and it was time to pick up speed. Of course, Angie never could obey any kind of command.

She proved that when she lifted up, leaving his dick cooling in the wind. Brett's eyes popped open, his hand unclenching from the edge of the counter where his fingers had dug into the pressed wood beneath the laminate surface. He wouldn't have been shocked if they'd left indentions, not that he cared.

All that mattered was the need pounding through him. It set fire to the blood in his veins, making them boil as he flushed. The silken strands of her hair felt cool by comparison as he wound his fingers through her dark tresses, but before he could pull her mouth back up his swollen length, Angie was licking her way back down it.

Her lips slid down his side this time, treating him to a wicked massage that left his dick weeping for more, and then he was spurting, gasping, his eyes rolling back into his head when she reached his balls and sucked one right into the moist, velvety depths of her kiss. Brett damn near crumpled to his knees as she licked and toyed with his balls, making him come in little fits and starts as his cock threatened to erupt.

He fought back, his hands returning to the counter to clutch at it as he bit down on his bottom lip and strained to hold back his release. He wasn't going to waste his shot in the air like some juvenile with a woody and no sense of what to do with it. Of course, Brett couldn't do with it what he really wanted.

Not yet, at any rate.

So, he stood there, clenched and silently swearing revenge as Angie finally nibbled her way back up to the top of his cock and began to fuck him with those slow strokes again. This time he didn't hesitate to take command. After all, there was only so much a man, any man, could take. Brett had taken his share.

Now it was time for Angie to take hers. This time when Brett buried his fingers in her hair, he molded them around her head, taking instant control. Forcing her to pick up speed, he began pounding her up and down his length and hips thrust forward, fucking his dick straight down her throat. She welcomed him, bobbing faster and faster until, within seconds, he ground his teeth and grunted as he came in a hard, molten blast.

Damned if Angie didn't pull back. Her fingers curled around his cock, directing the heated spray of seed upward and over his own shirt. She milked and pumped him, trying to wring every last drop out of his dick, but she missed a gallon or two because that is how heavy his balls still felt as the tension gripping his muscles finally eased and the sharp talons of rapture relaxed into a blissful ease that had him smiling down at her, despite the mess covering his shirt.

Angie was giggling, that sexy twinkle sparkling in her eyes. She'd thought she'd won, but she didn't realize that the war had just begun and her ass belonged to him. Maybe she did realize it. Maybe she read the intent in his gaze. Whatever it was that had her laughter fading into silence also had her stilling, but it was too late.

When she leapt up to flee, Brett was right on her heels.

Chapter 12

"I don't know where it could have gone," Heather insisted for like the hundredth time as Patton all but tried to shove herself under Heather's desk. "It was right there in the drawer. I swear."

She issued that plaintive assurance to Mike, who stood there wondering how he'd gotten himself sucked into this disaster. This was all Angie's fault. He'd always known getting mixed up with her would be a disaster...just not this kind of disaster, or the kind that happened in the kitchen before he'd left.

Mike didn't know what the hell that had been about and why he kept freaking out every time he touched her. What he did know was that he had to get this problem in control because it was one thing to choose not to do Angie. It was an entirely other thing not to be able to do her.

"I'm sure it's here, Heather, and I'm going to find it," Patton insisted somewhat desperately as she went crawling across the floor. "I'm sure it's around here somewhere. It just has to be."

"Don't worry?" Heather rolled her eyes and shook her head as she glanced over at Mike. "Don't worry, she says. It's just my ass in the fire if Alex finds out that I even had the damn thing to begin with."

Alex referred to one of Heather's current boyfriends or fiancés. Mike didn't really know their official status. That didn't mean he didn't know Alex. They went way back, and Heather was absolutely right. He'd be pissed.

Hell, any man would. The only reason Mike wasn't was because he wasn't on the flash drive. Thankfully. But if he had been, he already knew how his file would read. He was a wussy who was afraid of pussy.

"And what happens if you don't find it?" Heather demanded to know, finally earning a look from Patton, who frowned over her shoulder at the other woman.

Not all pussy, Mike corrected himself. Just the sweetest fucking one he'd ever dipped his fingers into. Mike admitted it. He'd licked his fingers clean after he ran back to his room the other morning. All he really wanted was another taste of that cunt. He wanted to lay Angie down and slip those perfectly curved calves of hers over his shoulders and have himself a feast.

"I guess then that means...somebody took it, but don't worry," Patton quickly added with a glance in his direction. "That's why Mike's here. To solve the mystery of who."

Mike perked up at the sound of his name, but they weren't talking to him. They were talking about him.

"Is that right?" Heather glanced back over at him with a frown. "And why are we trusting him? He's not a detective, but he is one of *them*."

The way she stressed that last word had Mike sighing, a gesture that had Heather's scowl only darkening and her doubt, clearly, expanding.

"Because we have to trust somebody," Patton argued as she came to the edge of a stack of boxes. "Besides, he's the only one willing to help. How long have these boxes been here?"

Heather didn't appear to hear that question. She was still studying Mike, and he could sense her reservations. She was right to be wary. They couldn't trust him. That was just why he stayed silent as Patton turned back once again to shoot Heather a pointed glance.

"Heather?"

That snapped the little round baker back to the moment as she returned Patton's glare. "You're not going to find it under any boxes. It's gone!"

"It didn't just disappear, and I am going to find it!" Patton shot back, bristling with an indignation that had Heather sighing along with Mike this time.

"Heather! We need help out here." Some young waitress had stuck her head through the swinging door and called out for assistance.

"Fine, then you keep on looking. I've got work to do." With that, Heather huffed off.

Mike snorted at that, though softly enough that Heather didn't hear. He didn't want her taking offense. After all, she was dating the sheriff, and he was trying not to get arrested. Not to mention he was a little intimidated by the woman. She had that mother thing going on that made Mike feel as if he was five again. Still, she couldn't be all that pure, not seeing as she was dating both the sheriff and a fireman.

"We need a Plan B," Patton declared as she lifted herself off the floor.

"And do you have one?" Mike asked, breaking his.

"Okay, let me correct that. *You* need a Plan B," Patton stressed with a bright smile. "Because you are my plan."

"And when did I agree to that?" Mike bit out a laugh, shaking his head at her. "I'm just here to make sure you don't get arrested."

"Please, don't be difficult," Patton begged, clamping onto his arm and gazing up at him with those magnificent violet eyes. "I'm—"

Patton fell ominously silent before breaking into a grin. Reaching out to latch onto Mike's wrist, she began trying to drag him toward the door. "Come on."

"Hey, where we going?" Mike begrudgingly followed, hoping like hell Brett called soon with the news that one of the Davis brothers was on his way to rescue him.

"Just come on," Patton insisted, her eyes sparkling with a dangerous enthusiasm. "I got an idea."

"Oh, God save me now."

* * * *

Brett whistled as he made the drive out to the Davis brothers' ranch. It was beautiful day. The sun felt warm against his skin. The grass was perfectly green and trimmed, the sky as blue as the clouds were white. The possibilities for adventure felt thick in the air.

That wasn't all that was thick. Brett smirked at that wayward thought, admitting that fucking Angie's ass a second time that morning hadn't done much to cool the raging tides of his desires. All it had done was feed them because now he knew how good it could be, and all he wanted was more. All he had to do to get it was convince Mike to take a chance on Angie.

How was he going to accomplish that feat? Brett didn't know, but he wasn't worried. He felt way too good to worry. Hell, he felt like whistling. That was just what he did as he turned off the highway and up the drive that led to the spread-out compound that served as the heart and hub of the ranch.

On any given day, the place could be full of commotion or, like it was that day, a ghost town. All the ranch hands, along with the brothers themselves, were out in the fields working. Brett ended up having to drive all over the place before he tracked down two of the three brothers. Unfortunately, Slade was not one of them.

Slade Davis, the middle brother, was known for his calm, reasonable approach. Chase, the oldest, was known for his command and arrogance, not to mention his hard attitude. Devin was the baby of the group and tended to be a little wild and reckless. From everything Chase had said over the years, that hadn't changed.

It wasn't a well-kept secret that Devin and Chase clashed a lot, and dealing with them together could be tiring. So no one would have blamed Brett for being braced for outrage and outrageousness, but what he got were two blank stares as both men blinked in his revelation and then shared a look between each other.

"Yeah," Chase finally responded with a heavy sigh. "We know."

"You know?" That Brett hadn't been expecting. "How do you know?"

"We've already been contacted and asked to pay ten thousand to keep things quiet for now," Chase admitted, still showing no real signs of life and confusing Brett all the more.

"And are you going to pay?" he asked, uncertain of what else to say but still shocked when Chase nodded.

"For now."

Brett hesitated, giving him a chance to go further with his explanation, but Chase didn't, leaving Brett just as confused as he'd been a second ago. "What the hell is going on here? You're being blackmailed, and you're not even the little bit pissed about it?"

"We're just playing this smart. Everybody who needs to know what they know knows it."

Brett blinked that in, trying to follow along and coming to the obvious conclusion that Chase was telling him to mind his own business, which he would gladly do except that there was one thing the brothers didn't know.

"Fine, but maybe you ought to give that speech to Patton," Brett advised him. "Because she's running around conducting her own investigation into the matter."

That got a response, this time from Devin, who scowled with unpleasant surprise as he turned on his brother. "Oh, crap. Now what are we going to do?"

"Mike's trying to keep her out of trouble," Brett assured him. "Of course, you know how Patton is."

"Yes, trust me, we know." Chase heaved a deep sigh and scowled, appearing to consider his options before pinning Brett with a hard look. "What I'm about to tell you stays here, between us. Got it?"

"Like I've got anybody to tell."

"He's talking about Angie," Devin shot back. "Whatever she knows, Patton will know, so she can't know anything."

"Got it. Angie will be kept in the dark," Brett assured them, curious enough to agree to just about anything. "Just tell me what the fuck is going on."

"Gwen Harold was blackmailing a whole bunch of people," Chase began, pausing to shoot Brett a pointed look. "Now she's dead. All the evidence she collected on her victims has disappeared along with the flash drive, and suddenly we're getting cryptic e-mails demanding cash. You put all that together and we've got a dangerous situation on our hands."

"Then you should warn Patton." And he should warn his brother before they stumbled into trouble.

"And send her running straight into the danger?" Devin shook his head. "No. What she doesn't know won't kill her…just as long as we can figure out a way to control her investigation."

"So I guess you better call your brother and give him a heads-up," Chase advised.

Brett was already reaching for his phone.

* * * *

Mike sighed as he flipped his phone closed and glanced over at where Patton was studiously trying to pick the lock on Howie's trailer. He could have helped her. He knew how to kick in a door, but she insisted. Given that Mike's sole purpose here was to avoid getting either one of them arrested, he'd agreed, but now his patience was wearing thin.

So was the light.

Mike frowned as a shadow darkened over them. Unless clouds came in the same of a person, they had company. Company that had snuck up on them silently enough that none of Mike's finally honed senses had been triggered until it was too late. Mike felt his heart lurch as he swung around to confront the Amazon smirking down at him.

It was Wanda.

He hadn't seen her in over ten years, but that didn't stop him from flashing back to when they'd been kids and she used to put him in a headlock. Mike had pleaded with the most wonderful Wanda in the world to gain his freedom. It had been humiliating.

"Oh my God," Wanda breathed out with a smile breaking across her face. "If it isn't little Mikey...and General Patton!"

Patton swung around at that greeting, and instantly, Mike knew that he was in trouble. Patton and Wanda were back together again. While Wanda had almost ten years on Patton, they still had a strong history as mentor and pupil.

"It's Wonderful Wanda!" Patton all but exploded upward, leaping off the top step of Howie's deck to launch herself straight into Wanda's arms.

Well over six feet, Wanda had the kind of muscle tone that scared most men but allowed her to catch Patton without toppling over. The two women squealed and hugged and then started babbling out questions and answers in an endless avalanche of chatter that boggled Mike's mind. He didn't stand a chance of keeping up with their conversation.

He didn't even try. Instead, Mike's attention was caught by the sudden rattle of the back door's knob. It turned, glinting in the sun, and once again, he was caught off guard as GD threw the open door. He didn't look happy. With an aggravated motion, he snapped at them in a pissed-off whisper as he glanced all around.

"Will you three idiots get in here before somebody notices you?" The big man stepped back and motioned for them to hurry up.

"Oh no." Wanda sighed and shook her head. "Somebody is grumpy."

"Don't start with me, Wanda," GD snapped.

"Wouldn't dream of it, shorty." Wanda slapped the big man on the arm as she followed Patton up the steps and into the dark confines of Howie's small kitchen.

Mike brought up the tail, leaving him as the one who had to deal with GD's scowl as he shut the door behind them. The big man didn't even have to start. Mike knew what he was thinking and held up his hands in surrender.

"I'm just the following the redhead. How your cousin came to be here, or what I'm doing here, I don't have a clue," Mike swore, earning him a snort from the large and irritated man before him, but thankfully, GD followed his comments and turned his attention on the two women smiling at them.

"What?" Patton dared to blink innocently up at GD. "Why are you looking at me like that?"

"Why shouldn't I be looking at you like that?"

Patton smile didn't dip with that obnoxious retort, but neither did she answer GD. "How long have you been in here?"

"What the hell are you doing here?"

That was at the beginning of an argument that quickly included Wanda, who apparently had been following GD around for the past two days. A bounty hunter by profession, she was testing her stalking skills and considered GD to be really out of practice. Of course, he was indignant that she'd just waltzed into town and started harassing him.

Apparently, GD was doing Wanda some kind of favor. In repayment, she was annoying the shit out of him pretending she was a detective. In reality, Wanda made a career out of hunting down men who had dared to harm a woman or a child. She insisted that was the same as working any dipshit case GD took.

The very fact that Wanda dared to insult the big man to his face went to prove what kind of crazy GD's cousin was and just why Mike stayed away from that battle. Moving into the living room, his nose wrinkled as he took in the dank, depressing room. It was small and cramped, decorated as if they were still in the seventies, but it was also strangely, perfectly clean. The cook sure as hell hadn't looked that clean back at the diner.

Clean it might be, but fresh smelling it certainly wasn't. The heavy scent of age weighed on the stale air, adding to the oppressive feeling of the orange shag carpet and the cavernous wall-to-wall paneling.

"I don't think we have time for you to go through the twelve theatrical stages of a hissy fit." Wanda's sharp retort drew Mike's gaze back to the sight of the two Davis relations facing off. His money was on the Amazon. "So why don't you go do whatever it is you're here to do, and I'll help Patton do whatever it is she's here to do."

"Fine," GD snarled.

With his ears burning and cheeks glowing, he was flushed and looking ready to blow as brushed past Mike and stormed off down the hall. Mike would have been glad to let him go, but from the look Patton shot him, he knew that wasn't her plan. It was clear from the way she nodded her head after GD what she wanted, but still Mike hesitated until she snapped at him.

"Mike!"

"Fine." Mike heaved a sigh and plodded after GD.

The long, narrow hall that led to the back bedroom was lined in snipped and flattened soup cans, which could almost have been attractive in a rustic sort of way if it weren't for the birdhouses tacked up along with them. The creepiest thing by far, though, was the collection of birds.

Never a big fan of any pet that didn't bark, Mike especially didn't like stuffed ones. They weirded him out with their plastic eyes and their too-still postures. He couldn't help but give them a wide berth as he finally stepped into a strangely cheery bedroom.

Painted a bright yellow, with a matching floral bedspread, the room contrasted sharply with the image of the rough and greasy cook Mike had gotten a glimpse of earlier. Whoever this room belonged to, it wasn't Howie. Either that or they didn't know Howie well enough. For that, Mike was thankful.

"This place is giving me a bad vibe, man." And Mike had learned in the marines to pay attention to his vibes. They'd save his ass more than once.

"Tell me about it," GD retorted as began to slide his hands across the wall. "While you're at, why don't you tell me what you are doing with Patton?"

"Angie," Mike answered in one word as he watched the big man continue to inspect the walls. "What you hoping to find there?"

"A hidden camera," the big man answered succinctly, pausing only long enough to cast Mike a pointed look over his shoulder. "And it would go faster if you would help."

"It would go faster if I knew what the hell was going on," Mike muttered, even as he began inspecting the far wall.

"You don't really want to know the details, do you?" GD asked, returning his attention back to the wall he was checking.

"No, probably not," Mike admitted. "But since I have now been tasked by Chase to keep Patton distracted and out of trouble, I kind of need to know where not to let her roam."

That revelation had GD stopping to turn and gape at Mike. "You're kidding me? I'm working my ass off here to save this town from completely imploding and they're letting fruit-loops run around playing private eye?"

Mike shrugged, not sure how to answer that question. "I don't know, man. I don't even know what is going on."

"This shit's got to stop." GD shook his head and headed for the door.

"Where you going?" Mike hollered after him, turning to follow, but his attention got caught by the stuffed bird perched damn near over the doorway.

His nose wrinkled as he eased past it in disgust. It almost felt as if its black, lifeless eyes followed him, but that alone had him pausing as he realized the sensation wasn't just nerves or a trick of the light.

The damn thing's eyes were following him, and it was the only bird with black ones.

Something was wrong, and Mike really didn't want to touch the damn thing. GD had taken off, though, leaving him to suck in a deep breath and touch the dead, stuffed animal. He'd never actually touched one before, but the moment he wrapped his fingers around the damn thing, he knew something was inside it.

That was GD's problem.

Mike didn't feel the least bit bad about dumping that headache on the big man. It didn't even matter that GD was actually helping him out by letting Patton in on a few little facts she didn't know. Catching only the tail end of GD's revelations, Mike still heard enough to know that GD had outed the Davis brothers.

That was exactly what they weren't supposed to do, but GD was clearly annoyed that everybody was trying to play detective. They were all getting in his way, an observation that had Wanda snorting. Patton, on the other hand, turned an enraged gaze on Mike and demanded to be taken back to the ranch.

"Sure." Mike had no problem divorcing himself of this mess and was more than happy to pass off his recent find to GD. "Here, man, I think this is the dead bird you were looking for."

GD lifted a brow at that but accepted the stuffed animal without comment as Mike turned to follow Patton back out the door. She bitched non-stop for the next half-hour but thankfully didn't require Mike to respond to any of her rather colorful comments and speculations. That was a good thing because he really wasn't paying her any attention.

His thoughts drifted back toward Angie and what he was going to do about her. Mike really didn't know. He wanted her in a way he'd never wanted any other woman. Strangely enough, he couldn't seem to take her. There could be a way around that problem. He just needed to get Angie to agree to his conditions.

Fortunately, Mike spotted his brother's truck parked out front of the big main house dominating the cluster of buildings that made up the main compound of the Davis brothers' ranch. Patton had jumped out before he'd even come to a complete stop.

She was racing up the front steps even as he was pulling the key from the ignition. Patton didn't wait on Mike but disappeared into the house. By the time he'd reached the front door, the yelling had already started.

Mike followed the hollering into the brothers' study, where he found Patton confronting Slade over the thick wooden slab of his desk. Brett was kicked back on the couch across from it, watching the two with a small smirk pulling at his lips.

"Hey, man." Mike slumped down on the seat beside Brett as Slade stuttered desperately in a vain attempt to keep up with Patton's accusations.

"I…no, we….Patton!"

"What's up?" Brett greeted him with a nod.

"And don't think I don't know why you don't care about that stupid flash drive! GD told me the truth. It was a sham. A fake!"

"I've come to a decision." Mike glanced over to catch his brother's gaze before continuing.

"Yeah?" Brett looked over at Mike as Slade attempted to defend himself.

"That is the most ridiculous accusation. I would never…"

"Yeah." Mike had to bite back a smile. "I'm thinking you should marry Angie."

"You set me up, and I can prove it! Just you wait till…"

"Is that right?"

"Yep." Mike nodded as Slade came out of his seat.

"Oh, don't you take that tone with me! You wouldn't be in this mess if you hadn't stolen those damn files in the first place!"

"And let me take a guess. You're going to be fucking my wife, right?"

"Yep."

"Steal? Steal! Oh, come on!"

"That is if you can manage to fuck my wife without running away like a little girl." Brett smirked.

"I got a plan for that, too." Mike turned to see Brett's smug smile as he unveiled his brilliant idea. "I'm going to do her in her sleep."

"Her sleep?" Brett's mouth fell open as he blinked at Mike in shock.

"I'm going to ask her first," Mike retorted, enjoying the way his brother continued to gape at him. "What? You didn't think I'd sneak into her bed without permission. I'm not like *some* people."

That echoed loudly in the suddenly silent room, drawing both Slade's and Patton's gazes in their direction as if they had both forgotten that the brothers were there. Apparently, they weren't welcome either from the scowls each sent Mike and Brett. Slade, though, was the one who voiced his annoyance.

"If you two don't mind, I think I need to have a private word with Patton."

"Oh please." Patton snorted and rolled her eyes. "Private word, my ass. You just don't want any witnesses for what you're about to do."

"And you do?" Slade shot back, causing Patton to still for a second before she went screaming out of the room.

Slade was right on her heels, a grin breaking across his features as he rushed past Brett and Mike. Both brothers watched him disappear out the door, and seconds later, Patton's cries were breaking into loud threats that faded away with the slam of the door.

"So?" Brett picked the conversation right back up. "You're going to ask if you can sneak into her room and molest her while she sleeps? That's your plan?"

"You got a better one?"

Chapter 13

Angie sat her desk staring at the schedule before her. Her head was pounding, her neck strained. No matter how long she stared, the schedule refused to be sorted out. There were too many men, which was why they tended to double up. While a lot of seasoned members already had established partnerships, the younger ones were still sorting things out.

That was supposed to be GD's problem. Of course, he'd quit, and Brett had taken off to God knew where. As for Mike, Angie wasn't certain whether he was taking the job or not. Strangely enough, he didn't seem that interested in working at a club full of naked women. That would have made her love him more if it weren't for the fact that she was getting stuck carrying the load for both GD and Lana.

Patton was certainly of no help. She'd completely disappeared and wasn't answering her phone. Neither was Mike, which had Angie suspecting they were in jail. She was half temped to call down to the station and see if she had won her bet. Assuming she had, Angie still had to figure out how to claim her prize. Given Mike's tendency to run away, she might really have to tie him to her bed.

"Knock, knock!" Brett called out as he stuck his head through the door. "You ready for dinner?"

"Where have you been?" Angie glanced up with a scowl, not about to be seduced by that big, goofy grin of his. She was ticked, and he was going to know it. "I've been working my fingers to the bone all day and could have done with a little help."

"I'm sorry." Brett stepped all the way into her office. "I was with the big bosses."

"The big bosses?" Angie snorted at that, swiveling her chair so she could keep an eye on him as Brett started toward her. "Is that to say you spent all day gossiping with the Davis brothers?"

"Just with Slade," he corrected her. "And you'll be glad to know that the flash drive is no longer a worry."

"Really?" Angie lifted a brow at that. "Patton found it then."

"Nope." Brett shook his head. "It was a fake. Now, come on, dinner is getting cold."

"I have to work tonight," Angie argued, though she didn't put up any resistance as he hustled her toward the door. "And so do either you or Mike. I can't run this whole place by myself."

"Don't worry." Brett waved away her concern. "We got it all covered."

Angie was not reassured. "The schedule—"

"Will get taken care of," Brett assured her as he kept her moving down the path.

He steered her away from the main complex and into the maze of gardens that held all sorts of hidden delights. Angie couldn't help but wonder what he had planned. Neither could she stop from worrying over the schedule.

"How is it going to get taken care of?" Angie demanded to know. "I've been working on it for hours and—"

"You should have called in help," Brett cut in again, casting a quick grin over his shoulder.

"Yeah? What help?"

"Lana."

"Oh God. You didn't?"

He did. He had. It was clear from the twinkle in his eyes.

"Patton is going to kill you," Angie whispered. Then her friend would probably come after her. "You've got to send her away."

"What Patton knows won't hurt me," Brett shot back. "And who else is going to make sure this place doesn't crumble into chaos? Not me and, I'm sorry, honey, not you."

There was something about the way he said that assured Angie she was being insulted. "Why not me?"

"Because you are chaos."

"I am not!"

"And a little crazy."

"*I am not!*"

"But certainly not easy," Brett tacked on with a waggle of his brows that left no doubt that he was teasing her.

"You're playing a dangerous game, Mr. Mathews," Angie warned him as they rounded one last shrub to arrive a small garden nook.

It was aglow with candles that hung all around, casting a warm hue over the intricately set table. There was Mike, standing beside it at attention and looking as if he was awaiting orders. He must have had them drilled into his head already because he jerked into motion at the sight of them. He circled the table, pulling out the chair at the head as Brett led her to it.

"Well, this is…unexpected." Angie took in everything and couldn't help but wonder what they were up to. Whatever it was, there was one big problem that no amount of romance was going to settle. "And very sweet, but it's not worth throwing Patton into a panic when she finds out about Lana."

"Patton is not going to object to anything," Brett assured her, settling her down into her seat before he stepped back and allowed Mike to push her in.

"Right now, the Davis brothers are negotiating the sale of her share back to them."

That sounded distinctly ominous. Of course, that could have been Mike's tone. He did not look comfortable or the least bit relaxed. Angie eyed him as he settled down to the right of her. Brett took the seat to the left and, with a nod, set the waiters waiting in the shadows into motion.

"She isn't going to sell." Angie offered a smile up the man who lifted her wine glass up to fill it before turning her gaze back on Brett. "Patton has plans."

"Patton doesn't have a choice," Brett countered.

"She doesn't?"

"She stole personal, private information when she made that flash drive. Whatever guilt Chase and his brothers felt about keeping Lana a secret is gone, and Patton's ass is probably burning right about now," Brett promised her. "But that's not our problem."

"Says you." Angie snorted, distracted by the delicious smelling pot the waiter settled onto her plate. It was French onion soup. Her favorite. "Oh, that looks good."

"I ordered it especially for you." As sweet as the gesture was, Mike still sounded as though he pissed about something. Angie couldn't help but eye him with unease.

"Is everything okay?"

"Everything is great."

"Yeah…" Angie drew out the word as she continued to study him. "I don't know why I doubted it."

Brett laughed at that and shook his head. "Ignore Frankenstein over there. He's just working up his courage to ask you something."

"Really?" Angie quirked a brow at that, her attention remaining on Mike and the blush raging across his cheeks.

"No."

"Yes."

"Brett!"

"You're running the mood," Angie snapped, breaking into their disagreement before it could escalate into an actual argument. This time she pinned her gaze on Brett as she made her position clear. "If your brother needs time, give it to him."

"I don't need time," Mike retorted, clearly insulted by her attempts to side with him. "I just think there is a right way and a wrong one."

"And this is the wrong one?"

"Well, it is now," he shot back at her as if that weren't obvious.

"Fine." Angie nodded and picked her spoon up. "Then let's eat. I'm hungry."

Dinner passed by quickly after that. She and Brett kept the conversation going, as Mike seemed to slowly be working his way through whatever had him tense and scowling. By the time the desserts arrived, he appeared ready to talk. True to form, he started out as if he were negotiating some kind of battlefield truce.

"I think we need to discuss the terms of our agreement."

"What agreement?" Angie paused with a spoonful of ice cream hovering inches from her lips, not certain where this conversation was going.

"The one where we sleep together and then have to marry you," Brett informed her.

"That's not an agreement. It's a condition," Angie corrected. "And it is not up for negotiation."

"Yeah, but we both can't marry you," Brett countered. "So…"

"So you want to know which one of you I want to bite that bullet?" Angie had never considered that before.

Nor had she considered that the brother who wasn't legally married to her wouldn't be emotionally tied. That wasn't the dream. That was a nightmare. Angie suspected she knew just who to blame.

"You don't want to marry me." Angie pinned her look on Mike as she stated that obvious conclusion.

"Angie—"

"That's fine." Angie waved away Brett's interruption as she pushed her seat back. She rose up to stare down at Mike. "I get it. You don't love me. You don't believe in my gift, but I do. I love you and I'm not having sex with you until you can say the same.."

With that, Angie turned and walked away. It was up to Mike to make his decision because, the truth was, she'd waited long enough.

* * * *

Mike sat there staring after Angie and feeling a deep, irrevocable sense of loss. He told himself he should be grateful, but the truth was he was resentful. It wasn't Angie that he resented, though. He loved her.

It was his dad he hated. It was his dad who had turned him into the stupid bastard who had intentionally destroyed what could have been the best thing ever in his life. It was his dad that had sown that seed of fear. Mike just wanted to crush it.

Hailey.

Hailey would know how to do that. Though they'd never spoken about it, Mike knew his sister had been just as deeply affected by their father's abandonment. Yet, somehow, she'd managed to get over it, managed to trust again. She'd know how to fix this.

With that single thought, Mike shoved away from the table and headed for the exit, leaving Brett calling out after him. He didn't pay his brother any mind. After all, the one thing Mike was certain of was that Brett didn't have the answers he needed.

It was over a half-hour later when he pulled his truck to a stop in front of the house that Cole and Kyle rented together. They shared it, just like they shared his sister. He was just going to ignore that detail and pretend as though the three were nothing more than roommates. Of course that was hard to do when Cole opened the door wearing nothing more than a pair of baggy shorts and whole lot of sweat, along with a mean-looking frown.

"Hey, man. What the hell you doing here?" Cole asked, not bothering to open the door wider and invite him in. That snub tempted Mike to return the rudeness, but he held his tongue and managed a much more polite response.

"I'm looking for Hailey."

"She's out with Heather. They went to the mall down in Dothan and won't be home for at least another hour. So go away."

With that, Cole tried to slam the door on Mike's face, but he wasn't about to be so easily dismissed. Lifting a hand, he planted a palm firmly against the door and pushed. Cole might have been ripped with muscles that would normally have impressed most people, but he was still a good fifty pounds lighter than Mike. It was no competition. Cole slid back along the wood floor as Mike shoved his way through the door.

"Fine. Then I'll wait for her," Mike declared, turning to step into the living room but pausing as he took sight of their concept of deco. "What the hell is this? A gym? You two that worried about the upcoming competition?"

"Please," Cole snorted. "Don't flatter yourself. This is all a part of a compromise. Hailey wanted the spare bedroom so that she could lock us out whenever she got pissed. So, our stuff had to come out here."

And it had to be there because Pittsview didn't have an actual gym, which sparked an idea that flared briefly. Then it disappeared behind a fresh wave of irritation at the sight of Kyle coming out the hall bathroom, clutching a towel around his waist with one hand as he shoved the wet locks plastered to his forehead back.

"Shower's all yours, man," he called out to Cole before seeming to notice Mike standing there. "What does the fuckhead want?"

"He's looking for Hailey."

"Huh."

That was all Kyle seemed to have to say. With that, he turned and walked away, right along with Cole. Suddenly, Mike was standing there by himself with nothing to do but reconsider his idea. He didn't need to stand around here waiting to talk to Hailey. The person Mike needed to talk to was his dad.

Feeling more focused than when he'd arrived, Mike turned and stormed back out the door. He'd no sooner reached the bumper of his truck than a set of headlights cut across the road and Brett's truck came ambling down it with a low rumble. Mike stood there and waited as Brett pulled in along the curb. Brett left his engine idling as he hopped out and came around to greet Mike.

"I thought you might be here." Brett glanced over Mike's shoulder before pinning him with a hopeful look. "You didn't hurt Hailey's girlfriends, did you?"

"Nope." Mike shook his head. "Why you following me?"

"Why?" Brett reared back as if Mike had smacked him. "What the hell else would I do? I'm your brother. I know you better than you know yourself, and I know you're up to no good."

"Really? Then you must know where I'm headed now."

"Well, I don't know that." Brett huffed and rolled his eyes. "But I do know you're not going anywhere without me."

"I want to go ask Dad why." Mike needed to know but didn't expect Brett to understand. That didn't stop his brother from agreeing with him.

"Fine. Then let's go have a word with the old man."

* * * *

Angie muffled a yawn and stretched her hands over her head as she glanced over at the clock on the wall. It was two in the morning, and she and Lana had managed to put out all the fires. It helped that the party in the main hall had settled down. Most of the couples and groups had retreated to their fantasy rooms to continue on with the screwing.

That meant her day had finally come to an end.

It had been long, tedious, and unnecessarily hectic, thanks to Brett and Mike. Truthfully, she didn't know what she was thinking anymore, much less feeling. After all these years, seeds of doubt had finally started to bloom in her mind. Things were supposed to be easy. They were supposed to be a perfect fit. She and Brett were, but Mike...he just wouldn't let her in.

Angie hadn't ever realized just how truly screwed up Mike was, but now she did. It about broke her heart. She wanted to the one to help, to soothe away his worries and assure him that it would all work out. If it all could work out.

She was beginning to wonder about that.

The doubts that had always lingered gnawed at her again, but Angie pushed them away. She wasn't ready to give up. Maybe things weren't as simple as she'd envisioned, but that didn't change the fact that she still loved them. Her affection for both Mike and Brett was rooted in the bedrock of her very soul.

That was sort of the problem.

"You're thinking too hard," Lana cut in, seeming to read Angie's thoughts. That was a talent she was known for. "Whatever it is, it's not going to be solved by giving yourself wrinkles."

"It's not the wrinkles I'm worried about," Angie assured her, shaking her head as Lana lifted up the vodka bottle she was holding in an invitation. "No, thanks. I think dealing with Brett and Mike will be easier sober."

"They're giving you a lot of trouble, huh?" Lana topped off her glass before turning around to meet Angie's curious gaze.

"Not as much as Chase gives you." Angie pointedly turned the conversation. She didn't want talk about Brett or Mike or the decisions facing them. "I have to say I was shocked that Patton agreed to let you return to work, but even more amazed that you came back. I would have thought you'd had enough of this place."

There was a question buried in her comments, one that Lana first appeared as if she was going to ignore. She sat there for a long, silent moment, just watching the clear liquid swirl in her glass. Eventually, though, she shrugged and glanced up.

"I don't have anywhere else to go."

There was a sadness to that reality that Angie could share. If things didn't work out with Brett and Mike, where would she go? That question echoed through her. It sparked a fine thread of fear that snaked up her spine, but Angie squashed it, marshaling her defenses and offering Lana up the same assurance that she gave herself.

"Then we'll find you some place." Angie smiled. "After all, you are a beautiful, intelligent woman who can manage a whole club full of annoying men. That's got to be a marketable skill."

That did get a laugh from Lana, who lifted her glass toward Angie. "Well then, to new beginnings."

Angie didn't have a drink, but she gave nod in salute and lingered long enough to assure that Lana would be okay before taking off. She was tired and a little worried about Brett and Mike. They hadn't checked in all night. Neither were they answering her calls. Worse, there were no trucks parked in the driveway when she got home.

The house was dark and quiet as she entered. A quick peek into their room assured her that both bunks were empty. That couldn't be good. It was nearly three in the morning, and every bar was closed. Crawling into her own bed, she lay there and listened to the minutes tick by on her clock, wondering with every single second where they were.

It seemed as though she would never get to sleep, but she must have dozed off because somewhere in the middle of the night her worries faded away and dreams of both Brett and Mike began to flood her head. The things they did to her left Angie gasping and sweating in her sheets as she came to full awareness in a rush of ecstasy.

Chapter 14

Saturday, June 30th

Angie's eyes popped open as her back arched, her hips lifting into the mouth devouring her cunt. It was, in that second, that she realized she wasn't alone in bed. Mike really was there, his face buried between her legs as his fingers dug into her thighs, holding her pussy open to his ravaging kisses.

His tongue was wicked and wild as it licked up the trembling walls of her sheath. He drew out her release until it imploded on itself, becoming a seething whirl of need that had her straining to reach another climax. Angie buried her fingers in Mike's hair, pressing him closer as she begged with broken breath for more. He gave it to her.

Lifting his lips to clamp them around her clit, he began to torment the swollen bud as he pressed the flared head of a plastic cock past the clenched ring of muscles guarding her sheath. Her pussy sucked in the long, hard length as the pleasure of being stretched and packed full left Angie twisting with the delight starting to sparkle too brightly through her.

Then he was fucking her, hard and fast, driving her from one peak to another and giving her not a second to catch her breath. Angie was flushed, her whole body tingling and tense as the sensations blurred. It wasn't until Mike reared back and rolled her over that she realized he'd distracted her. All the while he'd been lubing her up, making sure she was good wet and ready for the hard ride he planned on taking her for. Mike didn't hesitate to take it, slamming the hard length of his dick deep into her ass.

He made his intentions clear with his first thrust. He pounded into her with all his strength and set up a rhythm that was too fast for her to possibly keep up with. Not that he expected her to do much but lie there and take her fucking. He didn't leave her any choice in that as he kept her pinned beneath him with a rough grip on her hips.

He took complete advantage of that, showing off his skills as he reamed her hard and fast, only to slow down every time she came close to coming. In those moments, Mike treated her to longer, slower strokes that only stoked the inferno of need consuming her. He didn't stop until she was crying, pleading with him to release her from the tension binding her so tightly that pleasure had become tinged with pain.

"Tell me you love me," he demanded, finally breaking his silence with a snarl, but Angie had no strength left to take offense at his tone or deny him what he wanted.

"I love you."

"Even if I fucked another woman tonight?"

That question brought tears to her eyes, but, still, she couldn't lie. "Even if."

"Shit!"

Angie didn't know what that meant, didn't have time to figure it out. Her whispered confession seemed to snap something within Mike, making him grow impossibly more savage as he took her without thought, without fancy moves, without any deliberations at all. She couldn't deny that as much as she loved him, she loved his fucking just as much.

White-hot rapture lit up every one of her nerves, making the whole world sparkle before her eyes. The glittery rush of delight bloomed ever fiercer with each pounding thrust of Mike's hips. He'd lost his rhythm and now pumped into her in long, hard, slow strokes as he milked the moment for all it was worth. Angie arched into each one, allowing the euphoric showers to rain down and drown her in their bliss.

She felt free to float there while, above her, Mike was grunting it out. He was flushed and sweaty, straining as every muscle he possessed clenched and flexed in a sexy motion that brought a drunken smile to Angie's lips. He was a thing of beauty, and he was hers. That thought flooded through her just as his seed did.

With a roar and one final thrust, Mike came hard. He made a face that would have been funny at any other time as he held still for a blinding second before collapsing on top of her. Seconds later, he was snoring and Angie was still smiling.

Mike had gotten over his fear of touching her. That was a good first step. The next was to calm him down a little. While she loved how rough and demanding he was, Angie sensed there was some other desperation driving him. Like maybe he really had made a mistake earlier that night.

That thought soured her mood and had her glancing over to where he was drooling on her pillow. There were no lipstick stains, but something darker stained his jaw. Angie frowned, reaching a hand up to brush his hair back from his face. Almost instantly, the bruises swollen along his cheeks and lips became clear.

He'd been in a fight.

Angie frowned, strangely not reassured now that she knew he hadn't been wasting time on another woman. Another woman she'd have, at least, understood. Mike's constant anger, she really didn't. It worried her slightly because he hadn't used to be like that. His temper seemed shorter these days.

She had a sick feeling she was to blame for that. That wasn't the kind of influence Angie wanted to be. Saddened by just the thought, her mood soured as the sweet glow from his loving faded away, and all she felt was sticky and stuck.

The first she couldn't do anything about until she managed to roll Mike off of her. That took some doing, given he was still stuck in her. Still sensitive from his fucking, she couldn't help but gasp as she wiggled free. Then she had to remove the dildo. Angie took a moment to pull the sheets out from under Mike and tuck him in before heading off to the shower.

It shouldn't have shocked her that not five seconds after she stepped beneath the warm spray of the shower Brett appeared, naked and pressing in behind her in the stall. He paused to scowl, though, as the first tepid drops of water hit him.

"Isn't that supposed to be hot?" he asked.

"No." Never one not to take advantage of the moment, Angie turned to press herself up against the smooth, hard planes of Brett's chest. "Hot water is bad for your skin. It *sucks* out all the moisture."

Brett's cock bobbed against her stomach at that stressed word, growing harder and longer until it all but poked her in the belly button. Angie smiled as she slid down to her knees, allowing her breasts to tease his hard length before finally taking him in her hands.

She understood now. This was a game. The game they'd agreed to. Porno date night had just begun, and she was about to have some fun. Dipping her head to allow her tongue to twirl over the fat, flared head of his cock, Angie settled down for a long, slow tasting.

* * * *

Brett arched his hips and gave himself over to Angie's torturous teasing. This was really how to investigate a suspect because he would have told her anything right then. Thankfully, she wasn't asking. She was sucking, and he was in heaven.

Time, reality, and even the cold pelt of water against his heated skin faded away beneath the pleasure flooding through him.

It twisted through his muscles, tightening each one until the strain became too much. Everything snapped in that moment, and with a mighty roar, he gave himself over to his release, allowing the primitive rapture to wash away all lingering signs of domestication.

That façade had already been thinned by the battle earlier tonight and the agreement he and Mike had come to while sitting in their jail cells. Angie was his. She'd bear his name and wear his ring, and Mike would be free. That was if he wanted to be. That was his problem, and Brett was Angie's.

He smiled down at her as she sucked him dry, or, at least, she tried. She couldn't succeed, though. She never would be able to because Brett's hunger for her would never diminish. He had a sense that it would grow only stronger over time, which was amazing because, right then, he was almost desperate with a need to taste his Angie once again.

Just the thought had him smiling and twisting his fingers through her hair to pull her back and free his cock. Angie blinked and glanced up, batting her long, thick lashes at him with a smile that held the promise of a lifetime full of wonder and pleasure. It was time to start living that life, and that began with claiming the woman who had always belonged to him…or, maybe, having to explain himself to her.

"What happened to you?" Angie's grin faded beneath a scowl that had her brows angling downward. She rose up, shrugging off the hold he had on her to reach up and cup his cheek.

Brett winced slightly, reminded of the well-earned bruises he had collected earlier that evening. "Mike and I seem to have forgotten that we got our size from our dad."

"Your dad?" Angie's frown darkened even further. "You got in a fight with your father?"

She already knew the answer to that. From the way her hand fell back to her side and she stepped back, Brett could already guess Angie didn't approve. That wasn't surprising. Women rarely understood that sometimes some things just had to be settled with a little aggression.

"Yep." Brett nodded, not about to lie or apologize for that truth. "Mike and I worked on our daddy issues."

"Oh for God's sake." Angie heaved an annoyed sigh.

"It's over now," Brett promised. "And Mike got what he needed to get out of his system."

Or, at least, Brett hoped he had. Even if Mike hadn't, Brett didn't want to argue about that now. Angie looked too good wearing nothing but a frown and slick sheen of water. The endless drops raining down from the shower head above dripped and rolled around her well-formed curves, highlighting them in a glistening glint that drew Brett's eyes to the lush and bountiful mounds of her breasts. Beneath his gaze, her nipples puckered, furling into tight points that begged for his attention. He had yet to get to play with those puppies.

"Do you mind?" Angie snapped, crossing her arms over her breasts and blocking his view.

Brett glanced up, wondering if she realized the vulnerability of her position. Probably not. If she had, Angie probably wouldn't have wasted time with the lecture.

"I'm trying to have a conversation with you. I want to know what happened between you and your father," Angie demanded, but she didn't give Brett a chance to answer before she was pelting him with even more questions. "And how did you end up involved? And, given there are two of you, I'm assuming your old man lost the war, right? Please tell me he's not in the hospital or anything. Oh, wait—the police aren't looking for you, are they?"

That thought had her eyes rounding on him with both shock and dismay. Angie had worked herself up, and Brett didn't figure it would help the moment any to inform her that they had gotten arrested but that their dad had decided not to press charges. That was the first nice thing he'd done for them in years.

Whether she wanted to admit to it or not, Angie had been right. Brett felt freer than he ever had before. It was as if some part of him was finally content to close the door on that part of his life and start on the next. That was all he really wanted to focus on right then. Angie, finally, seemed to be figuring that out.

"Why are you looking at me like that?" She backed away from him. Banging into the side of the shower, she began to inch toward the side, looking ready to flee in a second. "What? Aren't you going to say anything?"

Nope. He didn't have to. All Brett had to do was smile down at her, and that sent Angie running. Wet and wild, she tore out of the shower and went shrieking down the hall. He didn't even pause to turn off the water before he took off after her.

* * * *

Brett slammed through the bedroom door not a half-second after Angie tried to throw it closed, not that she put any real effort in to keeping it that way. Instead, she squealed and raced across the room, tripping at just the right moment to end up face down on the mattress. Mike ended up pinned beneath her as Brett came down over both of them.

Just as she planned, she was good and caught between the two brothers. Mike grumbled and shifted beneath her, rolling to his side as he glanced down and glared at them. Brett paid his brother no attention as he settled his heavy weight down over her. Sandwiched as she was, Angie felt both vulnerable and sexy as hell, especially when Brett snarled and jerked back.

He kept her trapped between his thick thighs, shoving his callused hands roughly down between her spread legs. There was no gentleness or tenderness left in him as he covered her cunt and claimed it as his own. Angie was wet and ready for the fucking, even if all he offered her was thick length of his fingers. He spread them wide as he turned and twirled the tips of his fingers into the sensitive walls of her sheath, spreading her wide and making her giggle.

Angie squirmed as she pumped her ass upward, brushing her cheeks against the naked length of his cock as she teased both him and herself. He was swollen, hard, and still sticky from his recent release, and he wasn't alone. Mike had his own dick pressed up against her thigh. While he was near to where she wanted him to stick it, Angie hadn't forgotten where he'd stuck it. That was why she planted her hand on his chest and shook her head at him.

"I'm sorry, cowboy, but you've got to go wash up before you take another ride," Angie warned him, drawing a snicker from Brett.

He hung his head over her shoulder and grinned down at his brother. "Yeah, stud. It's time to hit the showers while you let the real man handle the lady."

Mike growled at that, his eyes flashing with a dangerous look. Then he struck. Before Angie could even attempt to defend herself, Mike clamped a hand over his brother's and pounded his own fingers deep into her cunt. Stretching her muscles until the pleasure was tinged with a slight hint of pain, Mike forced Brett's hand into motion. He set up a hard, fast rhythm, fucking her with a speed that had Angie arching and crying out, but they had only just begun to toy with her.

Brett dug the heel of his palm into the swollen bud of her clit, making sure the small bundle of nerves was treated to a constant massage as he pumped his fingers deeper and deeper into her. His free hand lifted to capture her breast and torment the puckered tip. Just as sensitive as her clit, her nipple pulsed with a rapturous delight as Brett rolled and tugged.

Not to be outdone, Mike matched his brother, only he used his lips. Angie gasped and arched into the sweet, velvety wonder of his kiss as Mike sucked the pebbled tip of her other breast past the hard ridge of his teeth and into the warm, wet depths of his mouth. Angie's eyes fluttered closed as she savored the pleasure of the brothers' caresses.

This was what she'd always dreamed of...well, sort of. It was actually a lot rougher, harder, and faster than she'd imagined. Both brothers seemed to be in a frenzied rush to drive her completely insane. Angie didn't have the willpower to resist that kind of delight. Instead, it consumed her whole, leaving her crying out as her whole body convulsed with an ecstasy that clenched her muscles.

It was a climax that left her far from appeased. Just the opposite. Angie felt strung out on the pleasure, tense and straining for more. More was just what Brett gave her. He didn't even pause or hesitate to give any warning that this was the moment. Instead, he pushed Mike's hand away, lining the bulbous head of his cock right up with the clenched entrance to her cunt. Then he was pounding into her.

Angie's eyes damn near bulged out of her head at the first deep thrust. She'd been screwed over the years by many different sized toys, but none had been as thick, long, or hot as Brett's dick felt as he filled her sheath to the very limit of her capacity. Then he was fucking her with a speed no other had ever come close to. Brett didn't even give her a chance to adjust to the sensation of taking a real man into her body, much less spare her a moment to catch her breath before he was pounding into her with all the force of his wound muscles.

It was too much, and Angie completely forgot about Mike or even wondering where he had disappeared. All that mattered in that moment was Brett and the delicious tension beginning to twist out of her cunt and through the rest of her body. Angie's fingers dug into the sheets as she moaned and drooled, reduced to the status of a wanton ragdoll, completely at his command.

What Brett seemed to want in that moment was to claim her in every way possible. Either that or he was trying to drive her nuts. Whether he meant to or not, that was just what he did when he pulled free, leaving her crying out. Angie had just started to catch the rhythm, pumping her hips with his when, suddenly, she found her legs being lifted over his shoulders.

Brett's stubbled cheeks scraped against the inside of her thighs. The heated wash of his breath teased the folds of her cunt a second before he struck. Then there was no saving her.

* * * *

Brett ignored Angie's shrieks and squeals as he devoured her cunt, consumed by a hunger that grew only stronger as her heady, delicious flavor flooded his senses. He was like a man possessed, fucking his tongue over and over into the velvety clench of her sheath and taunting her with erratic licks upward to tease her clit.

It wasn't enough. It never would be enough. Not until he was buried once again in her tight cunt. This time he was going all the way. Until then, he'd just have to make do with her ass. With that thought driving him, Brett made Angie come not just once but two more times until the thick cream of her release dripped down in a slow tide that he easily directed to the clenched opening of her ass.

Releasing her molten flesh, he lowered her back down and quickly began lubing her up for the fucking to come, giving her all the time in the world to offer up an objection. Angie didn't voice a single one. Just the opposite. Her hips flexed upward as he screwed his sticky fingers into her tight channel, pumping herself against him in a demand for more.

He had all she would ever be able to take. All she'd ever have the opportunity to take again because Angie's ass belonged to him. With that vow made, he withdrew his fingers and flipped her over, lining up the weeping head of his cock against her ass. A distant part of Brett warned him that he was doing this wrong, that he should say something, that he should gentle his approach, but he didn't have it in him. The warmth that flooded through him fed the feral thrill as he began to sink into the tight clench of her ass. She was small, and her muscles fisted around him in blatant attempt to challenge his strength.

Brett knew it was intentional. The wicked woman still giggling into the sheets before him relaxed for just a second, sucking in a good two inches before clamping back down around his throbbing and pulsing muscles so that the whole room shimmered before his gaze as a rapture more intense than anything he'd ever known tore through him.

Always aware of his strength and size, he'd tamed his primitive desires long ago, but in that moment, he could no longer hold back on a need that had built through the years, and Brett gave in to the sharp demand of his body, flexing his hips and slamming his full length into her. He fucked a scream right out of Angie as her laughter broke into wanton, breathless pants.

Her heavy breathing matched the fast, hard pace he set up as he pounded into her with a speed that had them both slick with sweat in a matter of minutes. She tried to keep up, but there was no way she could match him. Instead, he held her still, keeping his hands clamped around her waist as he bounced against the flushed, plush globes of her ass.

Through narrowed eyes, he watched those apple cheeks split wide over the thick stalk of his dick as it plundered her tight depth, and he listened as Angie cried out, clearly enjoying every second of his fucking. Brett knew the second it all became too much for her.

Angie's skin blossomed with an impossibly redder hue, as every muscle down the graceful curve of her spine clenched and bunched with a tension that spoke to her on-coming climax. Brett wasn't about to deny her. Instead, he changed up his speed, mixing thrusts that were hard and deep and sent her moaning into the mattress as her whole body convulsed with her release.

Brett paused, giving her the moment to enjoy the pleasure and waiting until finally she relaxed all around him before he bent down and pulled her hair back from her neck so he could nuzzle his lips against her ear. The motion pulled his cock backward as he pointedly began to rock.

"You ready for round two, baby?"

That murmured question had Angie tensing beneath him as her eyes cut to their corners in a comical look that assured him the answer was no. Not that Brett intended to let that stop him. Angie had unleashed the beast, and he was having way too much fun running free.

* * * *

He was too late.

Mike had washed up as quickly as he could, but in the few minutes it took to him clean up, Brett had already claimed his prize and moved on. Now he was fucking Angie's ass with a relentlessness that had the whole bed groaning with each thrust.

The damn thing was grinding its way across the floor, the legs of the bedframe scraping up the hardwood as Angie clutched at the sheets, moaning and crying with a delight that had her features flushed with her pleasure. She was beautiful, a creature of lust and want that seduced with simply a look.

That was what Mike was—seduced.

He stood there transfixed, staring at the couple pounding it out before him as the need thickening in his balls grew unbearable. Shaper than any other pain that he'd known, Mike felt the talons of desire cut through him and draw him forward. He stumbled over his own feet, causing both Angie and Brett to still for a moment as he banged into the mattress.

An instant later, they were back to moving, to fucking, as Brett dismissed him without a second look. Angie, on the other hand, held his gaze, drawing him around the mattress as her eyes dipped down to the thick bulge of his erection. She licked her lips and bit down on the bottom one that left him in no doubt as to what she wanted. It was just what he wanted.

Hell, he was aching for it, harder and bigger than he'd ever been.

That revelation scared him a little, but not Angie. She was there to catch the flared head of his cock in her mouth as he stepped up closer to the bed. It took skill and talent and a hell of an ability to suck, but she managed to draw him in deep without using her hands at all. With her fingers still clenched in the sheets, she sucked him all the way back to the bend in her throat and still didn't stop.

Mike's eyes all but rolled back into his head as her lips clamped down and she kept on going. He felt the ticklish rumble of the sexy grunts Brett was fucking out of her, but nothing compared to the moment when she swallowed and tightened all around him, making Mike do a little growling of his own.

That felt good, but not nearly as good as he needed it to be. Taking command of the moment, Mike fisted his fingers in her hair, gathering the silken tresses into a tight ball that allowed him to not only control her motions but also watch as she bobbed up and down his cock at his direction.

Her cheeks were flushed, her eyes glazed and her lips swollen. Angie looked like a sexual goddess created for the pleasure of a man, for his pleasure, and he wanted it all. That might make him a bastard, but so be it.

Ripping her head back, Mike forced Angie to rear up. Brett moved with the motion, settling back onto his knees until Angie was all but sitting on his cock. His brother slowed down his own motions, catching Mike's gaze over Angie's shoulder. They shared a silent motion of recognition before Brett shifted, forcing his legs between Angie's so that he could spread them wide.

The folds of her cunt parted with them. Pink and swollen and glistening with arousal, her pussy looked like a delicate heaven Mike planned to plunder. With that, he accepted his fate and fitted the weeping head of his cock to the dark entrance that led him into the tightest sheathed he'd ever screwed.

She was tight, hot, and wet and clung to him like a velvety fist that pulsed and milked his length better than any ever had. Mike's fingers dug into Angie's hips as she twisted and moaned. Caught between the two of them, there was nowhere for her to escape. All her attempts did was ignite the burning embers smoldering in his balls as her cunt clenched around him.

In that moment, he lost all control. Mike wasn't even sure of what the hell happened next. All he knew was he was sweating, straining, and pumping his hips as fast and hard as he could while Brett pounded into Angie from behind. She was squealing and clawing at him, her beautiful tits bouncing with his thrust of their hips.

Then the whirl of rapture that was whipping around them exploded into an avalanche of pleasure. Mike strained and arched into the sensation, feeling every muscle he possessed go taut. He knew this moment well, but somehow it felt different. This synchronized dance that he and Brett had indulged in many times before had never felt like this.

This time, neither brother had been in control of the rhythm. Instead, it had been set by the need that had captured them all, driving them straight toward a white-hot eruption of pure bliss that sucked them all under.

Angie went first.

Her skin grew even pinker as she lost the ability to keep pace, finally giving up that last bit of control. Mike didn't have time to savor his victory, though, as he felt the heat in his balls boil over and flood his shaft. Then he was coming, flooding her cunt with his seed and silently longing for one to take root.

That thought should have sent him running, but Mike was way too weak to go anywhere. Instead, he wrapped his arms around Angie, pinning her to him and collapsing onto the mattress. A second later, Mike passed out. For the first time in a long time, he slept with no concern left for the world. He was at peace.

Chapter 15

Angie woke up several hours later much the same way she'd fallen asleep, pinned between two hard male bodies and being fucked from both directions. She was wet, sweaty, and sore but couldn't deny the pleasure twining through her muscles. She didn't even have the strength to fight it, much less the will.

Tipping her head back to rest on Brett's shoulder, she began to move in rhythm with Mike and him, following the flight of rapture beginning to lift her higher and higher. Her heart raced, her fingers clutched at Mike as his muscles bulged beneath, and his own hands clung to her hips, forcing her to fuck him back with the same strength he rammed himself into her with.

His fingers weren't the only ones digging into her flesh. Brett had just as tight a hold on her, though his fingers dug into the fleshy globes of her ass. He bounced them against the long, rigid length of his cock as he pumped his dick deep into her body over and over again.

There was barely any room for Brett, not with Mike stretching her cunt wide. This was what she'd dreamed of, but Angie had never imagined it would be so intense, so overwhelming. She couldn't help but fear the rush of ecstasy that drowned her in a sparkly delirium that cleared only minutes later, after Mike had already left the bed without a single word.

That was when Angie became aware of the sunlight and the numbers blinking on her clock. It was nearly noon, and she barely had the strength to pull away from Brett's hold, but she needed to get moving. She had a lunch appointment with Patton, who would come looking for her if Angie didn't show up.

The last thing Angie needed was for Patton to find her in this position. Patton would, no doubt be excited, and, worse, full of questions that Angie honestly didn't have answers for. She didn't know why it had happened, or why it had happened now. Other than a fight with their father, nothing had really changed.

Yesterday, Mike hadn't wanted to marry her. She'd made her terms clear, but in the grunting and groaning, he'd never once uttered a single word to make her think he felt anything for her other than physical pleasure. What was she supposed to think of that?

Angie didn't know. What she did know was that she was supposed to be happy. She'd gotten what she wanted, but somehow it didn't feel right. It didn't feel like the dream had.

Turning, she offered Brett a half-smile as he blinked up at her from his pillow. Even sleep-tousled and rolled up in floral sheets, he looked hard, his features cut with a firm hand.

"Mornin'," Angie murmured, looking quickly away. She felt strangely awkward and uncertain of what to say.

"What's this?" Brett lifted a brow as he reached up to brush his thumb over her cheek. She felt the heat growing beneath his touch and couldn't hold this gaze. "Never let it be said that the great and mighty Angie is suddenly feeling a little embarrassed and shy."

She was, and she didn't want to talk about it or the confusing mix of feelings churning in her gut. Instead, Angie focused on the practical and used it as a shield against the illogical doubts swirling through her head.

"You didn't wear a condom." That came out a little more blunt than she'd meant for it to sound, but there was no taking it back. Nor was there any denying the smirk that tugged at Brett's lips as he studied her for a moment.

"I didn't think one was necessary."

"Neither did your brother."

"What's wrong, sexy? You afraid we're going to knock you up and leave you hanging?" Brett teased her.

"That wasn't what I was thinking." Neither did she believe that they'd abandon her, but Angie could believe that they'd feel trapped by such an obligation.

"Then what the hell were you thinking?" Brett demanded to know, appearing to lose a little of his patience and his good mood. "Is something wrong, Angie? Because you can tell me if there is."

Angie frowned at that and glanced over at him, taking in the sight of the bruises that had darkened over the night. They bothered her. They left her wondering…

"No." Angie shook off those thoughts before they could gather and form into a problem she'd have to face. "There's nothing. I'm just a little tired, and sore."

That brought the smile back to Brett's lips. He cast a lecherous look down her frame as he patted he mattress in front of him. "Well, if you want to lie back down, honey, I'd be glad to give you a full-body massage."

Angie snorted at that, certain that he would. "I think I'll just go wash up."

"You sure?" Brett watched her slip out of the bed with open disappointment. "I give a really good oral massage."

That had Angie pausing and casting him a look. He greeted her doubt with a dirty smirk and waggle of his brows. She ended up rolling her eyes as she reached for her robe.

"Thanks, but I think I'll stick with the shower."

"Maybe I'll join you." Brett shoved back the sheet, revealing not only a hard body that rippled with muscles but also an erection most men would brag about. "I can help clean those hard-to-reach places."

"Yeah, I bet," Angie muttered and quickly looked away from the cock that was all flushed and swollen and tempting in ways she'd never guessed one could be. Already she was growing wet as an ache that she feared would never die bloomed to life once again, but this time it held the tinge of a frantic emotion that didn't sit well with her.

"If it's all the same to you, I think I'll just take care of that problem myself."

With that, Angie escaped out of the bedroom and rushed toward the already steamed bathroom. This time when she shut the door, she locked it.

* * * *

"I think we're in trouble."

Brett closed the bedroom door and pinned Mike with a worried look as if he needed that added weight to take his brother's words seriously. Mike knew things were screwed up. He knew whom to blame.

Himself.

This was all his fault. He hadn't been easy on Angie. He hadn't been the kind, gentle lover that a virgin deserved. He'd probably hurt her. He couldn't even remember. Never in his life had he been that far out of control before.

The worst part, though, was that he couldn't seem to focus on anything other than the memory of Angie's cunt clenched tight around him like a velvety glove. She'd milked the very seed from his balls not even a half-hour ago, and yet, they were full and hard again.

Mike wanted her. The need, the hunger, it didn't abate. It only grew. It threatened his very sanity, rendering him almost completely irrational. Mike knew that was a problem. Brett's grim pronouncement only confirmed his fears.

"She looked happy to me when I went to get a shower," Mike grumbled as he rubbed a hand over his face in a vain effort to wipe away the guilt. "Maybe it's just you that's in trouble."

"No, I'm telling you something is not right," Brett assured him. "Angie's acting weird."

That had Mike dropping his hand as he shot Brett an annoyed look. This conversation was not helping his sense of panic in the slightest. That damn emotion had returned to poison his thoughts, even as he tried to reason with it and his brother.

"Angie is weird."

"She's worried about condoms."

"So?" Mike shrugged, stretching with the gesture and arching his back. He was sore and tense, not at all like he normally was after getting laid. "That seems sensible."

"Not if you're in love with a man and planning on marrying him," Brett shot back, clearly growing flustered with Mike's attitude. "I'm telling you something is not right!"

"Whatever." Mike shoved off the bed, desperate to escape this conversation and the insecurities it awakened within him. "I'm going to start breakfast."

With that, he yanked the door open, forcing Brett to get out of his way as he slammed out of the room. Ten minutes later, when Angie joined him in the kitchen, Mike already had the eggs going, the bacon baking in the oven, and the coffeepot filled with a fresh brew that seemed to lure her toward it like a zombie.

Without meeting his look or even bothering to offer him a basic greeting, Angie shuffled across the floor. She was wearing a long skirt and a loose top, a drastic change from her normally too-tight outfits. Mike watched her with the growing sense that Brett was right. Something was wrong.

Angie was having regrets.

Well, that was too damn bad. She'd made her bed and forced him into it. Now she was just going to have to live with the consequences. They had a deal, and she wasn't backing out now.

Intent on reminding her of that fact, Mike stalked up behind Angie and crowded her against the counter. Caging her between his arms, he pressed in tight, making sure she felt the thick length of his erection as he ground it into her ass.

"Morning."

"Morning," Angie returned after a moment's hesitation. "Was there something you wanted?"

Mike didn't answer her. Not with words. Instead, he showed her, sliding a hand down her side and bunching a fist into her skirt. He dragged the hem up slowly, aware that the motion had caused Angie to tense against him, but the catch in her breath assured him she was far from annoyed, despite her tone. So, he didn't stop until he felt the silky press of her skin beneath his fingertips.

Smooth and flushed, Angie skin only grew hotter as he slid his hand along her thigh. Mike slid his fingers up until the tips brushed against the small slip of lace barely covering the swollen, wet folds of her pussy. With a slow, easy movement, he slipped his fingers beneath the elastic edge of her panties and teased those puffy lips before dipping down between them to discover the soft, velvety flesh of her cunt.

Mike took his time, stroking over her intimate folds as he listened to the soft mews that began to fall from her lips. He took his cues from the little gasps and sighs, allowing Angie to tell him without words just how she liked to be petted, to be fucked.

Capturing her clit beneath the flattened tip of his thumb, he began to roll the sensitive bud, making Angie tense against him. She liked that best of all. He knew she'd like what he planned next, but Mike had barely begun to tease the tight ring of muscles guarding the entrance to her cunt when the back door banged open and Hailey came walking in like as if she owned the place, which she did.

"Oh for God's sake!" Hailey spat, stumbling to a halt as she took in the two of them. "You know I'm happy you two are working everything out, but really, I have to work at some point! Don't you guys have a club where you can play these games?"

"Sorry, Hailey," Angie apologized, not sounding the least bit contrite, though she did shrug away from Mike's hold.

Squirming out from where he still had her pinned against the counter, she stepped to the side to toss first Mike and then Hailey a quick smile that held a hint of nervousness.

"I have to get going anyway. I have a meeting this afternoon."

Mike didn't have anything to say to that. Instead, he turned to lean against the counter and watch her leave while he lifted his fingers to his lips. The heady scent of Angie's arousal clung to them, along with the creamy proof of how ready she was for him.

The temptation was too great, and he found himself sucking his fingers dry as Brett came stumbling into the kitchen seconds after Angie fled out of it. He paused and glanced around before shooting a look at Mike.

"Angie."

"Left."

"Oh," Brett sighed, his shoulders slumping as he cast a disappointed look at Hailey. "Hey, Hales. What you doing here so early?"

"It's not early! Not for people who work," she shot back with enough annoyance to have Brett and Mike exchanging a look.

Mike stepped aside, allowing his brother to reach for the coffeepot as he headed toward the back door. "It's Saturday. People don't work on Saturdays."

"People who want to get paid do," Hailey retorted. "And don't think I haven't heard about what you two got into last night."

That accusation had Mike stiffening up. "What do you mean by that?"

"I'm talking about our dad." Hailey hesitated as she narrowed her eyes on him. "Why? What did you think I was talking about?"

"Nothing."

"Uh-huh."

"How do you know about our catching up with Dad?" Brett turned the conversation, but the speculation was still there in Hailey's eyes as she studied them both while she answered.

"I had an unpleasant call from his wife. She was not particularly pleased about the brawl that broke out in her front yard." Hailey hesitated again, but neither brother had anything to say. "Well? You want to tell me what you two were up to?"

"I think you call it getting closure." Mike had gotten some. He'd like a little more but knew better than to go back for it. After all, their dad could give what he took.

"That's not funny, Mike," Hailey snapped. "You should just be glad he didn't press charges. And don't think I don't know that you stopped by my house before going down there. We all know why, too."

"Oh, don't start, Hales." Brett groaned, his eyes closing as he grimaced theatrically. "Mike didn't hurt your pretty boys."

The two of them took up that argument as Mike stood there between them, his thoughts centered on what Brett had said. He hadn't hurt Hailey's pretty boys, but he feared he might have hurt somebody else. Angie had taken off without her purse or shoes, and she hadn't snatched her keys off the counter.

Wherever she was going, she was walking barefooted, though he suspected she really was running. Brett had been right. Something was wrong with Angie. The question was, what?

* * * *

"What the hell happened to you?" Patton stumbled to a halt, her mouth gaping open as she took in the sight of Angie waiting on the bench tucked beside the entrance to the Bread Box.

Angie had been waiting there for over ten minutes, feeling more than a little self-conscious, thanks to the looks she was getting. Patton's bug-eyed look of horror didn't help.

Reaching up to finger her hair, Angie knew she must look worse than a mess, but still, she sought some kind of reassurance.

"Do I look that bad?"

"Yeah." Never one to coddle anybody, Patton offered her a sad smile and a quick nod. "I'm sorry, honey, but…did you drop your brush in the toilet or something?"

"Or something." Angie felt her eyes flood inexplicably with tears as her voice broke over those two words. She didn't understand what was happening to her, but Patton seemed to.

"Oh, honey, noooo!" Patton rushed over to settle down on the seat and swooped Angie up in a big hug. "It's going to be okay. You just tell me what is wrong, and I'll take care of it."

That was Patton. Commanding, dominating, and, in her own twisted way, a big softie. She was a good friend. For some idiotic reason, that thought had Angie bursting into full-on sobs. Patton tucked Angie's head against her bosom and rocked her as if she were some kind of baby.

Distantly, Angie knew they were probably making a spectacle of themselves, but she didn't care. Neither did she worry what anybody would think of the sight of her cuddled up against Patton. Maybe elsewhere in the world, it would have been weird, but in the south, people were huggers. Huggers and patters.

"There, there." Patton patted her on the back and rocked Angie as if she really were a child.

It didn't help. The crying did. While Angie felt no less rational when the tears finally dried up, she was, at least, a little more sedate. Pulling back with a sniff, she rubbed at her eyes, certain that she looked even worse now.

"Look at me." Angie snorted and shook her head pathetically. "Look what they've done to me."

Because she was certain this was Brett and Mike's fault. Patton seemed to instinctively understand that as well. She leaned back to do just as Angie had ordered and studied her with a critical eye. It wasn't shocking that she saw the truth almost instantly.

"Oh my God!" Patton breathed out like a prayer. "You…Mike, Brett…isn't this supposed to be congratulations?"

It was, but for some reason, it also wasn't. Angie didn't have an answer for that bit of confusion. She didn't need one. Patton seemed to understand perfectly, or, at least, she thought she did.

"Oh my God!" She gasped once again as her eyes rounded with another wave of shock. "They aren't any good, are they? I would never have thought…I mean, given their reputation—"

"Patton!" Angie snapped before the other woman could upset her further by following that thought to a comment about all the women they had been with. "They're good."

"Then you—"

"Yes!" Angie could feel the flames consuming her face, which made absolutely no sense. She'd never been shy about sex, but then she'd never had the real thing before. "Many times."

"Hmm." Patton seemed to consider that as she continued to keep her narrowed gaze focused on Angie. "Then why exactly are you sitting here dressed like some hobo with no shoes on, no purse in sight, your hair sticking damn near straight up, and crying your eyes out? Because that's how *good* they are?"

Angie shot Patton a dirty look for that and reached up to try to pat her hair down. It was pointless. Without a blow dryer or any of her products, her hair was doomed to be larger than the rest of her head. A brush, though, would have helped with the knots. Angie eyed Patton's purse, betting she had more than simply a brush in there.

"Oh," Patton sighed, drawing Angie's attention back toward her. "I get it. You feel used, don't you? You thought it would feel special, and it wasn't, was it?"

Those words cut right through Angie, making her freeze from the inside out with a bitter recognition. That was exactly it.

Chapter 16

"I don't want to talk about this." Angie hopped off the bench in a sudden rush to avoid that conversation. She couldn't have it. Not until she had some amount of time to consider the matter herself. "I'm hungry, and, obviously, you're buying breakfast."

"Here." Patton passed her purse over to Angie. "Run on into the bathroom and try to clean yourself up a little. I'll get a table."

"Fine, but if the waitress stops by, order my usual."

"Usual?"

"Coffee and raisin-bourbon pancakes with caramelized maple syrup sauce."

"Not a problem, but don't let Heather see you're not wearing shoes," Patton warned.

Angie frowned down at her feet and found her first real smile of the day. "Yeah, you want to go get pedicures after this?"

"Sure." Patton smiled. "We can get them done at the club."

"Um, you're not allowed at the club...are you?"

The answer was no. Angie could see it in Patton's gaze, but the other woman's smile just grew bigger as she opened the bakery's door. Angie hesitated before rushing in and past the curious glances. That conversation was not over, but first, she really did need to do something about her hair.

Thankfully, Patton had more than just a brush in her purse. She had a rubber band and some powder and even a tube of mascara. By the time Angie was done, she was, at least, presentable, if not actually bordering on cute, in a hippy sort of way. More amazing than her transformation was the fact that Patton had managed to snag a booth.

"Okay, I called this meeting because we are at DEFCON 5, and we're all out of stages!" Patton declared almost the instant Angie's ass hit the seat.

"Uh...Patton—"

"The flash drive was a fake!"

"I know."

"What? *Why didn't you tell me?*"

Angie heaved a heavy sigh and shrugged. "It wasn't like I knew when I talked to you yesterday, and shouldn't we happy about this? Like, maybe, only at DEFCON 3 or 2?"

"Three or two?" Patton gaped at her. "We've been duped, played for fools, we got—"

"Lucky," Angie cut in with a pointed look that had Patton sulking back into the booth.

"Fine then." Patton stuck her chin into the air and settled back against the wall of the booth. "I guess all we have to talk about is your, Brett's, and Mike's evolving relationship."

"So, we're at DEFCON 5, huh?"

"And sinking fast." Patton nodded as she leaned forward again. "I had to sell out my share of the club...and agree to let Lana work there."

"I know."

"Of course you do." Patton hesitated, lifting a brow in Angie's direction. "Aren't you going to thank me or marvel at my generosity in letting her return to work for, at least, a little while?"

"No." Angie snorted, finding a laugh buried in that idea. "You weren't being generous."

"How do you know?"

"Because I know you. This move benefits you in some way." Angie paused to study Patton for a second before admitting, "I just haven't figured out what way, yet."

"I want male strippers."

"What?"

"And I'm not talking about those cheesy, wiggle-around kind. I'm talking about hunks who know how to move it!"

"Patton—"

"I know a few back in Atlanta that…oh my God, did they test my vow to be faithful to—"

"Patton!" Angie cut in, feeling her frustration level rise as she tried to rein in her friend's more extreme ideas. Unfortunately, all of Patton's ideas were extreme. "I don't know what the hell you're talking about, but if you think you're bringing male strippers into the Cattleman's Club, think again."

"I'm not talking about *their* club," Patton shot back. "I'm talking about *my* club."

"Your club?" Angie repeated, hating to point out the obvious because she already knew Patton had a comeback, and she feared what it was. "You don't have a club."

"I'm going to start one."

That was exactly what Angie had known she was going to say. "Patton—"

"Oh, come on!" Patton cut her off with a frown. "We're over forty years past the sexual revolution. Women should be allowed to get their groove on."

"And where are you going to find these women?" Angie demanded to know, already certain she knew the answer. Based on the smirk Patton shot her, she wasn't wrong.

"Well, I do have a list of female clients who already enjoy, shall we say, an active lifestyle. I also happen to have a good friend who knows how to recruit even more women."

"Okay, fine." Angie knew when not to argue a point. "Let's just say you got women…where are you going to put them? A club will require a massive amount of capital investment."

Patton just smiled, and Angie knew that look. It sent a cold chill down her spine, but before she could give voice to her fears, Heather came shuffling down the line of tables with a fresh pot of coffee, refilling mugs as she went. She paused by their table, but before she could get a word out, Patton was already speaking up.

"Tell Angie you'd go to a club where the women ruled and the men walked around on leashes, wouldn't you, Heather?"

Heather stilled for a moment, glancing between the two of them before reaching over to refill their mugs. "Your orders will be up in just a moment."

"That's not a no!" Patton hollered after her as Heather moved on. Turning back to confront Angie's pointed look, Patton still refused to give up the argument. "Like Heather is our target member. She's a prude."

"You asked her," Angie reminded Patton, as if that were needed. "And she can't be that big of a prude. She's all but engaged to the damn sheriff *and* his best friend."

"Yeah, well...Alex was never much to look at," she muttered resentfully.

"Patton."

"Konor, on the other hand..."

Patton tipped her head and watched the big fireman strut up with two plates. She was all but licking her lips, and Angie didn't think she was checking out the food. She shot Konor a smile as he came to a pause by their table.

"I got a raisin-bourbon pancakes with caramelized maple syrup sauce," he announced, lifting a brow along with a delicious smelling plate.

"Right here." Angie had expended enough energy last night that she deserved a good lunch.

Of course she always came up with a good excuse to eat well in the first meal of the day. Breakfast was her meal, and, apparently, a tight ass was Patton's weakness. She didn't even make any bones of checking out Konor's ass as he set Angie's plate before her.

"There is some toasted walnut butter on the side," he informed her before turning back to Patton, who glanced up quickly at him as if she hadn't been guilty of anything. "And you must be the three-egg omelet with bacon, cheese, and chives."

"Mmm-hmm." Patton nodded, studying Konor's well-cut features for a second before horrifying Angie with a question Patton should have known better than to ask. "Say, Konor, you don't happen to know how to dance, do you?"

"Patton!"

"What!" Patton obnoxiously shot back with the same outraged shock, earning her a dirty look from Angie and a smirk from Konor, who didn't bother to answer her question before turning to walk away. He did pause, though, to shake his ass at them, causing Patton to laugh as Angie heaved a sigh.

The man had no idea of the danger in encouraging Patton's outlandish ways. Nobody did. Not even the people who knew her well enough to love or hate her. There was one person who Angie was pretty certain did hate Patton, which made it all the more deranged that Patton actually had the audacity to bring Lana up as a possible business partner.

Apparently, Patton had it all figured out. She'd sold her share back to the brothers with three conditions. They cut off a part of the club's lands and titled over to her. They gave her a whole lot of money to spend how she wanted, and they replaced Lana within the next two months.

That was when Lana would be taking her punitive trip across the country with Cole Jackson's bone-headed cousins in an RV, no less. Despite the fact that had to be the cruelest of all things Patton could have dreamed up, she still seemed absolutely certain that Lana would buy in and partner up with her in her new adventure.

"Do you even hear yourself?" Angie finally had to ask. "Lana *hates* you."

"So?" Patton shrugged. "I hate her, too."

"Then why the hell would you want to partner up with her?" It made no sense except, maybe, to Patton.

"Because she knows how to run a club," Patton shot back, as if that weren't obvious.

"No, you're not getting the point." And she was driving Angie insane in the process. "Why would she want to work with you?"

"Money."

That actually made some sense. Sort of. That is if Angie refused to consider the obvious, which Patton clearly was. It almost pained her to point it out, but somebody had to.

"You do realize that's not why Lana worked at the club?"

That blunt question got little more than a shrug from Patton. "Yeah, I know, but if everything goes to plan, Lana won't be lusting after Chase for long."

Angie stilled at that comment. Lana had been lusting after Chase for almost all of her life. Why Patton thought she'd soon be distracted made little to no sense to her. She almost didn't want to ask but had to know the reason for Patton's certainty.

"And why is that?"

Patton just smiled and dug into her omelet, going silent for the first time that morning. She didn't have much else to say after that either, leaving Angie to worry over just what kind of plans Patton was making. She was worried because Patton had a history of getting things her way, which Angie guessed wouldn't be so bad this time.

The idea of buff, dancing, half-naked men wasn't all that bad.

What was bad was Patton suggesting they head out to the club to get those pedicures. Angie agreed, though mostly because she wasn't paying attention. That changed somewhere around the time that Patton was explaining her idea for luring away all the women from the Cattlemen and forcing them to negotiate with her club to get pussy.

In short, she wanted to be the madam of Pittsview, if not the whole of lower Alabama. Actually, Patton wanted Lana and her to hold that title. That was just the weirdest of all of Patton's ideas.

Angie couldn't wait to see her pitch it to Lana.

* * * *

Brett glanced around at the obstacle course and had to admit he was impressed. Nick Dickles had really built something spectacular here out at his camp. That wasn't shocking. Nick had always succeeded at everything he did, right or wrong. What did amaze Brett was that the horny bastard was all ready to settle down.

Of course, true to his nature, Nick had found himself a character and a half in Kitty Anne. She wasn't only hot. She was also currently showing Mike up as she raced through the course. Nick and GD's woman was clearly impressive. Definitely the kind of woman Brett would have picked out for himself if his heart hadn't already settled on one.

Angie.

He'd been trying to call her all day, but she'd left her cell at home and was never around when he called out to the club. By the fourth time, Brett got the message. Even if she was around, Angie wasn't speaking to him. He just didn't know why, and he was starting not to care why.

The woman couldn't do this. She'd pursued them. She was the one demanding that they marry her. The one saying she was in love with them and calling them her destiny. Now that he and Mike had finally given in, she ran cold?

That wasn't right. That wasn't fair. Brett wasn't going to let Angie get away with it either. They were getting married and living happily ever after. That was the deal.

"You okay, man?"

GD broke into Brett's brooding thoughts, reminding him that he was doing it again, loosing focus. Angie really had his head twisted around. Brett tried to shake it loose as he cocked a smile in GD's direction.

"I don't have a clue," Brett admitted honestly.

"Then you must have woman troubles." GD paused, his own smile taking on a wicked curve. "Angie troubles."

"Yeah."

"Can I give you a piece of advice?" GD asked and then promptly went ahead and did just that before Brett could respond. "Just give in. It's not worth the fight."

Brett didn't respond to that. He didn't have to. Something in his face had GD's gaze narrowing before his eyes widened, a chuckle falling from his lips.

"Holy shit! Ha! You gave in. You didn't even last a week."

For some reason, that just tickled GD. He didn't keep the mystery to himself but gloated with an ego that was apparently growing richer by the second.

"You just made me five thousand buckles. Man oh man."

Brett didn't say anything. He just stood there staring at GD as he laughed and shook his head. It took the big man a moment, but eventually he realized Brett wasn't cheering him on. Brett wasn't even smiling anymore.

"Uh-oh." GD heaved a deep sigh as he calmed down. "You did her, and you don't want to marry her."

"You got that reversed," Brett muttered, causing GD's jaw to go slack as the merriment twinkling in his eyes shined even brighter.

"You're kidding me!"

"I don't know. I don't want to talk about it." All talking about it was doing was giving him a headache. So, he turned his attention back to the obstacle course and dismissed GD's continued stare. "This thing is impressive. The kids really built it?"

"Yeah, well...they had some help," GD slowly admitted, clearly reluctant to follow the change in conversation but knowing he couldn't force Brett to talk. "The guys in town really pitched in. A lot of them are mentors, including Cole—"

"You mean Sally," Brett corrected him, but GD didn't even smirk as he ignored that dig.

"And Kyle. They're *very* familiar with this course."

"That almost sounds like you think they might beat us." Brett paused, waiting for GD to join him in a laugh, but all he got was a pointed look. "You do think that!"

"Just because you're bigger doesn't mean you'll be faster," GD warned him. "Hailey didn't pick two pussies, even if you don't want to admit it."

"Oh please. Mike and I wiped the floor with those two, and what the hell is that look for?"

"Just because somebody doesn't fight back doesn't make them weak." GD paused, instinctively glancing back over at Kitty Anne and smiling.

"She's impressive, too," Brett commented, amused by the way that compliment had GD's chest swelling outward with pride.

"That she is."

"That's a big rock on her finger, too."

"Yep." GD glanced over at Brett, his grin growing. "You planning on getting Angie one? Because I can hook you up with the jeweler."

"I think I'll wait until I know she's going to say yes."

Before GD could respond to that, Mike came jogging up. He'd been moody most the day, but right then, he was wearing a wide grin. Shirtless and sweaty, his brother glanced between GD's smirk and Brett's scowl before settling on the big man.

"This thing is an awesome workout."

"Better than Angie?"

Mike stilled at that question. His smile faded into a dangerous look as he narrowed his gaze on GD. "What are you talking about?"

"He knows," Brett warned his brother.

Mike blinked that in and then did just what Brett had. He changed the topic. "What happened with the dead bird, man?"

GD snorted, clearly irritated at both brothers' attempt to avoid the subject he clearly wanted to linger on. "It's a long story, and, trust me, you don't want to hear it."

"That bad, huh?"

"It's a camera imbedded in a stuffed bird and pointed at a bed. How can it not be that bad?" GD shot back. "Even worse, you got Wanda all worked up. You know how she feels about crimes against women. She takes it personally."

"Wanda." Brett shivered at just the thought of GD's cousin. She'd beat him up when they'd been little. He was not looking to running into her now that she was grown. "How long she sticking around for?"

"Too long."

That, apparently, was all GD had to say about that subject. He wasn't even subtle about it. He just walked away, leaving Mike and Brett with the uncomfortable silence that seemed to arise whenever they were alone.

"You get the feeling he's not thrilled with Wanda's visit?"

"Why should he be?"

Wanda was trouble. Always had been. GD hadn't been lying about her making everything personal, or her drive to protect what she considered the weak. In that one small way, Brett could respect her. He just also wanted to steer clear of her.

The awkward tension rose back up, but Brett couldn't stand it anymore. "So, when are we going to talk about the fact that Angie is pissed at us?"

"When I know what we're going to do about it?" Mike responded after a second. "Because, right now, I don't have a clue. You?"

"Not really…but dinner, a romantic dinner, heartfelt declarations, the whole prince charming thing, I would think that would be called for at this point." Brett just never had done any of those things. Neither had Mike.

"I just don't think it's that easy," Mike insisted.

"Why not?" Brett didn't understand why Mike was so hesitant when it was obvious that seduction was called for. At the very least, it couldn't hurt, but Mike was the brains, and he actually had a good reason for his concern.

"Because...I mean, Angie has been dreaming of us for *years*," Mike stressed. "She created a fantasy. She fell in love with it, and last night...maybe she felt the difference."

Brett blinked that in, realizing in that moment that Mike hadn't doubted himself. He'd doubted Angie. "You're saying she doesn't really love us."

"I'm saying she doesn't really know us, and that's not something you fix with a dinner."

"But dinner is the place where you *start* to fix it." After all, if she didn't know whether they were the same men she'd dreamed of, it was time to prove that they were.

"All right." Mike slowly nodded, though he still seemed reluctant. "We'll start with dinner."

Chapter 17

Angie's phone buzzed for the fourth time in as many hours. This time it was Mike's name that flashed across her screen, but still, she ignored its summons. Instead, she sat there tense and nervous, waiting for the sound to stop as Lana eyed her from the other side of the desk. She'd been showing Angie how she organized the schedule so that it was easily managed.

They'd been at it all day and most of the night. Lana was training her so Angie could train Lana's replacement. In the process, she'd started to type everything up and fill it into a book that was quickly becoming Angie's new work bible. Names, contact, how to operate every computer system, it was all there.

So were Brett and Mike.

They weren't going anywhere, and neither was her problem. It would be nice, though, if she could at least understand why her heart was racing. Angie didn't have a clue. All she knew was that the very thought of them made her panic. Lana seemed to sense it.

"Are you ever planning on talking to those boys again?" she asked, a hint of amusement softening her words.

"I might," Angie shot back with a shrug, trying to play it off as if she weren't half as freaked out as she was.

"I thought you said they were good," Lana reminded her, as if that counted for much.

"Technically speaking."

Angie could admit that, but that didn't mean she wanted to talk about it. So she did what she'd done whenever Lana had brought up either Brett or Mike. She changed the subject. Unfortunately, she was running out of subjects, but there was one big one she hadn't brought up yet.

"So, did Patton talk to you about her club idea?" Angie asked innocently, knowing she was about to blow Lana's mind.

"What?" Lana stilled at that, blinking in wide-eyed confusion. "Patton's starting her own club?"

"Yep."

"Don't they call those places asylums?" Lana leaned back in her seat with a laugh, clearly amusing herself. "Or is she planning on starting a clown college? What? I've got to know. What is Patton's club going to be?"

"The Cattlewoman's Club." Angie didn't hesitate this time, feeling more as if she was defending her friend than betraying her.

That answer certainly had Lana sobering up, along with straightening up. "The Cattlewoman's? You mean, she's going to find men to crawl naked on leashes?"

"I think she's thinking more along the lines of the Harem on steroids with male strippers to keep the women entertained."

At least, that was about as much as Angie had listened to, but that didn't mean she hadn't caught the general gist of Patton's grand plan. Neither was she unaware of the risk she was taking in revealing all to Lana.

"I think the real point of the club is to kind of unionize the ladies from this club and pool their power to have more say about how they interact with the Cattlemen."

"She wants to be head bitch." Lana summarized Patton's goal rather well, even if she was just a little off the mark.

"Actually, I think she wants you to be head bitch."

"*What?*" Lana's mouth actually fell open, and seconds later, laughter came rolling out. "That is the craziest thing I've heard in ages."

"Maybe." Angie didn't want to cast that stone because she beginning to realize that the craziest thing around was actually her.

She'd convinced herself that she was in love with Brett and Mike, but what if she wasn't? What if she was in love with a dream? What if Lana was, too?

"Actually"—Angie frowned as the idea growing in her head developed with each word—"I think maybe it would be a good thing. You know, you and Chase have never been equals, not in business, not in your relationship."

That observation had Lana's laughter drying up. Her brow began to narrow into a frown, but Angie barely noticed. She was too busy realizing just how much she and Lana had in common.

"That's sort of something Patton has with him that you don't."

Patton had always been in love with Chase, but it hadn't weakened her. It hadn't reduced her to his servant, but rather his match. That was where Patton's confidence came from, along with the certainty that she didn't have to fear Lana. Chase would always be hers.

"She's giving you a chance to have it." It was a setup. Angie could see that now. "Once you do, you'll realize that you can do better than him."

"Ha!" Lana shook her head at Angie. "You're as crazy as she is if you believe that shit. Nobody is Chase's equal. The man is an island. He holds himself above everybody else. Trust me, I know."

Angie didn't think Lana did. She didn't think Chase held himself above Patton, though she wouldn't deny that is what made Patton special. That was what made Angie feel less than with Mike and Brett. They weren't equal.

Angie had been chasing them for so many years. She was tired. She wanted to be the one who was pursued. If that was what she really wanted, then she was going to have to answer her phone.

"Angie!" Lana snapped a finger in front of her, making Angie start as she realized she'd drifted off. "You okay? You seemed to check out there for a moment."

"Yeah." Angie shook off her doubts with the determined reminder that her relationship with Brett and Mike could turn out differently than Lana and Chase's.

Maybe she had been a little naïve in thinking things would be perfect, but that didn't mean they couldn't be. Some things just required work. One thing Angie knew was that Brett and Mike were worth the effort…or, at least, her dreams were.

Angie glanced up at the clock. It was almost nine in the evening. There was still enough time to salvage the night. With that thought, she reached for her phone.

* * * *

"Was that Angie?" Mike tossed that question over his shoulder at Brett, whose phone had rung just a moment ago.

"I don't know," Brett muttered as he glared at his phone. "I think we lost the connection. I haven't got any bars."

"Eh." Mike shrugged off that concern. "We can give her another ring when we get back into town."

"Or maybe we could surprise her," Brett suggested. "Women love surprises. I think they consider them romantic."

"Depends on the surprise." After all, it was a surprise that had gotten them into this mess.

Mike knew that it had been a tactical mistake to slip into Angie's bed and molest her like he had, but the truth was, he hadn't been thinking straight. Actually, he hadn't been thinking at all. He'd been riding high on emotion, overwhelmed by the sudden sense of freedom.

He knew Angie would never understand. Mike didn't suspect he could explain it to her, but he really did feel better now that he'd worked off his aggression on his old man. All the frustration, all the resentment, all the bitterness, it was all gone. Now when Mike thought of his father, all he thought of was a pathetic, old bastard.

They'd been better off without him.

"What's that?" Brett straightened up in his seat as the sight of the lights that had glimmered in the distance grew brighter.

They were flashing, and there were people in the road. Women. There were women in the road, and they were waving for help. Mike slowed down, coming to a stop beside one seriously stacked brunette, who clung to his window as he rolled it down.

"Is there a problem?" he asked, certain he already knew the answer.

Their car was pulled over to the side. Four of the hottest women he'd ever seen were crowding in around the truck. They were barely dressed, and he couldn't help but think that this was the way so many pornos started. Even the brunette's answer sounded scripted.

"We've run out of gas, and our phones don't have any coverage." The brunette batted her thick lashes at him as she offered Mike a smile that he knew well. "Could you help us?"

* * * *

Angie bit back a yawn and glanced over at the clock. It was nearly two in the morning, and she still hadn't heard from Mike or Brett. She'd tried calling them several times but kept getting dumped into voicemail. She didn't know what that meant and couldn't help but be a little unnerved.

Those concerns remained only whispers thanks to Lana, who kept her busy all night long. The club was once again Master-less. What with Brett and Mike having disappeared, GD having quit, and the terms of the Davis brothers' truce with Patton being they hadn't worked when Lana was on duty, things had gotten a little crazy for a while.

They'd settled down, though, and now that she finally looked up at the clock, Angie was stunned at the time and suddenly a little panicked. God, she hoped they hadn't gotten into another fight, or worse. That right there was the problem. She didn't actually know them well enough to know what kind of trouble they would be likely to get in.

It had been years since they'd hung out. Truth was she'd thought they'd hold out longer, that she'd have more time to get to know them again, but now she didn't even know what to expect as she headed for the front of the club and the ride Lana had called up to the butler's station to arrange for.

There actually weren't any taxis this time of night, but a valet would work. What she got instead was Dean. The brash, young buck offered her a big smile and tip of his hat as she walked up toward him.

"Evenin'."

"I thought a valet was going to give me a lift," Angie responded, without bothering with a polite greeting or even acknowledging his.

"I'm headed toward town, so I offered." Dean smiled all innocently, but Angie knew better. There was nothing innocent about the man.

"Great." Angie heaved a deep sigh, wondering if she should insist on a valet.

"Oh, come on," Dean cajoled her as he tried to place a hand on her back to lead her toward the truck the valet had pulled up under the main entrance's carport.

Angie shrugged away from his touch, shooting him a sharp look. "Don't even."

"All right." Dean held his hands up in surrender, falling in step behind her as she led the way to his truck. "Don't worry. I'm not trying to make a move here."

Angie snorted at that. Dean was always making a move. That was just the kind of guy he was, but he wasn't dangerous or known to push. So, she allowed the valet to assist her up into the cab as Dean jogged around the hood to the driver's side.

"No, I'm serious," Dean said, picking up their conversation as if there had been no lull. "Why is it that women always think I'm hitting on them?"

"Because you are?" Angie snorted as she buckled herself in, already feeling confined as the valet shut the door and trapped her in the cab with Dean.

"See, that's what I don't get," Dean complained as he eased the truck around the lushly landscaped island that curved around with the cobblestone drive. "I ask an honest question, and you just dismiss me."

Angie couldn't deny that, so she simply avoided it. "You're supposed to put your seat belt on. It's the law."

"And if I do, will you tell me what it is I want to know?"

"Trust me, you don't really want an answer," Angie assured him as the thump of the road smoothed out into asphalt and the lights of the club began to fade into the background.

They weren't needed for her to see the look Dean shot her as he reached for his seat belt and snapped it pointedly into place. As if she couldn't read the intent behind that action, he prodded her almost instantly with a patient but firm-sounding command that only a Cattleman could perfect so well.

"I'm waiting."

"Fine." Angie gave in, but she had one condition. "Just don't get mad at me and leave me on the side of the road because you don't like what you are hearing."

"Trust me, honey, I'd never do a lady like that."

"There," Angie snapped, clearly shocking him with the sharpness of her tone. "That's the problem. You're a condescending punk, who talks and acts like he's a twelve-year-old with his first boner."

"I got my first boner when I was—"

"I don't care." Angie held up her hands in a bid to be spared that bit of information. "You asked. I answered."

"That you did." Dean nodded, and then, thankfully, he shut up.

As the silence and the road stretched on, Angie began to feel a little bad for being so brutally blunt. He had asked, though. Insisted, actually. Still, she could sense a decent enough guy lurking underneath all the attitude. He couldn't even be blamed for having an attitude. His reputation preceded him, but more importantly, so did his age.

Angie had been raised in an age when men were supposed to be men, all rough and hard. Dean was young enough to have been raised in an age when men were supposed to be boys, all hip and cool and smooth. Those terms would never be used on either Mike or Brett.

"Can I ask you a question?" Dean finally broke the silence, pulling Angie from her thoughts as she glanced over at him.

"If I say no, you're going to anyway, right?"

He flashed her a quick smile. "I'm just curious if the rumors are true."

"They rarely are," Angie informed him. "Especially about me, but you can go ahead and ask."

"Did you really just decide to be in love with Brett and Mike because of some dream?" Dean's smile faded slightly as his words seem to weigh on him. "I mean, can you do that? Just decide to love somebody and...love them?"

"Given the divorce rate, I doubt it."

"I'm being serious."

"So am I." That was the unfortunate part. Angie marshaled her defenses against her doubts and Dean's skeptical look. "As for the dream, it was something special. I really can't describe it."

"You can't even try?" Dean pressed. "I mean, it just seems like a dream is an awfully flimsy thing to base your life on. You can't just decide to be in love."

"Who says?" Angie argued. "Why? Why do you care? You got something besides a hard-on for some girl?"

"No," Dean answered honestly before busting into a grin. "I was just curious why you are so stuck on Brett and Mike, because they certainly don't treat you right."

"That's what you think," Angie shot back, not about to admit that he might have a point.

Instead, she played the moment off with a smirk as he finally pulled his truck into her drive. Sure enough, there were no other vehicles there. A fact that did not escape Dean's notice.

"It doesn't look like your men are home." Casting a sly glance in her direction, the boy just couldn't seem to help himself as he offered her a lame come-on. "Maybe I ought to stick around, make sure you don't get lonely."

Angie unsnapped her seat belt and shoved open her door before shooting him a tight smile. "Thanks, but I know how to entertain myself."

That got her a chuckle from Dean, and he waited there until she'd disappeared inside, proving that he did have a few manners. Maybe he'd grow into more. Even if he didn't, that wasn't her problem. Her problem was setting things right with her men.

She had a plan.

It started with stripping down to nothing and leaving a trail of clothes all the way to the bunk bed her two men still shared. Those would have to go. They'd talk about that and a whole lot later. Right then, Angie wanted them to understand one thing.

She was willing to work on this relationship.

She wasn't running.

Crawling into Mike's perfectly made bed, she tucked the sheets in back around her and settled into the far corner, planning on surprising him when he finally made it back home. That had been the plan, but his heady scent infused the sheets and filled her with a relaxing warmth.

A sense of peace invaded her and had Angie falling asleep within minutes, despite her best intentions to stay up and be waiting for her men.

* * * *

"Did anything about that seem weird to you?" Brett asked after they'd driven the girls to the gas station and back.

The women were all now safely packed back into their car. Brett watched as they pulled onto the road in front of Mike's truck and couldn't deny the sick feeling building in his stomach. It was late. Really late. They'd wasted a lot of time screwing around with those ladies, too much time, but things were finally settled. Sort of. They still hadn't heard back from Angie. That had him reaching for his phone, only to realize it was no longer clipped to his hip.

"Shit."

"What?" Mike glanced over at him, but Brett barely paid him any attention as he turned to glance back into the bed.

"I lost my phone."

"If it's back there, it's probably busted up by now," Mike warned him.

"I'm the one that got busted up." Brett snorted as he settled back into his seat. "Those women...I almost got molested."

"You're telling me," Mike retorted with a chuckle. "You should have been up here with grabby hands, or didn't you notice me swerving all over the road?"

"Sorry, I was a little distracted. I could have done with a stick to beat them off with."

That, for once, wasn't a brag. Neither was it worth gloating over. Brett hadn't been interested in any of those ladies. His heart already belonged to one.

"Give me your phone," he demanded, holding his hand out.

Mike shifted around in his seat, causing the truck to weave slightly, but he came up empty-handed. "I don't know where it is."

"Well, that's weird." And more than a little suspicious.

"It's unfortunate, but a little late to worry over it." Mike shrugged. "It's past two in the morning. Who were you really going to call?"

"Angie," Brett shot back. "At least now I know why we haven't heard from her."

"She's probably in bed," Mike suggested, but Brett didn't think so.

"She's probably at the club...and isn't that where the girls in front of us are turning toward?" Brett scowled as the car ahead veered to the right, turning onto the highway that led straight to the Cattleman's Club. It was in that shining moment that all the pieces snapped together.

"Oh son of a bitch," Mike whispered, the obvious hitting him just seconds after Brett. "We were set up."

"Angie was testing us." Because she didn't trust them, and that shouldn't have bothered Brett half as much as it did. Hell, he hadn't even been tempted. That thought actually did bother him a little.

"And if we follow far enough behind, we might just catch them reporting back to Angie." Mike sounded as though he savored that idea. The grin he flashed at Brett certainly held a hint of anticipation. "Then we can make use of the club's disciplinary items."

"Can't I just spank her with my own hand?"

"You can spank her with whatever you want," Mike assured him as he eased back on the gas. He killed his headlights and turned slowly onto the highway lit almost perfectly by a full moon.

Nobody would see them coming, and that was just the way they'd been taught to corner their prey in the marines. There was no denying they enjoyed exercising those talents. It just didn't get them anywhere. The ladies might have returned back to the club, but they didn't report back to Angie.

She wasn't there. She'd gotten a ride home with Dean Carver, or so the butler told them. Butlers didn't lie. So Brett climbed back into Mike's truck and headed into town. A half-hour later they were pulling into the drive and piling out to go wake up Angie and have a word with her.

The only problem was she wasn't there...and Dean Carver was a dead man.

* * * *

Hailey giggled and squirmed in Cole's arms, the plush, silken cheeks of her ass grinding back against him as she kept him hot and hard, tucked deep inside the tight vise of her sheath. He'd slid in there while she'd been asleep, but after he'd already spent a good half-hour getting her nice and wet. He'd known she'd been dreaming. The only question was whether or not it had been Kyle or him starring in her fantasies.

Probably both, because that was the way she really liked it.

Five days a week, that was just how they gave it to her. Fridays, though, were Kyle's alone and Saturdays were Cole's. As far as he was concerned, it was still Saturday, even if, technically, it had rolled around to Sunday. Besides, what was he supposed to do when he woke up to a soft, sweet, naked woman tucked along his side?

Ignore her?

Not hardly.

Only a fool ignored a woman like Hailey, and only an idiot wouldn't take advantage of the situation. Cole had never been either of those things, which was why he dared to lay claim to her ass once again. She had such a nice ass.

He was trapped in heaven, a utopia that was made only better as he tickled her again, making Hailey squirm and pant, the laughter tingeing her sleepy voice, even as she complained.

"Cole! I'm trying to sleep."

"It's six," he retorted as he buried his lips against the curve of her ear. "Time to get up."

"Time for you to get up," Hailey muttered and tried half-heartedly to pull free of his hold. "I'm not the idiot who bet my brothers they could beat them at some stupid obstacle course."

Cole rolled his eyes at that. What had she expected Kyle and him to do? They couldn't honestly fight back. Neither being a fool nor stupid meant he knew his limits. Hailey's brothers were big, really big and just out of the Corps. They'd kill him given the chance. He didn't doubt that.

"Aren't you supposed to go train or something?" Hailey grumped, her words blurring into a heavy moan as Cole slid a hand down from her hips and around to cup the smooth mound of her cunt.

"What do you think I'm doing?" he murmured huskily as he found her clit and pinned the swollen little bud beneath this finger.

With slow rolls, he stole her ability to speak, but not hear. Hailey gave a jolt when the cell phone sitting on the nightstand suddenly began dancing across the hard surface as it began to buzz. Cole went still along with Hailey, knowing just what she was thinking. Something bad had happened. It was his job to shelter her from the bad things, which was just why he reached for the phone.

He snatched it up before she could, cutting her words off with a hard thrust. Whatever Hailey's objections, and Cole had no doubt that she'd planned on issuing some, they got lost as he distracted her with a hard, fast fucking that had the sweat building up along his spine and his words coming out in breathless pants.

"What?"

"Where is my sister?" Brett shot back, his words sharp enough to cut.

"Busy."

That was greeted with a pregnant pause that held the weight of a promise as dark as his tone. "What are you doing?"

"Trust me, you don't want to know." Cole chuckled, knowing he was busted and unable to help taunting the jackass on the other end.

"I'm going to kill you."

"You can come on over and try."

But Hailey wouldn't let him, and they both knew it, which was why Brett should have smarted back. It was all the revenge he was actually likely to get. He didn't, though. Instead, he fell silent for another long moment. That was fine by Cole. After all, he was busy himself.

"We can't," Brett finally admitted. By then, though, Cole had lost the thread of the conversation.

"Can't? What?" He tried to fathom what the hell Brett was talking about, but the rapture pulsing out of his dick was damn distracting.

"Mike and I, we can't come over there and give you the beating you deserve."

"Huh."

"We're in jail."

"Oh."

"Are you listening to me?"

"No," Cole admitted. "Hold on a second and let me finish this up here."

He didn't wait for a response but dropped the phone onto the bed and rolled Hailey all the way beneath him as he reared up and got down to business.

Chapter 18

Sunday, July 1ˢᵗ

Brett really was going to kill Cole. He didn't care how Hailey felt about that matter. He knew what the son of a bitch had done to his sister. He'd heard them through the phone. That was when he'd had to hang up. There were just certain lines that could not be crossed, and listen to Hailey have sex was one big one.

He was scarred. For life. He was going to kill Cole. The little pussy had to know what he had coming to him, yet the dumbass showed up at the police station wearing a grin and flashing a wad of cash.

"Hey, man." Cole nodded to Brett, where he sat brooding on the bunk built into the wall of his cell.

"What the hell are you doing here?" Mike grumbled, rising off his own bunk to eye Cole suspiciously.

Brett hadn't informed Mike of what had interrupted his call. If he had, Mike would have gone for Cole, and Brett wanted that honor.

"I came to bail you out." Cole appeared to be fighting the smile tugging at his lips, but he wasn't winning. The laughter was all too clear in his tone as he tacked on an obnoxious, "Duh!"

"Fuck you, Sally," Mike shot back, his mood sour enough to rot eggs with just a look.

Brett was right there with him. The very light of the day felt like an insult, as though the world was laughing at them because they'd actually believed Angie's bullshit. She hadn't been saving herself for them. She'd been saving herself to make fools out of them.

"Didn't your brother tell you?" Cole lifted a brow, drawing Brett's dark gaze up to his sparkling ones. "That itch has been scratched."

"You're a dead man walking," Brett vowed, but that didn't seem to impress Cole in the slightest.

"Aren't we all?" he retorted with a snort. "Besides, it's going to be kind of hard to kill me from jail. So, you want to tell me why you felt a need to break into Dean Carver's house and beat the crap out of him?

"Not that I'm complaining," Cole rushed to assure them. "It's just that the bets are already flying down at the club. Personally, I put my money on you two being complete psychos, but others seem to think you had to have a reason."

"You think you're funny, don't you, Sally?" Mike stepped up to the bars and gave Cole a hard look. "But do you hear anybody laughing?"

"Yeah. Myself."

That had the two of them going silent as Mike tried to glare down Cole. It was pointless. Cole's smirk remained firmly in place. For the moment, he had all the power. It was time to be reasonable, something Mike seemed incapable of these days. That left it to Brett to be the grownup.

That was really why they were in jail.

Brett heaved a heavy sigh that broke up Cole and Mike's impromptu staring contest. "Where is Hailey, jackass?"

"Where do you think?" Tearing his eyes away from Brett's brother, Cole shot him a quick look. "Telling Angie that you two idiots got yourself arrested."

"She already knows," Mike muttered as he sulked away from the bars, even as his comment drew Cole's narrowed gaze back in his direction.

"How would she know that?"

"Because she was there," Brett snapped, borrowing a phrase from the little punk. "Duh!"

"Uh…no, she wasn't." Cole blinked, his grin growing out of control as he added up all the pieces. "Oh, don't tell me, you thought Angie and Dean…"

Cole burst into a laughter so deep it had him bending over and stumbling back into the cell across from theirs. Brett, however, was not nearly as amused.

"She was there," he insisted. "I saw her with my own eyes."

Actually, he'd just caught a flash of a naked woman before she'd locked herself into the bathroom, but that had to have been Angie. She'd gone home with Dean.

"No." Cole refused to back down. "She wasn't. She was at home, waiting for you…supposedly naked in bed, and she woke this morning without you there and came to the conclusion that you'd spent the night in a more entertaining fashion."

"She wasn't there," Brett repeated, having difficulty with that concept. "We checked her bed."

"Did you check yours?" Cole shot back, bursting back into laughter as Brett blinked, dumbfounded at that brilliant suggestion and the realization of what it meant.

"Then we beat up Dean."

"For no good reason," Mike finished, coming to the same conclusion Brett had just reached.

"This is all your fault!"

Brett turned on Mike, the relief he felt over realizing that Angie hadn't betrayed them morphing almost instantly into guilt over what they'd done to Dean. That burned right into anger at his brother, who'd set him up, even if he hadn't done it intentionally.

"You said she wasn't there, but she was!"

"I didn't see her," Mike defended himself, but he didn't sound convincing.

"I am going to kick your ass," Brett growled.

"See, psychos." Cole snickered. "You two need to learn you can't solve everything with your fists."

Mike turned on him. "How the hell do you know any of this?"

"Because she called." Cole shrugged. "She was all in tears. "She thinks you spent your night in a more entertaining fashion."

"And you didn't tell her the truth?" Brett roared. He'd have loved to tear into the other man and vent some of his building frustration, but the bars got in the way.

"She was carrying on too much for Hailey to get her to listen." Cole shrugged again as if that wasn't anything. "Why do you think Hailey went over there?"

Whatever Hailey had to say it wouldn't be as good as what Brett knew he'd come up with, like begging her forgiveness for ever letting Mike talk him into all of this dating insanity. That was coming to an end. They were going to put this mission back on track and stop with all these stupid games, but first, they had to get out of jail.

"Cole, go bail us out," Brett snapped, not that the other man jumped to obey.

"Oh, it's Cole now, is it? What happened to Sally?"

"Now!"

* * * *

Angie sat at the kitchen table, breathing deep and trying to calm herself. Everything was okay. Dean wasn't badly hurt, but this was the second fight in as many nights. If they kept this up, somebody was going to end up dead. That thought scared the shit out of her, especially because Angie was pretty certain she was the reason they were spinning out of control.

"Why? I just don't understand why." Angie looked toward Hailey for help, but she didn't have anything to offer.

"I…don't know," Hailey admitted with saddened frustration that they shared because they both knew the truth.

It didn't matter why. What mattered was the fact that her dream had been wrong. She wasn't good for Mike and Brett. She was bad for them. Heaving a heavy sigh at that thought, she couldn't help but wonder where that left her. The answer was obvious.

Hailey finally broke the heavy silence that had thickened between them. "What are you going to do?"

She glanced up, not even a glimmer of hope shining in her eyes because Hailey already knew the answer to that question. Still, Angie didn't have the heart to say it aloud.

"I'm going to do what I have to." That she would.

"Angie—"

"I think that's them," Angie said, cutting Hailey off before she could argue.

Both women cocked their heads as they listened to the sound of an engine pulling into the driveway. That was her cue. Shoving away from the table, Angie tossed Hailey a quick smile before darting for the door.

"I better get packing."

"Angie—"

"Don't worry, Hailey. Everything will work out." That was probably more of a hope than an assurance, but it was something to cling to.

Of course, she should have known that she wasn't going to escape that easy, but Angie, at least, bought herself a few seconds more to try and erect her defenses before Brett and Mike banged into her room. She heard them coming. Hell, she'd heard them from the second they slammed into the kitchen and started arguing with Hailey.

"What the hell were you two thinking?" That was Hailey's greeting.

Brett's was no less abrupt. "Where the hell is Angie?"

"Where the hell are Cole and Kyle?" Hailey shot back.

"Those two pussies ran away almost the second they let us go," Mike retorted, his voice sounding closer, as did Hailey's.

"They bailed you out," Hailey complained, her words somewhat muffled by the heavy pound of footsteps coming down the hall. "You think you'd be a little nicer to them!"

That got no response except for the slam of the bedroom door against the wall. Brett burst into the room, his gaze cutting across it to land on Angie, where she stood by the bed. Mike was right on his heels with Hailey bringing up the rear.

"What are you doing?"

"Why do you have a suitcase out?" Brett followed up almost instantly on his brother's demand for an explanation.

She could tell that this was about to get ugly. Actually, it already had. Ugly and hard. Sucking in a steadying breath, Angie glanced over both men's shoulders, ignoring them and their questions to address the worried looking woman lingering behind them.

"Hailey, do you mind giving us a little privacy?" Angie asked, knowing what was to come was best done without an audience.

"Are you sure?" Hailey hesitated, sounding both concerned and uncertain.

Angie knew she understood what was about to happen. She wasn't alone. The panic rising in Mike's gaze was as clear as the anger darkening in Brett's. This was not going to be easy, but that didn't change her answer.

"Yes."

"Okay then." Hailey slowly nodded before casting a dark look in her brothers' direction. "I'll go, but this isn't over yet. We're going to talk about this. Got me?"

"Fine."

"Sure," Brett echoed his brother once again.

Neither man spared their sister so much as a look as they crowded into the room, shutting the door on Hailey and confronting Angie with matching scowls. That wasn't what had her cringing as she finally glanced up at them. It was the sight of the bruises, proving that Dean hadn't gone down without a fight. It also made her worry that he might be in a lot worse condition, but she was just too afraid to ask that question.

"What did the two of you do?"

"Where the hell were you last night?" Mike countered. "Cole said you were here, but we looked and—"

"I was in your bunk bed." Angie cut him off, irritated by the accusation in his tone. "I left a trail of clothes to your door. Didn't you notice?"

That caught them both by surprise. She could tell from the look they shared they hadn't noticed, or if they had, they hadn't figured out that obvious message.

"We just thought you were messy," Brett finally answered for the both of them, drawing a frown to Angie's brow as she puckered up at that comment.

"What? I'm not messy." Angie huffed, amazed he'd even suggest such a thing.

"Uh-huh," Mike agreed without a hint of sincerity as he glanced pointedly around the room. "This is just organized clutter, right?"

"What?" Angie glanced around the room, not certain what he was trying to say. The room looked clean enough to her. "This is normal. I'm sorry if I don't starch my sheets and run white gloves over everything, but I live in the real world…the one where you don't go around *beating people up*!"

"What is that supposed to mean?"

"We thought you had hooked up with him!"

This time it was Mike talking over his brother. He actually had the audacity to take a step up with that retort, as if he were confronting her with it, but Angie wasn't impressed.

"So?" Angie shot back. "That doesn't give you the license to beat the crap out of him. This is the real world where people are expected to settle their problems without violence. Of course, you two seem to have a problem *with* violence."

"What the hell is *that* supposed to mean?" Mike snapped as if she hadn't been clear enough, leaving Angie no choice but to be brutally honest.

"That means…I'm not good for you."

Just the idea had Angie fighting back tears, but she couldn't control the trembling that started deep within her stomach. She could feel herself breaking down as the reality of her decision started to cut through her. There was just no hiding that kind of pain.

"Angie—"

"No."

She cut Brett off, holding her hand up for him to stop both trying to talk her out of what had to be done and to assure he didn't tread any closer. It wouldn't take him much, not more than a plea, a kiss, and her defenses would crumble. That was the problem with love. It made strong women weak.

Sucking in a deep breath and letting it out slowly, Angie tensed every muscle she had and forced herself to say what really needed to be said. "I'm leaving."

"No."

That popped out of Mike's mouth, a hard command filled with pain. Angie hated to cause him even a second of anguish, but she had to do this.

"Yes."

"Angie—" Mike tried again to get a word in, but she couldn't afford to give him that chance.

"No. This has to be done."

Angie didn't know if she was talking to them or to herself. They all stood there, frozen in the moment, before Brett finally broke it as he stepped back and lifted his chin.

"Fine. Then go."

"No!" Mike turned on his brother. "You can't just let her walk away."

"She wants to leave." Brett breathed in deep and shrugged. "I'm not going to force her to stay."

"But you don't want her to go...oh God." Mike gasped as if the truth had finally hit him. "You're giving up. You're just like Dad! Son of a bitch! *I trusted you!*"

Mike's tone grew from a horrified whisper into a roar that ended as he launched himself at Brett, proving just why Angie had to leave. Now they were fighting among themselves. This wasn't an argument that was just a little out of hand. They went crashing to the floor in a heap of legs and arms that quickly began kicking and punching out in a whirlwind that would have caught her up in it if Angie hadn't leapt out of the way.

She darted for the door, fleeing without a backward look.

Chapter 19

Patton was waiting on the back porch to greet Angie with open arms. Angie didn't ask how the other woman knew what had happened or how badly she would need a friend right then. It didn't matter. All that mattered was that Angie could break and not worry over the consequences.

So, she did. She sobbed and rambled on as Patton prodded her toward the truck waiting at the curb. She sniffed and bemoaned fate as Patton drove her back toward the club. Then she finally let Patton hand her over to the sympathetic spa attendant who escorted her back into the Harem for a no-frills-spared day of pampering.

That didn't make Angie feel better, but it didn't make her feel worse either. Dean managed to do that. He showed up at the edge of the Harem, demanding to speak to Angie, and she didn't have much right to deny him. She did don a robe, though, before joining him in the courtyard area in front of the entrance to the Harem.

He was sitting, waiting with his leg stretched out before him. It was sheathed in a white cast, and a pair of crutches were leaning against the side of the garden bench. As if that didn't make her feel bad enough, Dean's face was as bruised and swollen as his knuckles. It was clear from the sight of him that he had lost the battle, but that didn't make him any less of an ass.

"Angie." He cast a critical eye over her, just one because the other was swollen shut. So, too, were his lips too puckered to really draw up in a smirk, but she could sense him making the effort. "You're looking good, if a little overdressed."

"Dean...I'm so sorry." Angie chose to ignore the last of his comments to focus on the reality of his situation. "I never even dreamed this would happen."

"Eh, my dad used to beat me worse." He waved away her concern with that failed attempt at humor. She wasn't even sure if it was a joke. Not the way he sighed and shook his head. "Of course, he never got put into jail for it."

The implication was clear. Dean was pressing charges. Angie knew she should have seen it coming. She certainly had considered it, but knowing now that they really would be going away cut deeper than she had anticipated. She felt her knees weaken and quickly settled down on the bench beside Dean. He watched her with a one-eyed gaze that clearly saw too deeply.

"You don't want Brett and Mike to go to jail for it either," he murmured, his words slurred slightly by the swell of his lips.

She didn't, but neither did Angie have the guts to admit that to Dean. The last thing she could do in good conscience was plead their case because they simply had no case. That should matter. That should change things, but it didn't. Angie still loved them. She was just really bad for them.

"You care about them," Dean stated, a hint of disgust in his tone. "Even after all of this, you don't see what kind of monsters they are?"

"They're not monsters," Angie shot back, instantly bristling. "They were just jealous. Really, this is all my fault."

"You believe that?"

"I do. If you're going to blame or punish anybody for what happened, it should be me." That sounded noble and grand, but Angie didn't honestly expect him to take her up on the offer. She was in for a shock.

"Okay," Dean agreed without a moment's hesitation. "I got a deal for you."

Angie had a sense he'd had one all along. Why else would Dean have sought her out? It was as though thought occurred to her that

Angie realized she was probably already in trouble. So it was with a sense of foreboding that she prodded him along.

"Yeah? What kind of deal?"

"First, you'd have to agree not to see or talk to either Brett or Mike until after our deal is completed," Dean stipulated, giving her a pretty big hint as to what was coming next.

"Then what?" Angie lifted a brow. "I have to sleep with you?"

"Please, I don't need to blackmail women into my bed," Dean snapped, instantly insulted. For a second Angie felt bad, but Dean ruined the moment when he qualified his denial. "I just want the chance to convince you that I can satisfy you better than either of those assholes can."

Angie doubted that completely, but she didn't take up the argument. Instead, she narrowed her attention on the three little words that mattered the most. "And by a chance, you mean…"

"A date."

"And?"

"And I'm going to make some passes."

"And?" Angie pressed, certain there had to be more, but if there was, it was up to her to figure everything out.

"And nothing." It looked as though he tried to smile again. "I'm just looking for a chance here, Angie. An honest one…though, it might be a month or so before I'm back to looking normal enough to make any passes. So, like I said, you can't have any contact with either Brett or Mike."

She didn't want to have contact with them. If she did, she'd crumble. Angie knew she didn't have the strength to resist them. In fact, she knew she should flee, but she couldn't leave them to end up in jail.

"Fine." Angie pinned Dean with a hard look. "I'll give you the time and go on the date, but you can't press charges against either Brett or Mike. Deal?"

* * * *

It took over a half-hour for both brothers to wear themselves out, and by then, Angie was long gone. Brett kind of figured that was a good thing, given they'd trashed her room. Actually, Hailey was the one who would probably be pissed. It was her furniture, after all, that had gotten broken.

Lying there with his legs bent over the busted-up bed with his back stretched across the floor, Brett stared up at the ceiling as he silently categorized all of his aches and pains. He hurt, that was for sure, but he didn't think anything was broken. Anything more than his relationship with Angie.

She'd left. Walked away. Just like their dad.

As much as Brett told himself he didn't care, he knew it was a lie. So maybe he did have some daddy issues himself. Maybe pounding on the old man hadn't helped relieve them. Maybe there wasn't anything that could. Nothing that is but Angie.

Brett wanted her back already, and she hadn't even been gone a whole hour. Pretending as if he didn't care didn't change that fact one bit. That didn't mean that Brett knew what to do, as if he had the energy to do anything other than lie there beside his brother, staring up at the popcorn on the ceiling.

The seconds ticked past into minutes, and slowly, the heavy pants of breath that filled the air quieted back down, allowing the silence to thicken around them until finally Mike spoke up.

"I think we should buy the house out from Hailey." That came out as if they were having an actual conversation, which they had not been having. That didn't stop Mike from continuing on. "Then we can build a second story with bigger bedrooms and open up down here into one big living space."

Brett turned his head, allowing his cheek to rest against the cool wood floor as he studied his brother for a moment. "What do we need a big living space for?"

"For the kids," Mike shot back, his own chin dipping to the side so he could shoot Brett a dirty look. "This house isn't going to be big enough for the family as we grow, and I don't really want to do renovations while Angie's either pregnant or trying to keep up with whatever hellions we spawn."

"Angie?" Brett blinked, wondering if Mike's head had taken a blow. "Angie left."

"We'll get her back." Mike shrugged as if that weren't even a problem. His nonchalance was just shocking, and Brett didn't even know what to make of his brother's attitude.

"We will?" Brett cocked a brow. "It's just that easy? You're not even the slightest bit *panicked* over the matter?"

Mike blinked and shook his head. "Nope."

"Nope? *Nope*?" Brett felt like hitting his brother all over again. "That's all you have to say? Nope."

"What else is there to say?" Mike countered, giving Brett a moment's pause.

"I don't know," Brett finally snapped. "But I do know two days ago you couldn't touch the girl without wetting yourself—"

"I never wet myself." Mike took instant offense at that, but Brett wasn't listening.

"And now, all of a sudden, you're all relaxed and unconcerned. What the hell is with that?"

"What's the point in getting all upset?"

"Are you on drugs?"

"What?" Mike drew back as he stared at his brother in shock, but Brett wasn't backing down.

"You can tell me. Did you pop some happy pills?"

"Yeah. I took happy pills. That's why I helped you redecorate Angie's room." Mike snorted and rolled his eyes before answering in a more serious tone. "No. I'm not on drugs. I just…enjoyed the workout."

"Maybe Angie's right," Brett muttered as he shook his head and turned his gaze back to the ceiling. "Maybe you do have an issue with violence. After all, this is the second time you've appeared happier after a fight."

Before Mike could respond to that accusation, Chase's voice rang out from the kitchen as he called out a greeting. Neither brother responded as they both lay there silently listening to the stomp of footsteps and the rumble of voices. Chase hadn't come alone. He'd brought his brother Slade. From the direct route they took out the kitchen and down the hall to Hailey's room, Brett was betting he knew who had sent them over.

Angie.

She'd obviously gone running to the Davis brothers. Actually it was more likely that she'd gone running to Patton, who had sent her men after them. The only question was what they wanted, because Brett wasn't up to another fight.

* * * *

The morning breakfast crowd at the Bread Box was loud and lively. The weekend news was full of juicy tidbits, and the gossips were having a field day, just about everybody mulling over the rumors and adding their own interpretations on to them.

All anybody wanted was a little proof to run with, which explained why almost everybody fell silent as Chase and Slade led Brett and Mike into the bakery. A heavy wave of anticipation and expectation followed the four men as they cut a path to the back booth Heather had reserved for them. Even she glanced at them with speculation glinting in her eyes as she came over to offer them menus and take their drink orders.

Chase and Slade went first. Brett went next. When Heather's eyes finally landed on Mike, he tipped his chin up and spoke loud enough to assure everybody could hear him.

"I'll take a coffee, and the answer to the other question you're wondering about is, yes. I am going to ask Angelina Motes to be my bride."

Heather's eyes rounded as Brett groaned, and both Davis brothers shared a look, but it was too late for any of them to do anything about the bomb Mike had just set off. Already the aftershocks were rippling through the diner as the conversation around them grew once again. No doubt by the end of the day there wouldn't be a single person in the county who hadn't heard Mike's grand declaration.

"You know, it is traditional to ask the woman first," Slade pointed out with a hint of amused exasperation lightening his tone.

"Do you really think she'll say no?" Mike shot back, because he didn't believe she would.

Sure, Angie was a little upset with them, but they could get over that hump. Mike was even willing to vow never to fight again if it helped. Of course, he would need some other way to relieve the tension that seemed to build up in him, but he had an idea about that.

"Actually…" Slade let that dangle out there.

Though the ending was clear, it remained an unfinished thought as Heather returned with four coffees and a batch of napkin-wrapped silverware. She lingered only long enough to take the rest of their orders and then scurried off toward the kitchen as Chase went directly back to the topic at hand.

"Angie's not going to say yes." That was Chase, blunt as always. "She can't."

"What do you mean, she can't?" Mike didn't like the ominous sound of that. "Is she married already?"

"No." Slade hesitated, clearly not wanting to elaborate.

"But," Mike prodded him, feeling the tension gathering again in his muscles.

"She's agreed not to see you," Chase spoke up, filling in all the details before either Mathews brother could ask for them. "If she does, then Dean is going to press charges."

"What?" Mike snorted in disbelief. "He can't do that."

"He did it and more," Slade shot back. "Angie's agreed to give him one month to try to seduce her—"

"*What?*" Mike gaped at Slade, completely unable to reason through that revelation. So he rejected it out of hand. "No!"

"Yes," Slade insisted. "And she's not allowed to have any contact with you during that time."

"Or he'll press charges," Chase repeated with a pointed look.

"I'm going to kill that son of a bitch," Mike muttered, not certain if he meant it or not in that moment, but Chase clearly believed him.

"Do that and you'll not only end up in jail, but you'll also lose Angie forever. Is that really what you want?"

No. What he wanted was to find her and plead his case. He also wanted to know how he'd ended up in this mess. It was a disaster, one of his own making, and that just boggled his mind. Never before had he so thoroughly screwed up. Hell, he'd never even screwed up before.

Mike always succeeded at everything he did. He succeeded because he'd always had a plan. His plans were always well thought out and executed. Not this time. This time he'd been driven by pure emotion, which was just as dangerous as he'd always suspected.

"You need to get a grip," Chase stated as if he were reading Mike's mind. "Angie loves you, sure, but dealing with two total psychos would drive any woman away."

"We're not psycho," Brett grumped, clearly insulted but also sullen enough to prove that he knew they weren't acting right.

"You've started three fights in two days," Slade retorted with obvious disgust. "You're completely out of control, but then again, that's why we're here."

"Because we've been there," Chase assured them before pausing to shrug. "But we didn't take the bait. I'm afraid you did."

That sounded very ominous, and it put every single one of Mike's nerves on edge. "What do you mean? The bait?"

Chase and Slade shared a look, and Mike knew in that instant the story started with Patton. He was right.

"Patton was a little upset about how you treated her friend," Slade started, as if that excused whatever came next. "So, last night she decided to test you."

"The women." It all clicked then. Last night Mike had figured the women broken down on the side of the road had been test. It wasn't shocking that they had been Patton's idea, but it did leave one question unanswered. "Did Angie know?"

"No." Chase shook his head. "Not as far as we can tell."

"And Dean?" Brett pressed. "Was he in on it?"

"No." Slade hesitated yet again before finishing off the tale. "That just seems to be an unfortunate twist, but she did delay you and is feeling guilty about the fact that left Angie without a ride."

Everything had just escalated from there. Mike wanted to blame Patton for this mess but knew he couldn't. That was on Brett and him. They'd screwed up, and now they had to fix it. The question was, how?

Chapter 20

Monday, July 2ⁿᵈ

Brett woke, banging his head into the ceiling once again. He'd made a small crack now in the drywall but didn't care. Instead, he sat there hunched over and brooding as he considered that he could have spent the night in Angie's room but hadn't dared. There were too many memories, even if there were really one a couple night's worth.

Not that his bed had been any kind of sanctuary. He'd lain there last night much as he was sitting there today wondering what he'd do if Dean convinced her to date him instead. Even if they didn't date, what if they slept together?

That thought was like acid, burning through all his layers and eating away at his soul. It didn't help that a small voice whispered to him that this was just what Angie had to live with for years. For years? He couldn't survive that long. He really would kill somebody. That thought scared him most of all.

Shoving off the bed, Brett jumped down to the floor and shuffled his way into the kitchen, looking for the pot of coffee that filled the air with its rich, heady scent. He plodded past his brother without a word. Mike was hunched over the kitchen table with some mess of papers spread out before him.

Whatever his brother was up to, he was absorbed by it, but Brett wasn't awake enough to care. All he cared in that moment was about pulling a mug down from the cupboard and filling it with the blackened brew that assured every morning was a good morning.

Brett downed half the cup in one gulp and refilled it before feeling enough like a human to finally settle down at the table.

The first thing that he noticed as he claimed a seat across from his brother was that Mike didn't have papers strewn across the table. He had greeting cards. At least a hundred of them. As he reached out to sift through the pile, Brett got a good idea of what his brother was up to.

"Love letters?" It took all his self-control to hold back the laughter that those two words evoked. "You're going to write Angie love letters?"

Mike didn't respond at first but finished whatever sentence he was working on before glancing up to pin Brett with a look he knew well. "I've got a plan."

"Mmmm." Brett glanced down at the table. "To overwhelm her with greeting cards? What's next, balloons? Oversized stuffed teddy bears?"

"Don't be an ass," Mike growled. "I actually have a good plan."

"Okay." Brett downed another half a cup of coffee in a gulp, fortifying himself before glancing up and nodding at his brother. "Hit me with it."

Mike rolled his eyes at Brett's theatrics but didn't bother to nag him about them. Instead, he leaned forward with an eagerness that Brett couldn't help but find a little amusing. "We're going to write her letters, every day."

"And?" Brett prodded when Mike just stopped.

"And nothing."

Brett hesitated, not certain if it were him or Mike who had lost it. After a moment's consideration, he was pretty certain it was Mike.

"And what is that going to get us?" Brett pressed. "We need to have something more than letters."

"No, the letters will work," Mike insisted. "She'll get to know us, and that will help her fall in love with us."

"She's already in love with us!" Brett snapped, wondering how his brother couldn't see the obvious. "That's not the problem."

"No?"

"No!"

"Then what the hell do you think is the problem?"

"Us," Brett shot back. He couldn't be any clearer than that, but the scowl that darkened Mike's brow warned him that he had better try. "Look at us. I work at a sex club. You're unemployed. In the last two days, we've picked fights with just about everybody. The day before that you got shitfaced and trashed the house. Your plan to look like a complete ass that no woman wants to be married to? It was a success!"

That seemed to cause Mike a moment of consideration before he finally snorted. "Huh. I guess you're right."

"And that makes you smile?" Brett couldn't fathom why his brother was suddenly grinning, but Mike was.

"Well, yeah." Mike nodded. "I mean, maybe it was a bad idea, and maybe now I do have to undo what I did, but as you just pointed out, I succeeded."

Brett's head hit the table as the weight of his own exasperation felled him. He couldn't believe Mike sometimes. Of course his brother did have some redeeming qualities.

"Oh, don't worry," Mike continued on. "If the problem is our listless and pointless trajectory, I've got a solution for that."

* * * *

That Monday was the longest day of Angie's life. It was a perfect storm of misery. Her heart ached with a pain that didn't relent for even a second. Her body ached, too. She'd spent the whole day on her feet, overseeing the setup for the Fourth of July frenzy that was now less than two days away. Of course, frenzies built kind of like the headache she'd grown throughout the day as the club began to swarm with ever-growing crowds.

As Lana had explained, the membership list was near to six thousand, but most days, there were less than a thousand members actually at the club. A majority of those were locals who stopped by on a routine basis. Over the Fourth of July, though, the club could swell to over four thousand. It stopped there only because that was peak capacity.

It didn't help that the Fourth was in the middle of the week. It extended the celebration, as half of the crowd arrived before and left immediately after the holiday while the other half arrived immediately for the holiday and stayed through the end of the weekend. Then there were those who couldn't make the holiday but came for the weekends, assuring that the club and all the problems of running it kept Angie moving all day long.

While she'd always had a great deal of respect for the job Lana did, Angie was really impressed now by how easy the other woman made it all seem. It was going to be hard to find her replacement. One thing for sure, it wouldn't be Angie.

Even if the job had been fun, she couldn't stay in Pittsview. It had been a battle all day not to give in to the longing and the urges and call Brett or Mike. She wanted to say she'd made a mistake, even though she knew she hadn't. Angie also knew she couldn't fight this battle every day. It was going to be hard enough to do it for a whole month.

They didn't help the matter.

Just because Dean had demanded that she have no contact with them, he hadn't apparently demanded that they have no contact with her. If he had, they weren't complying. Angie wasn't going to rat them out, though they weren't doing much to keep their attempts secretive.

That was the last thing anybody would use to describe the balloons that Mike had scent. A card attached had simply read,

Balloon ride? Angie didn't know exactly what that meant, but she suspected he was asking her out on a date.

Apparently, it was more than a date. That had become clear with the next gift that had arrived. It was a teddy bear. An eight-foot-tall teddy bear with another note pinned to it. This one was more pointed. It read, *Alaskan cruise? Whales and bears, oh my.*

Those words held more significance than simply the offer contained within them. Angie had been on an Alaskan cruise and written Mike all about it. It had been so romantic and beautiful that she'd felt so alone and had written him every day, describing the trip as if sharing it with him. She had seen whales and bears. He'd remembered.

Angie had almost crumbled in that moment and gone running back to Mike, and she would have if Lana hadn't been there to stop her. Lana had done the very job Angie had demanded of her the previous night. She kept Angie from giving in during those moments of weakness. They came at least once an hour, which was the same for the gifts that kept arriving.

After the teddy bear had been sent back, the flowers had arrived with a note asking if she'd preferred to swim with the dolphin through tropical reefs. She'd sent those back as well, along with the Belgian chocolates that asked if she wanted to take a sweet tour through Europe.

By the time the homemade pasta and meatballs had arrived, Angie was too hungry to send the delicious meal back. Instead, she devoured it and waited eagerly for the dessert to follow, but nothing came. She didn't have time to worry over whatever they were up to now.

The rest of the evening passed in a blur. It wasn't until after three in the morning when Angie was finally given a chance to take a minute's break that it dawned on her that she hadn't heard back from either Brett or Mike. She didn't know what to make of that and didn't really have the energy to make anything of it. Angie barely had the endurance to make it all the way back to the room she'd been assigned.

The club had a lot of staff. While a good portion of their workers came from in town, they still housed a good number of people at the club. Hidden in a thick grove of pines and oaks, the servants' quarters were more like a well-equipped campus accessible from the main club areas by golf carts.

Angie was too tired to drive her own. One of the butlers took her and assured her along the way that somebody would be by with breakfast by seven in the morning. The food sounded good. The timing not so much. She didn't object, though.

There wasn't time to sleep in. Not this week. For the rest of the week, Angie knew sleep would be a hard-fought-for commodity and so didn't even bother to turn on the lights as she stepped into the studio apartment she'd been assigned. Letting the door slam shut behind her, and knowing that it automatically locked, Angie kicked off her shoes, dropped her purse on the floor, and stumbled across the dark room to fall face first onto her bed.

She lay there like that for several minutes before it dawned on her sleepy mind that her cheek was resting on something softer and warmer than her blanket, something that smelled like Mike, warm and enticing. Levering herself up onto her elbows, Angie blinked drowsily down at the bed and then decided that whatever it was she didn't care. Angie certainly didn't care enough to bother to turn on the lights.

So she flopped back down and burrowed herself deeper into the comforting scent. Content for the moment, she passed right out, and it wasn't until morning that she realized that she had Mike's shirt wrapped around her like a blanket. There was a note crumpled beneath her.

She pulled it out and unfolded it, settling back into her bed to read it with a smile pulling at her lips. Mike hoped that the scent on his shirt helped her dream of him because he would be dreaming of her. It had. She'd had the sweetest dreams of both him and his brother.

That morning, Angie wondered if maybe things were salvageable after all. That hopeful seed took root and blossomed into a full sense of optimism over the next couple of weeks. Brett and Mike wrote to her every day, telling her all about their decision to start a gym in town and the renovations they were working on doing on Hailey's house.

They were getting it ready for Angie, getting themselves ready to be the kind of men she deserved. It was sweet and very touching. What it wasn't was just for show. Apparently, they really meant what they said. Hailey assured Angie that her brothers had bought her house, though she retained the right to use the garage as her studio until Cole and Kyle finished building her a better one out at the house they were restoring for Hailey.

Everybody was getting houses, Angie included, because Hailey also came around bearing blueprints and plans that Brett and Mike wanted her to approve. Of course she'd hesitated, trying to explain to Hailey why she'd walked out on her brothers. Hailey wasn't hearing it, probably because Angie wasn't really selling it all that well.

The truth was she had fun poring over the layouts, given that they were going to completely renovate the whole house. Truthfully, she couldn't wait to pick out finishes and see how it all came together. Even as that thought occurred to her, Angie knew she was folding.

Dean didn't stand a chance because Brett and Mike were turning into the thoughtful, hard-working men she knew them to be. Not that Dean was putting in much of an effort to woo Angie. That was a little peculiar, though Angie didn't notice it until she stumbled onto Dean and his buddy giving a brunette a workout.

They were buried out in the garden maze and didn't catch her spying. Angie did linger, her own memories and desires spurred on by the sight of the two men frantically fucking the woman caught between them. Actually, technically, only one man was doing all the work. Dean was lying there on the ground with his casted leg outstretched and his hands stacked behind his head. He was clearly simply enjoying the ride his buddy was putting the brunette through.

It was clear that he wasn't the only one enjoying the moment. Flushed with her passion, the woman was moaning and drooling, matching the pace the man behind her set with the flex of her own hips. It was clear she was lost in the moment. That was what it had been like the one time Brett and Mike had come together to love her.

It had been a wild, insatiable ride. Even the memory had her toes curling and her cunt softening. Angie wanted to go find Brett and Mike right then and there. She would have, too, if it wouldn't have cost her their freedom. So, instead, Angie retreated back to her apartment to do as she had done for most of her life, handling the matter herself.

It wasn't until an hour after that, as she was luxuriating in a bathtub full of bubbles, that it finally dawned on her that there was something odd going on with Dean. Even if he didn't know that she'd find him out in the gardens, he had to have known that she would hear about him having a tryst with one of the girls.

While she wasn't jealous and hadn't expected any sort of fidelity on his part, Angie had expected to receive some attention from the man. After all, he'd gotten beat up because of her. If nothing else, he should really want to stick it to Mike and Brett. Angie had certainly assumed Dean did, given the terms of their arrangement.

Truthfully, their arrangement was a little odd. It kind of reminded Angie of another similar deal that had been recently struck. The more she considered the matter, the more Angie realized that there was only one twisted mind that would have come up with either idea.

Patton. Somehow, someway, she was involved. Angie could just sense it, which was just why she called up her dear friend and arranged to meet her at Riley's for a beer and a heart-felt conversation.

Angie arrived first and settled into a booth in the back with a pitcher and a basket of tater tots covered in chili and cheese. Typical of her nature, Patton was late and came rushing in with a gust of enthusiasm that didn't allow for Angie to get a word in for the first several minutes.

"Oh, I am so sorry I am so late," Patton apologized without any real hint of sincerity as she dropped her purse onto her side of the booth and slid into the seat. "But I've been working so hard on the details of my club idea. I've decided to wait until after Lana comes back from her romantic vacation. I figure even if she doesn't feel like she owes me, which she will, then, at least, she should be in a better mood. Oh, look a pitcher."

Patton shot Angie a quick grin as she reached for her glass. "That's a lot of beer. That must mean we have a lot to talk about, and I can easily imagine what. After all, Hailey has been keeping me abreast of all the details.

"Those two have really whipped into shape, haven't they? They're almost becoming the perfect men, aren't they?" Patton finally paused to pin Angie with an expectant look. "Well? Aren't they?"

Angie sucked in a slow, deep breath, refusing to allow herself to be sucked into Patton's gleefulness. She was here for answers and knew how to get them from her friend.

"I know what you did," Angie confronted Patton, keeping her tone as hard as her glare. "I know you convinced Dean to offer me that deal. Now I want to know why and how much it cost you."

Patton could have denied it, and probably would have if Angie had shown a second of hesitation, but she didn't. Finally Patton sighed and shrugged, offering Angie an answer she didn't expect.

"I felt guilty," Patton admitted.

"Guilty?" Angie blinked, not understanding that. "For what?"

"Well…" Patton drew that word out as she shifted in her seat. "I kind of set Brett and Mike up to be tested the night that Dean took you home, and that's why they were late and weren't there to give you a lift home themselves."

"Whoa, whoa, whoa." Angie waved Patton to a stop. "Back up. What do you mean you had them tested?"

Angie figured she already knew the answer to that question. Patton's smile assured her that she did, and so did her words.

"I mean I had a few of the girls hit on them and see if they were likely to stray, which, by the way, they're not." Patton offered her that bit of news with an uptick in her tone that sounded more desperate than cheerful. Angie knew why.

"I should kick your ass."

"Didn't you tell Brett and Mike that you were leaving them because they had an issue with violence?" Patton instantly countered. "And I only had your best interests at heart, and it wasn't like I knew you'd get a ride home from Dean, and—"

"Patton!" Angie broke into her long, winding justification. There really was no point in letting Patton go on like that. Not when she'd already forgiven her friend. "It's all right."

"It is?"

"Yeah. You didn't make Mike and Brett go after Dean. Neither could you make them cheat. If you and some of the girls want to waste your time trying…go ahead."

Angie knew that she wouldn't have had that confidence two weeks ago, but now she knew how special she was to her two men. Special enough for them to actually write letters and get their shit together. They wouldn't throw that effort away on some quick screw.

"But I still don't get how you came up with this second twist or even how you got Dean to go along with it."

"Dean?" Patton snorted. "I paid him off."

"Why?" It wasn't just guilt that had Patton hesitating to answer. "What? What is so bad you don't want to tell me?"

"Nothing."

"Patton."

"It's just that, you know, you run away from things." Patton hesitated over her words, cringing backward as if she expected Angie to take offense.

She was too shocked, though, to take offense. "What? What do you mean I run away?"

"Well, I mean, you avoid difficult situations."

"I do not."

"Oh no?"

"No!"

"You've been faithful to two men who you have barely seen in ten years." Patton paused as if that said it all, but Angie wasn't impressed with her reasoning.

"So? You saved yourself for Chase, Slade, and Devin."

"And I saw them constantly. I had an active relationship with them. You used Brett and Mike to avoid having any relationship with any man," Patton shot back. "And don't deny that your first instinct when things got difficult with them was to run away."

How could she deny it? She had run away. The truth was Angie had never truly felt understood. Her premonitions and intuition had left her feeling alienated. Angie probably would have run farther if Patton hadn't lassoed her with the deal she'd struck with Dean. Angie wasn't running anymore, though, and Patton wasn't apologizing. Far from it.

"Now that you know the truth, you know that you owe me."

Chapter 21

Tuesday, July 14th

Mike smiled as he glanced around the field and nodded. It was flat, hard land, making it ideal to train on. The lot was large, big enough for Brett and him to build in all the courses they wanted. There was even a barn that, with a great deal of work, could be converted into a sizable indoor gym. Most importantly, they were only a ten-minute walk from town.

"It's perfect." Turning to cast a look over at Brett, who stood there taking it all in, Mike pressed his brother for an agreement. "Don't you think?"

"I think it's going to be a lot of work," Brett returned, but he shrugged as if his words didn't faze him. "But then a boot camp is supposed to be a lot of work, right?"

"That it is," Mike agreed, not dissuaded from the challenge before them in the slightest. "Though I think starting a business is going to be the harder part."

Actually, they were getting kind of lucky because they already had investors. The Davis brothers were lending them the cash to buy the land and even putting up the capital to help them get everything built and prepped. Of course they'd demanded a pretty hefty chunk of the company.

There were buy-back plans and liquidation rules that Slade and Mike had hammered out. In the end, Mike was content that they'd gotten a good deal. That confidence wasn't based completely on arrogance but partly on the fact that they already had guys calling to ask when they'd be taking clients and inquiring on how much membership was going to cost.

Those were all good omens, and Mike wished he could say the same when it came to Angie. Not being able to see her, touch her, to hear the sound of her voice, it was killing him. Mike couldn't help but wonder if Angie felt the same way.

Hailey thought she did, but Mike wasn't certain if he could trust her judgment. Hell, he wasn't even sure he could trust her. Mike knew what Hailey thought, knew she considered him and Brett high-strung. She didn't want to set them off, no doubt afraid of what they'd do, but they weren't going to do anything.

Brett and Mike had already talked the matter over. They knew what they needed now. They needed direction, goals to accomplish. More importantly, they needed to work out, to wear out the buildup of frustrations and aggravations. On top of all of that, they needed Angie.

Things just weren't the same without her around, which was funny because she hadn't been around all that long. While that might have been the technical truth, the reality was he'd been carrying her in his heart a lot longer than he'd ever realized. Thanks to all those letters she'd sent, her words, her voice had wormed its way into his head until he could almost hear her making little comments as he went through his day.

It was as though she was a part of him. That just made the past two weeks all the more aggravating. Being separated from Angie was slowly eating at him, but now he knew how to cope. Mike, quite literally, tried to outrun his pain. He was clearing damn near twenty miles a day now, and that included two workouts with his brother.

Brett was there with him step by step, and his brother was the only one that he was allowed to hit. He and Mike kept their hand-to-hand combat skills sharp, though they wouldn't be teaching any of those moves to their clients. They just liked to stay sharp, and Mike did like to hit things.

"Maybe we should put in a boxing ring."

That got a laugh from Brett. "You need to stop adding on, man. We haven't even bought the property yet."

"I'm just saying."

"You don't even know how to box!"

"Yeah?" That might be true, but Mike did know something. "That won't stop me from kicking your ass."

"I'd like to see you try," Brett shot back and then paused to frown. "Is that GD?"

Mike turned around to watch as a big pickup pulled off the highway and rolled slowly over the red dirt to come to a stop beside his truck. Even if he hadn't recognized the oversized vehicle, Mike could easily recognize the man behind the wheel. It was hard to mistake GD's massive bulk for anybody else.

"Yep."

"Wonder what he wants," Brett murmured, echoing Mike's silent thoughts as they both watched the big man hop out of his truck. The massive vehicle swayed slightly as he slammed the door. The smile GD shot at them was a warning all of its own.

"He wants something."

Mike was certain of that, but he'd give GD a chance to get to that point himself. After all, the man wouldn't ask for anything that Mike couldn't give, or wouldn't. Not only did GD know better, there really wasn't much Mike wouldn't do for his friends.

"Hey, man." He nodded toward GD as he came sauntering up. "How's the dead bird?"

"Rotten," GD spat with a disgusted shake of his head. "Thanks for asking. How goes the search for a place to put your gym?"

"Better than rotten," Mike admitted as he took the hand GD offered him. It was that offer that assured Mike whatever it was that GD wanted was big. Hell, he even shook Brett's hand.

"Hey, man. How is it going?"

"Not bad." Brett bobbed his head before pointedly glancing over the lot around them. "We're thinking this might be the spot to start Mathews' Gym. What you think?"

"Not bad." GD echoed Brett's words as he took everything in. His gaze narrowed on the barn for a moment before his brows lifted and he shot Brett and Mike a curious look. "I take it that's going to be the gym."

"Yep." Mike nodded, all but anticipating the question that came next.

"Then what are you going to do with the rest of this lot?" GD looked across the large dirt field. "Build a really big parking lot?"

"More like an obstacle course," Mike corrected him, breaking into a smile along with Brett as GD snorted.

"I should have known."

"The kids love it and so do the adults." Brett shrugged. "So we're going to have a boot camp for the hard-core soldier wannabes. Then something a little more punk and alternative to pull in the teenagers who need to burn off energy. It'll be great."

"Yeah." GD nodded, his smile growing as he considered the matter. "It's not a bad idea, but I'm betting you're going to need a little help getting all this done."

"Everybody needs help," Brett shot back, sharing a look with Mike.

"Why are you worried what we need?" Mike glanced back toward the big man. "You offering to help?"

"Yeah, in a way." GD took a deep breath, and Mike could tell the big man was bracing himself, but he still had no idea what was about to come out of GD's mouth. "Rumor is you're willing to sign over fifty percent of the business for an investor, so I'm here to tell you that I represent an interested party who will take thirty-three percent and an *active* role in the company."

The stress on that one word made it clear what he was really offering. What wasn't clear was whom the big man was talking about. Mike had only one fear.

"This isn't about Wanda, is it?"

"No." GD snorted. "It's about Kitty Anne."

Relieved to hear that, Mike managed to find a smile as he considered GD's answer. "What's wrong, man? You having woman problems, too?"

"It's not woman problems," GD corrected him. "It's an occupational issue."

Mike busted out laughing at that. Brett joined them as GD flushed and scowled at them both.

"I don't mean it that way," GD grumped. "Kitty Anne is smart, determined, and...a woman."

"Yeah, we got that." Mike nodded, not certain what GD was getting at. "Noticed it right off, but I'm not sure what that has to do with anything."

"Nick runs an all-boys camp."

"And Kitty Anne causes problems." That Mike could believe.

GD and Nick's woman was well built and quite attractive. Those could be two detrimental things to a young boy who was trying to focus on his studies and improving his circumstances. Hell, even an ugly woman could be detrimental to those two goals, and the boy didn't have to be that young. All a man really had to be for women to be distracting was alive and interested.

Unless, of course, they were already distracted by a different woman, which was why neither Mike nor Brett was interested in Kitty Anne. At least, not that way, but she might actually make a good business partner. After all they'd seen the woman kick GD's ass on the obstacle course. That had been impressive.

Mike shared another look with his brother and got the nod that had him turning back to GD with a smile. "So, why don't you buy us dinner and let the woman negotiate her own deal?"

* * * *

GD did one better than that. He invited them back to the cabin he shared with Kitty Anne and Nick for a home-cooked meal. Not that any one of the three of them had cooked it. Instead, they'd ordered up a meal from the mess hall down at the camp. Some of those boys could really cook.

Brett had to admit he was impressed. Impressed with the meal and the woman sitting across from him. Kitty Anne had some great ideas. She was certainly enthusiastic and would help expand their client base when it came to women, but if they took her up on the deal she was offering, he and Mike would not only be gaining a business partner but also losing a good chunk of cash.

The Davis brothers, on the other hand, could give them more money and less interference, but they'd be taking more of the profits and offering less help. It was a hard call, which was just why Brett let Mike sort it out. That just what Nick, Kitty Anne, and his brother spent most of the night doing.

Brett and GD, on the other hand, headed down to the game room at the boys' camp to shoot pool and gossip. That was just what they did. GD told him all about how they were buying a house for Kitty Anne's mother and that they'd planned to build their own but that Kitty Anne asked if they could spend the money investing in Brett and Mike's idea.

Apparently, fundraising wasn't really her thing.

Brett got that. He'd rather be working his ass off, too. He'd also like to ask about Angie but held his cool, waiting for GD to finish complaining about his cousin before he pressed the other man for the details he really wanted.

"So, how are things going out at the club?" Brett finally asked, not even bothering to try and play it cool. There was no point. From the smirk GD shot him, the big man already knew that his curiosity was killing him. So, Brett just gave in. "Angie getting along all right?"

"I guess." GD shrugged. "I don't actually see her much, given I don't really go out there much."

"Then who is the master?" Brett stepped back as GD circled the pool table to check all the angles.

He shot Brett a quick look and an even faster answer before he bent over to take his shot. "I don't know."

Brett waited until after the balls had stopped clacking into each other and didn't bother to move when GD sank the ball he'd been aiming for. That didn't mean he stayed quiet.

"So, you haven't seen Angie...or Dean?"

GD snickered at the clear difficulty Brett had getting that name out without cussing. He shook his head at Brett and took his shot before straightening up and answering.

"I've seen Dean. I've seen him chasing after some brunette."

"Really?" Brett perked up at that. "You think maybe you can point that out to Angie?"

"Please, the boy has never stood a chance with her." GD rolled his eyes. "She'd never let him touch her."

"Huh." Brett frowned as he considered that. "So, you don't think we stand a chance with Angie?"

"What I think is that it is your turn," GD shot back. "On the other hand, I *know* that Dean doesn't stand a chance with Angie. Hell, everybody does. There's not even a bet in the book because nobody will take the other side. Not even Dean."

That should have reassured Brett, but for some reason, it bugged him. He kept turning what GD said over and over as he lined up his shot. He missed, but by the time he straightened back up, he had the problem figured out.

"Then why the hell did he make the deal?" Brett pressed, as if GD had any answers.

The big man didn't. He just shrugged and nailed his shot, along with the next three. By the time GD stopped, he'd won, which was just perfect timing. No sooner had GD straightened up, wearing a smile of victory, than a young guy came running into the room.

"GD! Kevin is—oh, hello there." Coming to a stumbling stop, the stranger blinked up at Brett with the most brilliant violet eyes he'd only ever seen once before.

Patton had eyes like that and hair a few shades lighter but with the same reddish streaks. In fact, if the two of them were standing next to each other, Brett would have sworn they were siblings, but that couldn't be...could it?

"I'm sorry. I didn't mean to interrupt." The guy seemed nervous and was shooting GD pointed looks. "If I could, though, have a moment with you, Mr. Davis?"

"Sure." GD slapped Brett on the back, jarring him out of his stupor as he walked past. "I'll be back in a moment, buddy."

"Sure," Brett echoed, shaking his head free of the ridiculous thoughts that had caught a hold for a moment.

Patton didn't have any siblings. She had a mother who had run off and a father who had been murdered, but no brothers. Even if she did, there was no way GD would be hiding that fact. He was tight with the Davis brothers. Not as tight as Brett and Mike, but pretty damn close.

They'd all gone to school together. Who they had not attended class with was Dean. That bastard sure as hell didn't owe Brett or Mike a single thing. Just the opposite. He had every right to his revenge.

Mike and Brett had been completely in the wrong. That wasn't something that sat well with Brett, especially not if Dean wasn't really after Angie. That still left him curious about what the other man was after. He put that question to Mike not a half-hour later.

Some kind of emergency had erupted with one of the kids, requiring not just GD and Nick to go off to assist, but Kitty Anne as well. They'd all rushed off, leaving Mike and Brett to figure out what to do with the rest of the night. There was a lot of night left, but that didn't change the direction Mike turned in as they reached the end of the drive.

They were headed home for another long, lonely night. That grim thought took Brett back to the reason they had to suffer—Dean. Dean and his deal. Something was wrong there. Brett could just sense it, but he couldn't figure out what it was.

"Brett!" Mike snapped, shooting him an annoyed look as a semi whooshed past, headed in the opposite direction. Its bright lights cut across the cab and illuminated Mike's frown as Brett blinked and glanced over at him.

"What?"

"Weren't you listening to what I was saying?"

Brett blinked and frowned, straining to think of the right answer. It was pretty obvious. "You talking about Kitty Anne and the deal you two were working out."

"And?"

"And…it's a go?"

"Brett." Mike sighed, assuring Brett that he had guessed wrong.

"So, it's a no."

"I didn't say that," Mike snapped, confusing Brett all the more.

"Then what the hell did you say?"

"That you weren't listening to me!"

That retort had Brett growling as he all but threw his hands up in frustration. His brother was determined to be difficult. Well, so was Brett. Dismissing Mike and his woman-like hissy fit, Brett went back to mulling over their current predicament.

While GD might not have had much to say about the matter, Hailey had tons. She lectured them almost every time she saw them. Brett put up with it only because she was also willing to pass messages to Angie and relay back more than just the answers.

From Hailey's perspective, Mike's plan was a roaring success. Angie seemed to be melting beneath all the attention. Knowing that only made it all the harder to stay away, which was just why Brett really wanted to know what had motivated Dean to make the deal he had. Especially if Dean knew he couldn't win.

That question bugged the shit out of Brett. He couldn't just relax back into the couch and watch TV while Mike spent another night going over numbers and plans. His brother was obsessed with calculating their future down to the very penny. He barely noticed as Brett cut through the kitchen and headed out the back door.

Brett didn't bother with either his keys or his wallet but headed off on foot down the shadow-lined streets. There were very few sidewalks in Pittsview and very little traffic to worry over. In fact, not a single vehicle passed Brett as he cut through the large neighborhood that surrounded the city's south side.

The sheriff did jog by with a kid keeping pace beside him. Both were wearing flashers and appeared lost in the silence of their run. Alex cast a nod in Brett's direction, but his steps never faltered, and neither did he break the rhythm of his breathing to call out a greeting.

That was just fine with Brett. He was lost in his own thoughts. Those thoughts led him directly to where he'd been warned by just about everybody not to go. Twenty minutes after he walked out of his own back door, Brett found himself staring up at Dean's front door.

Brett knew he should turn around, but he didn't. Instead, he walked up the three steps that led to the top of the yard and the path that ended at the arched wooden door. That was when he definitely should have turned around, but he didn't. Instead, he knocked and waited until Dean appeared, wearing a pair of jeans that had been split up the side to allow room for the cast covering his leg.

"Oh God," Dean groaned and banged his head into the side of the door, "Why me?"

"Don't panic." Brett held his hands up in surrender, deeply bothered by the sight of the bruises still marring Dean's clean-cut features. Then there was the cast that had him leaning slightly on his good leg. "I'm not here to hit you again."

That got a snort as Dean looked up toward the heavens in exasperation.

"I just wanted to…"

Brett faltered as Dean finally turned his gaze on him. He wanted to know why Dean had offered Angie the deal he had, but Brett didn't have the audacity to ask that question with the man's eye still discolored from his beating. There was really only one thing to say.

"I'm sorry. We shouldn't have hit you."

"No. You shouldn't have," Dean agreed with no hint of annoyance. "But apology accepted. Good night."

"Wait a minute." Brett stepped up, smacking a hand against the door Dean tried to close in his face. "Why are you being so bitchy?"

"Because you beat the shit out of me?" Dean offered that with a lift of his brow. "Now—"

"Dean?" The sultry call of a woman in heat to the lover she desired echoed out of the hall across the living room and drew Brett's gaze over Dean's shoulder.

The other man groaned, his eyes fluttering shut, even as Brett's connected with the woman who was wearing next to nothing as she came to a pause in the entrance to the hallway. For a second, both of them froze, the brunette with horror and Brett with shock. In the next breath, she took off down the hall as Brett turned his amazed gaze back on Dean.

"You're doing the mayor's wife? She's like sixty!"

That had Dean's eyes snapping open and his hand swinging out to fist itself in Brett's shirt. Before Brett could brace himself, Dean yanked him into the living room and slammed the door closed. Despite his broken leg, the other man lorded over him with an intimidating scowl and a fierce look of determination that hadn't been there two weeks ago when he'd been squaring against both Brett and his brother.

"You're a real ass, you know that?" Dean snapped.

"It was her." Brett paid little attention to the other man's insult, as finally some of the pieces started to fall into place. "She was here that night, and that is why you don't want this to be a big deal."

"I don't know what the fuck you're talking about," Dean denied and then dared to threaten. "But I suggest you keep your wild speculations to yourself unless *you* want to end up in the cast."

"Those are awfully big words for a man who is actually in the cast," Brett shot back, feeling less and less guilty about having put Dean into that cast. "I can't believe you are doing a married woman. That's low."

"Please." Dean snorted. "They're not doing anything their husbands don't. Women of any age with something to prove are a whole hell of a lot of fun."

Brett blinked, wondering how the hell Dean knew that. However he knew it, one thing was for damn certain. Angie was way too good for this weasel. Brett intended to make sure she knew it, too.

"Well, I guess that is your business. I should probably leave you to it."

Brett tried to brush past Dean but didn't dare to actually bang into the man, not about to be accused of knocking him over. Dean knew it, too. He shifted his weight, intentionally blocking Brett's way as he held him up.

"What you're about to do now doesn't matter to Angie, but it will to a whole lot of other people," Dean warned him, expanding his threat with a pointedness that had Brett bristling. "Being at war with the local government isn't exactly the best condition to start a business with. So just remember, *they* are not doing anything *their* husbands aren't."

The way Dean stressed those two words left no doubt that there were not only more but that their husbands held positions that had the kind of authority nobody in a small town wanted to piss off. Brett didn't really care. Not as much as he suspected Dean did.

"But it matters to you." Brett stepped up to openly challenge Dean's attempt at intimidation. "Because you'll be their primary target. So, you know what you are going to do tomorrow?"

"Free Angie from our agreement?" Dean guessed accurately.

"You're a smart man." Brett complimented him with enough disdain in his tone to make a mockery of his words. "Now step aside."

Dean didn't say a word but eased back, allowing Brett to pass. He headed out the door, not even bothering to look back when it slammed closed behind him. Dean could slam all the doors he wanted. That slime ball wasn't going to get anywhere near Angie. That was all that mattered.

What mattered was that tomorrow Angie would be free and this was the last night he had to go to bed alone. That thought turned his attention from Dean to just what he planned to do tomorrow once Angie came home. He didn't even consider Mike until he pushed open the back door to find his brother just as he'd left him.

Mike appeared completely oblivious to the fact that Brett had been gone for over an hour. He glanced up as if startled by Brett's sudden appearance. As always, Mike didn't take well to being surprised.

"Where the hell are you coming from? I thought you were watching TV."

"I went for a walk," Brett retorted, shutting the door behind him and turning toward the fridge. He fished out a beer and popped the top as he turned back to his brother, trying for complete indifference. "I actually ended up running into Dean."

Mike stilled at that, his gaze narrowing as he tensed. "Yeah. That's odd."

"Not really." Brett shrugged. "We were at his house."

"Brett."

"I didn't hit him."

"That doesn't mean he won't claim that you did," Mike shot back.

"I don't think so." Brett smiled. "I kind of caught him in the act with the mayor's wife."

Mike blinked at that, clearly not certain how to take Brett's comment. Enjoying his brother's look of disbelief, Brett slid into the seat opposite Mike and regaled him with even more salacious tidbits.

"And from what I gather, she is one of many."

"No!" Mike whispered, his eyes beginning to twinkle with merriment. "The mayor is like seventy. His wife is like sixty."

"According to Dean, she's only gotten better with age."

Mike didn't even seem to hear him but appeared lost in the wonder of the moment. "Wait until Angie finds out."

"Mums the word." Brett shook his head. "Dean's going to let her out of their deal, but we've got to keep our mouths shut. Understand?"

"I understand." Mike's momentary smile faded as he glanced down at his papers. "All my plans…nothing is ready."

* * * *

Dean sat there on the edge of his bed, listening as Mrs. Rebecca Winters rushed about the place. To most people, she was Becky, the warm, sweet wife of the mayor. She was involved with all the right associations, went to all the right functions, and threw parties for the poor. In short, she was the perfect small-town mayor's wife.

Unfortunately, she was married to a letch. After Dean had proved that point to her, little, innocent Becky had turned into an angry and outraged Rebecca and fucked Dean's brains out. The woman might sag here and there, but she was tight, hot, and wet in all the ways that counted.

Beyond that, she paid well.

"Here." Rebecca slapped a thin stack of fifties down onto Dean's nightstand before turning to offer him a hopeful smile. "Next Monday?"

"Yeah. That's cool." Dean nodded slowly, wondering just why he wasn't happier.

Rebecca could have really wigged out about the Brett thing, but instead, he'd stumbled back into the bedroom to find her playing with herself and hungry for dick. She'd fucked him damn near raw, and that was normally a good thing. Not tonight.

Tonight he just felt wrong.

"Try not to brood too much, darling." Rebecca reached a hand out to cup his chin and tilt his face up. "Even if Harvey finds out about what we're doing, he's not going to do anything that would risk his political career."

Dean offered her a quick smile and nod. After leaning up for the chaste kiss she dropped on his lips, he sat there watching her go, knowing that wasn't the problem. He didn't give a shit about Harvey Winters, even if the fat bastard was the mayor. What Dean cared about was Gwen. She was gone now.

Nobody really cared besides him. The only family that had shown up for the funeral had been her cousin Kristen. She'd looked nervous, sending him curious glances that didn't hide the speculation in her gaze. Dean knew she was wondering if he'd killed Gwen.

She wasn't the only one.

Chapter 22

Wednesday, July 15th

Angie woke up slowly, coming to with a reluctance that weighed on her. She lingered in bed, unwilling to get up as she considered that she had no real reason to. Lana was running things fine without her. The book she was building would make it easy enough for anybody to step in and take over her job, even if finding somebody was going to take a while. So was sorting out how she felt.

Patton had really forced her to face a truth that Angie had long avoided admitting. She was afraid. Falling in love with Brett and Mike had been easy because they had been a custom-made fantasy. The question now was really whether or not she could love the real men that they were, even if they were flawed.

Angie so wanted the answer to be yes. The letters and gifts that Mike and Brett had showered her with just went to prove that some things could be better than her dreams. Dean's bruises were a reminder that they could also be worse. Those thoughts just had her going around and around until she finally rolled out of bed to escape them.

Feeling as if her limbs weighed a ton, she shuffled into the bathroom, where she took twice as long to get everything done. Even once she was freshly showed, groomed, and dressed, Angie still felt deflated and unable to move any faster than the slow pace she set as she started up the path from the servants' campus toward the main lodge.

It was a long walk. That didn't help. Neither did the cup of coffee she ordered up once she made it to the dining hall. Accustomed to her presence, the men ignored her, allowing Angie to brood over her breakfast as her thoughts continued to churn. They didn't stop until a shadow fell across her table.

"Angie?"

"Dean."

Angie looked up to find him staring down at her with eyes that both opened and closed. He was almost back to looking human again. She knew he was definitely back to fucking, cast or no cast.

"Can I have a seat?" Dean asked, nodding to the chair opposite her, and there was really little Angie could do but agree. After all, the man was standing there balanced on crutches and one foot because of her.

"Of course." Angie gestured politely to the chair, watching as Dean made a show out of settling down. Only once he'd rested his crutches against the side of the table and glanced over in her direction did she finally continue on. "So? What can I do for you?"

"Actually, it's what I can do for you that I'm here to talk to you about," Dean corrected her, but Angie still wasn't ready for his big revelation. "I'm letting you out of the deal."

"What?" She'd specifically told Patton that she didn't want to have the whole thing called off. That would leave her to have to deal with the Brett and Mike situation too soon. "I don't—"

"Brett stopped by last night to apologize." Dean paused, his eyes lifting for a moment as his lips thinned. "He convinced me to break our deal."

"He did?" Angie stiffened at that announcement. "How?"

She feared she already knew the answer to that question. It was the answer to all her questions, or maybe not. Dean surprised her once again as his gaze dropped back to hers and he smirked.

"Not in the way you're thinking. He didn't threaten me or hurt me," Dean assured her. "As I said, he apologized."

"And you just forgave him?" Angie asked, not believing that story for a moment.

"Something like that." Dean studied her for a moment before leaning forward slightly and dropping his voice to a whisper that assured nobody overheard him. "Trust me. I wouldn't give in to threats or intimidation. Only blackmail."

With that confession, Dean reached for his clutches and hefted himself back onto his feet. Once again, he paused to smirk down at her and offer a final suggestion.

"I'd count myself lucky if I were you. After all, look at the lengths those two idiots are willing to go for you."

With that, he took off for the main door, leaving Angie to watch him leave and wonder if he didn't have a point. Brett and Mike had fought for her, had wooed her, and according to Hailey, they were even getting their shit together for her.

To be worthy of her.

Angie's own words echoed scathingly through her head as she remembered telling both brothers she was too good for them. She'd been half joking and half responding out of annoyance, but she wondered if her words hadn't been truer than she'd wanted to admit.

The truth was that she did think a lot of herself, but she'd always considered herself confident, not vain. It was clear now, though, that had been a defense mechanism against all the teasing and patronizing responses people gave her simply because she was different. Angie believed in dreams.

Didn't she?

That was a question that kept her occupied through most of the day as she went about her tasks with little thought for them. The only conclusion she could come to was that she wanted to believe in them. If she believed strongly enough, they would come true.

That thought had her glancing across her desk later that afternoon at where Lana sat, her hair pinned up and her features furled into a frown as she studied the schedule before her. Lana seemed to become aware of Angie's scrutiny slowly. Her chin lifted reluctantly as her gaze shifted up to meet Angie's. They held each other's stare for a moment before Lana broke down and asked the obvious question.

"What? Do I have something on my face? Is my hair out of place? What?"

"Do you think I'm being stupid?"

"What?" Lana reeled backward as she shook her head. "No, and I have no idea what you are talking about…unless you're talking about Brett and Mike, *again*."

Angie sighed, her shoulders slumping with guilt as Lana rolled her eyes.

"I should have known." Lana offered Angie a half-smile that was filled with pity. "Look, Angie, maybe you should stop trying to tie yourself up into knots and just accept that you were happier with them than you are without them."

Angie blinked at that, wishing it were that easy. "Life isn't that simple."

"Maybe. Maybe not." Lana shrugged. "But you know what Patton has that I don't? I mean besides Chase. She's willing to fight for her happiness, and I never did. Now look at where we are."

Angie wanted to tell her friend that she could fight now, that it wasn't too late, but she couldn't because if Lana tried she'd end up crushed. It was too late. Chase belonged to Patton.

"I'm wasting time, aren't I?"

Lana nodded sadly. "And you're letting life make the decision for you. Destiny has to be a choice, otherwise it's a shackle."

Hadn't she thought the same thing just recently? Destiny had to be a choice and Angie was making hers. She was in love with Hailey's brothers. That was what that. Angie simply decided to love them, but the truth was that if she wasn't capable of loving them then she wouldn't, but she did.

Who really cared how or why Angie had come to feel that way? It didn't matter. What mattered was that she did love them. As for her feelings of superiority? She'd let that be their problem. Angie had no doubt that Brett and Mike would find a suitable way to dissuade her of that notion. More importantly, these past two weeks they'd already proven that they would be willing to try.

Maybe it was time to prove she was, too, and she knew just how to prove it.

* * * *

"Is everything ready?" Mike asked for like the millionth time, making Brett glower as he glared at his brother.

"Doesn't it look ready?" Brett demanded to know. He was tired of saying yes. Even more tired of Mike's fussiness, which seemed never ending.

"I don't know," Mike muttered as he glanced around. "Do you think it's enough? Or maybe too much? What if all these candles start a fire? We don't even technically own the property yet."

"Would you stop!" Brett grabbed his head, trying to contain the pounding that was beating through his skull. This was all Mike's fault. "All damn day. Good God, man, it's been all damn day! Don't you think blue would be better than red? Do they make blue flowers? I don't know, maybe we should go with pink? Do you think crystals or glass? Balloons? Streamers? Blankets or quilts? Should we right her name in the sky? What about serenading her? Ahhh! I can't take it!"

Brett bugged his eyes out with that last proclamation as he pinned his brother with a crazy stare that Mike met with a frown and a touch of annoyance sharpening his own tone.

"You don't have to be all melodramatic about it. I just want everything to be perfect."

"Why?" Brett shot back. "It's not like Angie's perfect."

"I'm going to tell her you said that."

"Go ahead, as long as that means we're moving past the decorating stages."

Because Brett was not a decorator, and no matter how much sparkle and bling Mike tried to drape the old barn in, it still smelled and looked very much like a ruin. It was not what he'd call romantic, but he didn't doubt a woman would. They went in for effort, and the barn clearly looked as though it had taken a lot of effort.

"Fine," Mike snapped. "Then the next stage would actually be going to get the damn woman."

Yes, it would. After two weeks without Angie, Brett was damn anxious to see her once again. Anxious and not moving. Neither was Mike. Instead, they stood there staring at each other at the revelation that now was finally the moment of truth. They'd either succeed in wooing her or...

"What are we going to do if she says no?" Mike whispered, giving voice to the very fear that had lingered between them all week.

Brett had only one answer. "Then we ask her again...maybe in a hot air balloon with streamers hanging down."

"We could send an elephant to pick her up and have her arrive like she was on her way to a wedding." Mike perked up.

"You are not marching an elephant down my streets," Alex broke in, startling both brothers with his sudden appearance. He was standing in the open barn door, glancing around with a funny look on his face. "This place looks like some three-year-old with a pink princess obsession went on a tear through here. I thought this was supposed to be some kind of gym."

"It will be," Brett assured the sheriff, though he didn't seem to convince him.

"Yeah, right." Alex smirked. "That's why your business partner is named Kitty Anne."

"Was there something you wanted?" Mike asked with clear exasperation. "Or are you just here to annoy us?"

"Well, actually, I do have a purpose." Alex pinned Mike with a hard look as his smile faded away. "I've been informed by Heather that she was in possession of a flash drive that you and Patton are searching for. Though I'm not sure if I believe her. I mean, you teaming up with crazy—"

"It was a fake." Mike cut off Alex's wandering tale. "The Davis boys slipped Patton bad information just to mess with her."

"Hmm."

"What? Hmm?" Mike scowled. "Don't you believe me?"

"Yeah, but that begs the question about where the drive is and who would have taken it," Alex pointed out.

"I guess those are your problems, and as you can see, we have our own to attend to." Brett nodded to the pink palace behind him. "You think Angie will like it?"

"I think it smells like shit in here." Alex glanced around before shrugging. "But I'm not a woman. To them, it's the thought that counts."

That was pretty much Brett's theory, too.

"Anyway, if that's all you know about the drive, I'll get out and leave you two to whatever this is." Alex turned but paused to glance back and offer them one final bit of advice. "If you ever do get rid of the pink and actually turn this place into a gym, you should try to get a contract with the city council. I've been lobbying them for years to set up a gym for the deputies. I bet they'd pay for the membership if you cut them a deal."

"Thanks, man." Mike nodded. "I'll keep that in mind."

Both brothers watched the sheriff saunter off back to his patrol car. He pulled around in the big dirt yard and out onto the highway with a final honk of his horn. Mike and Brett waved back and waited until the sound of Alex's engine had faded into the darkening night.

"Well?" Mike looked over at Brett. "You figure out yet how we're going to go get our girl?"

"Yep." Brett smirked, enjoying what came next. "Let's blow out the candles and get dressed because we're about to infiltrate the Cattleman's Club."

* * * *

They needn't have bothered with getting all dressed up and going through any effort to get past the club's front gate and into the main lodge. Not only was there no real security, they weren't barred from coming into the club in the first place.

Mike didn't point out that fact to Brett, though. His brother seemed to enjoy pretending he was executing some kind of high-risk operation. The only risk here was that Angie would refuse to go with them, but Mike already had a surefire way to keep her from saying no. He was going to stick his tongue in her mouth. He figured, as long as he was kissing her, Angie couldn't object, except to the kiss, which Mike was certain she wouldn't do.

Of course that didn't mean things were going to be easy because the hard part turned out to be finding Angie. According to Lana, she wasn't working and hadn't been seen in hours. With that news, and assuming she was out with Hailey or Patton or some other girlfriend, they'd retreated to her room to surprise Angie when she returned.

Only she didn't return, and by midnight, Mike and Brett started to get alarmed. They started calling around and found out that nobody had seen Angie that day. Everybody was kind of annoyed that they'd waited until that late to call.

It felt like déjà vu, a test by fate that they dared not fail. Neither was in agreement on what to do. Brett kept trying to call her, but she wasn't answering. So he decided to set up camp and flopped down on her bed to take a nap, leaving Mike to do whatever he wanted.

He wanted to start calling every hospital and police station around to assure nothing bad had happened to Angie, but he curbed that impulse, certain it was a leftover feeling of the panic that came from caring about another person. If he wanted to move past those frantic thoughts, then he'd just have to ignore them.

Mike would act sane, normal even. Maybe one day he would be both of those things again. Then he'd feel like himself again. It had been a long time since he'd felt like that. Years even. That revelation depressed the shit out of him.

By the time he'd made it back to town, he didn't feel much like doing anything but settling down onto the couch and drinking himself into a stupor. That probably was, sadly, a normal thing to do, even if it probably wasn't emotionally healthy.

Mike debated that silently as he turned into his neighborhood. He didn't have an answer by the time he pulled into the drive, but he forgot the question at the sight of Angie's car parked in his space. Perking up at that sight, he wondered if maybe life hadn't finally cut him a break as he blocked her in and hopped out of the cab. The answer to that question was yes.

That was clear the second he shoved into the kitchen and found the table set for a romantic, candlelit meal and a dinner that still smelled delicious hours later. That was when he realized that fate hadn't really cut him a break. Nope. Instead, the truth was he'd screwed up again because, clearly, Angie had been planning a surprise that he and Brett had ruined once again.

Maybe that explained why she wasn't waiting there with the plates and dishes. Mike didn't find Angie in either bedroom but passed out on the couch in the living room. Curled up on her side, she looked like an angel in a lace dress that clung to her lush curves in a way that would tempt any man into sinful thoughts.

Only a man who loved her, though, would feel more guilt than lust as he knelt down beside her to take in the tired rings around her eyes. Apparently, Angie hadn't been getting any more sleep than him these days. Maybe that was what they needed. A good night's rest.

That thought brought a smile to Mike's lips as he brushed a wayward strand of hair back from Angie's pale cheek. She murmured, turning into the gentle caress as the thick forest of her lashes fluttered upward. She blinked sleepily up at him with a sweetness that made his heart clench.

"Mike?"

"Shh," he whispered back as he shifted, allowing his arms to slide beneath her and roll her into his embrace. "Go back to sleep."

"Mmm," Angie moaned softly as he hoisted her up and began carrying her off to her bedroom. She burrowed her face deeper into his chest as she murmured tiredly. "I made dinner."

"I know." Mike kept his voice pitched low as he made his way through the dark house.

"It was good."

"I'm sure it was."

"It was supposed to be a surprise." There was a slight hint of sadness mixed in with that wishful whisper.

"It was," Mike assured her as he finally shouldered his way past her door and into her room.

"But I wanted to show you that I could do normal." Angie sighed as Mike settled her down onto her bed. She breathed in deep and let out one final deep breath, along with a last mumbled confession. "I'm not crazy."

Mike stood there staring down at Angie as she passed back out, amazed by her comment. Angie definitely was crazy. The right kind of crazy. The silly kind. The fun kind. The kind that made him smile and laugh.

So why wasn't he happy?

Chapter 23

Thursday, July 16th

Angie woke up the next morning with a thick set of arms wrapped tightly around her. She was snuggled tight against a hard chest and knew instinctively it was Mike. Only he would tighten his hold and try to keep her close as she turned to face him.

His eyes were wide open with no hint of sleep lingering on his features. Angie stared up at him, admiring the sheer perfection of his face. There were nicks and scars, and his brows had a funny little curl to them that was all Mike, just like the frown that settled over them.

Brett and Mike might have been born a carbon copy of each other, but they'd grown into two distinct men. If it had been Brett holding her this close, Angie had no doubt she'd already be sweaty and moaning, but Mike just studied with an intensity that left her slightly unnerved.

"How long have you been awake?" Angie asked, her voice rough and raspy with the sleep still tugging at her senses.

"I never went to sleep," Mike answered, his own whisper thick with a huskiness that was equal parts want and hardness.

"Oh."

Angie wasn't certain what to say about that, but she could sense that Mike had been doing more than simply holding her through the night. There was an intensity to his gaze that assured her deep thoughts were swirling within him, but she didn't dare press, not wanting to force him to be anything other than what he was. Mike would share that with her when he was ready, not when she made him.

That was a lesson that had taken Angie years to learn and even longer to accept, but now she got it. She wanted to be loved unconditionally but had put conditions on her own affections. That hadn't been right. That was what was really eating at her.

"You don't have to marry me."

With those six words, she gave Mike back his freedom, but he didn't celebrate with a smile or even a look of relief. Instead, he offered her his own confession and about broke Angie's heart with it.

"I'm not a good man, Angie." Mike paused, adding a weight to his words that assured Angie he meant every single one. "I've done horrible things. Things that I can't escape, that I can't forget. They've eaten away at me, and as much as I want to be the man you fell in love with all those years ago, I don't think I ever will be again."

Angie felt the tears flood her eyes as she watched him struggle with those truths. It made her ache to watch him suffer so, especially because she knew she couldn't simply take away the pain. That didn't mean she wouldn't be there for him to help carry it. Swallowing back the pity that she knew he'd never accept, Angie spoke up, offering him what she could.

"And I'm not the girl you left all those years ago. Nobody stays the same, but that doesn't mean that our love doesn't grow with us." Reaching up to cup his cheek, Angie offered Mike a small smile as he turned into her touch, seeking what comfort she could offer.

"And did it?" Mike's lashes lifted to reveal the hope that he dared to cling to as he gazed down at her. "Did it grow, Angie?"

"Stronger every day," she assured him.

Angie caught a flash of relief in Mike's gaze seconds before his lips settled over hers, breaking her mouth open so that his tongue could lay claim to her with a hunger that left Angie shaken. She could sense the frantic desperation in his kiss. There was no skill, no gentleness, no hesitation to the hands that began to tear the clothes clean from her body. The emotions pouring through him were too volatile to be tamed.

Angie didn't even try. Instead, she wrapped her arms around Mike's neck and clung to him, allowing him to take what he needed because it was what she wanted. She'd ached for him every day she'd been gone, dreamt of him every night. Not just him, but Angie didn't have the time or the breath to question where Brett was.

Mike was on the move, his lips following the trail of his hands. He nibbled his way down Angie's neck, scraping his teeth against her sensitive skin and making her shiver and arch up into the wet, suckling kisses he shifted to as he began to trace the flushed, swollen globes of her breasts. Around one, then the other, higher and higher, he treated her to a slow devouring that had her nipples straining and puckering with anticipation of the lips coming ever closer.

It felt as if her whole world was focused on the slow, sensual march of his mouth. Angie's breath caught, her muscles tensed, and she quivered with expectation. Yet, she was still caught off guard by the sudden rush of lust that consumed her the second his lips finally broke over her tit.

It was at that very second that the hand cupping her now naked mound struck as well. Angie had been so absorbed with his delectable nibbling, she'd lost track of what else Mike was doing. He'd stripped her naked and now plundered the creamy depths of her cunt with the same savage intensity that he used to ravaged her breasts with.

His other hand came to capture her other nipple, even as he pinned the swollen bud of her clit beneath the fat, callused tip of his thumb. That quickly, the world spun away from her, narrowing down to the three beaconing points of pleasure vibrating through her body. Mike rolled her tits along with her clit in a rhythm that wound through Angie until she felt like a string rolled too tight and ready to snap.

Mike sent her sailing as he abandoned her clit to fuck his fingers hard and deep into her, making Angie cry out and arch with the rapture that pounded through her. She was barely aware of Mike raring to watch as she came undone before him, but Angie knew the exact instant he slid down the bed to bury his face between her legs and allowed his tongue to replace his fingers because that was the instant her climax bloomed into a whole new tier of pleasure.

He sucked and fucked and pumped, tickling the sensitive walls of her sheath with the heavy stroke of his tongue and making Angie come all the harder. Still, he didn't stop. Without any mercy or any hint of stopping, he devoured her pussy until her head was thrashing across the pillow, her hair whipping in all directions as she twisted in the strong hold of the hands gripping her hips.

It wasn't until she sank her nails into Mike's own silken strands and balled her fingers into fists, pulling his hair damn near out as she tried to free herself, that he finally paused long enough for her to catch a breath. That was about all she caught before the smooth, heated, engorged head of Mike's cock slid between the plump and swollen lips of her pussy to lodge against the clenched opening of her weeping cunt.

Then he was forging inward, stretching her with his thick, hard length and making Angie mew with the delight that shot out of her pelvis in a sparkling shower that drowned her in an excitement, which only escalated as Mike's hips begun to flex. He went slow and steady at first, allowing her to savor the feel of the cock stretching her fantastically wide. The sensitive walls of her sheath spasmed with the pleasure.

Those ripples rolled outward, causing Angie's tired muscles to contract once again as she felt twisted into a knot of tense anticipation. Mike was fucking her too slowly, but she didn't have the ability to form the words to demand more. Instead, she let her body do the talking for her. Tightening her cunt down around his dick, Angie used muscles she'd never before worked so hard as she pumped his cock with a series of rapid pulses that had Mike snarling.

His gaze cut from where it been locked on the sight of his dick pillaging her pussy to meet Angie's gaze, and for a moment, she could see the truth. Mike was mesmerized. He was in love with her. She could almost sense the words ready to fall from his lips, but what came instead was a growl.

That feral sound heralded a shift in Mike's demeanor as he came down over Angie, capturing her wrists in her hand and pinning them to the bed as he began to pound into her, fast and hard and completely out of control. The wild rhythm sent one release slamming through her after another until she was caught completely within the euphoric bliss that lulled her right into the sweet abyss of oblivion.

* * * *

Angie passed out with a smile on her face as Mike thrust one last time with a roar that matched the might and strength of his own release. Then he collapsed on top of her, giving into the exhaustion pulling at his body and the peace enveloping his soul. Mike barely had enough sense to roll to his side before he smothered Angie.

It was hell sliding free of the tight clench of her cunt, and the urge to pound back into her hadn't faded, even if his strength had. It was heaven, though, to curl up along Angie's side and tuck her into his hold. With the sweet scent of her hair tickling his nose and the soft, lush feel of her breast filling out his palm, Mike finally gave in to the darkness shadowing out the bright sunlight streaming through the windows.

That light had barely faded when he was abruptly woken not even an hour later by the sound of Brett hollering out as he came pounding into the bedroom. It had taken his brother long enough, and he didn't sound all that shocked as he came to a stop.

"I should have known it!" Brett spat as he glared at the bed. "Where the hell did you find her last night?"

"Here," Mike muttered as Angie groaned and shifted in his arms, clearly trying to avoid both the light and the noise. "And keep your voice down. Angie needs her sleep."

That drew a dark glare from Brett, but at least he shut up. Reaching for the hem of his shirt, he stripped down before nodding at Mike.

"Move."

"Go fuck yourself," Mike shot back almost instantly as he snorted. Brett was nuts if he thought Mike was budging even an inch.

"Come on, man." Brett whined. "You had her all night, and that bed isn't big enough to sleep all three of us."

"Then go buy a bigger one and leave us the hell alone," Mike grouched, but Brett wasn't going anywhere.

"Don't make me raise my voice," Brett threatened, even as he started to do just that.

The idiot pushed it a little too far, rousing Angie. Her features furled into the cutest scowl as she blinked against the light and grumbled at both of them.

"What the hell are you two arguing over? I'm trying to sleep."

"Mike won't move," Brett complained, as if he were ratting Mike out to their mommy. "And there is not enough room for all three of us."

Angie's frown darkened for a moment, but she didn't argue with Brett or tell him to get lost. Instead, she turned in Mike's arms and pushed him over until he was lying on his back. Then she climbed up on top of him and settled down with a mumble.

"There. Now you have room."

Brett did, but he wasn't half as pleased with the situation as Mike. He flopped into the bed with a huff as Mike snuggled Angie into place. She felt good against him, all soft and plush and rounded in just the right ways. She was also warm and sweet smelling and then gone.

Angie let out a squeal as Brett reached out and all but dragged her off of Mike onto his chest. Mike shot up onto his elbow, suddenly quite awake as he glared over at his brother, but Brett wasn't paying him any attention. He was too busy smiling and settling Angie into place. The damn woman didn't object. That didn't mean Mike wasn't going to.

He reached out to grab Angie's arm, ignoring her heavy, pointed sigh as he began to drag her back into his arms. Brett didn't let go without a fight, though. He latched onto Angie's other arm and tried to tug her back. She ended up trapped between them, and it took only a few seconds for Angie to snap at both of them.

"Enough!" Jerking her arms free, she cast a glare over both brothers as she scrambled out of the bed to tower over them. "I'm going to go take a shower. Since all three of us can't fit, I'm going to take it alone!"

With that, she stormed off, her ass sashaying with a sexy sway that had Mike's cock swelling with renewed interest. He could have put that erection to good use if it hadn't been for Brett. Turning a dirty look on his brother, he found Brett eyeing Angie's ass with a similar interest.

"Don't even think about it," Mike snarled as he stomped out of the bed. "You and I, we need to have a word."

"I think you've already had more than one," Brett snapped, matching Mike's motions with his own agitated ones. "Why didn't you call me last night?"

"Because I needed some time alone with Angie." That was the truth. He could share her with his brother, but that didn't mean he didn't need time to be with just her. He wasn't the only one.

"What about me?" Brett paused with his jeans in hand to ask that. "Don't you think I would enjoy having some time with her myself?"

The answer to that question was too obvious to bother with, so Mike focused on fishing his own jeans off the floor, only to find that he'd broken the zipper. He'd ripped the damn thing almost clean out. That was how out of control he'd been. That was how badly he'd needed Angie.

"We need to settle this," Brett insisted, drawing Mike's attention back toward their argument. "Come on. I'll get the pen and paper, and we'll write up some rules."

* * * *

Angie knew she was in trouble when she found both brothers seated at the kitchen table with a pad of paper in front of them. The shower had relaxed her. Taking the time to not only dress but to do her hair and face had helped revive her spirits, and she was ready to start her day. The sight of that paper pad, though, dented her enthusiasm.

"Oh God," Angie groaned. "You two aren't making up more rules, are you?"

"Don't worry. They're not for you," Brett assured her with a grin as he beckoned her forward. "Though I do think it would be appropriate for you to kiss your future husbands when you walk into the room."

Angie snorted at that, but Brett wasn't joking. He tapped his lips pointedly as he tilted his chin into the air with an expectation that Angie considered denying, but he was too cute to refuse. Of course, it turned out to be a trap.

No sooner had her lips brushed against his than Brett's arm snaked around her waist and he jerked her down into his lap. His mouth took command of hers as his tongue invaded, dueling with hers as they fought for control of the kiss. He cheated, winning only when he slid a hand up her skirt.

Or, maybe she won because Angie wasn't wearing any panties.

The second Brett discovered that fact, he growled, his grip tightening around her as the callused tips of his fingers left a searing trail down the curve of her naked mound. She was soft and wet, her pussy welcoming his touch even as she parted her thighs, giving him more room to torment her.

Brett took instant advantage, dipping his fingers between her swollen folds to tease the sensitive bud of her clit. He toyed with it, making Angie gasp as she twisted free of his kiss. Brett let her go, his mouth dipping down to catch the pebbled peaks of her breasts. Her nipples had hardened into tight nubs that pressed through her shirt with pointed demand.

As Brett's mouth settled over her swollen globe, his teeth snapped down around her sensitive tit, holding it captive for the tongue-lashing he treated her to. Angie went wild as the motions matched the hard press and grind of his thumb over her clit. Her whole body began to spasm with a release that bloomed even higher, as suddenly Mike was there.

His hands felt rough, his grip almost punishing as he knelt beside Brett's chair and latched down onto her thighs. With a jerk, Mike pulled Angie free of his brother's tormenting touch and into the open-mouth kiss he placed over her cunt. In an instant, the callused tips of Brett's fingers were replaced by the velvety torture of Mike's tongue as he fucked with quick strokes that tickled the walls of her sheath and made Angie come all the harder.

Still, that wasn't enough. Not for Mike. Not for Angie. When he pulled back, she eagerly followed. She pushed him back onto the floor as she slid completely off Brett's lap. Mike shoved his sweats down and freed his magnificent erection eager to be mounted. As much as Angie's cunt quivered with the thrill of the thought of being filled by his thick cock once again, this time she wanted a taste first.

She caught him off guard, making Mike moan and jerk as she captured the bulbous head of his dick with her mouth. With slow precision, she sucked him past the tight clench of her lips and into the warm constriction of her mouth. Nursing him with every inch she slid down, Angie took Mike to the back of her throat and then down it.

Then she set about tormenting him with a slow pace that lasted no more than a minute before he growled and snarled a hand in her hair. Clenching his fingers into a fist, Mike forced Angie into a fast-paced rhythm that matched the hard pounding pace of the cock that screwed its way past the spasming walls of her sheath as Brett came out of his chair. He settled behind her, his fingers biting into the soft flesh of her ass as he held her still for his wild fucking.

Angie didn't object. Far from it. She fought free of Mike's hold to lift clear of his dick and cry out as her whole body clenched with a sharp, steep climax. She felt the ripples of pleasure race down her spine and spill out of her cunt as wave after wave of heated cream eased Brett's path and filled the air with the scent of her release. A release that only left her wanting more, but she didn't have the breath left to demand it.

Instead, she panted with each pounding thrust of Brett's hips as the pleasure twisted through her once again. It exploded a second later when Brett pulled free and slammed the full length of his sticky dick straight up her ass. Like a fireball, the rapture whooshed through her with such intensity and speed that she nearly blacked out for a moment. Then Brett was riding her rough and hard, making Angie drool all over Mike's chest.

Mike grunted, his hands coming to settle over her waist. Then with a hard jerk, he ripped her free of Brett's hold and claimed her cunt as he all but dropped her down the thick length of his dick. Behind her, Brett snarled and jerked forward, and that quickly, Angie found herself sandwiched between both brothers as Brett gripped her ass and spread her cheeks wide.

Angie knew what came next but still didn't have a chance to brace herself for Brett's invasion before he was stretching her back channel wide as he pounded back into her ass. She was impaled on two meaty dicks, each one grinding into her tight sheaths and setting off endless waves of delight. They tore through her with a frenzied rush.

This was heaven.

This was Angie's heaven. She gave herself over to the two brothers who not only claimed her body but her heart and soul as well.

* * * *

Brett closed his eyes and savored the sweet rush of ecstasy that flooded out of his balls and into the clenching depths of Angie's ass. There was just no denying it. This was heaven. He never wanted to leave. The only problem was he didn't have the strength to leave there.

Instead, he collapsed into a heaving, sweaty, quivery heap on the kitchen floor. Brett's only solace was that he wasn't the only one left too weak to do anything but gasp for breath. Mike and Angie were both there with him as well. Though it was with a little embarrassment that Angie recovered before either one of them.

Rallying, she managed to hoist herself up onto her arms and snicker down at Brett as she teased him. "So is that the appropriate way to greet my two husbands whenever I walk into a room? Because I've got to warn you, we might scandalize some people."

Brett laughed at that, though he highly doubted they would scandalize very many people. Pittsview had to have the largest most perverted population of any town he'd ever visited. He was glad to fit in.

"We could make it a rule if you want," Brett teased Angie back. "All you have to do is hand me that pad of paper up there, and I'll add it to the list."

Angie snorted at that as she shoved herself all the way to her feet, lording once again over Mike and Brett. "I think I need another shower."

"You need—"

"No!" Angie cut him off as she stepped over Brett. "I don't need any help."

"Yeah, well, don't use all the hot water," Mike shouted after her as he lumbered to his feet. "Other people need to bathe, too, you know?"

"I know!" Angie hollered back a second before the bathroom door slammed shut.

"And I'm next." Mike shot that at Brett, who rolled his eyes and scrambled to his feet.

"Whatever, man." Brett shrugged and jerked his jeans up. "I'm hungry, and not for a cold dinner."

They'd cleared the table when they'd settled down for their negotiations, but the food and plates remained stacked up on the kitchen counters, a reminder of how they'd screwed up last night. Angie didn't seem interested in holding any grudges, though. Technically, she'd screwed up their plans, too.

Still, Brett figured it would be best not to point that out. Instead, he set about cleaning the kitchen and then making up his famous waffles. By the time he poured the first of the batter into the iron, Mike and Angie had swapped places. Once again she was wearing little to nothing, which was a very distracting quality. Brett almost burned the first waffle.

Angie noticed, or, at least, that was why he assumed she was smiling. On the other hand, it might have been the list. Pulling the pad of paper closer, she began to read it out loud, as if Brett didn't already know what was written on there.

"Each man gets two nights a week…to do what?" Angie glanced up, raising a curious brow.

"You," Brett answered succinctly as he flipped the second waffle out.

He glanced up in time to catch Angie's snicker and the sight of Mike shuffling past the doorway wearing nothing but a towel and a few drops of water. He disappeared a second later, and the bedroom door slammed shut.

"I should have figured," Angie muttered as she glanced back down at the list. "All disputes will be settled with a competition?"

"You don't want us fighting, do you?"

"Of course not." Angie scowled, as if the very thought was insulting, but she didn't stay focused on that point for long. "And what is this? Bedtimes? Dating ages? Who helps with what homework? What are you planning, to start an orphanage?"

"No." Brett flipped out another waffle, not daring to glance in her direction as he explained the logic of the situation. "But a good plan makes for a good parent."

"Or maybe an obsessive one," Angie mumbled as her frown darkened. "And how come the boys are allowed to date earlier than the girls? And you have a whole different list of firsts for them. Do you have any idea how sexist that is?"

"Yes." Brett braced himself and met Angie's gaze, knowing nothing he had to say would appease her. "But that's just the way it is."

"Oh? Okay." Angie ripped the page of rules off the pad and crumbled it up, tossing it directly into the garbage can.

"Hey!"

"Sorry, that's just the way it is," Angie shot back. "Besides we don't need rules. We have my intuition."

"God save us," Brett muttered, earning him a dirty look before Angie nodded at the growing stack of waffles.

"Now hook me up. I'm hungry."

"We haven't even put a ring on her finger and already she's trying to boss us around." Mike shook his head as both Angie and Brett turned to find him standing half-dressed in the doorway.

His brother had pulled on another pair of sweats that did little to hide the massive bulge that assured everybody knew that he was still hard and ready. Brett suspected that was just why Mike was wearing sweats. They came off a whole lot easier than jeans.

"Oh, waffles." Mike perked up as he strode across the room to snatch up the stack of fluffy goodness. He paused only long enough to shoot Brett a hopeful look. "Syrup and butter?"

"On the table."

"You're the best brother." Mike tossed Brett a wink, and it hit Brett in that second that something was a little different about his brother.

It had been a long time since Mike looked so relaxed, much less went around winking. Brett watched him settle down at the table beside Angie and knew just whom he had to thank for Mike's transformation. She smiled over at his brother, and Mike melted like the butter he was spreading across his waffle. There was no denying it. Mike was in love.

So was Brett.

Flipping two more waffles out of the iron, he turned it off and pitched the empty bowl of batter into the sink before joining Mike and Angie. She turned to cast her smile over at him as he settled into the seat across from her, and Brett found himself nearly melting just like his brother beneath her praise.

"These are excellent. Thank you."

"It was nothing," Brett mumbled, actually feeling the heat tingeing his cheeks.

While Angie had the decency not to comment on his strange response, Mike snickered and pointed out his strange moment of bashfulness.

"Are you blushing?"

"No," Brett spat, offended and lying.

"You are," Mike insisted with a laugh.

"Oh go to hell," Brett muttered.

"That's enough." Angie rallied between them to cast a disapproving look in Mike's direction. "Stop picking on your brother."

"And if I do, what will you give me?" Mike asked, shooting Angie a lecherous look that left no doubt what he wanted.

"It's more of a question of what won't I give you if you don't," she shot back with enough snotty distain to make Brett laugh.

"You better watch out, brother. I think our woman is challenging you."

"No!" Angie's finger shot up to ward Mike off as he started to ease closer. "Don't even think about it! Stay back!"

Mike smiled and relaxed back into his seat with confidence that Brett knew well. Mike knew Angie's weakness now, and his brother wasn't above exploiting it. Angie knew it, too, if the way she narrowed her eyes on Mike was any indication.

"Fine." Mike lifted a brow in her direction. "What is it you want to talk about?"

"I don't know." Angie shrugged. "Maybe talk about the gym I hear you two are opening? Or we could talk about those house plans you sent Hailey out to the club with? Or we can talk about what I expect in terms of a proposal, or where I want to honeymoon, or—"

"Hold up." Mike held up his hand as he cut her off. "Let's clear some of this up. Yes, we're opening the gym."

"And we can handle the proposal," Brett chipped in.

"And you're getting two honeymoons because we each want our own separate ones," Mike quickly added.

"And the renovations?" Angie asked, going straight to the one question they both had skipped over.

She'd correctly deduced that there was a reason for that. Brett didn't want to be the one to tell her what it was. Neither did Mike from the look he shot Brett. They silently waged a battle as Angie waited patiently for one of them to fold. That was always going to be Mike because Brett could sit there all damn day. He wasn't the impatient one in the family.

Actually that was Hailey, but Mike was a close runner-up.

"We don't have the money."

"What?" Angie blinked as if that didn't make any sense or it hadn't been hard as hell for Mike to admit to in the first place.

"We don't have the money," Mike repeated, sounding as if he were strangling on the words.

"But I do." Angie smiled. "In fact, I've been saving money for years."

"We're not taking your money." Brett rejected that idea without hesitation. "That's not right."

"What?" Mike shot him a look as if he'd lost his mind. "Of course we'll take her money."

"Hold up." Brett couldn't believe what he was hearing. "You'd take the money?"

"Why wouldn't I?" Mike shot back, only to be immediately seconded by Angie.

"Yeah, why wouldn't he?"

"Because…" Brett didn't want to say it, but Angie was clearly not going to let him avoid it.

"Because?"

"You're the woman." Brett knew he was wrong and digging a deep hole for himself, but he was just being honest. "We're the men. We're supposed to take care of you."

"That's sweet." Angie offered him a smile that Brett didn't trust for an instant. "Really sweet. Still, I think I'd rather take care of myself."

"And how can you do that if you give us all your money?" Brett shot back, not certain how she couldn't see the obvious.

"Because I'm investing in you." Angie sounded just as exasperated as him. "You *are* my future…aren't you?"

* * * *

Angie's breath caught when neither brother answered. They shared a quick look and then pinned her with matching frowns. It was in that instant that she knew everything would be all right. They had a plan. She could tell. Even if she couldn't have, they told her.

"Did we not just say we had the proposal under control?" Brett demanded to know, as if he had any right to sound upset. "And don't try to change the subject. I love you. I am willing to spend the rest of my life with you, but I will not take your money."

Angie blinked, torn between being overwhelmed by his pledge and outraged by his stubbornness. She didn't get a chance to choose an emotion before Mike was offering her up his own solemn vow.

"I love you, too, and I have no problem with allowing you to help finance our future."

Angie's heart was a flutter. This had to be the best day ever. They loved her. She'd known it, but it was still good to hear. That didn't mean she couldn't figure out that they were teasing her. While their words rang true, the smiles tugging at their lips assured her both of the brothers were fighting back the chuckles. So she responded accordingly, giving them each a stern look.

"I love you both, too, but *that* had better not be my proposal."

Epilogue

Sunday, July 20th

Angie smiled as she watched the ground float away. The deep-throated rush of the fire the hot-air balloon captain fueled with the mere pull of a cable added to the sense of adventure that had filled the day, and it wasn't barely past noon. Who knew what else lay ahead?

Angie knew. Happiness. Contentment. Excitement.

Most importantly the future held promise. Standing there in the basket as the balloon sailed gracefully higher, Angie felt nothing but grounded and secure with Brett's arm latched around her waist and Mike's arm resting across her shoulders. She was tucked tightly between the two, just where she belonged. Finally, she fit in.

"Do you really like the property?" Brett asked for about the millionth time, clearly concerned that she didn't approve the place they'd picked out to build their gym and obstacle course.

"It's perfect," Angie assured him with a smile. "Everything is perfect."

It was.

The pink carnival they'd turned the barn on the property they were looking at had been a perfect expression of their affection. It had also been a little much. The balloon ride, on the other hand, was a soothing salve to her overstimulated senses.

"It's beautiful up here," Angie whispered, not wanting to ruin the soothing melody of the fire burning overhead. It had a tranquil kind of lull to it.

"But not as beautiful as you," Mike murmured before dropping a quick kiss on her forehead.

"Not nearly as beautiful as the life we're going to build together," Brett added on as he dropped an identical kiss on the other side of her head.

He had that right. Visions of happy chaos filled Angie's head even as she considered how calm the town below looked. Nestled among the trees and the fields, Pittsview small town center looked charming and welcoming. The image was completed by the lake sparkling off in the distance like some idyllic mirage.

The only thing that disrupted the illusion was the distant sound of an engine buzzing through the sky. Angie squinted into the sun as she looked for the small plane that sounded as if it were approaching. She'd just caught sight of it when smoke began to appear from its tail. For a brief second, Angie thought the pilot was in trouble, but then the plane began to twirl and twist, spelling out her name followed by the question everybody town could read.

Will you marry us?

There wasn't a single hesitation in her answer. "Yes, but only if I get my bears and whales."

* * * *

Wanda glanced up at the sound of a small plane circling overhead and frowned. Some idiot had wasted his money on another completely pointless romantic gesture. She didn't go in for that kind of crap herself, but then she could pretty much guess how most relationships were going to end—badly.

"Well, isn't that sweet," Dean muttered, drawing Wanda's gaze back to where he sat on the picnic table.

He was smoking a cigarette and looking shifty as hell. Then again, Wanda had a good radar when it came to spotting lies. That was about all this man was full of.

He was the no-good type, which probably explained why he'd been involved with Gwen. From her preliminary research, Wanda had figured out a few things about Gwen. She was a bitch and, worse, a blackmailer. While both were motives for murder, neither was a justification for her death.

Wanda planned to make sure Gwen found justice, even if it was too late to save her. After all, that's what she did, hunt down men who hurt women and, especially, children. Dean and his attitude weren't going to stand in her way.

"So you don't know anything?" Wanda pressed. She was giving him a chance to come clean, though, she knew he wasn't going to take it. Dean didn't disappoint her.

"Gwen and I weren't that close." Dean shrugged as if he weren't lying through his teeth. "Wish I could be of more help."

"Oh, think you can." Wanda smiled, showing all her teeth as she eyed him like a meal she was intent on devouring. "And I guess I should tell you right about now that I've talked to Gwen's cousin, Kristen."

That caught Dean's attention. He stilled, glancing up at her with a speculative gleam in his eyes that matched the sudden tension holding him stiff.

"Is that right?"

"Yep." Wanda nodded.

Dean studied her for a second before asking her the obvious question. "And just what did Kristen have to say?"

"Wouldn't you like to know."

THE END

WWW.JENNYPENN.COM

ABOUT THE AUTHOR

I live near Charleston, SC with my biggie, my dog. I have had a slightly unconventional life. Moving almost every three years, I've had a range of day jobs that included everything from working for one of the world's largest banks as an auditor to turning wrenches as an outboard repair mechanic. I've always regretted that we only get one life and have tried to cram as much as I can into this one.

Throughout it all, I've always read books, feeding my need to dream and fantasize about what could be. An avid reader since childhood, and as a latchkey kid, I'd spend hours at the library earning those shiny stars the librarian would paste up on the board after my name.

I credit my grandmother's yearly visits as the beginning of my obsession with romances. When she'd come, she'd bring stacks of romance books, the old fashion kind that didn't have sex in them. Imagine my shock when I went to the used bookstore and found out what really could be in a romance novel.

I've worked on my own stories for years and have found a particular love of erotic romances. In this genre, women are no longer confined to a stereotype and plots are no longer constrained to the rational. I love the 'anything goes' mentality and letting my imagination run wild.

I hope you enjoyed running with me and will consider picking up another book and coming along for another adventure.

For all titles by Jenny Penn, please visit
www.bookstrand.com/jenny-penn

Siren Publishing, Inc.
www.SirenPublishing.com

Lightning Source UK Ltd.
Milton Keynes UK
UKHW02f2018280318
320173UK00006B/799/P